GIRL ON THE RUN

BOOK TWO OF DANIELA'S STORY

PETER WOODBRIDGE

BEARWOOD
PUBLISHING

VANCOUVER, CANADA

This is a work of fiction. The names, characters and incidents portrayed are the work of the author's imagination. The story is set in the context of recent historical events. However, any resemblance to actual persons living or dead is purely coincidental. Locations of certain police and security services buildings have been disguised.

Copyright ©2022 by Peter Woodbridge
All rights reserved.

No part of this publication may be reproduced in any form, or by any means, electronic or mechanical, including photocopying, recording, or any information browsing, storage, or retrieval system, without permission in writing from Bearwood Publishing.

For Inquiries: info@bearwoodpublishing.com

ISBN
978-1-7775735-4-6 (Hardcover)
978-1-7775735-3-9 (Paperback)
978-1-7775735-5-3 (ebook)

FICTION, THRILLERS, ESPIONAGE

Cover Design by Spiffing Covers: www.spiffingcovers.com

Production Services by FriesenPress: www.friesenpress.com

Distributed to the trade by The Ingram Book Company

ALSO BY PETER WOODBRIDGE

The Girl From Barcelona
Book One of Daniela's Story

Girl With A Vengeance
Book Three of Daniela's Story

For more information, visit peterwoodbridge.com

Dedication

To Kit, my wife and best friend.

Principal Characters

Ahmed	ISIS explosives expert, working in Spain for al-Qaeda.
Antonio Valls	Detective Inspector, Mossos Homicide Squad in Barcelona.
Aurelia Périgueux	Gold expert, working for Spain's TFPU anti-money laundering unit.
Claudia Ramirez	Chief Inspector leading Spain's National Police GEO Group 60.
Colonel Scott	CIA chief, covert operations in Europe; politically ambitious military officer.
Condesa	Widow of Count Carlos; a former government minister in Madrid.
Daniela Balmes	A spy and former Civil Guard officer in Ceuta; involved with Jamal and Antonio; codename Felix.
Diego	Moroccan-born Deputy Inspector with GEO Group 60.
General Bastides	Leader of a coup d'état to overthrow the Government of Spain.
Isabel	Antonio's sister; a former teacher turned courtesan.
Jamal Ismet	Former surgeon from Homs, Syria; now an al-Qaeda-linked rebel commander.
Lord Garwood	British GCHQ officer; senior diplomat in the Middle East.
Luis	Special aide and chauffeur to General Bastides.
Maria	Accomplished defence attorney; divorced, Antonio's live-in partner.
Michael O'Flaherty	ISIS operative; undisclosed other covert roles; codename Fidelity.
Nicolas	Nicolas Julio de Granada, 15th Marquis of Tarragona; banker.

Raphael Robles	GEO 60 senior officer, aka Mustapha; head of al-Qaeda in Spain.
Syrian Minister	Diplomat; influential friend and ally of President al-Daser.
The Russian	Alexei; officer with Russia's Spetsnaz GRU military intelligence in Syria.
The Sniper	An unidentified assassin.
William	Mossos hacker; former member of China's Cyber Blue Hacking Team.
Xavi	Detective Sergeant, Mossos Homicide Squad; Antonio's buddy since childhood.
Yussef	Younger brother of Ahmed; an ISIS operative.

Al-Nusra Front	Jihadist rebel fighters, later known as Hay'at Tahrir al-Sham.
Civil Guard	Senior military force for Spain's border security and other policing roles.
FATF	Financial Action Task Force, an anti-money laundering global initiative.
GEO Group 60	Fictitious anti-terrorism unit within Spain's National Police, Special Operations.
GRU (officially GU)	Russia's military intelligence service, Moscow.
Mossos d'Esquadra	Catalunya's primary police force.
National Police	Spain's civilian federal police force, including domestic anti-terrorism units.
TFPU	Terrorist Financing Prevention Unit, Government of Spain.

CHAPTER 1

A Hurried Exit

It hurts.

Being different hurts.

Growing up, we don't want to be singled out and treated differently. We yearn to belong, to be accepted.

Daniela was eight years old when her life changed. The shock and trauma of her parents' deadly accident and loss of her only sibling made her different. At the convent school, her friends treated her like fragile glass—the tragic orphan. She began to resent the pity-laden looks of sympathy from the nuns.

Why had she been spared? She wasn't with them that day; perhaps she should have been.

Then the evils that came later. Systemically abused by her uncle and guardian, Raphael Robles, she'd learned to survive—to cope on her own. Constantly watching, she'd trusted her instincts and was rarely wrong.

So, years later, on the drive out to Sabadell, when Antonio received a phone call from Diego, her senses were alert—scanning for subtle signals.

Antonio was clever, a smart policeman. Better than most at not revealing his hand. But she knew immediately. It was just a glance, a quick furtive movement of his eyes. His breathing deepened almost undetectably—an involuntary action as his brain reverted to attack mode and demanded more oxygen. In heightened anxiety, he stiffened. Only slightly, but she didn't miss it.

Sensing her own fear, she felt her mouth go dry. Her heart rate kicked up as her brain's autoresponse—a surge of noradrenaline—prepared her body's defences. Those few seconds confirmed it. The game was up. He'd found out about her.

She had to escape.

"You've gone quiet, boss," she said, shifting up a gear to pass a convoy of slow-moving commercial vehicles. "Anything wrong?"

He shook his head. "Just thinking."

No small talk now, she noted. Another confirmation.

"I hate these recruitment presentations," he said eventually, sounding relaxed, but his voice was still edgy. "The worst is, they're not an option. Just part of the job. Thanks for driving, by the way."

"Doing my job, boss. We should be there soon. Fifteen minutes. We've made good time." Past the convoy of trucks now, she shifted down. It was just a question of time, who could outsmart the other. If she was right about the phone call, he'd be thinking hard about trying to gain the upper hand. She was a step ahead of him. Gradually, she accelerated—figuring that, at high speed, he wouldn't risk a crash by trying to snatch his Glock out of its holster on the back seat. He'd be forced to wait.

He could text ahead for help, but then he would know that she knew. Besides, it wasn't his style; he'd use his brain to try to outwit her. She could handle that. Reduce the tension, she told herself. He'd remain on full alert, of course. But she only needed a few seconds. Enough time to stay ahead of him—a chance to make her escape.

"Diego called you," she said, attacking right down the middle.

He hesitated. Only slightly—a giveaway.

"I stole the money from the farm," she said quietly.

"He told me," Antonio replied.

"Did he tell you who I work for?"

"That you're an al-Qaeda spy? A double agent?"

"It's a bit more complicated than that," she said. "You're going to arrest me?"

"Tell me that Diego is wrong."

She knew he was stalling. "He isn't wrong. It's only part of the story." He glanced at a highway exit sign. "You have ten minutes, Daniela. Tell me the rest. Convince me."

"You wouldn't believe me."

"Try me."

Her reply was a cynical laugh.

"Look, Daniela, I don't know what you've been up to exactly. But what you're doing now is wrong. We've come a long way together. There has to be a better way than this. I'll help you—I promise."

She had little faith in his words. She'd been a jihadi extremist operating among some of the worst terrorists imaginable. He was head of the Mossos Homicide Squad. If Diego had told him she was an al-Qaeda spy, she had no doubt that he would arrest her. Possibly even kill her.

There was only one way out.

Wrenching the steering wheel violently, she aimed their vehicle at the flatbed of a heavily-laden bulk container truck. It would be like hitting a brick wall, she knew, as she smacked the passenger side into the unforgiving metal. Antonio's door buckled in, and his window shattered. On instinct, he covered his face with his hands as the twisted roof caved in and a metal strut narrowly missed his forehead. Using the force of the collision impact to power their vehicle away, she fled the scene.

"Holy shit, Daniela, are you trying to kill us?" Then he felt the barrel of his Glock as she thrust the gun against his carotid artery. He froze in disbelief. "No, Daniela."

"Sorry, but you're leaving me no choice." Moments later, she swerved across two lanes of traffic to the hard shoulder. "Get out," she yelled. "I don't want to shoot, but I will if I have to. Get out. Now!"

Keeping his hands hovering in the air, in her line of sight, he kicked out the damaged door and exited the vehicle. He stumbled onto the gravel hard shoulder.

"We're on the same side, Toni. Trust me," she shouted, revving the engine. Removing the magazine, she threw his disarmed firearm onto the grass verge. With the damaged passenger door still swinging open and engine screaming at a high pitch, Daniela released the clutch, causing several cars to swerve as she rejoined the traffic. Minutes later, in sight of a gas station, she abandoned the vehicle and ran up a grass verge.

It was only a short sprint to reach the fence. Clambering down the embankment to the local road on the other side, she calmly thumbed a ride.

The middle-aged driver couldn't believe his eyes. It wasn't every day that he could pick up such a great-looking young woman. He pulled up sharply. "Where are you going?" he asked with a lewd smile as she climbed into the passenger seat.

"Mossos . . . police!" she replied, thrusting her badge in front of his face. "Get going," she ordered. "I need a ride into town. Now move it!"

The startled driver glanced at her. "Where to?" he asked. He couldn't have been more respectful.

"Head for the Diagonal," she ordered. "I'll let you know." Yussef's apartment was not far away, but she mustn't give away her destination. Antonio would figure out her plan too quickly.

"Down here," she instructed later, as they approached an underground car park.

"I've got to get back home," he pleaded.

"Park first, then you can go."

In the darkness of the parking spot, she slammed the trunk on the terrified driver, throwing his keys and phone inside the car. Someone would find him soon enough. It would be a long time before he'd try another pick-up.

Back on the street, she called Yussef's number. Three rings, three times. Then she called him again and let it ring. "Yussef," she said rapidly when he answered. "Are you still in Barcelona? We have to talk."

"Why?" he demanded, his voice laced with suspicion.

"Are you at the apartment?"

"No. Why you ask me?"

"You mustn't go there. It's dangerous."

"My brother, Ahmed."

"Ahmed is at the apartment?" she asked, aware that he'd just confirmed it. "Yussef, I am coming to meet you. I'm not far away. Meet me at the park nearby. Stay out of sight and do *not* go to the apartment. The police will know about it. You'll be captured. Our jihad will be at risk. Stay away from the apartment," she repeated. "Mustapha wishes it. Promise me!"

There was silence as he cut the call.

"Damn!" she exclaimed. She tried again, but he wouldn't answer. She must get there quickly. As far as she was concerned, Ahmed could take his chances; it was Yussef she needed. Muscle power to help her move the gold and banknotes.

Getting to his apartment would be difficult. The metro wasn't an option; it had security cameras. Neither was a cab; she would be easily remembered. Then she saw an answer. The hop on/hop off tourist bus was a slow mode of transportation—slower than she would have liked, but at least it would get her close.

Perfect cover.

The sniper's sensitive fingertip gently touched the polished gunmetal trigger of his modified Mauser 86SR. Pausing his breathing, he steadied his shot. It was a standard technique learned early in his career to keep his body immobile. Nothing must disturb his aim, as he waited to release the 7.62 mm projectile along its trajectory.

There was static in his headphone. No orders came.

Resuming his breathing, he waited for approval to fire. "Target in my sights," he confirmed to Control. Reminding them should not have been necessary. Somewhere along the chain of command, someone was hesitating. His opportunity for a shot wouldn't be available much longer. He'd been on his own, returning to base, when the call came through. Control had intercepted a Catalan police communication. A Mossos squaddie had caught a glimpse of Daniela scrambling down a grass embankment off the autovia. She'd been given a ride almost immediately.

At first, the squaddie had ignored the incident. But events were unfolding. Very soon afterwards, he'd heard on his radio about the incident involving the truck and a badly damaged BMW abandoned on the autovia. A Mossos detective inspector had been ordered out of the vehicle at gunpoint. He'd wasted no time reporting it.

A nationwide APB for Daniela Balmes had been issued. Control had been monitoring the communication channels. Now they had a confirmed sighting. An alert patrol officer in a Barcelona suburb saw her board a red hop on/hop off bus. He'd called it in. His call had been intercepted by the sniper's Control. Now they knew exactly where she was.

Girl On The Run

The bus was travelling in the sniper's direction. With only a few minutes to prepare for her arrival, he selected the vantage point of a low-rise commercial building overlooking a passenger drop-off point. It was late afternoon, and the November light was fading. Moments later, the bus stopped to allow a handful of weary, straggling tourists to get off.

He located the girl. From Control's description, he recognised her immediately: it was Daniela. Through his spotting scope, he made a positive identification.

His orders were simple: eliminate her.

Control would decide the timing.

She was sitting partially obscured in an aisle seat downstairs. Her spatial awareness was superb, he observed. By instinct, she was making herself a difficult target. He respected that. Now, just for a moment, he had a clear shot. The opening might last another six or seven seconds.

Across the street, a Catalan flag, flapping in the light breeze, provided confirmation of the direction and strength of the wind. He made a final check of the firing parameters displayed in fine orange lettering below the crosshairs of his telescopic sights. Distance to target: 103 metres. Wind: full value. Angle of attack: constant.

The projectile would have to travel through the laminated glass window of the bus, absorbing some of the bullet's energy. From experience, he knew the resistance of the glass wasn't enough to deflect the bullet from its intended path. He would need only one round. The suppressor he'd fitted to his rifle would muzzle the supersonic crack. His target wouldn't have a chance to hear the sound. By that time, she'd be dead.

Nothing from Control. He reconsidered his shot.

With a full body view, killing was easy. Wounding the target without risk of a bleed-out required far greater skill. The sniper knew that his opportunity for a centre-mass shot, where the compound bullet would penetrate the middle of her body and destroy her vital organs, was no longer an option. That had been available to him seconds earlier. Now, less than fifty per cent of her body mass was visible.

There was no other choice, he decided. It had to be a headshot.

If the bus driver started the bus moving again, the timing for a clear and decisive delivery would diminish significantly. His eye returned to his rifle scope. The decision to proceed, or not, was up to Control.

Still nothing.

"Four seconds." He breathed the words calmly into his headpiece microphone. "Clear shot."

The bus was one of several on the busy street. The sniper was sensitive to the risk of collateral damage. He was a professional, too experienced to allow accidents to happen. There were no children on the bus. Only once in his career had he made a collateral killing. On his first mission—a child in Afghanistan. The young boy had run out suddenly from his hiding place and had taken the shot intended for his heavily-armed mujahid father.

It was the low point of the sniper's career. His memory of the child, alive and bleeding out onto the desert sand, still recurred in his worst nightmares, haunting him. Reassuring words from his commanding officer had done little to lessen his remorse. The incident was unfortunate, the senior man had told him. But it happens. We're at war. Get over it.

After "the incident," he'd changed his set-up routine. Vestiges of guilt burned deeply into his subconsciousness. Today, as a reflex action, he glanced away from the telescopic sight and quickly scanned the surrounding area. No apparent collaterals. All seemed clear.

"Two seconds. Clear shot," he breathed into his microphone, and waited.

His focus turned to the crosshairs of his telescopic sights targeting the side of Daniela's head. Adjusting his aim slightly low, he compensated for the setting angle of the evening sun. For an instant, it seemed to him that she glanced up—looking almost directly at him. It was as if she knew her time had come. He didn't want to look into her eyes; it would curse him forever.

There was a crackling sound in his headphone. "Affirmative. Proceed," came his instructions.

The bus started to move, but he held her in his sights, automatically adjusting his aim to account for the sudden movement. Slowly, he squeezed the trigger, feeling almost no recoil. There was a ballistic crack but little else. The suppressor had done its work. Lifting his eyes slowly above the telescopic sights, he checked the impact—anticipating that Daniela's skull would be slumped sideways in a terminal bloodied trauma. Instead, he saw her eyes widened in surprise.

"Failed," said the sniper into his microphone.

He was aware that, having survived, Daniela could now trace the trajectory of his shot. She would be able to see the spider-web penetration of the bullet's journey through the laminated window. At that instant, she looked up at his position on the rooftop. Both of them had a clear view of each other.

"Abort," came Control's instructions, precluding any chance of a second attempt.

The sniper disconnected from his target in an instant. His mission was over. Standard operating procedures were to extract himself safely and without incident from his position. Withdrawal routines drilled into him during training required him to avoid drawing hostile fire. Most likely, she was unarmed; there would be no return of fire. Even so, he knew his biggest risk was complacency. He was aware that the advantaged circumstances of his withdrawal might not be so one-sidedly in his favour on a future occasion.

Following the protocols established for disengaging from his position, the sniper kept his head and body low and rolled onto his back.

Removing the rifle's pivot pin, within seconds he had packed the disassembled rifle into his kitbag. Mindful of his training, he pocketed the still-hot spent shell casing. Retrieval was his unit's standard procedure: Don't give them any information. No signatures. The spent bullet couldn't be traced to his gun. Embedded somewhere in the frame of the bus, it was now a lump of compacted cupronickel.

Swivelling the peak of his baseball cap back to the front of his head, he climbed through the metal door rooftop entrance and headed down the concrete stairs to a side street exit.

Daniela was not aware that the shot had passed just in front of her face.

Yet, somehow, she'd sensed it.

Moments later, she'd heard a crack. The bullet, travelling at over eight hundred metres per second, had entered through the window to her left. She knew immediately she'd been the intended victim of a targeted shooting. Swinging her legs into the aisle, she looked past the shattered window—searching for where the shot had originated. Tracing its path, she caught a brief glimpse of the sniper and his hasty departure preparations on the rooftop.

Realizing that her life had been saved because the bus driver had applied his brakes sharply to allow a speeding moto to pass, she knew she'd been lucky. The bullet, she guessed, probably had embedded itself somewhere in the metal frame of the bus. It was unimportant. What she wanted to know was who was trying to kill her.

Scrambling to get off the still-moving vehicle, her first thoughts were about the sniper, then about Antonio. She could understand that he'd want to arrest her. She couldn't believe he would want her dead. By an assassin's bullet? It was too hard to believe. Yet, if it wasn't Antonio who'd ordered her killed, who was it?

For a moment, Daniela hesitated. Several thoughts passed simultaneously through her brain— questions fuelled by a sudden jolt of adrenaline, rising anger, and resentment. The sniper might already be relocating and setting up for a second shot. Her training yelled at her to withdraw to safety, but her need to know compelled her to confront her assailant.

She had to find out.

Sprinting towards the building, she glanced up to examine the aging structure. The sniper would have few choices of an escape route from the roof. Hiding out of sight in a doorway, she waited. He emerged moments later. Seeing him, Daniela pulled back into the evening's gathering shadows—watching as he looked left and right, cautiously checking his escape route. He wore a baseball cap pulled over his forehead and carried a heavy sports bag, confirming the profile she'd expected.

Hesitating, she withdrew from sight as two Mossos motorcycle police swept by—their emergency sirens blaring. She saw that, instinctively, the sniper also had pulled back out of sight. His defensive action confirmed Daniela's hunch—that he was anxious not to attract police attention. Commencing his exit route, he walked briskly northwards. It would allow him to avoid a group of Mossos squaddies arriving at the next junction to set up a barricade.

She doubted that this level of police activity was anything to do with the sniper. The whole of Barcelona suddenly seemed alive with police. She could see them and hear them. There was something going on, something really big—and she had a shrewd hunch that she was the focus.

How they'd located her so quickly was a puzzle. The scale of the police response was scary. Obviously, Antonio had not been convinced by her reassurances. He was organizing a dragnet over the whole area. A complete lockdown.

She was on the run.

From his behaviour, the sniper wasn't from the Catalan police; she was sure of that now. But she had to find out whom he was working for. Who wanted her killed? On the street, she paced him, keeping close to the concrete walls of the nondescript commercial buildings that blight some of the eastern suburbs of Barcelona. She noted that he paused briefly several times, using storefront windows to check behind him and survey the path ahead.

Then, for Daniela, a fortuitous event occurred. The sniper glanced back and failed to see a delivery bike emerge from an alleyway. He and the rider collided, ending up in a pile on the sidewalk. Recovering quickly, the cyclist yelled an expletive and continued his journey. His ankle twisted, the sniper hobbled forwards for several minutes—eventually stopping in a deserted narrow walkway. Daniela seized her chance. She hit him before he could look up, while he was off balance. Grabbing his collar, she dragged him forwards—smashing his head into the graffiti-covered concrete wall.

He'd tried to kill her, and she felt no remorse in hitting back. Concussed and bleeding, he lay sprawled on the ground. He wouldn't have any identification. She knew there was no point in searching him. As a Mossos cop, she would have had other resources to find out who he was. That was all gone now. She needed to be quick. The narrow walkway was deserted, for now.

Unzipping his sports bag, she examined the modified Mauser. No markings. No serial numbers or manufacturer's identifications; they'd been filed off. A professional. The search told her nothing. He could be working for anyone. The army or Spain's federal security forces, maybe? He could be an independent: a contract killer? Nothing inside his bag yielded any clues. She didn't care about leaving fingerprints. They already knew who she was, and she wanted them to worry that she might know who *they* were. It gave her a psychological edge.

The sniper, head bleeding profusely, was coming around and trying to sit up. She had only a few seconds to identify his employers. "Who the hell sent you?" she demanded in Catalan, quickly repeating her question in Spanish. Watching his eyes narrow—not from fear but defiance—she knew he wasn't going to tell her a thing. He was too well trained.

There was no time for more forceful questioning.

She spotted the heavy gold pendant he was wearing—a talisman, officially forbidden, but snipers are highly superstitious creatures. It was hanging on a leather thong around his neck. An unusual design—the shape of two numbers intertwined. Wrenching it from his neck, she thrust the pendant in his face. "I'll find out who you are, soldier," she said. "I'll be coming for you."

Glancing around, Daniela confirmed that no one was watching. Picking up the metal stock of his rifle, she held it high and slammed it down on his right hand, instantly breaking all his fingers against the hard concrete. He cried out in intense agony. She repeated the process with his other hand.

Walking away, she looked back to see him writhing in pain. By nature, she detested violence. But this man had tried to kill her. He knew the risks. Her actions had simply evened up the score, making sure his career as a sniper was finished. She had no qualms. He was a good-looking man in his early thirties. Lots of other careers would be open to him.

An hour ago, she had been a valued member of the Mossos Homicide Squad, working with the complete trust and support of Antonio.

Now she was a fugitive.

She had to collect Yussef and get to her aunt's place; she must complete what she'd set out to do. First, get past the blockade.

With heavily armed police everywhere, it wasn't going to be easy.

Yussef

Darkness overtook the day.

A good omen, she thought. All her life, it had been her friend. It had protected her. Tonight, she would need all the help the night shadows could provide. Walking alongside a young couple, she kept pace with them—making it look like they were three friends going out for the evening. Ahead was a barricade. Flashing red and blue lights reflected off the walls of buildings, illuminating the area like intrusive laser probes. Armed, serious-looking Catalan police were blocking off the main street, checking IDs. Their faces were concealed behind intimidating black balaclavas.

National Police and Civil Guard vehicles were arriving and officers on foot began filling the streets. That meant additional trouble for her. The feds didn't need permission from the Mossos to be there. Under Spain's ambiguous policing laws, they had jurisdiction too. Daniela was aware that if she were up against the Mossos alone, her task would be easier. With the feds involved, there was an added element of professionalism and quick-response combat experience.

She regretted now not going directly to Yussef's apartment. She had wasted precious time. In retrospect, her altercation with the sniper had been an expensive diversion. Escaping from the city was going to be really tough. Confirming her worst fears, progress on foot was slow. Several times, she took refuge in small local shops to avoid being stopped by patrolling groups of *Brigadamòbil*. Like a thief in the night, she threaded her way past them, with several close calls.

She needed to get to Sant Andreu and secure Yussef's help before the police searched the area around his apartment and apprehended him. At her current rate of progress, and exit routes blocked, she began to doubt she would make it at all. It was obvious that the security forces were searching for her: a young woman travelling on her own. Worse, by now, they would have circulated her description. Daniela decided she needed to have wheels.

A Catalan, about her own age, wearing a chef's apron was exiting the door of a side-street café. He was lifting up the seat of his moto, taking out his helmet. They spoke for a few minutes. He'd just finished his afternoon shift. He couldn't take her to her destination, he said, handing her the passenger helmet. But, as a *partisano*, he could give her a ride part of the way. She took his white apron and fastened it around her waist, thinking it might help as a disguise. On impulse, she gave him a kiss. One Catalan to another.

His moto was old and underpowered; it made slow progress. For Daniela, the journey was frustrating. Several times, they saw roadblocks ahead. The chef, who had little time for the police, took diversionary measures. Following the lead of several other moto drivers who shared his distaste for the law, he nimbly diverted around the blockades. He must have changed his mind en route, thought Daniela, because he dropped her off very close to where she wanted to go.

She caught up with Yussef as he was pacing the park near his run-down high-rise apartment building. Pulling him into the shadows, she tried to talk to him. He needed to understand why the manhunt was under way.

"I must go and warn my brother," he said, pulling himself away.

"Yussef, listen to me," Daniela said. "If the police have captured your brother, they'll be inside the apartment waiting for you. You'll be arrested. How are you going to help Ahmed if both of you are in jail? Besides, they'll never let you near him. They know you're a terrorist, don't you understand?"

"I saw him a few hours ago only," the young Arab boy protested. "I will go to there and find him. I will tell him. I must warn him."

Daniela could see that the boy was scared, but he was overly sure of himself. It was a weakness of youth. Love and unquestioning family loyalty would not allow him to abandon his brother. He wrenched himself away from her and continued walking.

"Go!" she said loudly. "If you want to act only with your heart, then go ahead! If you want to be a hothead, we are doomed. They will capture you; they will torture him. Both of you will die. Then what good will you be to the jihad? Answer me, Yussef," she demanded, catching up with him and grabbing his arm. Finally, he stopped struggling. She could see that her words were affecting him.

"Please, sit down and talk. Not here. They are watching for us." She glanced around the park. "Over there." She pointed to a wood bench next to a weathered stone statue of an ancient saint. "From the apartment building, they will not be able to see us." She knew that she had only one chance to gain his confidence. "Yussef, answer me these questions." Daniela grabbed the boy's sullen face and forced him to look into her eyes. "Who was it that sent me to meet Ahmed and you?"

He considered her question for a moment. Daniela was aware that he knew the answer; he was delaying because he was trying to think through the situation. "Who sent me, Yussef?" she demanded.

"Mustapha," he answered in a thin, reluctant voice.

"Yes, it was Mustapha," she repeated loudly. "Do you trust Mustapha?"

"Why you question his word?" The boy's eyes suddenly blazed at her in anger. "He is our leader in this country. He take care my brother and me. We obey him, not you." His dismissive look of derision alarmed her.

"They have captured Mustapha," she said quietly. "I know this because I was in the police; I was spying for the jihad. It was Mustapha who arranged for me to be accepted into the Civil Guard, to be trusted by them. Mustapha ordered me to find out what the Spanish government knows about us. To find out how much they know.

"Months ago, Mustapha told me to take the hawala money to Jamal—for the jihad," she continued. "I did what he commanded. I went to Syria—to your country. Jamal was grateful. He sent me back with important information for Mustapha. You know that. But things have changed. Our bombing attempt, it has failed. They have arrested Mustapha. Now they hunt for me. And for you too. The gold and money we took—it belonged to the general. He has been arrested. The general's man, the chauffeur whom your brother Ahmed knows, he also has been captured by the police. We—you and I, Yussef—we are the only ones who remain free to continue our mission. The jihad needs the money we took from the general. Jamal needs it in Syria. We must continue our work, don't you see?

"If he were here, Yussef, what do you think Ahmed would say to you?" she demanded again. "What would he tell you to do? Would he say to you 'run inside the apartment building and get shot dead by the police?' Or would he tell you to use your head?" Daniela tapped her forehead. "What would he tell you? He would say that the only important thing is the jihad."

The boy didn't reply. He was in conflict—his tense body told her he was struggling with his decision. Finally, he nodded. His narrowed eyes burned into hers. "First, I must know if Ahmed has been captured. I see that, then I believe you." He pointed two fingers at his eyes.

Daniela shook her head. "No, Yussef. It is too dangerous to go near your apartment. They are looking for us; they will be waiting." She pointed to the sky. "It is dark. They will be on the rooftops. They will use special equipment. Like those night glasses we wore to steal the money at the farm. You remember?"

Yussef shrugged. He did not care. She knew he wanted to see his brother—to see for himself if he could help Ahmed escape.

Daniela shook her head. The boy was infuriating; he was so stubborn. Making up her mind quickly, she said, "I will prove to you that they have captured him. But you must do everything I tell you." Without another word, she walked in the direction of the apartment. Moments later, they emerged from a side alley. She knew they would be hidden from the direct line of sight of any police guarding the apartment.

17

Several people were walking along the street. Too few to provide close cover for their movements, she decided. Then she spotted a bread delivery van parked outside a café. "Come," she said. Glancing at the café window to make sure they were not being observed, she snatched two trays of freshly baked bread rolls from the back of the van. One of them she handed to Yussef and walked briskly across the street with the other. By now, they were under the canvas awning of a novelty store, concealed from view. The store was dark and closed for the evening. They hid and waited until the bread delivery van had disappeared up the street.

"Come on," urged Daniela. "Hold the tray on your shoulder, like this." She demonstrated how he should pile up the bread to hide his face from view. Several unmarked vehicles were parked outside his apartment building; heavily tinted windows hid the occupants from view. "There," she said quietly to him. "Do you see them? They are Mossos squaddies." He followed as she continued walking.

Moments later, Daniela turned a corner. A car was starting to move off from the traffic lights. She darted behind it, deftly placing one tray on its flat trunk as it pulled away. Swinging around the corner, the driver—unaware of his cargo—passed close to one of the Mossos squad cars. The metal tray slid onto the road with a loud clatter, scattering a fusillade of fresh bread rolls onto the street.

Moments later, at the traffic lights on the adjacent corner, Daniela did the same with another car. Within seconds, dozens more bread rolls flew on the road—rolling under the wheels of cars, scattering like a panicked family of fleeing chubby white rats. Vehicles swerved, passers-by stopped to gawk, and traffic came to a stop. For a brief time, the situation was bizarre—freshly baked buns strewn ludicrously across the grimy grey tarmac.

Daniela's ruse had the effect she intended. The Mossos reacted swiftly. One of the officers jumped out of a squad car and started to direct the traffic while several others began to pick up the errant bread rolls. As best he could, one of officers stowed the squashed and misshapen buns into a black plastic bag and thrust them into his trunk.

As Daniela and Yussef watched from the shadows, the street was cleaned up quickly and the Mossos squaddies returned to their vehicles. There was no doubt they wanted to get back to their surveillance without delay. Daniela looked at Yussef. "You saw them. Now do you believe me?" she demanded.

Eyes wide, he nodded.

"We must get out of here," she ordered. "Next time, we may not be so lucky." Minutes later, they sheltered in the safety of a deeply recessed storefront several blocks away. "You and I, together, we can rescue Ahmed," said Daniela looking directly into Yussef's eyes. "I can help you get back to Syria. I promise! You can be together again. When you get home, Syria will need you. But, right now, I need you more. Our jihad needs you. You saw them, Yussef," she continued. There was no hint of satisfaction in her voice. The diversion had achieved what she hoped: it had been a necessary tactic to gain his trust—and submission.

Perhaps it was a pragmatism that came from Yussef's ability to survive in the uncompromising war zones of northern Syria, Daniela wasn't sure. But after a moment of processing her words, he slowly nodded his head in agreement. A great sadness filled his normally bright and vibrant eyes as he breathed out deeply. "I understand," he said grudgingly. Then he looked alarmed. "Money you have given us. It is in apartment."

Daniela took his upper arms in her hands and squeezed them. "Now the police have it, Yussef. Forget it. We have hidden away more money than we need; you know that—you have seen it. I will give you more. Now we must go and move it to safety. Before the police find it. The money we hid—it belongs to the jihad," she added, her eyes blazing. "Trust me, Yussef."

Getting away from the neighbourhood proved even more difficult than Daniela's escape from the inner city. She'd wasted more time convincing Yussef than she'd intended. It had been necessary. Now, in hindsight, she worried it might prove too costly. More blockades were being set up. Daniela could see that backup assistance from the National Police was arriving. The situation had become really serious. Plainclothes officers had joined the hunt. Maybe they had figured out her little ruse. They weren't fools; they knew how to spot fugitives and they knew the tricks criminals use to avoid being caught.

Several times, she cursed that she had to drag Yussef along with her—he was a liability. As an illegal entrant into the country, always in hiding, he was unfamiliar with the city and depended completely on her. He seemed almost casual about their predicament. She would have been much safer if she were travelling alone, but he was vital to the next stages of her plan. Pulling him into the shadows, she explained that it was no longer safe to use the side roads. They would have to make their way through neighbourhood backstreets and along the storm drain channels. It would slow them down, she admitted, but it was less risky for two fugitives travelling together.

Yussef shrugged, seemingly indifferent to her heightened concern. In the war zones of northern Syria, he said, he had become adept at such tactics.

Daniela knew that, in a way, he admired her. But she was a woman. In his culture, women could not be trusted to understand these things. He was a man; the need to take risks was his natural way of life.

"Where it goes?" he asked, pointing to a fully laden municipal recycling truck waiting at a traffic light.

"I don't know," said Daniela. "Somewhere out of town, I think. Maybe not where we want to go."

Yussef ran to the back of the vehicle and grasped one of the two hold bars. Seconds later, a surprised Daniela did the same. The driver and homeward-bound crew were relaxing in the cab and didn't see them.

Two yellow safety vests, smelling of garbage, were crammed into a side pocket. Daniela and Yussef quickly put them on. It worked. They rode several kilometres before jumping off. The terrain had become more rural, but Daniela knew they were travelling in the wrong direction to get to her aunt's house. There was one compensation: at least there seemed to be fewer police around, she noted thankfully. It would be stupid to hotwire a car and give away their location. Somehow, they had to get another ride—this time, in the correct direction. Public transport wasn't safe, so what?

Fortune was on their side. Close by, a well-lit driveway led to a resort hotel—a favourite among budget tourists visiting the area. She explained her idea to Yussef. Minutes later, they walked through a side door, entering the lobby where Daniela saw what she needed. Walking with confidence past the concierge's vacated desk, she picked out two suitcases from a neatly organised pile waiting to be transported to the airport.

Pulling a five euro note from her pocket, she tipped the doorman and pointed to a taxi. They needed to go to the airport quickly, she told him. They were late for their flight. Could he help with their baggage? Soon afterwards, Daniela judged it would be safe to dump the taxi. She asked to be dropped off at a third-rate hotel. "That other one was too expensive," she explained to the puzzled driver. Still, the tip she gave him wasn't bad. Minutes later, they abandoned the stolen suitcases and continued on foot.

As the pair drew closer to their destination, police security on the roads once again seemed to become more intense. Daniela knew the area, and so far, they'd managed to avoid most of the roadblocks. Walking into a blind junction, they'd narrowly missed being stopped and questioned by a group of Mossos squaddies. It had been a close encounter, but it gave Daniela an idea.

She'd spotted an unoccupied patrol car parked on a side street. The time she'd spent with the Mossos Homicide Squad had yielded useful knowledge of their mobile operations. She knew that, for emergency reasons, the vehicle wouldn't be locked. Within seconds, she was sitting in the driver's seat keying an information request into the communications console. The reply that she hoped for came back almost immediately. The farm at El Canós—from where, days earlier, they had stolen the massive pile of gold ingots and currency—was no longer classified as an active crime scene. She breathed a sigh of relief. That meant that the police, for now, had completed their investigation there.

Daniela knew that the chauffeur had been arrested, and she guessed that the farm would be deserted. A new plan formed in her mind. It involved a huge additional risk, but the people looking for her likely wouldn't be thinking she would use the farm to hide away. Getting out of the police vehicle, she walked away casually, nodding for Yussef to follow. She doubted her illicit use of the vehicle's communication equipment would be detected. After all, the Mossos wouldn't be monitoring routine operational enquiries made by their officers from inside a patrol vehicle. Frowning with distrust, Yussef followed her up the street.

They had a short window of opportunity, she figured. She and Yussef would be safer if they moved the treasures of Aladdin's Cave from her aunt's house back to the farm. They could stay at the farm for a day, maybe two at the most. After that, it would be necessary to move again. In the short time they had, there was much to be done, she told him. The thought of the money was foremost in her mind; she couldn't risk losing such a fortune.

Without it, her efforts would be for nothing.

They arrived at her aunt's empty house more than five hours after Antonio's dragnet had commenced. Their journey had involved several close encounters. Now, at least, they'd be able to rest for a few hours. Using a spare key she kept hidden in the woodshed at the end of the garden, they entered the house. She warned Yussef not to turn on any lights.

Meanwhile, Daniela went to the garage and inspected the stolen truck they'd driven there just a few days earlier. It all seemed so unreal, she thought. She breathed a sigh of relief when she saw that the gold and wood boxes of currencies were exactly as they'd left them. No one had been here. They were safe, for now.

After what she had been through, she needed to clean up. She was surprised how unhurried Yussef was—and his insistence that he, too, must wash before they continued. He had missed his sunset prayers and now must offer the night prayer, *Salat al-'isha*. Without a word, she went quietly to another room, knowing it was her place to stay out of his way.

An hour after midnight, they pushed open the rusting garage doors. It was a rural area, and the village was quiet. Beckoning to Yussef to reverse the heavy truck onto the street, she locked the garage. She knew they would have to be careful at this late hour to avoid the police patrols. Using back roads she'd known since childhood, keeping the old vehicle's main headlights switched off, they reached the farm at El Canós without incident.

Through the night, taking only short rests, they unloaded the heavy ingots and wooden boxes. Both of them were sweating and exhausted, and their hands were sore, but she felt exhilarated. Glancing at her watch and seeing the first signs of the approaching dawn, Daniela instructed Yussef to stay with the money. She drove the vehicle back to her aunt's house, locking it securely in the garage.

Before sunrise, she left the house for the last time. It was no longer safe to be there. From a rack, she took down the bike she'd owned as a teenager. It had been such a long time ago; she gulped—her throat suddenly becoming tight. Terrible memories of the past came flooding back: the shock of the accident; her aunt informing her with a mean, indifferent face that both of her parents, and her brother Alejandro, had been killed. She recalled the haunting memories of the funeral, the sale of the family home she loved so much, and being forced to move in with her aunt. She wanted to erase every single recollection of her time at the convent—and the dreaded visits of Raphael Robles to her bedroom. Daniela felt her heart palpitate. She breathed in deeply, pushing away the terrible memories, banishing them to the far reaches of her consciousness.

As best she could, she inflated the tyres with an old bicycle pump. She left the house without looking back. Travelling on the same back roads and pedalling across farm sidetracks to avoid meeting any early risers, she arrived back at the farm. Yussef was visibly relieved to see her. He looked surprised when she entered the farmhouse and slammed the door angrily behind her.

His eyes widened as she stormed across the bare stone floor to face him—her face dark and blazing. Without warning, her mouth turned downwards in a tight arc, her jaw set hard, she began to howl. It was an animal's sound, a deep and explosive screech that seemed to shock the boy. She railed against his chest with her fists, all the time sobbing and yelling. Alarmed, he tried to fend her off, but she fought like a woman possessed.

Yussef grabbed hold of Daniela's wildly lashing arms and pulled her close to him. Instinctively, his arms knotted tightly behind her body as she kneed and kicked at him. She fought, struggling to get free, unaware of her intense strength. Unable to punch him, she tried to claw her fingernails into deep ridges down his chest. Eventually, panting and out of breath, she stopped fighting. Burying her head deeply into his shoulder, she sobbed. Her entire body trembled.

"What?" Yussef asked. "What is it?"

Daniela knew that he had no knowledge of the tragic events of her upbringing, or the abuse she had suffered many years earlier at her aunt's house. He seemed to realise, though, that her attack was not directed at him. "What?" he asked again. "Tell me."

She just shook her head. Burying her face still deeper into his shoulder, she uttered words he didn't understand. Gently, he placed his hand under her chin, forcing her to look at him. Her eyes were black and wild, her face contorted with pain. Yussef was shocked. Despite her trauma, despite her sobbing, Daniela had been unable to shed a single tear—a condition brought on by stress and repressed emotions.

Moments later, she pushed her face onto his; her eager lips found his mouth and forced his lips apart. Greedily, she pushed her tongue into his mouth, devouring him. At first, he resisted, not understanding her emotions. But, as she pulled him towards her, pressing and rubbing her body against his, he quickly became aroused. Within moments, her lithe liquid movements had whipped him into a frenzy.

The adrenaline rush she'd built up during the night and the violent release of her tortured emotions needed a physical outlet. Her pent-up energy did not go to waste. Nor did the heavy stacks of gold ingots, which, in her absence, he had piled neatly together on the stone floor.

Yussef was already exhausted from the strain of unloading the gold from the truck. Yet, he found reserves of youthful energy as Daniela ripped away his clothes and forced him backwards against the clunky, solid metal stacks. Despite the chill of the early morning and the cold metallic roughness of the ingots, they were soon locked in a steamy carnal embrace. It was an intense coitus driven by lust and their own unfathomable, deeply private emotions.

For both of them, when eventually it came, it was a golden climax.

CHAPTER 2
Luis

The chauffeur knew he was being observed. He was aware that every word he said, every move he made, every action was being recorded and carefully noted. Days earlier, he'd been captured at the farmhouse by the Mossos and handed over to the National Police. They had transported him, chained inside a windowless padded vehicle, to a holding cell. It was somewhere in Madrid, he supposed.

To him, his interrogators were predictable. At first, they'd tried their standard routines to get him to talk. He'd said nothing. Their pathetic attempts had made him smirk. His silence and condescension only served to incense them further. Shackled to the desk in handcuffs and chains, he had laughed in their faces.

"Well, Luis," said his interrogator entering the room, "are you going to talk to me this morning?" It was more of a statement, a precursor, than a question. Luis knew it contained a lie. They had allowed him no sleep for days. He hadn't seen daylight since his incarceration, but he knew it was late in the evening. It was a feeble bid to disorientate him. Inwardly, he scoffed. Working for the general, he himself frequently had used the same technique when forcing information from his prisoners.

Luis scowled at him. Normally, one glance would warn off even the most seasoned police officers. He knew they regarded him as a hard case. Tall, dark, and creepy, he was aware that he might pass for being merely strange and abnormal—except for the chilling sense of evil that exuded from every pore in his body. He was proud of it. Then there was his disfigurement.

"Your hand, Luis," said the interrogator—as if reading his thoughts. His finger gestured dismissively to the chauffeur's right hand and wrist. "An acid burn, perhaps?"

Luis did not flinch. They'd taken away the leather gloves he used to cover up his physical deformity. It was such an amateur attempt to rattle him, he thought. The interrogator would have to do much better if he wanted to unsettle him. Luis prided himself on his self-control. He would not permit himself any giveaway muscle spasms. No involuntary twitches, no tell-tale eye movements.

He faced his interrogator, avoiding direct contact. Instead, he gazed steadfastly at the middle of the man's forehead where a fully formed brown mole riveted his attention. It was a convenient flaw of nature, Luis decided. He knew that his unrelenting gaze eventually would unnerve and fluster the man. With an exaggerated frown, he studied the mole with the detached interest of a surgeon deciding how best to cut out the offending growth.

It was amazing that these fools were still in charge of the country, thought Luis. General Bastides, as old as he was, would have led Spain to a much better future. The general had been a mere junior cadet in the last years of General Franco's regime—yet he had carried the generalissimo's mission forward as if he had been appointed to do so personally by the *caudillo*.

The common people just did not understand the modern world, Luis lamented. Leaders need to be strong and decisive. The general had said as much to him . . . many times.

Luis's captors would not give him any information; he was starved of news. He knew that *Operation Ferrol* had failed, that the general and *el ejecutivo*—the members of the coup's executive government-in-waiting—had been arrested. They had been betrayed. Luis was certain.

Women were to blame; they had interfered in the work that should be done by men. The condesa had spied for the government; he knew that now. She was behind the failure of the bombing attempt at Mossos Headquarters; there was no doubt in his mind. He'd wanted to strangle her on the night she'd visited the lodge. The general had given his permission, but her husband, Carlos, had been weak and emotional. Luis would have taken pleasure in cracking the condesa's long beautiful neck and disposing of her body, letting it sink to the bottom of the cold dark lake.

Then there was the girl. The Arab boy had called her Daniela. She'd been clever, that one. Luis had been taken by surprise. He never should have allowed himself to be captured, but her audacious nighttime raid on the farm had happened so quickly. It was embarrassing. Momentarily, he had let down his guard and been captured by two young kids. They had trussed him up and left him for the Mossos to find the next morning. He'd struggled to free himself. Yet, every time he had strained at the ropes, they seemed to become tighter.

She had placed a single ingot of gold at his tightly bound ankles. It was just one of the many hundreds of gold bars he'd been guarding. Gold which she and the Arab boy had stolen from him that night. It was an inspired tactic by the girl, he had to admit. The gold linked him directly to Aladdin's Cave—to the general and the murdered priest. With that evidence, the police had conclusive proof that he was a central part of the attempt to overthrow the government. No doubt they would search the farm and find the body of the builder he'd thrown down the well.

It had taken almost a decade for the general and his rich and influential friends to build up the massive slush fund. The money was intended to finance the coup. The general had told them that once the democratic government had been overthrown and Spain's security forces had pledged allegiance to the new regime, support for their cause would grow rapidly. The smart money would flood in. Business leaders would hesitate initially, some of the general's close advisors had cautioned him. They would wait, just to make sure. Eventually, they would find a back door—untraceable ways to support the new regime. The Spanish people would welcome a strong return to law and order. The old ways.

They would put the separatist leaders from Catalunya in prison. They would find ways to demoralise the misguided separatist masses. The last of the Basque resistance cells would be infiltrated. Soon there would just be one united Spain—the Old Spain, free of the foolish European democratic experiment.

A firm hand would be at the helm. It would mirror the security that the generalissimo himself had provided for the country after the setbacks of the civil war. Luis did not believe in God, but he believed that the wealth accumulated over many years at Aladdin's Cave had a divine destiny. Its purpose was to help free Spain from its dangerous flirtation with republicanism. The coup would re-establish Spain's independence and sovereignty. The king and monarchy would be fully restored.

"We have captured the girl," said his interrogator, interrupting Luis's thoughts.

He absorbed this new piece of information, not knowing if it was true. Instead, he forced himself to continue concentrating on his interrogator's mole.

"The general's gang has been captured, and we have arrested the al-Qaeda operatives—your friends. We know all about Aladdin's Cave," his interrogator continued.

Luis was infuriated by Señor Mole's incompetence. The man had no idea who he was dealing with—did he think that Luis was a mere lackey? A simple-minded chauffeur whose only purpose was to drive a vehicle for the general? It was astonishing. Luis's professionalism was deeply offended. The man was abandoning cardinal rules of the art of interrogation. He was stupid. Even the most inexperienced apprentice into the art would know not to give away so much information—not without receiving vital intelligence in return.

It was a game that Luis knew well.

In his youth, he had dissected mice and the neighbourhood's stray cats while they were still alive. He had developed impressive skills, surgically dismembering the animals—one bone, one organ at a time. He considered his experiments a scientific endeavour, unaware that his curiosity lacked the usual filters. For Luis, it wasn't cruelty; it was a quest for knowledge. It excited him too, yielding a profound source of perverse pleasure. He was puzzled when classmates and teachers had considered his procedures repulsive. It was difficult for him to understand why they, too, would not want to explore the boundaries of pain. He'd heard whispers of words such as freak, mutant, and monster. Their taunts simply drove him to greater efforts; they shunned him even more.

It seemed to Luis that most people have little self-discipline and are unable to tolerate physical distress. He had observed that they quickly develop an aversion to pain. People will do many things to avoid discomfort, he noted—and almost anything to avoid the agony of intense suffering. There were exceptions, of course, and he was one. He had experimented in his youth on a variety of subjects, not regarding them as victims but as a necessary component of scientific discovery. Luis had not spared his own body: his scars bore witness to his exceptional level of tolerance of severe pain.

Later in life, working as a special aide to the general, his interrogations of their country's enemies had followed a similar path. His most effective method of torture was slow painful dismemberment—extracting information as his prisoners lost their self-respect and dignity, pleading for mercy. The pain that Luis inflicted on his prisoners was excruciating. He was a master of the art—always keeping the victim's mind sufficiently alert, making sure he could bleed them dry.

Girl On The Run

His mind switched back to the interrogation. Señor Mole had just divulged information about the capture of the girl and the general. They were items of information that Luis had not known before. They might be true; they might not, he thought. Their veracity was not the issue. His interrogator's clear lack of skill infuriated him. What an amateur, he fumed.

The interrogator's mention of Aladdin's Cave, however, concerned him. The horde was a fortune, and obviously the police had found out about it. It had been apparent to him, at the farm, that the girl was connected to the Mossos. She had not been acting in an official capacity, he was sure of that. With help from the Arab boy, she had driven off with the stash. He had heard them drive the stonemason's truck down the farm track to the road. After that, he'd heard nothing except his locked-up dog barking. The Mossos had arrived the next morning—no doubt tipped off anonymously by the girl.

She wouldn't get away with the heist, Luis resolved. The general had powerful friends. Many people sympathised with the cause. It wouldn't be long before some of the general's supporters ascertained what had happened to the money. If they decided to kill the girl and the Arab boy, Luis felt it would be appropriate—although he would really like to have the opportunity to deal with her himself. He would make a thorough job of it. She would die slowly and painfully. It would hardly be full retribution for the trouble she'd caused, but a well-deserved pleasure nevertheless.

For now, Señor Mole was just floundering away in the dark. Luis had no idea what the man hoped to gain. He had failed to engage his prisoner and he'd extracted nothing in the way of information. The National Police were not stupid. Surely, they would replace him soon by someone more competent?

He didn't have to wait long. The interview room door cracked open a few centimetres, and something was said that Luis could not hear. Abruptly, Señor Mole got up and left the room without another word.

He was replaced a few minutes later by a shorter, stocky muscular man with closely cropped hair. He looked Moroccan, thought Luis, sensing that his new interrogator was far more skilled than his predecessor.

"You did well in the army," observed his new interrogator, sitting across from him at the table. "You received an honourable discharge, along with several commendations. It says here that you are known by many people to be devoted to the general." He did not look up from reading the file and did not seem to be expecting a response from Luis. "You served in North Africa, again with distinctions," continued the interrogator. His chin stiffened and his mouth twisted downwards. "That deserves respect," he said, not looking up—as if he was talking to himself.

Luis was pleased that the man seemed impressed; the compliment sounded genuine. Not gratuitous or condescending. Even so, it was most likely a trick—designed to lull him into a false sense of trust.

"Before that, you had a difficult childhood." His interrogator shot him a quick glance; it meant nothing by itself, but Luis had the feeling that the new interrogator was not going out of his way to antagonise him. An impartial gesture of camaraderie perhaps, nothing more. Possibly, that had been the purpose of sending Señor Mole to interrogate him first. Luis recognised softening-up techniques when he saw them.

The National Police could be clever. They would want to discover his vulnerabilities. His devotion to the general was well known, and Luis was proud of it. He was determined that it would be the only weakness they would discover. He would have to be on his guard. It was no longer the incompetent Señor Mole who was interrogating him; this new person seemed far more professional. Much smarter.

His interrogator's approach was measured and relaxed. It was difficult for Luis to determine what the man knew and what he didn't. He wished that he would not dwell so much on his past: his school years, his army service, and his time under the general's command.

Several times, he'd asked about his relationship with the general. Nothing was said explicitly, but the interrogator had inferred the existence of something, well, not quite normal. Luis had felt his blood boil but retained his composure. The nascent mutual respect that had been forming a few moments earlier now quickly evaporated. He didn't want the interrogating officer to continue this line of questioning. There was absolutely nothing of that sort going on; there never had been.

He was relieved, almost grateful, when his interrogator switched his line of questioning. An alarm was ringing in Luis's head. He realised that he had been in full eye contact with the Moroccan since the man had entered the room. In future, he would have to be more disciplined, he resolved. He would find a weakness in his interrogator's character and exploit it.

The weather had been warm recently, and the temperature in the windowless interrogation room was high—almost deliberately so, Luis suspected. Another of the Moroccan's interrogation tricks perhaps?

There was a buzzing sound.

Luis frowned; he hated flies. This was a large fly.

Since he was young, he'd taken great pleasure in capturing them alive for surgical dismemberment. He couldn't see it, but he knew that the fly in this room was a large house fly, perhaps a blow fly—a class of the insect species that Luis despised and feared. They were unclean and could bury their eggs under the skin of a human. Unless treated, the larvae would feed off nutrients under a person's epidermal layer. On a dead body, they could hatch into maggots within twenty-four hours. Luis had witnessed it several times.

Still out of sight but within his hearing, the persistent pest seemed determined to explore every crevice of the room in its quest to escape. For a time, it settled on the wall behind Luis's head. With difficulty, he shifted his position—sitting upright in his chair. The Moroccan continued his interrogation seemingly unaware of Luis's growing discomfort. Trying to give the man's questions his full attention, just as he had done with Señor Mole, Luis answered nothing. He was determined to focus precisely on what this man was saying.

A second blowfly seemed to have entered the room—or was it still just one of them? Luis began to feel stressed. His mouth became dry, and he wanted to brush the back of his head with his shackled hand. With effort, he remained still. The Moroccan seemed to find nothing amiss. There was a loud buzz as the fly flew directly between them, settling on the wall to the left of where Luis was chained to the table. His eyes widened. When the Moroccan looked down to consult his file notes, Luis managed a furtive look at the insect. It seemed to be cleaning its wings, he thought. Or perhaps getting ready to lay its eggs? Perspiration gathered on his forehead.

"When did you first start working for the general—after your army service, I mean," asked the Moroccan.

A bead of sweat dropped from Luis's brow and splashed on the dry wood table. His interrogator seemed not to notice and gave him an enquiring look, waiting for an answer. When none was forthcoming, he scribbled a few notes in his files and continued. He seemed almost bored by their encounter.

"I can see that you're not going to cooperate, Captain," said the Moroccan addressing Luis respectfully by his military title. "That's it for this morning. If you want to talk to me anytime, my name is Diego Abaya . . . Deputy Inspector Diego Abaya. Thank you for your time, sir."

He got up and left the room.

Moments later, through the one-way glass in the viewing area outside the interview room, Diego studied his prisoner. On his phone, he scrolled through his picture gallery to locate the photos that the murdered priest had mailed to the condesa. There were several of the chauffeur and the builder loading the gold and boxes into the stonemason's truck.

Linking the chauffeur to the general and the failed coup was the easy part. He needed to pump the prisoner for information about al-Qaeda and Raphael Robles. There was much more to this operation, he was certain of that. He'd been sidelined by Madrid colleagues in Ceuta after he and Antonio had stumbled across the capitán's clandestine operation. Then came the revelations about Daniela's journey to the jihadist camp in Syria. Someone had wanted Antonio and him shut out of the investigation. He was determined to find out who it was—who'd been working with Raphael Robles and al-Qaeda.

He looked at the guard. "Time to release a few more of those blowflies into the room, please, Sergeant," he requested. "Within half an hour, they'll drive him crazy. And he can't do a thing about it."

"Do you want some released into his cell too, Deputy Inspector?" asked the guard.

Diego shook his head. "No. He's too adept at catching them when he isn't chained down. Don't worry. His imagination alone is going to keep him on edge. He hates those things. He'll have nightmares. Give him a couple of days and he'll crack."

Both men looked on and watched as Luis involuntarily ducked his head to avoid the flight of one of the insects close to his head. The prisoner's eyes widened, and he twisted his head around several times as they became airborne. In the excessive heat that Diego had ordered to be pumped into the interrogation room, the perspiration on Luis's body seemed to exude fear. It served only to attract the insects to him.

"Let him stew for half an hour, then take him back to solitary," ordered Diego, receiving a respectful nod from the guard.

Later that day, Diego reported on the encounter to his new boss. "How did you know about the prisoner's muscaphobia?" he was asked.

Diego shrugged. "I'm not going to take any credit. It was a sharp-eyed young officer—a member of the squad that raided the chauffeur's apartment. He found about a dozen flies in various states of dismemberment in a saucer on the kitchen table. We found the same thing at the farm where he was arrested. I noticed his aversion to flies when we brought him in for interrogation. He flinched as one came close to him. It happened again later; the insect spooked him. To him, flies are dirty and loathsome," continued Diego. "It's a deep-seated phobia."

"He's evil and sadistic. But he has information we need."

"If I have to send him over the edge mentally to get it, I will."

Antonio

Somehow, Daniela had got away.

Antonio knew he'd made some serious errors. He had allowed his personal feelings to affect his professional judgment. He realised he'd made a mistake recruiting her onto the Mossos Homicide Squad. Not going through the normal hiring and interview process had been a personal decision; he'd cut corners. He'd been blind to what she was doing behind his back—trusting her when he should have been far more careful with the squad's information, and his own.

He'd done what he normally never did—and ignored the warning signs. Xavi and others had tried to alert him. They'd tried to tell him, but he hadn't listened. As if that wasn't bad enough, he'd screwed up the trust he had with Maria. He'd upset her and probably ruined their relationship.

It wasn't just a lapse of judgment on his part. He knew now that he'd allowed himself to be flattered and driven by his ego. Daniela had beguiled him, luring him into the trap she'd set. Emotionally, he'd been naïve. Professionally, he had lost sight of his objectives. He'd been duped: everyone knew that she'd made a fool of him. Worse, he'd let them down. Over the past several days, every time he looked in the mirror, Antonio had despised what he saw.

It was early afternoon, and he'd just returned from a difficult meeting at the Generalitat. The Catalan president had refused to accept his resignation. Fate had not been as kind to the chief: his father was close to retirement and a search was under way already for his replacement. His dad was a scapegoat. Antonio knew that he'd let him down.

"We foiled a terrorist bombing attempt—and a plot to overthrow the Madrid government," the president had kept reminding everyone at the meeting. "We've done well. This situation with the stolen stash of laundered funds—it's not our doing. Let's make sure we lay that stinking pile of puppy poop at Madrid's front door. They'd do the same to us if they had the chance.

"Antonio, you foiled the bombing attempt. You're a hero," the president had continued. "The media says so, and the public loves you. Most importantly, I say so too. I want you take a more prominent role going forwards."

No matter how much Antonio protested, the president had insisted. "In collaboration with the federal police, Catalunya is going to put more resources into the fight against terrorism," he announced. "When we become the Republic of Catalunya, we must be a world-class policing and security agency," he'd told the media immediately after the meeting, deftly sidestepping questions about Catalan separatism. "The fight for independence from Madrid is a totally different issue."

Hardly anyone believed his claim, but the media gave him credit. The president was an astute politician, playing his political cards with the flair of a master statesman. Yet, there were whispers that not all was well within his administration. Several of his colleagues were in jail, charged with sedition—prisoners of Madrid. They'd become popular local folk heroes. He was not. That would come when he successfully created the Catalan Republic. It was not far off—his advisors were certain.

None of the praise heaped on him made Antonio feel any better. His promotion to full inspector stuck badly in his throat; he knew it wasn't deserved. He'd called Xavi and told him about the meeting. His friend was upbeat and happy to hear Antonio's news. Antonio was feeling too defensive to share Xavi's cheerful feelings. He was aware his family and friends were relieved that the truth about Daniela had come out at last. They just weren't talking to Antonio about it. They weren't saying anything—not to his face, anyway.

Antonio glanced at his watch. He'd arranged to take Maria out for dinner that evening, just the two of them. They needed to talk over things—about them. He was determined not to repeat the mistakes of his recent past. For now, there was work to be done; he had even more responsibilities than before. He intended to make changes. Big changes.

The hunt for Daniela continued to be the highest priority for the Mossos and the federal police. Antonio intended to catch her and bring her to justice. Despite what the Catalan president had said about the stolen stash of laundered funds, Antonio knew that he'd almost had the money in his grasp. He'd been stupid. He'd allowed Daniela the opportunity to locate Aladdin's Cave and steal the massive fortune. She'd used Mossos resources and abused Antonio's trust, whisking away the stash from under his nose. He was determined to get it back.

He thought again about Maria. Tonight's dinner was going to be difficult. She'd been wonderfully supportive of him and understanding. He was aware that Daniela had been vindictive, almost succeeding in sabotaging their relationship. Now Daniela was a fugitive. Diego's investigations had linked her directly with al-Qaeda, as well as the attempted bombing of Mossos Headquarters. An international arrest warrant had been issued for her. A red alert. When caught, she'd be charged with theft and terrorist conspiracy, and probably a long list of other crimes. Meanwhile, she was on the run—dangerous and vindictive.

Antonio knew he had to protect Maria. To do that, he couldn't allow her to remain a target of Daniela's wrath. If anything happened to Maria because of him, he'd never forgive himself. He would explain his plan to her at dinner.

She would understand.

She didn't understand.

Maria didn't agree with Antonio; she didn't believe her life was in danger.

"You don't know who we're dealing with," Antonio protested. His words came tumbling out and they sounded angry. "I've talked to Diego. What she's been doing is far worse than I knew. She's part of a well-established al-Qaeda terror cell somewhere here in the city. We all know what ruthless bastards they are."

"I don't understand what you're suggesting," said Maria.

"I want you to stay in a Mossos safe house. Take time off from your job until this is over. If I get called out at night, or if I need to travel, I'd feel much better knowing our best teams are taking care of you," said Antonio.

"Is there something you're not telling me?" asked Maria. "Has she threatened to kill me? Why do you think my life is in danger?"

"No, nothing like that. But she's been trying to sabotage our relationship. You know that. She wants to get at me—and she'll continue to target you to achieve it. You've seen the manhunt we have under way to catch her. She's a dangerous criminal."

Maria was unconvinced and thought he sounded a bit paranoid. Antonio had told her about the texts that he'd discovered had been deleted from his phone by Daniela. She knew about Daniela's really sneaky trick at the flower shop. He'd been really embarrassed. There was probably a lot more he wasn't telling her, she figured. He was incredibly self-conscious about how stupid he'd been and found it hard to talk about. His male ego had been badly bruised. She didn't want rub his face in it. Instinctively, she avoided the subject.

"I want to be with you," she said adamantly.

He shook his head. "*Cariñyo*, I've screwed up badly already. We must find that woman and lock her away before she inflicts any more damage. You have to understand that we are dealing with a terrorist group, and Daniela is one of their most effective agents. We know that now. We didn't before, but we do now. She knows where we live. She wants you out of the way. I know her, sweetheart, and I understand her mind—how she thinks," he added forcibly.

Antonio was only trying to protect her, Maria was sure. But he hadn't been perceptive so far about Daniela. Before her cover had been blown by Diego, Antonio had been completely fooled by the girl. Mesmerised might be a better word. Daniela had been a clever little vixen, and she was really evil. Maria knew the real truth: Antonio had been seduced by the young girl's charm.

He'd been blind to what was happening. For too long, he'd refused to admit what had been clear to almost everyone who'd encountered the little bitch. Maria wasn't going to say that to Antonio. It would be too much of an affront to his masculinity; he would hate her for it. That was the problem she was struggling with. He was persecuting himself and overreacting to his poor judgment. He wanted to make amends—quickly and powerfully. Everyone knew it had become a vendetta. He was on a witch hunt, and Daniela was the wicked witch.

"There is one other thing," he started to say—and failed to make eye contact with Maria.

She looked at him with concern. "What?" she demanded.

"I think we should break up."

Maria gasped.

"I don't mean that we should break up. Not really. Just for appearances' sake—to fool Daniela into thinking that you're no longer with me, that we are no longer together."

"Toni, you must be joking," said Maria, starting to cry. "I don't want to be shut away out of contact with the world. I'm not some kind of delicate flower. We could face this thing together. I can help you; I want to help you."

Antonio shook his head. "Don't you see? We must give the appearance of a clean break. It's what she has been hoping for. It's what she has been working towards, forcing us to split up."

Maria couldn't believe it. Tears streamed down her face. She could feel her make-up coming apart. Her natural instincts were those of any other woman who loves her man and wants to be with him, to help protect him. She knew they'd be safer together than apart. But it didn't seem that way to Antonio. For a moment, Maria thought of telling him what had crossed her mind a few minutes earlier. If they continued to live together, she'd been thinking that maybe she could help lure Daniela—help trap her. Maria was willing to act as bait. But she knew that was precisely what Antonio feared. He would never allow her to put herself in the path of a direct threat. She knew that acting as bait carried other risks. The person out to kill her might not be Daniela herself—it might be an al-Qaeda professional killer. Yet, she feared the alternative much more. Breaking up—even if it was a subterfuge and just for a short time—was not something she was willing to do.

Finally, Maria relented. She wanted to put conditions on it—to limit the damage it would do to their relationship. Yet, suggesting that to Antonio would do no good, she told herself. As she frequently did with him, Maria acceded to his demands even though she was terrified of the consequences. The prospect made her feel ill. She conceded that as a policeman, Antonio had the weight of logic on his side. But, as her partner, he was making a terrible error. Nothing good would come of a staged break-up. If they knew how close she and Antonio had been for so long, few women would be fooled by such a contrivance. Certainly, Daniela would not be convinced by such an obvious ploy. The witch would see their break-up as an opportunity. She'd find a way to turn the knife—and make sure they'd never again have the chance to get back together. Manipulative, conniving, and unscrupulous women like Daniela would never allow a wounded competitor to escape. They would never take that risk.

Maria knew she'd been a target for Daniela's wrath. Now, she realised with horror, she would become the focus of the spurned woman's fury. Daniela would close in for the kill. Maria felt deflated, cast out, and rejected. It was not what she had expected of Antonio. Where had their love gone? she asked herself. Did he really want her, or was he still secretly infatuated with that devilish woman?

Her tears dried, and she entered a bitter, dark world where disillusionment and treachery walked side by side. It was a bleak place, without promise that any good would ever re-emerge. Maria wondered if they really had a future together. Yet, even that formerly happy prospect had lost its allure.

It was over, she admitted.

At that moment, she realised that she no longer cared.

CHAPTER 3
Daniela

Daniela knew they couldn't risk staying at the farm at El Canós. Not for long anyway. One more day perhaps, but that was it. It would take only one curious Mossos d'Esquadra patrol to drive up the farm track and check on the supposedly empty premises. Then it would be game over.

The farm was a distance away from the nearest village. Except for its brief occupancy by the chauffeur, it had been deserted for years. She could understand why he'd chosen it: the farmhouse and outbuildings were well-built and in good condition, made of stone from a local quarry. It had been an ideal hideout for him—and a clever place to store the gold and banknotes from Aladdin's Cave.

There was electricity and cold running water but no heating. The windows hadn't been cleaned in years. It smelled unpleasantly of wet dog. She shivered. It was a dank and depressing place. Despite its shortcomings, it was a temporary home. They and the treasure were safe—for now. As the hours passed, living in almost constant gloom and darkness, she and Yussef were irritable and constantly on edge—both listening for the slightest sound of impending danger. Without an escape route, there would be no way for them to elude capture. Their brief tenure as fugitives would be over; they'd be arrested and taken into custody.

Daniela felt cut off from the world. Without a computer, Wi-Fi service and a phone, she knew she was at a significant tactical disadvantage to the police and security forces. Getting back online—finding out what was happening, regaining control—was a vital lifeline. There had to be a way to re-establish it soon, she told herself.

Overnight, unable to sleep, she had tussled restlessly with her options. Eventually, an idea had emerged. Her most urgent priority was to create a new identity for herself. After that, they would have to move the gold and boxes of currency a second time—to a more permanent place of safety.

It was still early morning. She hadn't slept, and her eyes looked red and puffy. In the winter months, the nights were long and the days short. At night, it was cold—an almost constant chill. The farmhouse was austere and uncomfortable. She had insisted that Yussef should sleep on the old sofa in the main room. Telling him she was fine, she curled up on an uncompromising and unforgiving old wooden chair.

Forcing open the rusting metal-framed windows, she tried to get rid of the smell of the chauffeur's dog. Her thoughts kept going back to the night they'd carried out their daring raid. She'd taken a risk leaving Luis trussed up for the Mossos to find. Early the next morning, she'd made an anonymous call to them. During her last few days working for the Mossos—before her cover had been blown—she had heard that the chauffeur had been arrested. She was glad that the man was no longer around. He was pathologically evil.

Examining the room, it was evident that no one except the chauffeur had lived there—not for a long time. She knew it would be stupid to get a wood fire going. Smoke from the damp chimney would be noticed by the locals; questions would be asked and someone would call the police. They would have to make do, she told Yussef. Water from the ancient metal tap was icy cold—suitable for drinking but freezing for any other purpose. The place seemed to echo the austere character of the chauffeur. She shivered, yearning to get away from the bleak austerity of the place.

The previous day, she'd cut her hair. After a wash in the frigid water, it had looked a lot better. Today, she wasn't so sure. Leaning forwards, she examined her appearance in the cracked mirror in the cramped bathroom. It wasn't really a disguise, she admitted, but it would do for now—until she could create something more convincing.

Yussef was shivering. He'd found it difficult to sleep in the frigid conditions. Both of them were hungry, and that made the cold worse. Going outside into the damp morning, she rode her ancient bike in the direction of the local market town, shivering uncontrollably en route. In the harsh morning air, it was hard to warm up—even when she pedalled briskly. The chain and wheel hubs had not been oiled for years; the unlubricated metal surfaces made a harsh squeaking noise. The tyres were almost flat. She was relieved that no one was around to witness it.

Heaving against the pedals, she thought about her next steps. New documentation was her top priority. If she was stopped for questioning, she had nothing. That would sound alarms bells. Unless she was very lucky, almost certainly she would be detained for questioning. Then it was only a matter of time before a routine fingerprint check would reveal who she was.

She had money now—lots of it. What she urgently needed was someone else's identity—a young woman around her own age. A stolen passport would be ideal; she could doctor it herself in no time. Stealing a passport in this rural area, however, might draw attention. In Barcelona, it would mean nothing. Theft of passports was an everyday occurrence; black market IDs were easy to buy in the city. There was no other option: she would have to start small and modestly. Stealing a driver's licence, ideally from a tourist, might not be reported. Her English wasn't bad. At least it might get her past any immediate scrutiny if she were stopped for questioning.

It was breakfast time and most outdoor cafés in the town were closed for the season. The area was popular with cyclists, even in off-season—so a few places remained open. This morning, they were frequented mostly by locals. At one of them, a couple was sitting in the weak November sun, sipping steaming hot coffee and enjoying a relaxed start to their day. Mentally, she shook her head. The demographic was wrong; they were too old.

Minutes later, a group of noisy cyclists flashed by in their colourful outfits—tight spandex, muscular tanned bodies, and well-contoured legs. Their lead outrider, a man in his mid-thirties, she guessed, was talking loudly in English. Soon the group pulled up at a café where a waiter was wiping the overnight dew from the tables. The place had just opened.

There must be thirty of them, thought Daniela, an idea forming in her mind. She dismounted and walked slowly back towards the café. Loud noise and laughter soon confirmed they were Americans. That would work for her, she figured. There were several women in the group. She watched from a distance, waiting for an opportunity. One thing for sure, she thought, they wouldn't be loading up on heavy English breakfasts. Most likely, they'd set out early that morning and had been riding for several hours. They'd drink water or coffee and eat something light, she decided. That would give her twenty minutes, maybe half an hour at most.

The waiter, working alone, had not been expecting such a large influx of customers—and so early. He seemed bewildered by the energy and incessant foreign chatter of the group. Stopping his task of cleaning the tables, he was now handing around the café's menus. He hurried to the kitchen for the first orders for coffee and croissants. Minutes later, he was back with a loaded tray—trying his best to serve those who'd ordered them. He nodded his head vigorously as the cyclists barked out new requests for food and drink.

Daniela saw her chance.

Two or three of the women were similar to her in size and build, she had noted. One had caught her attention—she seemed Hispanic. Perhaps Mexican extraction, thought Daniela. Following the example of her friends, the young woman had placed her helmet and daypack on an empty table behind them.

Striding towards the kitchen, Daniela almost ran into the harassed waiter hurrying out with another tray of coffees. "I'll take that," she said in her best rendition of an American accent. "We need seven more espressos—and quickly!" He nodded his thanks and returned to the kitchen. Aware of the legendary penchant of Americans to be far too generous with their gratuities, Daniela guessed that the kitchen staff would pull out all the stops to be accommodating.

"Five espressos," announced Daniela in passable English as she arrived at the tables. "Plus, two Americanos." Collecting some empty dishes, she turned her back and placed them on the table behind her—alongside the helmets and the young woman's daypack. In the ensuing scramble, as the coffee allocation was sorted out by the riders, it was effortless for Daniela to open it and remove the cyclist's wallet.

"Hot croissants coming up," she told them, grabbing the tray and heading back towards the kitchen. Thirty seconds later, she had collected her bicycle and was pedalling briskly towards the far end of the market town. Out of sight, she examined her haul. The young woman's purse held a small amount of money, which Daniela pocketed. More importantly, she found her new identity—she was about to become Susan Garcia from Albuquerque, New Mexico. Aged twenty-four, she was just a few years older than Daniela. It was perfect.

The prize among the items she'd stolen was a family photograph. Susan Garcia had a brother. He could pass for being around Yussef's age, she noted. Her newly acquired parents gazed back at her from the photograph. The family was standing outside a building that clearly was a Christian Mission. A fortuitous cover story, thought Daniela, grateful for her unexpected luck.

For the next several hours, she stayed away from the café area. The real Susan Garcia would have discovered her loss by now, she figured. But the cycling group would have a schedule, and Daniela figured that the stolen purse would be a minor incident—even if it was reported to the local police. With luck, they wouldn't even connect her with the theft.

Figuring it was safe, she rode back into the town centre and set out to fill her shopping list. Her first purchase, using the girl's cash, was a lightweight backpack. Then, at a school supplies shop, she paid in cash for a second-hand laptop. At a farmacia, she bought make-up and some personal items, two cheap but convincing wigs, and some video games to keep Yussef occupied.

Walking past a novelty store, something caught her attention. She emerged a few minutes later with a pair of cheap glasses with slightly tinted unmagnified lenses and round frames. They changed the shape of her face and took attention away from her normally compelling eyes. With the judicious use of make-up, she figured, she could make herself look less attractive. Looking increasingly like a student, she wanted her new image to be unremarkable and commonplace. It might be difficult to achieve, she admitted. Her natural good looks made her stand out in a crowd. That was the last thing she wanted right now.

Finally, she purchased a dull but well-insulated jacket for herself. It appealed to her because a small American flag had been sewn by the manufacturer onto the front pocket. It was just the branding she wanted. She wore it right away. The same store provided two nondescript baseball caps. Already starting to be weighed down by her purchases, her final buys were a hoodie and a thick pullover for Yussef.

It was a risk remaining in the town, but she wasn't finished. Earlier, she'd evaluated the least risky among the public Wi-Fi options that seemed to be available. She'd decided on using the local public library. It was a small place and didn't seem to be covered by security cameras. Finding a quiet corner, she covered the desk with books to look like a student at work. She wanted to dissuade conversations with other patrons as she went online.

Within an hour, she was up to date with the news. She hacked into several websites and the personal online accounts of strangers selected at random. One had a VPN account, and she soon located several unencrypted files that had not been wiped clean. The cache history was full of promising leads. Within ten minutes, she'd created a convincing electronic trail to reinforce her new identity. Searching the geography of her newly acquired home town in the United States, she felt comfortable with her new cover story.

Daniela developed the beginnings of her new identity as Susan Garcia—an art student from New Mexico.

Keying into vacation properties in an area she'd targeted earlier as part of her plan, Daniela located what seemed to be an ideal property. It wasn't far from the farm at El Canós. Reserving it for several months with a local agency, she added some online requests. She was a visiting post-graduate student from the United States, she wrote. She would be arriving that evening with her brother; their parents would arrive shortly.

The agent replied almost immediately. Yes, the cottage was somewhat isolated, but it had reliable and strong Wi-Fi and would be a quiet place for her studies. It was furnished and available for immediate possession. The agency would require a down payment and a security deposit. Those could be paid when she arrived. The address? Of course, the agent replied. Naturally, Señora Garcia would want to check out the property online; he understood that. She made an appointment with him for early the next day to sign the rental contract.

Looking up from her laptop, she saw that the library was becoming busier. She rearranged her books to build a fortress of academic texts—dissuading anyone from talking to her.

Scanning several art websites, she subscribed to free emails using her newly acquired name and address. Knowing that most of them would on-sell email addresses in bulk to other commercial enterprises, she figured that within a few days, she would begin to receive piles of junk mail. For once, it would be welcome. She would have to buy a mobile phone legally. Probably two. With only the stolen driver's licence for identification, she needed tangible proof of her new identity as soon as possible. The junk mail would help for ID, especially if the storekeepers weren't too fussy. Hacking into a local utility company's server, she got access through a poorly protected minor supplier account. She linked to their change of address requests—using an account that had been closed recently but had a perfect credit score history. Duplicating the information onto two government sites, she cited the utility as a credit reference.

Her final visit, before she rode back to the farm, was to the local produce market. She chose several items of food that she thought would appeal to Yussef's Middle Eastern tastes and a fresh baguette.

Pedalling back to the farm through the back roads she knew so well, Daniela focused her mind. Recalling as many American television personalities as she could, she practised a low-key accent that she imagined would be representative of a Hispanic girl from New Mexico. Nothing too complicated—it just had to be believable. She would use the bottle of hair dye she'd just purchased to streak her hair blonde and enhance her physical transformation. It wouldn't be perfect; it just had to reasonably convincing, she thought.

Reflecting on her recent escape from Barcelona, the more she thought about the sniper's attempt to kill her, the more she was convinced it wasn't Antonio. That meant a lot to her. If the online news was anything to go by, his stern face during a recent interview left no doubt in Daniela's mind. He had completely dismissed her reassuring words to him. There was no doubt: he was on a vendetta—and out to get her.

He wasn't trying to kill her. But there was still the prospect of the long jail sentence that he clearly had in mind.

Daniela shook her head. He just didn't understand.

He didn't get it.

Daniela barely slept again that night. As much as she tried, she couldn't get Antonio out of her mind. If only she could talk to him—explain things. She had convinced herself that hunting her down like a criminal was not what he wanted for them . . . not really. He had his job to do, yes. He was a good detective. She knew that, and she admired and respected his sharp mind. But he was still her Antonio. If the night they'd almost shared together had gone differently, she was sure she could have convinced him about their future as a couple. She could help him see things—other possibilities of what to do with his life. Her plans were not beyond his comprehension. He wasn't weak, but he had allowed himself to be influenced by others. By that sister of his, and Maria.

She felt her blood pressure rise as she thought again about the words that Maria had texted to Antonio . . . the words she had quickly erased from his cell phone:

"Toni, I love you so much. I agree with you. Let's start again—a fresh new beginning. It will be just like the old days. Call me quickly. I can't wait to see you. You have my heart. I am all yours. M."

Daniela hadn't given Antonio a chance to read Maria's words. They were juvenile and a complete distraction. Maria was wrong for him. He would never be satisfied with such a relationship. Antonio with Maria? It was absurd. Daniela knew that he would be much happier with her. They had the same interests, the same intellect. A shared destiny. He might be satisfied with Maria for a time. It wouldn't last. It was just too comfortable, lacking the challenges that she and he could undertake together. With Maria, he would grow old. Gradually, disillusionment would set in. His sense of fun would be stifled; his brain would become dull. She couldn't allow Maria to do that to Antonio.

She wouldn't allow it.

Finally, she fell asleep, her mind exhausted—her body coiled tight with determination and resolve.

Next day, the sun shone and it was a bit warmer. The night had been cold, worsened by the creeping dampness of the farm buildings. Their new clothing helped make it slightly less uncomfortable. Daniela left early.

She cycled to a small town just south of where she'd stolen her new identity. Keeping a wary eye out for the American cyclists she'd encountered the previous day, she was able to find the rental agency without any problem. It was located on the main street.

The place seemed deserted. Likely, it was busy during the tourist season, she guessed. Not at this time of year. The middle-aged agent was expecting her and spoke passable English. She thanked him for his efforts and switched quickly to broken Spanish, which seemed to impress him. She intended to learn the language, she said. If he didn't mind, she'd like to practise.

He seemed charmed. Yes, he was pleased to arrange the off-season rental for the American oil painter and her younger brother. The cottage had enough bedrooms for their parents when they arrived from the United States, he told her. It was an isolated place in a rural setting. Lots of room. Plenty of space for their parents to park their car when they arrived from the airport, and it had a lockable garage. The local train service was a bit sporadic. But it was easy to use, if she needed to go into the city to buy painting supplies or visit galleries.

Daniela, stumbling in broken Spanish, apologised profusely to him. Would he mind if she paid in cash? If she were able to secure a confirmed place at the university, she explained, she would apply for non-resident status and open a bank account. For now, it would have to be euro banknotes. No receipt necessary. The beaming agent was reassuring as he pocketed the money. Not to worry, he said. The owner of the cottage lived in Argentina. He was sure the man wouldn't mind not having to deal with credit cards and all that tiresome paperwork.

What kinds of subjects did she paint, by the way? He himself liked to dabble, he admitted, smiling sheepishly. Just a hobby really. Not a lot of talent—they'd told him many years ago at school. Yet, painting gave such a sense of freedom, didn't it? It was therapeutic. And there were so many wonderful subjects to paint around here. The cottage was fully furnished, he confirmed. She and her younger brother could use the bicycles stored in the garage to go into the village and buy groceries. It would be good exercise, he said.

Daniela, struggling clumsily with her Spanish, found a way to tell the agent that her parents in New Mexico had chosen to adopt a handicapped Navajo boy. Out here in the fresh air and Catalan countryside, the boy would be less self-conscious about his speech impediment and limp, she intimated. Daniela made sure the agent took a good look at the stolen photograph she handed him. "That's my younger brother," she explained.

His sympathetic glance at the photograph of the handicapped boy conveyed his admiration for her compassion. It must be difficult for her, his look said. It's a wonderful-looking family, he agreed, handing the photo back.

"We love each other," said Daniela, her eyes turning downwards as if in a silent prayer. "And in the sight of God, we are all equal."

The agent nodded with polite enthusiasm. He was sure their whole family would enjoy their extended vacation in Catalunya. And, of course, if her parents should ever consider buying a summer cottage here, he'd be delighted to show them around. Prices in this part of the country were still quite a bargain, he said—handing her several business cards.

"By the way, Señora Garcia, your Spanish really is quite good," he said, smiling as he gave her two sets of keys. Coming from New Mexico, and with Hispanic parents, obviously she had an ear for it. She would soon pick up the language, he predicted.

Pleased with her transaction, Daniela retrieved her bicycle and started her ride back to the farm. She had been wrestling with another problem—she needed a better mode of transportation. Something quick and more mobile. A strong vehicle that could carry a lot of weight.

On her way into town, a distance from the rental agency, she'd noticed a used-car lot. It seemed to be a marginal enterprise. Under the circumstances, she thought it might serve her purpose. She had dismissed the idea of renting a car at one of the global agencies. There were far too many risks—and anyway, especially as a tourist, they would require a passport and credit card. Riding her bicycle into the used-car lot, she leaned it against the front of the sales office—aware that the salesman sitting inside was already sizing her up.

"How can I help you?" the young man asked. He smiled approvingly at her.

"I need some wheels," she said in Spanish heavily laden with an exaggerated American accent. "I'm a student, but I need more than that thing." She pointed at her bicycle. "Something reliable." She explained her recent arrival from the United States and residency in the area as an arts student. "My younger brother has a handicap; he's in a wheelchair," she added, giving the salesman a baleful look. She walked over to a beat up old green sedan. "Maybe I could buy this one?" she asked. "I have money, that's not the problem. I can pay you in cash."

Glancing around the lot, Daniela guessed they didn't sell many vehicles. He seemed alone in charge of the place. He was young and quite likely the son of the owner, she guessed. If he made a sale today, it might be a big boost to his ego—and the business.

"Oh, I really like your jacket," she said, coming close to him and running her hand up and down the lapel. She flashed him a flirtatious look. "We have these in the United States, but this looks really good on you." She broke away and opened the driver's door. "How much is this one?" she asked, giving him a generous smile.

"Sticker price is fifteen hundred euros. For cash, I can let you have it for twelve hundred. It's old, but it still has a few kilometres left on it. A good runabout."

"What about insurance?" she asked. "I haven't set up any banking arrangements yet. Can I just pay cash for that too?"

That won't be a problem, he assured her. He had a friend who could write-up a policy, and she could drive the vehicle away without delay. Her bicycle could be loaded into the back.

Daniela knew that she had no interest in the green sedan. It was a wreck. She needed a vehicle that could carry weight. A lot of it. She made a quick calculation. Each gold bar weighed twelve kilos; she'd confirmed on the internet. Fully loaded, even the largest compacts on his lot could transport a maximum of seven people. That was equivalent to about a half-tonne carrying capacity, she estimated. To save weight, they could keep low on fuel. Even so, with a driver and passenger, each payload would be a maximum of forty gold ingots. When they'd moved the gold from her aunt's house to the farm, she and Yussef had counted nearly eight hundred of them. That would mean twenty trips in total. It was impossible.

None of the cars would be strong enough to move the gold from the farm to the cottage in a single journey. They would have to make multiple trips. It would take too much time. Even worse, it would increase the risk of a heavily laden car being observed.

Far too risky. She had to find a better way to transport it. The stonemason's truck had been the ideal vehicle: it was built to carry heavy loads. She needed something similar.

"I'm not sure," she hesitated, walking away from the green sedan. "Maybe I should wait until all my residency papers have arrived. Besides, I don't think this one is best for me. My parents are arriving soon. It's too small. My dad is a big guy; his legs won't fit."

"I've got something larger over here," the young man said, beckoning her over to a more recent model—a shiny red compact. "The price is higher. But, if you're paying cash, I can cut you a deal." He grinned at her.

She shook her head. "It's a bit too flashy—even for an American." She laughed. "What's that?" she asked, pointing to the army-style green and brown Humvee at the far end of the lot. It was dirt-ridden and looked like it had seen better days.

"Oh that," said the car lot operator. "It's a trade-in. Two German guys used it to tour around last summer. They stripped everything out. Good vehicle, but it needs cleaning. It's reinforced for heavy loads. Do you need something that big?"

Daniela noticed his crestfallen face. It was obvious he'd been hoping to sell her a more expensive vehicle. "I've got to buy some furniture for my place," she lied. "And it would be good for carrying heavy things, including our suitcases."

"That's for sure." He laughed. "That thing can carry house-loads of furniture. Difficult to park in the city. You'd better off with the lower mileage red compact I showed you."

Daniela had opened the doors of the Humvee and was already looking inside. "Hey, when my parents arrive, we could go touring Europe in this," she said excitedly. "How much is it? It could fit my brother's wheelchair too," she added.

"Yeah, I suppose it could." He seemed to realise that he'd dissed the vehicle and it was time to extol its merits. Now that he knew this was the vehicle she wanted, thought Daniela, he'd be turning on his charm to sell it to her.

He patted the side of the vehicle, as though it was an obedient dog. "She's a great old lady, this one," he added, warming to his sales pitch. "Plus, I could throw in a new battery," he offered—probably covering up for the fact that the current one most likely would be as dead as a rock, she thought. Judging from its dusty condition, the vehicle hadn't been started up in months.

"I don't trust cheap batteries," she said. "I'm always having problems with my laptop. I'll pay extra for a really good one."

He smiled. "Don't worry, señora. I have a new industrial heavy-duty one out back. If you can wait a few minutes, I'll install it myself. Why don't you wait inside?" He held up the palm of his hand to indicate the start of a rain shower. "I'll put on new windshield wipers and give it a wash too."

"I'm not sure. How much do you want for it?" she asked, pulling back.

The young man gulped. Obviously, he was aware that it was an older model, although solid and strong. The upholstery was aging, and the engine likely had seen better days, but Daniela guessed that he wouldn't want to give it away. He was probably thinking it might sell as the warmer weather approached. "How about . . . Let's say forty-five hundred?" he ventured. "In cash. Everything included."

He waited while she pondered the transaction, watching the contortions of her mouth as she tussled with her decision.

"Wow, that's over five thousand dollars," she calculated, biting her lip. "Okay it's a deal. But my father is a minister of the church. He will be mad at me if I mess up and everything is not complete. Can I trust you to make sure the insurance and all that stuff is done properly? I don't know what the law here requires."

"Don't worry, I'll fix everything," he promised, patting her patronisingly on the shoulder. "You can bring in your identification papers anytime. Now go inside and get out of this rain. There's coffee in there. I'll have this old lady ready for you in no time." He hurried off to get his tools.

Alone inside the office, Daniela looked around. The young man had his back turned and was busy installing the new battery. She sneaked a look inside the old metal filing cabinet and glanced at the vehicle sales files. Soon, she found the information she wanted. From one folder, she removed a photocopy of an apartment rental agreement belonging to a previous customer. From another file, she found several character references. Using his photocopier, she printed a copy of the driver's licence she'd stolen from Susan Garcia—but made sure the number was blurred.

Taking a roll of money from her pocket, she counted out the purchase price, making sure that she included several small bills, so that it looked as though she'd had to pool all her available cash to pay for the vehicle. She didn't want to leave the impression that she could easily afford it. Then she sat back and waited.

She faked a grateful smile as the young man returned, wiping his greasy hands on a cloth rag. "I do have a copy of some documents that might be useful—until I can bring my identity papers. You can use this for the insurance, can't you?" she asked, handing him the photocopy of Susan Garcia's driver's licence. "And here is my lease agreement for my apartment near here," she added quickly, piling it on top. "Here are some references. They are in the name of the person we are sharing the apartment with. Is that okay?"

He laughed as he took the documents. "Oh, that's more than enough. I'll make a call to my friend and get the insurance done over the phone. You're lucky—the vehicle is licenced until late next year."

Half an hour later, her bicycle stored in the back, Daniela drove the freshly washed and fully legalised vehicle off the lot—and was heading back to check on Yussef at the farm. She was worried it looked ex-military, but they needed something that could carry a lot of weight. Later, she planned to find somewhere quiet and steal a set of licence plates from another vehicle. Then it would be virtually untraceable to the car lot owner. Besides, the young man seemed happy with his cash. She was sure he would bask in the glory of a profitable sale—soon forgetting that she'd failed to return with her ID papers. It was an old vehicle anyway. She figured the owner of the lot would write it off, pocketing the cash. The tax man would never hear about it.

With the right financial incentives, the used-car business worked to perfection, she reflected as she approached the gravel road leading up the farm. Importantly, she had acquired a vehicle they could use to move around. If the police got too close, they could quickly get out of the area. Now she could turn her attention to transporting the massive fortune they'd stolen from Aladdin's Cave.

She already had an idea that would take care of the heavy wooden boxes stuffed with cash. The paper money had to be put back into circulation as soon as possible. The gold bars were a different proposition; they could be kept much longer. The heavy reinforced chassis of the Humvee was strong enough to move the gold to a safe and more permanent storage place—in one journey.

Daniela knew exactly where to hide it.

Her choice of their new hideout was inspired, thought Daniela. The cottage she'd just rented was perfect: the location was exactly where she'd wanted; it couldn't have been any better. It had several bedrooms, a fully fitted kitchen and, just as the agent had promised, it was fully furnished. She was confident that the place would be clean and tidy, and inviting.

She was anxious to leave the depressing atmosphere of the farm—just as soon as she'd taken care of business. Firstly, the cash.

When that was taken care of, they would move the gold.

To a place where Antonio would never think of looking.

Nicolas

Nicolas Julio de Granada, 15th Marquis of Tarragona, stood alone and dispirited on the expansive marbled sundeck of his family's seaside chateau located on an exclusive part of the Spanish Mediterranean coast. He managed to wave cheerfully, with feigned enthusiasm, to his young wife and their two children as they climbed into the tender that would take them out to his yacht anchored in the bay.

He was becoming expert at such facial masquerades—a skill he'd perfected to an art form over the past several months as his desperation had increased. He was determined they must not discover the reality—that he was on the verge of personal bankruptcy, and so was the family's bank.

His children were too young to understand the impending catastrophe; their recriminations would come later. It was Cristina's disappointment in him that he dreaded most. Many times recently, he'd imagined the scared and disappointed look that would cloud her beautiful face as he confessed the truth. The disaster, he would have to admit to her, was entirely due to his imprudent investments—his greed and stupidity. She might excuse his foolishness; she could never forgive his deception.

He had failed her and their children.

By next week, the yacht along with ownership of the Banco de Familia Tarragona and all his properties would fall into the hands of bankruptcy administrators. Some time ago, he'd placed some minor assets in his wife's name; the rest he had heavily mortgaged. Now he hoped that the sentiments of his lawyer would prove to be correct—that his creditors would not push too hard in trying to claw his wife's townhouse and car back into his estate. They would be a consolation prize. For his family, it would be traumatic—a complete loss of face and social status.

His fate, unless there was a miracle, was pre-determined. His destiny was sealed. Miracles . . . ha! He'd given up believing in those many years ago, abandoning the charade of praying to a supposedly most merciful God. As he watched the vessel's tender reach the yacht, he turned and moved back towards their chateau. It, too, would be seized by the bailiffs, he reflected with a shudder.

Seven years earlier, he had promised Cristina's father that he would take care of her. He'd assured the elderly man that he would prudently manage the substantial investments he'd entrusted to Nicolas's care at the bank—one of Spain's oldest and formerly most respected financial institutions.

Girl On The Run

The crisis at the Banco de Familia Tarragona was a known secret within the banking community. Whispers and rumours were part of bankers' currency—alongside avarice and deceit. The holy grail of public confidence in the country's banks, it was claimed, was based on a rock-solid bastion of trust. In reality, the financial community was a sham, thought Nicolas. His fellow bankers followed a self-serving herd instinct. Threatened by outside forces, bankers are a band of brothers. Yet, he knew that at the first sign of any weakness within their group, they would turn into a pack of hyenas—circling the weaker member, savouring the spoils of a kill.

Some years earlier, the global economic downtown and crisis in Europe had inflicted widespread cutbacks. The band of brothers had appealed to Madrid and received a sympathetic ear. Bailout funds had been provided, more than once. Even as the heavy leather belt of regulatory austerity imposed on ordinary working people was cinched tighter, Madrid sheltered its banks. Nicolas knew that many of his competitors had been treated less cordially than he. It was perhaps a recognition by Madrid of the good standing in which his family, and his predecessors at Banco de Familia Tarragona, were held by the central government. Not least, generations earlier, by General Franco himself.

Despite the crutch of bailout funds, Nicolas had been unwise; he had gambled. Lured by the prospect of quick returns in the construction industry, he had invested the bank's remaining capital badly. He'd known it was rolling the dice; he ignored warning whispers in his ear that preached prudence and urged caution. Now even his most loyal investors and trusted friends had abandoned him to his fate.

Ugly rumours were beginning to swirl, propelling depositors towards a public rout—a run on the bank. In two days, after the holiday weekend, the regular banking week would resume. The outlook could be summarised very simply, his closest advisors had bluntly informed him. If the bank's depositors panicked, there would be insufficient cash to meet demands. Preferred lenders would be the first to demand repayment of their loans. After that . . .

Nicolas was unconcerned about the working-class families and others who had trusted their life savings to him. That was the risk they took, he felt. When the bank had done well, they had too. Anyway, by government regulation, they would be able to recoup a small part of their losses through the industry's insurance fund. Nor did he have sympathy for his unsecured investing friends, especially those who'd deserted him in his time of need.

Truthfully, he cared little for the burdens of his family's heritage. In the context of all those respected generations of his family before him, this would be their most glaring ignominy. A long time ago, he had shrugged off that unwieldy responsibility. He had been nobly born, yes, but he hadn't exactly inherited the fortunes of El Dorado.

It was Cristina he worried about, above all others.

He did not want to lose her.

Or his children.

Inevitably, she had heard some of the gossip, but Nicolas's words had reassured her. Her father's and their family's financial future were not at risk, he'd lied. It was just business and he—Nicolas, the 15th Marquis of Tarragona—would take care of them.

He'd thought dispassionately about suicide. It didn't seem like a feasible option. His life insurance policies were sizeable, but an accidental death would have to be convincing. Besides, he admitted, he didn't really have the appetite for it—or the courage.

"May I get anything for you, señor?" asked the voice of an older woman.

Nicolas turned, his face now frozen in a confident and seemingly relaxed countenance. It took him a second or two before he realised what the servant was asking. "Perhaps an espresso," he answered brusquely. "I'll take it on the terrace. Oh, and a glass of water too," he added, fingering in his pocket the plastic container of tablets prescribed by his doctor for high blood pressure.

In the shade of a juvenile palm tree, he looked again at the email he had received earlier that morning. It was from a female vice president of a medium-size, second-line Canadian bank. Its message was terse: *"We can help you, but this must remain confidential. Tell no one."*

It was an unusual message, especially as it purported to come from a well-known, reliable overseas source, thought Nicolas. This really wasn't the way such communications were handled. And there were no follow-up instructions. He was tempted to dismiss it as a hoax, as malware-generated spam. It was about on par with similar scam letters from Nigeria. But how had they found his name and his private email address? he wondered. Not just that, the Canadian bank was a credible name in the business. The email wasn't quite legitimate, for sure, but its offer of hope stopped him from deleting it.

He conceded that utter desperation might have something to do with his hesitation. In any case, he would not be foolish enough actually to reply. Surely it was a spoof? Perhaps someone in the media embarked on a fishing expedition. Instinctively, he was inclined to junk it.

His espresso arrived on a tray, along with the water. He smiled thinly at his elderly servant and mumbled his thanks. When she was out of sight, he removed the cap from its plastic container and swallowed four tablets. The coffee took away the sour taste of the medication.

His phone sounded. A second text had arrived from the same source. This time, it was much more convincing. Astonishingly, it contained two attachments. The first was a confidential board of directors' summary of their cash liquidity position. It was from the previous day. Nicolas couldn't believe it. Fewer than five people had seen that document.

The second document contained several months of near-term projections of cash flows for Banco de Familia Tarragona. Only three people were in possession of this information. It was unbelievable. Nicolas immediately leapt to the conclusion that Russian hackers must have compromised the bank's elaborate security system—in which case, a ransomware demand would quickly follow. Either that, or the email had to be from an insider. And a very close insider at that, Nicolas quickly concluded.

He would have to tread carefully. Very carefully.

Could this be a lifeline?

Surely not, but . . .

Hooked

Daniela sat back and thought about the two emails she'd sent.

There could be no doubt that Banco de Familia Tarragona was on its last legs and its owner would be desperate. She had researched Nicolas in considerable depth. It was not hard to guess that his current frame of mind would lead him to take risks that no one in his position normally would consider.

Her plan was simple. She had no expertise in laundering such a large amount of cash. Yet, she was certain that such skills were close to the hearts and business practices of many bankers.

Nowadays, she knew, banks had to navigate intense international controls. The new rules were strict—and reasonably well-policed by sophisticated regulators and elaborate tracking systems. Having paid huge fines for their past transgressions, most banks were staying well away from the more flagrant nod-and-wink layering practices of the past. Of course, laundering was too lucrative a business to abandon altogether. Backroom experts and greedy traders employed by the banks would find better scams: new angles and creative loopholes. Soon, they would move a step, maybe two, ahead of the regulators.

Initially, Daniela had assembled a short list of secondary and regional banks in Spain—ones which, like Banco de Familia Tarragona, were desperate to survive and maybe even more willing than normal to be unusually creative, despite the regulatory risks. Like Nicolas, they had a dire need for funds, especially ready cash. Daniela had a matching need: to put the banknotes from Aladdin's Cave back into circulation before they became stale and obsolete.

A perfect match, she'd concluded.

She had no intention of doing anything immediately with the gold bullion she'd acquired. It was a highly desirable commodity and could be put back into circulation anytime. But she was aware that even temporary storage was risky. The gold was heavy and difficult to transport over long distances. She had already figured out somewhere more permanent to hide it.

Her priority would be to offer the banknotes to Nicolas, surmising that he would leap at the opportunity.

Of course, she needed to make sure he could be trusted. After some searching on the dark web, she had stumbled across a well-hidden and embarrassing secret from his past. It was confirmed by a photo file she had found concealed on his laptop. Now she had a hook into him that would ensure his silence and loyalty. At the right time, to make sure that Nicolas knew she was not to be underestimated, she would text him an innocent message—along with a photograph of his wife and two children that Cristina had taken that morning on their yacht. Her text would say very simply *"To Daddy with Love."* It was Daniela's code for *"Do not betray me. I can bring you down—anytime."*

Concerns about the safety of his family would ensure Nicolas's loyalty. After all, she smiled, desperate men will do reckless things in crucial circumstances. Now there were just a few other steps in the process.

Within days, she anticipated, he would provide her with untraceable and fully negotiable bearer bonds issued by Banco de Familia Tarragona. They could be cashed anywhere by anyone, anytime, without need for explanation. They were a perfect liquid currency.

As part of her deal with Nicolas, she would require him to carry out a further transaction, which, as an experienced banker, he would know how to do—with the facilities and credibility to do it.

Overall, it was an arrangement that would net her just under six hundred and fifty million euros in gilt-edged securities, she calculated. The bonds would be fully convertible when the timing was right into clean and untraceable euros, dollars and sterling. They were perfect for her scheme.

For Nicolas, if his dark secret ever became public, it would be an even worse fate than personal bankruptcy.

There were embarrassing personal weaknesses that he would not want revealed.

To anyone—ever.

Unit 22

On the steep barren slopes of the Sierra Morena, a small underpowered compact was struggling to make headway against the incline. Strong crosswinds buffeted the vehicle from time to time, tossing it around like a plastic beachball. Several times, Diego had to wrench back control, fighting hard to steer the vehicle away from the narrow gravel shoulder. He'd been perilously close to the edge a few times; it hadn't been a nice feeling. The sheer unprotected sides dropped precipitously into deep, uninhabited dark valleys below.

He'd seen the strong-wind warning signs a few kilometres back. Shifting to a lower gear, he was thankful to be travelling slowly. No one else was on the road. It was deserted. He couldn't remember the last car he'd seen, and trucks were strictly prohibited from using this route. Even at the best of times, it wasn't the place to have an accident or a breakdown.

Diego concluded that the authorities had chosen a forbidding location for Unit 22. It was ideal for its purpose. Perhaps because he knew about the elaborate security measures surrounding the secret facility, he had an uneasy feeling that despite the bleak landscape, there would be eyes-on everywhere. Hidden cameras watching each move he made. He imagined a drone or two out there observing him with the eyes of a hawk. That was fine with him.

Still, it was a bit unsettling.

At least, they'd be tracking him and be able to guess at his arrival time.

Diego wasn't feeling good. It wasn't anything physical. More a feeling of disquiet. A sense of unease that had enveloped him for weeks—ever since they'd arrested his former boss. He felt betrayed. He'd admired and trusted Raphael Robles. And he'd learned a lot from him too. Now, at GEO Police Headquarters, smiles had vanished—replaced by furtive glances and narrowed darting eyes. Trust was in short supply; suspicions were easily aroused. It was hard for Diego to understand why Robles would choose to be a traitor to his country.

The irony was that he came from one of Spain's noblest families. They'd earned exemplary status over many centuries. Their Christian pedigree extended well back into history. His ancestors had distinguished themselves in battle and commerce long before Ferdinand and Isabella seized the last remaining territories held by al-Andalus and created modern Spain. The Robles family was bedrock Christianity.

An awkward question hung in the air: Who else might have been involved in the plot?

Adrenaline from the wild car drive had pumped Diego's emotions; he wanted to get back at his former boss. Since his arrest, Robles had been held at Unit 22 without charges. It was a legitimate limitation of his civil liberties—allowed under the country's anti-terrorism laws. No lawyers. Confined under ultra-maximum security, he was the most senior agent of al-Qaeda that Spain's security forces had ever taken alive.

At the beginning, Robles wasn't talking.

Not at first, anyway. It was just a matter of time. Eventually, he did . . . more or less. That was the problem with administering truth drugs to prisoners—they weren't infallible, Diego reflected. They could loosen a prisoner's tongue, but they could also make them anxious to please their captors. Sometimes, it was hard to sort out truth from fiction. Often, prisoners simply told their captors what they thought they wanted to hear. Diego figured that, at Unit 22, he'd be able to do better. He had an inside track. His new boss had given him the green light to interrogate Robles—with strict preconditions. He mustn't reveal certain things that the prisoner desperately wanted to know.

It was growing dark as the last of the day faded. Heavy black-grey clouds blocked out the last of the natural light. Already using his main beams, Diego wished he'd insisted on a better rental vehicle. Arriving late from Madrid hadn't helped. The best ones among the tired and nondescript fleet had already been picked through. He'd argued with the clerk, but it wasn't the kid's fault. Upgrading Diego as best he could, he'd comped him a handheld GPS. Diego knew he could have pulled rank. His National Police credentials nearly always terrified the crap out of members of the public. But he was travelling under an alias. His new boss didn't want his visit to arouse attention.

Over the weeks since Robles's arrest, his interrogators had learned a lot about al-Qaeda in Spain—subversive cells they had no prior knowledge of but suspected existed. They knew that Robles was the mastermind of terrorist jihadism in the country. Not just that, but his warped mind had created a new monster—an unholy alliance of Old Spain with vicious modern-day terrorists. His arrest wasn't public knowledge, and it had been kept that way under the orders of the prime minister. It was a smart move, thought Diego. Goodness only knows, the country could do without any more scandals and destabilising crises. Enough was enough. Modern Spain was a fledgling democracy vulnerable to subversion by home-grown separatists. Not to mention self-interested, highly-placed people scheming a return to the old ways.

Shifting gears, Diego made use of a straight stretch of road. Accelerating, he figured he might be able to clip a few minutes off his journey time. His thoughts drifted back to how he would interrogate Robles.

Surprise was always an invaluable weapon in warfare, and there was no doubt in his mind that, within GEO, they were engaged in a constant and vicious war against terrorists—of all kinds and persuasions. Tomorrow, when Robles saw him walking into his cell, Diego wanted the element of surprise. He wanted to unsettle him—before he could gather his wits. He intended to pump the bastard for information that he was certain he had—but which the prison interrogators hadn't been successful getting out of him.

Diego was convinced that Robles had an accomplice.

He suspected that senior people in the Spanish government—and maybe the Civil Guard and the Army too—had been complicit in his activities. His new boss agreed. They were convinced there was a conspiracy of silence—and it involved Madrid. Since Robles's arrest, high-ranking people had been protected, and Diego was determined to find out who they were. He knew he'd have to be as clever as his former boss, even though that was a formidable challenge.

At Unit 22, Robles's interrogators knew they were dealing with a very smart enemy agent. They had taken the view that they'd be able extract quality intel if they avoided the transactional game he'd prefer to play. They needed the ace card of controlling his mental state. Eventually, he would want to trade—his need for information was so intense. Diego knew his former boss's way of thinking. Robles might be willing to starve his body, but his mind was ravenous.

Encountering a sharp and dangerous switchback, Diego slowed almost to a crawl. Changing up, he focused only on his driving. He was near the summit and soon would head downhill for the rest of his journey. Not wanting to miss his turning, he took the opportunity to clean his windshield. Scratching angrily against the grimy glass, the blades left wide streaks of dirt. Visibility was only marginally improved.

It was hard to tell with diehards like Robles, he thought. Political prisoners are a different beast from the usual crowd of common criminals. For one thing, they don't respond to threats against their personal safety. They don't fear the prospect of long periods of incarceration. In most cases, they aren't driven by greed or the need for notoriety. Nor are they motivated by any of the myriad other reasons parroted by criminal psychologists as drivers of criminal activity. Political prisoners, especially religious zealots, are in a class of their own—and it's very large and rapidly growing. They are extremists by any definition.

Dealing with terrorists, Diego was aware that they don't see themselves as being criminals. In their own minds, they answer to a higher authority. One that is not the established order of things. They're willing to sacrifice themselves and almost everyone else for their cause. They have a completely different frame of reference from everyone else. For them, acts of terror are a means to an end. No remorse, no conscience, no pity. Wild animals have more compassion.

Then, occasionally—unfortunately, very rarely—Diego had found himself interrogating a confirmed terrorist who actually seemed to have a more open mind but with a warped social conscience. He knew they had no regrets about the deaths and vicious destruction they'd wrought. Yet, he could sense that they struggled to understand why other people couldn't comprehend the justification for their heinous crimes.

Ironically, at the time, Diego had even discussed it with Robles. "Some of them *do* care that we can't understand. They *want* us to understand," Diego had told him. Robles had said nothing, but Diego recalled a smile and his boss's intense look. Thinking back, with twenty-twenty hindsight, it seemed that Robles was delighted with his protégé's insight.

Encouraged, Diego had continued his explanation. Robles had listened attentively, like a proud mentor. "It's not a weakness in the resolve of such zealots," Diego recalled himself saying. "It's a reflection of their fundamentalist fervour. They feel the need to reveal the true path to others—and demand strict obedience to it. They are just as intolerant of alternative beliefs as their foot soldiers, and always ready to kill. Given a chance to preach, they almost can't stop. Bin Laden was a preacher: he was a missionary. Abu Bakr al-Baghdadi was the opposite: he killed on a whim," he'd told Robles.

Diego's fingers gripped the steering wheel—unaware that he was squeezing the life out of the inert object. If only he'd had just a hint of Robles's duplicitous dealings, he would never have had such a conversation with the man. Back then, it had just been two colleagues discussing a serious subject relating to their work. Now, as he drove to Unit 22 to interrogate him, he realised how convincing his former boss had been—fooling everyone.

It worried Diego that Raphael Robles didn't seem to fit neatly into either of the stereotypes he'd described that day. They'd worked closely for several years. Being in the same proximity, he'd learned a few things. He wasn't sure what Robles's IQ was, but he was willing to guess that it would be right up there at genius level—in his case, an evil genius. Robles was a brilliant manipulator, of course, and certainly a very smart detective. One thing Diego had learned: his weakness was his body language. He had lots of nervous energy, and it showed.

Over the years, he'd learned to get insights into his boss's thinking by observing him closely. When they next met, he wanted Robles to remember he possessed these informed perceptions. Diego wanted it to be part of his technique to unsettle the prisoner. If Robles was sluggish from a sleepless night, as he'd been assured he would be, he might let down his guard. Diego liked that. He imagined that, at Unit 22, softening up prisoners before interrogation would be one of their black arts. Mind games would be their specialty.

He was watching closely for his left turn when suddenly his headlights illuminated the sign he was looking for. He nearly missed it. Anyone reading the lettering, if they managed to see it at all, would learn that the dirt road sloped abruptly, leading down to one of Cordoba's reservoirs. It was marked strictly off-limits to the public. Diego slowed his vehicle to a crawl. The drive downhill went on for several minutes. Negotiating a cattle grid, the unforgiving metal strips jarred his vehicle so hard he was worried the suspension might break. Minutes later, he arrived at a high reinforced gate. A sign warned uninvited visitors of significant fines for entering the protected water table.

He was almost blinded by a series of intensely bright blue-white lights. Out of sight of the main road, they bathed him and his vehicle in a pool of scrutiny. Slowly, a high metal gate swung open, and a green light—which seemed to be concealed in an authentic-looking tree trunk—flashed a signal for him to proceed. The whole process of entry was controlled electronically. Diego had no doubt now that Unit 22's security cameras had picked up the presence of his vehicle kilometres away. He figured he was probably infra-red scanned as soon as he'd turned onto the dirt road. They know exactly who I am, he thought. I'm expected, and I'm more or less on time—when they adjust their arrival estimates to compensate for the crap car I'm driving.

A subdued light warned him that the speed limit was fifteen kilometres an hour. A snail's pace. In that satanic darkness, he didn't know if he could crawl his vehicle forward at more than five. Eventually, he saw a few dimmed lights on the approach road. The facility itself was well disguised as a series of farm buildings. It looked peaceful and innocent. Diego figured there would be electrified razor wire around the perimeter fence embedded inside innocent-looking green hedgerows. Well-armed guard patrols too. He doubted if anyone could get near the place, and that was reassuring. There was no way for anyone to force their way in, or for Robles and any of his fellow inmates to escape.

After he'd reported in and had been met by two seriously scary military guards, his successful retina scan allowed him to proceed to the next level of security. He was relieved of his SIG P226 and spare magazine. A guard gave him a receipt for them and a few other minor items. They took his car keys. He guessed that in a few minutes his vehicle would be stored somewhere out of sight, probably in a holding area excavated deep underground.

A genial senior officer greeted him. "Welcome to Unit 22, Deputy Inspector. I'll show you to your quarters. You can get a shower and a meal before turning in for the night."

Diego had overnighted at maximum security prisons before. He'd never thought of them as being holiday camps, but they weren't bad. Visitors' quarters usually were a bit spartan. They were never allowed to forget they were subject to the very strict rules of a well-managed and intolerant prison system. Diego respected that.

Unit 22 came as a complete surprise. It was so different from the norm. Incredibly modern, almost futuristic in design. He was amazed how few people there were. It was almost ghostly, like being beamed up into an alien spaceship. Considering what Robles had been up to and the power he'd wielded within certain neo-fascist groups in Spain—not to mention al-Qaeda—Diego was content knowing about the ultra-high security keeping the bastard in here.

Figuring he'd be able to get a few hours of sleep, he asked the officer for an early start for his internal briefing before he interrogated Robles. The officer grinned and assured him that Robles had no warning of his visit.

As Diego unpacked his overnight bag, he knew he'd have to find out why someone with Robles's background—coming from one of the most established Christian families in Spain—had become such an unapologetic and vehement jihadist. Inadvertently, Robles might let something slip that would help them track down Daniela. Frankly,

73

he doubted he'd have much success on that score. Those two seemed as thick as thieves.

He would focus instead on finding out who in the government and federal security forces Robles had been working with—who he was protecting. Powerful people in Madrid were involved in all of this; Diego knew it.

His visitor's bedroom was palatial but without real windows. In their place, a backlit pastoral scene offered a surreal feel of the world outside. Before he'd arrived, he'd expected to be sleeping on one of the usual hard military cots. Instead, his bed was pristinely comfortable.

Setting his phone alarm, he noted that the only giveaway that this was a military facility was the faint smell of chlorine bleach on the prison-cleaned bedsheets and pillows.

Diego slept like a baby.

CHAPTER 4
Jamal
Taybat al-Imam, North of Hama, Syria

His pain-racked body now in spasms, his face contorted with agony, Jamal struggled to examine the bloodied bandage covering the deep wound gouged into his left shoulder.

He guessed it might be a bullet, although he had no recall. Their position had been hit by a barrage of mortar fire. After that, the regime fighters had sprayed the building with gunfire as they moved through. They would assume that he and his rebel fighters were dead but would make sure with a short burst into each of the bodies. Insurance against a bullet in their backs.

His shoulder wound might have been caused by a piece of shrapnel; he couldn't turn his face close enough to the entry wound to see. It had missed the subclavian vein at least. Thanks be to Allah! I'm not quite dead yet, he thought. As for his scapula, the bone might have been hit. It could mend and was the least of his worries.

Gritting his dust-caked teeth, he reached again for his medical pack. Before the mortar shell had exploded, the bag had been slung across the front of his body. Now it was trapped behind him. Using his free right arm, he was able to work the canvas bag around towards his chest.

Much earlier, before he had passed out in pain, he'd tried to locate exactly where the object had penetrated his shoulder. He'd been careful, knowing that shifting its position by accident could tear into the vein. Better to leave it, he decided. The bandage had helped. Most of the heavy bleeding had stopped.

He was concerned about his left leg. It was trapped under a slab of fallen concrete. He could feel nothing: wriggling his toes yielded no sensation. As a doctor, that worried him. If blood supply stopped getting through, he could lose his foot or part of the leg. The onset of gangrene was his worst fear. The searing pain in his twisted thigh was intense. The last of his local anaesthetic had been used up days ago. He had one pre-packed syringe of morphine remaining. Somehow, he couldn't bring himself to use it. Not on himself. There would always be someone in his brigade in greater need. Jamal slipped back into a fitful sleep, knowing he desperately needed water and medical help.

He dreamed about Daniela. Then woke with a sudden start. Yelling out, he did his best to glance around. She wasn't there. He lapsed back into a fitful slumber.

Later, he was aware of artillery and the sound of an incoming tank shell. Distant at first, his ears recognised the tell-tale whistle sound. He waited as the noise of its approach became louder . . . still louder. It would land close to him, he realised without any emotion. Was this it? A wayward shell fired off target would be the instrument of his death? It was ironic really, he admitted, after all he had been through, and this time he was not even the intended target of the incompetent artilleryman. He hadn't even used the last of the morphine; he allowed himself a wry smile.

The shell hit about ten metres on the other side of the building. The percussion and shock waves shook his body. His ears lost all hearing. His lungs tried to cough out the tsunami of dust that now swirled past him. Trying to cover his eyes with his free hand was to no avail. The incoming grit gouged into his eye sockets. His rapid blinking acted like a piece of coarse grade sandpaper scratching inexorably against the sensitive membranes of his bloodshot corneas.

Jamal passed out.

He awoke sometime later. The dust had settled, and he realised that his immediate surroundings had altered. There was a large hole in the wall opposite him created by the explosion. Jamal could see that his leg was now freed. His boot was missing, and he could see dark congealed blood surrounding his ankle. He tried to flex his toes but felt nothing. Knowing that even a tingling sensation would be a good omen, he forced himself to exercise until his calf muscles became too agonisingly sore to continue. If he could stand, even on one leg, he reasoned, there was a chance he might be able to escape. Right now, it did not look good.

He heard the sound of a helicopter. Two, maybe three of them. Their powerful rotors punching the air, chopping, creating heavy pulses of aggressive sound. Then came the feathering. Still incredibly loud. Landing somewhere close. Sikorskys, he guessed from their powerful motors. But whose?

Over the past several months, the regime had pushed far north of Damascus, emboldened by well-armed and experienced Russian air strikes and, more recently, by their ground support troops. The Russians were providing armaments to al-Daser, helping swing the balance of military power against ISIS and the rebels. Jamal knew that the Iraqi Army would soon be ordered to fight against the Syrian Defence Force and the Kurds from the Iraq border. In the civil war, President al-Daser would accept nothing less than complete victory over the whole of Syria. Now that he was supported by Russian equipment and confident Moscow attitudes, and assisted by his allies Iran and Lebanese Hezbollah, the way was open for him to achieve total victory.

The Russians were the white-skinned saviours of a crippled and immoral regime, Jamal thought resentfully. They were strategic friends of Tehran and Damascus. They were temporary friends of the Turks and would be until the Kurds had been rendered impotent. Two wars in Syria were being waged in parallel. The Coalition's fight against Islamic State was being won. But the internal war of genocide, the so-called civil war, would continue unabated. Jamal knew that the international fight against President al-Daser had been weakened by America's dithering and lack of resolve. Indecision—the ultimate incompetence of a head of state during wartime. Jamal despised the Western powers. Yet, even he regretted that in recent times the United States had forfeited its manhood. It had lost its way.

Jamal knew that ISIS had been beaten on the battle grounds. They were a vicious bunch of savages, hated also by his own brigade of rebels. They both fought for an Islamic victory, but he detested the methods that ISIS used. They would be reviled and despised by the civilian population for generations to come. Al-Qaeda, which had been pushed to the background, now relished their former allies' demise.

In the final stages of the civil war, ISIS freedom fighters captured alive were being treated to the same brutalities they had meted out as they'd spread the evil of the caliphate. Like cats playing with half-dead mice, the victors denied captured ISIS fighters any swift justice. The prisoners begged to be put under the knife, but their captors' memories were long and bitter. There would be more torture, more agony. Retribution.

There were revenge killings too. Memories and tribal resentments were not just generations old but grudges carried over the centuries— handed down as a right-of-passage from fathers to sons, from mothers to daughters. Violent discord within families. Blood cousins pitched against blood cousins. Entrenched hostilities between neighbours, often for reasons long forgotten. Endless feuds persisted between tribes. Fealties betrayed. Nothing was considered excessive in the pursuit of vengeance—all in the name of family honour.

As an educated man, Jamal was aware that the words *"Vengeance is mine, saith the Lord"* appeared as an instruction in Deuteronomy—but he knew they held no place in the beliefs of those who had occupied these lands for thousands of years. In the view of such people, there could be no forgiveness. An eye for an eye. Blood money could be paid, but wrongs were rarely forgiven—and never forgotten.

Girl On The Run

There was no beginning to it; there was no end to it.

Drifting in and out of consciousness, Jamal pictured the vengeance that would be wrought on the soldiers of the caliphate. Many would be caught, tortured, and executed, yet tens of thousands would escape—to fight again somewhere. It was inevitable. His volunteer brigade of rebels was a militia. Ordinary civilians like himself had grouped together to fight al-Daser, to fight for the jihad but not to wage an unholy war. They had fought under several flags, merging with other rebel groups as became necessary, to consolidate their numbers and increase their military effectiveness.

Two days earlier, Jamal had received a direct order from al-Qaeda provisional headquarters. It had been handed down from Ayman al-Zawahiri himself. The order was for Jamal to transfer leadership of his brigade to his deputy. His immediate presence was required by the high command, said the order.

Jamal had ignored it. Hama—currently the focal point of al-Daser's systemic genocide—was still worth the fight, even though the prospects of a rebel victory were slim. On the outskirts of the city, Jamal's rebels had fought a series of skirmishes against the emboldened Syrian Army. Russian airstrikes had forced his rebel forces to disband into smaller, more mobile, platoons. Then, yesterday, there had been a massive counterattack from the regime on their base position at Taybat al-Imam—a comparatively small town but strategic in the battle for control of the land corridor from Damascus to Aleppo. Many of Jamal's men had been killed.

Drifting in and out of sleep, at times becoming delirious, he tried to stay awake but failed. Then . . . new voices. He was aware of an officer's commands being shouted. He tried to make out what was happening, then lapsed into a confused world of overlapping images and sounds.

Straining to open his eyes, he could make out the blurred shape of a Syrian Army soldier. In his sights, the laser beam of his captured M16 assault rifle centred on Jamal's forehead. The soldier's eyes burned with the wild fury that only pure hatred can engender. Next to him, a tall, thin Russian officer was yelling—ordering him to lower the weapon.

Jamal watched the encounter, aware that his imminent demise was in the balance. He did so with little emotion, but an impending feeling of dread. As his eyes cleared, his gaze focused on the man who was trying to save him. The Russian's black brassard indicated a blue and yellow crest. On it, a bat was superimposed. Jamal's heart sank. The officer was a member of the Spetsnaz special forces. Within Syria, they were mobilised as part of Russia's military intelligence, the GRU. The Russian's interest in him was not a good sign, Jamal knew at once.

The Spetsnaz officer won the argument and came over to kneel by him. Brusquely, he searched through the pockets of his tunic, finding his identification papers. His eyes widened as he read through them. Then smiling triumphantly at Jamal, he said in fluent Arabic, "Well, commander of al-Nusra, we find you at last." Turning his head, he gestured in the direction of the Syrian Army soldier and spoke to Jamal. "He will not be your executioner. Not today. We have other plans for you."

The Russian stood up and spoke rapidly in his own language into his lapel radio. Minutes later, soldiers could be heard scrambling over the rubble inside the building, attempting to climb onto the small concrete ledge which was all that remained of the floor. They were Russian ground force troops.

Jamal was aware of someone close to him. He heard a voice in a language he didn't understand—but it sounded Russian—a heavily accented Chechen voice, perhaps. It was a young voice, kindly—not that of a killing machine, thought Jamal. He felt something cold on his lips. Someone was wiping away the encrusted dust. A squirt of fresh water was delivered inside his mouth. Something soft was dabbing at his eyes, removing a few layers of dust from his encrusted eyelids.

Slowly, Jamal was able to make out the red insignia of a young medic. His gaze fixed on the young man's tunic and identified several battle citations. He saw the soldier's eyes—an intense blue; they flickered as the medic thought through his next steps. Jamal no longer cared. He had no power to influence his fate. The pain in his leg became intense, as his sense of feeling returned. The Russian lifted his hand and swung it in a short arc, backwards and forwards across Jamal's face like a pendulum. All the time, the medic was watching Jamal's eyes.

He wants to know if I'm scared, or defiant, thought Jamal. Maybe he thinks I'm lying on top of an IED. He returned the stare of the Russian, who was now shining a thin pencil light into his eyes. Jamal winced. He tried to grin, as a thought entered his mind—maybe he thinks I'm stoned on jihadi pills!

The young medic seemed satisfied and re-examined Jamal's leg.

The ensuing pain was unbelievable! In the agony, Jamal's eyeballs disappeared upwards into their sockets—only the whites remaining. He screeched with pain. Eventually, he looked down. The Russian had turned his broken leg back into a forward position. A spear of broken fibula that had stuck out of Jamal's leg—an ugly splinter of raw crimson bone—was now back in its place.

The Russian leaned over to his medical bag and took out a phial of endomorphin. He made the injection straight into Jamal's shoulder, through the tattered cloth. It took only a few seconds to work.

Jamal was asleep. He was unaware that the Russian was still working on his leg. The medic gave his patient several injections of antibiotics. He grafted on layers of artificial skin and bound the wound with a splint. All the time, the Spetsnaz officer hovered in the background.

With care, Jamal was placed on a stretcher and lowered out of the ruined building. He did not know that his rescuers had slipped many times in the process, risking their own safety. Their orders were clear: this captive must be kept alive. He awoke briefly as they carried him towards a field ambulance. He saw again the face of the young Russian medic. The boy examined him and looked up at the Spetsnaz officer for instructions. The officer gave him a nod of approval. Looking at Jamal, the medic tapped the clear plastic cylinder of a syringe to remove a small air lock.

The action told Jamal that he was no longer going to be loaded into a field ambulance. The tall, thin Spetsnaz officer had received new orders on his radio. As the drug took its effect, Jamal realised that he was about to be loaded into one of the helicopters. His status as a prisoner of war had just been elevated. Now he was a prisoner of Russian military intelligence.

Jamal regretted not having died alongside his men.

Then he passed out.

Jamal
Latakia, Syria

They were good to him.

Even in his weakened, often delirious state, Jamal knew that he was receiving exceptional medical care. They seemed determined he would recover. His training as a surgeon helped him recognise the signs—the constant stream of specialists and senior experienced nurses; his medications and almost nonstop monitoring of his vital signs. It confirmed what he'd suspected on the day he'd been captured: he was a high-profile prisoner with a price on his head.

In those first few weeks, during the times he regained consciousness, he sometimes wondered why they were working so hard to keep him alive. They wanted him to recover—even though, for years, they would have done almost anything to kill him.

After several months, Jamal no longer speculated. He was certain they had a role for him—if only as a pawn in some elaborate game of war chess. He had only one question: What was it they intended him to do? He had received no clues during his repeated interrogations, not a single hint. There was nothing in their pattern or tone that might have tipped him to their thinking—their plan for him.

Even when his health and physical condition improved and when, with the aid of crutches, he could shuffle around his heavily guarded private ward, he could not glean their objectives. There was, however, one thing he knew: the Russians were close allies of President al-Daser—and they could not be trusted.

One day, long after the interrogations had ceased, he was interviewed by the senior Russian officer whose tunic bore the fearsome bat emblem of the Spetsnaz. Jamal was still being kept in solitary confinement, but they had continued with his exemplary medical treatment. For the past several months, he had been provided with specialist training in calisthenics. He was given spa treatments twice a week.

"What do you want of me?" he asked before the tall, thin Russian could speak.

"You do not remember me, perhaps?" queried the officer. "I rescued you from the building where you had been trapped, where your men had been killed—and you too, almost."

"I am grateful," Jamal nodded. "Yet, I am fearful of the price I must pay."

"The price you have paid—already it is more than most men," the officer replied. His tone was sincere and respectful, thought Jamal. The compliment was not unwarranted, but he waited for his captor to reveal his real agenda. "You are regarded highly by your people," said the Russian. "A hero, maybe. Even with your considerable injuries, there are things you can do to help your country. Actions you can take to help the peace process."

Jamal glanced at the metal crutches with which he was learning to walk, and said nothing.

"The medical experts . . . they say you will make a full recovery. Perhaps some residual pain, but you have no fear of that," said the Russian. "You have strong constitution, commander of al-Nusra. We will help your body recover as well."

CHAPTER 5
The Cottage

It was another risk, thought Daniela.

Yussef seemed impressed by the Humvee—happy they had a vehicle at last.

Feeling the jangle of the vehicle's keys in her pocket, she resolved to keep them with her. Yussef was young and impetuous. He might be tempted to take the vehicle—and whatever money he could carry. She'd delivered him a stern lecture about their dire predicament. He'd promised he wouldn't do anything stupid.

For now, she just had to trust him.

The cottage was situated on farm land and had a panoramic view of the surrounding area. She knew that the nearest neighbour was at least a kilometre away. For her purposes, the privacy was perfect. It had an added advantage: it was surrounded by a copse of trees—which made the cottage hard to see, yet she could see anyone approaching. It was exactly as she'd viewed it on Google Earth at the library. She'd studied the area carefully and had memorised all the important details. It was almost like she'd been there several times before.

At the cottage, there was none of the damp coldness of the farm at El Canós. It was inviting and comfortable. The electricity was on, and she turned on the hot water boiler, adjusting to its maximum setting. At last, they could wash properly; she almost laughed aloud. Plenty of clean linens and three comfortable bedrooms. The Wi-Fi worked, just as the agent had promised. A strong signal.

Deciding to explore outside, she checked the detached garage alongside. It had no windows and would suit their purposes, she quickly concluded. Walking down the track leading from the road, she cut across the ploughed fields. Daniela knew exactly where she was going but hadn't expected to meet her neighbour quite so quickly. They saw each other at exactly the same time. She knew who he was immediately: Antonio's grandfather was out walking his dog. He'd just left his own cottage on the far side of the hill.

There was no alternative other than to continue walking until they met. Rapidly, she mentally rehearsed her cover story, hoping that her Americanised Spanish would fool the old man. Getting closer, she wasn't fully prepared for their encounter. He looked so much like a much older Antonio that she nearly gasped. Bright and intelligent. Fortunately for her—friendly, like his dog.

She introduced herself and relayed her cover story. He was charming and welcomed her to the area. Speaking, she made sure her Spanish included several grammatical errors common among foreigners. Excusing herself, she fussed for a moment with his dog, wanting to make friends. It would be useful cover for the plan she'd developed.

"I know it's an imposition," she smiled sweetly before they parted, "and totally outrageous, but I'd love to hear more about the area. Do you think we could meet in the village for a cup of coffee? And please bring Trieste."

Antonio's grandfather beamed with delight. "Well, you're new to the area—and my new neighbour—so please allow me to invite you for lunch. There's a very nice restaurant here. About a thirty-minute walk. I can make a reservation when you're settled in, Susan."

Daniela laughed. "Oh, there's not much to settle in. We don't have much luggage; that's arriving with my parents. I'm available anytime."

"What about your brother?" he asked.

"He's a bit shy and has a learning disability," she answered quickly. "He's taken to painting and would be much happier doing that. Why don't you bring your wife, though?"

His face clouded for a moment. "I live alone, actually." Then, looking brighter, he gazed down at his dog. "Except for Trieste, that is." He laughed.

"Not even a housekeeper or a gardener?" she asked.

He shook his head. "I do it all myself. Keeps me on my toes."

"Trieste must come as well then," insisted Daniela. "She's such a lovely dog."

"How about Friday?" he asked.

"How about tomorrow." She laughed, flirting with him. "I have nothing else to do. And I have so many questions to ask you. Would tomorrow be all right?"

As they parted, he extended his hand. Ignoring it, Daniela leaned forward and kissed him on both cheeks. "There," she laughed. "I'm learning to become a European."

Watching as the old man and his dog continued their walk, she knew she didn't have long to scout out his property. At least she knew now that he lived alone and she wouldn't be disturbed. Ten minutes later, she found exactly what she'd expected. The detached stone garage next to his cottage was a serendipitous find. He didn't have a car; the garage was disused and empty. Similar to the garage at her aunt's house, it had a sunken repair pit made of strong concrete walls. The empty pit was covered over with thick planks of wood and hadn't been disturbed in decades, she guessed. All the gold bars could be fitted into the space—and be completely hidden out of sight.

Taking a series of photos with her phone camera, she closed the garage door and headed back to the cottage. She couldn't imagine a safer—and more unlikely—hiding place for the hoard.

Daniela and Nicolas

She'd seen online photos of him before, but when he entered the café, Daniela thought that Nicolas looked haggard. He was a handsome man. Of that, there was no doubt. Tall and slender, with thinning but still abundant silvery grey hair swept back without a parting. His tanned face was angular, as a patrician's, suggesting a high-born aristocrat.

He wore casual clothes, as she'd instructed. *"Don't be conspicuous,"* she'd warned, not realising that his noble breeding would stand out anywhere. As much as he tried to downplay his background, Nicolas's imperious, aloof attitude had been indelibly bred into his genes over many generations. One glance would tell you that he was not a man of the people. Wearing slacks with a high-necked navy cashmere pullover, he looked elegant, she thought. Perhaps a little effete. She watched from across the street as he purchased two cups of coffee and sat alone in a window seat—as she'd instructed. He seemed nervous—which was a good sign, she felt.

Daniela had no intention of entering the café just yet. She had to check if he'd brought along any helpers. Thugs, or worse—the police. There were no signs that he had, but she intended to put him through another test or two before she could be sure. He would be desperate to get his hands on the money she'd offered, and such men might be tempted to do anything.

She'd arrived early, anticipating a set-up. Everything appeared normal, but she knew that meant nothing in the shadowy world of surveillance. He'd parked his car along the street from the café and seemed to be alone. He must be in such dire straits and needing the money so badly that he'd heeded her warnings, she thought. Her most recent message to him had been clear: *"Try to trick me, and I'll be gone in a split second—so will your chance of getting the money."* It seemed that he'd listened and was obeying her instructions.

She called the private number he'd given her. Watching as he put down his coffee cup and answered, she instructed him to leave the café immediately. "Walk to your car and place your keys on top of the trunk. Then go back inside the café and wait."

Minutes later, she casually pushed a baby stroller in the direction of the vehicle and picked up the keys. Opening the trunk, she took a weighty backpack from the stroller and placed it inside. It was a quick operation taking no more than a few seconds. Keeping the keys with her, she walked back up the street—lingering inside a vegetable stall in the market.

It had been a risky move. If their rendezvous had been under surveillance, almost certainly she would have been observed. He could have set up cameras. She wasn't convinced yet that she wasn't being watched, but knew it was a chance she'd have to take. There was no other way to carry out the transaction. She rang his phone. "I have your keys. The trunk is open. Check the bag inside. Count it. Check for an electronic tracer, too, if you wish. There isn't one. Wait for further instructions."

Daniela saw Nicolas do exactly what she'd told him. She scanned the area carefully. Nothing, as far as she could see. She had time on her side, and he wasn't going anywhere without his car keys. Continuing up the street, she walked away from the café. He could wait another ten minutes while she did her next check.

The stroller had served its purpose. Abandoning it, she climbed the steps of a multi-storey car park. She'd explored the area earlier and knew it offered a panoramic view of the street and rooftops. Satisfied they were not under surveillance, she joined him a few minutes later at his table. "You've seen what I have. Do you want to do business? Do you want the full six hundred and fifty million?"

Nicolas's mouth gaped open. "You're so young," he gasped. "I had no idea . . ."

"Never mind that," she snapped. "Your part of the deal is the bearer bonds. Oh, and a couple of other things I will need from you. You'll receive details later. Keep the money in the backpack as a gesture of goodwill. Here's another present for you." She handed him a memory stick. "Just in case you decide to trick me, take a look at this. I hacked it from your laptop—the private one you keep. You probably can guess which files I'm talking about. They are my insurance policy. If you keep your side of the deal, no one else ever sees those files.

"I'm trusting you with six hundred and fifty million euros in cash," said Daniela, looking hard into his eyes. "You are trusting me not to fuck up your life. Remember that I can put you in jail for the rest of your days." She tapped the memory stick with her finger. "For the bad-boy stuff you've been up to, they don't offer early parole—even if you're able to survive the special treatment the other inmates will give you. Don't mess me around, Nicolas."

She looked across the table at him, his jaw gaping open in astonishment. "You'll need a truck to carry nine very heavy wooden boxes stuffed with euros," she advised. "If we have a deal, bring the bearer bonds with you. I'll let you know at the same time about the other things I will need. Don't call me; I'll call you." She gave him a grim smile. "This deal can be painless and beneficial to us both. The cash is clean, unmarked, and untraceable. It needs to be put back in circulation. Terms and conditions as I outlined to you in my email."

There was no reason to discount the loan she was making to Nicolas's bank, she'd told herself. After all, she was saving his skin. Besides, if he'd borrowed from the mob, they would have been far less generous. It was a clean transaction. She was a businesswoman; she might as well make a profit on the arrangement.

She tossed his car keys at him.

"Nice meeting you," she said, and left the café.

Nicolas Julio de Granada, 15th Marquis of Tarragona, remained sitting at the table, squeezing the handle of his cold cup of coffee between the tips of his elegant and well-manicured fingers. He wondered what had just happened. Six hundred and fifty million euros—almost too good to believe. It would save his bank, and his marriage.

Perhaps he should believe in miracles after all.

If he went to the police, they'd confiscate the money and he'd go bankrupt. If he did as she told him, all seemed likely to go well. For a moment, he considered the ploy of accepting the money and later finding a way to renege on his side of the bargain. After all, that was part of bankers' stock in trade.

Then he glanced at the memory stick she'd given him and acknowledged that she was a very smart operator. Nicolas was under no illusions. The girl was far from being a Good Samaritan. Her terms and conditions were tough and commercially clever. There wasn't a single doubt in his mind he would agree to the deal.

God had not sent him an angel, he concluded.

His benefactor was a she-devil.

He had no wish to see the compromising files of himself made public.

─────

Making her way back to the cottage, Daniela was aware that, very soon, she would be taking several huge risks.

Keeping Nicolas waiting for twenty-four hours would help minimise some of them. By then, she figured, he would have made discreet arrangements to transport the money. She would wait until the following day before calling his private number—and give him the address of the farm at El Canós.

"I need your help tonight, Yussef," she told the boy. Reluctantly, he dragged himself away from the painting he'd started. "We have to move the gold—bring it here for a time. We can't risk leaving it at the farm any longer."

It wasn't that she didn't trust Nicolas to keep his side of the bargain—in fact, she expected that he would. Why tempt fate? she asked herself. It would be a smart move to transport the gold away from the farm before Nicolas and his men arrived to pick up the wooden boxes stuffed with euros. There was no need for him to know anything about the bullion.

However, that gave her very little time to move it. She and Yussef would have to transport the gold from the farm to the cottage—that night.

"Again?" complained Yussef. "Why it is necessary we move it again?"

"It isn't safe at the farm—*we* are not safe at the farm," she explained for the second time. Her face darkened. It was annoying that he continued to question her. "It won't be the last time either," she added with impatience. "We will have to move it again, very soon. Tomorrow, in fact. Look, here is where to hide it." She showed him the photos she'd taken.

"This is dangerous," he objected.

"Dangerous? Yes," she replied in an abrupt tone, trying to resist sneering at him. "Is that what you said to them, when you committed yourself to the jihad?"

His face went red with embarrassment. "That is not what I meant."

"I know, Yussef. I know you are not afraid of the danger." She placed her hand on his shoulder, aware that she did not want to provoke him. She still needed his help. "Sometimes, we have to take small, cautious steps. As a soldier, you know that. Sometimes, big steps are too risky. Please trust me." It had been a useful outburst, Daniela reflected later. She knew that Yussef was becoming frustrated. It was hard for him to visualise what all of this meant for the jihad and how it would help them find his brother, Ahmed.

That night, Yussef worked hard at the farm at El Canós, loading the gold into the Humvee. Daniela insisted they must move every bar in a single journey. There were still roadblocks throughout the area, she warned—perhaps fewer than before, but the Mossos remained alert. Yussef was an energetic worker and, wearing the gloves she'd purchased, carried most of the gold single-handedly into the vehicle. She was pleased with his change of mood and attitude.

He had only one question: "Why are we leaving the boxes of cash behind at the farm?"

"We cannot leave it with the gold," she replied without hesitation. "It's safer to separate it. If we are discovered, we will lose everything. It is better for the jihad to keep it in two different places."

He nodded his understanding and seemed to approve of her caution. "You're clever, aren't you?" he said, half in provocation. "Ahmed told me so. He trusts you."

Daniela liked what Yussef was saying. It reinforced her standing. "Yussef, you must remember that Mustapha trusts me. It is hard for me to explain everything I do." Absent-mindedly, she fingered the blue sapphire necklace around her neck—the one that Jamal had given her. "You must learn to trust me."

That night, they drove the heavily laden Humvee through the back roads and reached the gravel path leading to the cottage. The military-looking vehicle was perfect for the job. Even so, Daniela negotiated the roads cautiously, not wanting to leave behind tell-tale tracks or break an axle because of the heavy load. It was a difficult and tense journey. They had to rely on the vehicle's sidelights for navigation.

"We don't have to unload the gold," she told him as they locked the vehicle in the garage at the cottage. "It can remain in the vehicle. Tomorrow, you must take it to the place I showed you—the place where the old man and his dog live. They won't be there. I've made sure of that."

Granddad

Next day, Daniela strode with confidence across the restaurant floor to the table where the old man was sitting, his hands clasped together, resting gently on his stomach. Trieste recognised her instantly. The dog got up from its resting place next to the man's legs and rushed to greet her. Daniela fussed with her for a moment.

She moved towards the table and kissed the man on his cheek, squeezing his shoulder with her hand. Antonio's grandfather smiled. "Well, it's a long time since a beautiful woman did that." He seemed almost embarrassed.

"You look wonderful," she exclaimed, genuinely impressed. Previously, she had seen him in well-worn casual clothes when they'd met while out walking. Shaved and dressed-up, he looked much younger and quite elegant. By nature, he was softly spoken, but she guessed that, at one time, he must have been quite debonair. He was certainly well bred and charming—perhaps something of a playboy and a little bit devilish, she imagined. She thought again how very much he looked like Antonio.

"How are you?" she asked, sitting down. The waiter gracefully pushed forward on her chair.

"I took the liberty," he announced proudly. "I don't drink much these days, but this I know to be from an excellent vineyard. He indicated a bottle of white wine in the ice bucket. "Would you like to try it?"

She nodded eagerly and tuned her mind to Susan Garcia mode. "Mum doesn't drink, but Dad does," she confessed to him. "At home, as kids, we were allowed a little bit of wine with meals." She took a sip. "What kind is it, a Riesling?" she asked, deliberately making a beginner's error.

He smiled. "Actually, something more local." He was careful not to embarrass her by pointing out her mistake; it was understandable from a foreigner. The wine waiter smirked knowledgably and refilled the old man's glass. "Well, tell me about your day," he invited, keeping direct eye contact with her.

Daniela was startled for a moment by the directness of his gaze. She giggled. "It's a bit crazy, isn't it?! We live practically next to each other . . . well, close to each other. Now, here we are arriving separately for lunch. It's almost like a formal date." She bent down and slipped a treat to the dog. "Tell me, did you take her for a good walk already today? Trieste is so well behaved," she added, rubbing the dog's head.

"Oh, she gets spoiled a little—but that gives me pleasure," he answered happily.

Very soon, Daniela had the old man talking. He loved his dog; that much was clear. She fibbed to him about a Labrador they used to have at home. He'd lived until fifteen, she lied. She tried to steer the old man towards talking about his family. She wanted to ask how long he'd been a widower, but he seemed reluctant to discuss the subject.

"My brother is showing a real interest in oil painting," she said, understanding the need to divert the conversation.

"He's . . ." the old man began to ask, clearly a bit embarrassed to broach the subject.

"Yes," said Daniela. "He's nineteen and . . . How would you say it in Spanish? He has some development problems." She stumbled with her Spanish, getting the tense wrong. She tapped her head.

Antonio's grandfather nodded with understanding. The kindly creases around his eyes told her that he sympathised with her family's situation—and that he admired her positive attitude. He didn't feel the need to preach, she thought.

"Not everyone looks after their family members," he said. "It's the same everywhere in the world. Yet, there are those who do . . . like yours. They show a level of compassion that is heart-warming. Well done," he raised his glass to toast her.

As they clinked, Daniela smiled her gratitude to him, yet she felt phony and contrived. She was aware that she was deceiving this nice old man—Antonio's grandfather—to further her own agenda. But her survival was necessary, and she needed to keep the old man away from his home while Yussef hid the gold in his garage. She wasn't proud of her conduct and hastened to change the subject.

An hour later, they had eaten their meal and drunk most of the wine. "Holy Toledo, that was good," she exclaimed. "Much, much better than the food we have in New Mexico. It's delicious. Good thing I'm riding a bike; I need the exercise," she said, leaning forward and placing her hands over his. "Oh, I'm enjoying this so much. Thank you for an excellent lunch. How are you getting back home?" She was doing a quick mental calculation.

"Oh, I always walk," he said. "It's just half an hour. I shop three times a week, just a few items. So, I'll do that as well. I always bring Trieste. Today is special." He flashed his eyes at her. "Today, she gets an even longer run-out."

Through her questions, Daniela had made sure she knew all about the old man's habits and how long he stayed away from his house when he walked to the village—sometimes visiting with friends. It had been important to know his schedule and his absences. She had to be sure that Trieste wouldn't pose a problem for Yussef.

He'd be there now, under cover of the old man's garage. She imagined he'd be sweating as he laboured to unload the heavy cargo from the Humvee. She'd calculated that the gold from Aladdin's Cave was worth three hundred and fifty million euros. All of it would be stored safely under Antonio's nose. Unless they screwed up badly, it would be a hiding place he'd never discover. Right now, she needed to call Yussef and find out how he was getting on with the move. If he needed more time, she would have to find a way to delay the old man.

"You looked very thoughtful there, for a moment," he said, looking across the table at her.

"I miss Mum and Dad," she improvised quickly, adding a convincing sniffle. "They've had to delay their arrival for a few weeks."

He leaned forward and brushed back the hair that had fallen over her eyes. "Oh, that's disappointing. I'm sorry, Susan."

"You're very sweet." She smiled and touched his hand again. "Can you excuse me?" she asked, dabbing tears from her eyes. "I'll be back in a few minutes." She got up from the table and went to the washroom.

Dialling Yussef's phone, she received disappointing news. He said he needed more time—he'd been delayed. The farmer had been out in his fields, so Yussef had kept the Humvee out of sight until he'd left. "How many have you unloaded so far," she demanded.

"I'm only halfway through. They are heavy, Daniela. I'm tired."

Daniela wanted to yell at him. It didn't matter that he was tired. Didn't he know how important this was? Instead, she controlled her response. "Yussef, we have to succeed. Think of Jamal. Think of the jihad." She made a quick calculation. "I'll get you another half hour," she told him, "Please make sure you clean up afterwards. Don't leave any tyre marks near his house. I'm relying on you, Yussef." She was hoping that passing farm vehicles would erase any tracks he would leave on his exit.

On her way back to the table, a good-looking man in his thirties—who fancied his chances with her—blocked her way as she walked past the bar. His amorous intentions were obvious. From the corner of her eye, Daniela could see that the old man was about to haul himself up and intervene, but there was no need. Within a few seconds, the amorous beau was doubled up on the floor writhing in pain.

She shook her hair as she returned to the table and sat down. "Sorry, but he became rude. I kicked him in the nuts."

"Why is it that we men think that we have the right to accost attractive women?" he asked, embarrassed by the event.

"Probably because you men have penises, and we have vaginas," she said without a blush.

He burst out laughing, eventually wiping the corners of his eyes to remove the tears. "Ah, you're a refreshing change, Susan," he conceded. "So, why me?" he asked, emboldened.

She nodded, fully understanding his question. "Well, it helps that you're probably the only man in this room who's not trying to take my panties off," she replied matter-of-factly.

He flushed red.

"Plus, you're mostly honest about your intentions. It's a pity. I would like to have known you when you were younger. Much younger," she said with a laugh, "in case we go off track. Also," she started to say, breathing in deeply, "please don't take this as an offence, but you remind me of my own grandfather."

He smiled but had not missed the significance of her choice of words. "You know I'm a grandfather?"

Daniela looked surprised. "You told me," she said quickly—trying to cover up her blunder. "You told me yesterday, when you were out in the fields walking with Trieste. Don't say you're losing your memory," she scolded him with a forced laugh. "If you do, I won't have any neighbours to talk to."

He laughed.

Her answer, she thought, probably was enough to assuage any doubts he might have. But she had made an error and his guard was up. He was a smart man, and his mental faculties were fully intact. She'd have to be more careful in future. In a way, she was pleased that he was so mentally sharp. It wasn't just wishful thinking: she saw a lot of Antonio in the old man. He was a shrewd judge of character, and she cautioned herself to be careful. She mustn't assume that his age was a weakness. If Antonio was anything to judge by, he was quite capable of thinking laterally. That could put her plans at risk.

She leaned forwards and caressed his hand. "Your wife," she asked, thinking of the additional time that Yussef would need. "You were married only once—and she was the love of your life?"

He stiffened, then regained control and started to relax. "Another guess, Susan?" he said, not intending it as a question. "Yes, you're right." He paused as emotion took over. "Men are supposed to go first." His voice had become heavy as his larynx constricted.

Daniela could feel his struggle and felt sympathy for him. He was a nice man, and she disliked having to play-act and deceive him.

"It's not something men expect," he continued hoarsely, his voice forcing itself over the lump now swelling in his throat. "We're not prepared for it. You women are, but we men are not. I had never thought about it really until she was diagnosed. Then you don't have much time to get prepared. Life suddenly has only one priority. Then, one day, you wake up and you're by yourself."

"She always talked too much," he added, tears starting to well. "I told her many times. She always had something to say." The hoarseness in his voice now was beyond his control. "Give me a few minutes of quietness, please, I used to implore her—before they discovered her tumour.

"You know something, Susan," he said suddenly, looking up at her. "I wish I had let her talk . . . just chatter on, as much as she wanted to. I miss her voice, the sound of her. Just having her around was a priceless treasure. I'd give anything to go back and relive those times. I'd tell her that I love her and that she could talk as much as she liked. Now, I live with lots of silence."

Daniela leaned forwards and squeezed the old man's arm. His head was down as he forced back a wall of tears. With a sideways glance, Daniela saw that the man at the bar who'd propositioned her was no longer there. Damn, she thought, I hope he's not lurking outside wanting to make trouble. It's the last thing I need.

99

"I miss her, Susan," the old man said simply, and kept his head bowed.

Daniela kept hold of his arm, saying nothing. Sometimes, there was nothing to be said—at least nothing that would help such a wonderful old man in his grieving. She wanted someone to love her the same way. Sniffing back an unwanted emotion, she forced the thought from her mind.

It made her think of Antonio.

After lunch, Daniela arrived back at the cottage. She found Yussef lying on his bed looking exhausted. His face was still flushed from his lunchtime exertions. He had wiped himself down with a bath towel; it was saturated with sweat. "How was it?" she asked.

He shrugged his shoulders and closed his eyes to sleep.

"Thank you for doing it," she said simply, and went to her bedroom.

Immediately, her guard was up. Something didn't seem quite right. At first, she couldn't tell what it was; everything seemed to be in place. She wondered if Yussef had searched through her things. Her laptop had been hidden under her mattress. The bedclothes were ruffled and just didn't look the same.

She looked for the tell-tale thin sliver of clear adhesive tape she always placed on the edge of the laptop. There was no doubt: it had been pulled away—she was certain. There was only one explanation: Yussef must have tampered with the device. Starting it up, she looked for clues that he'd been successful in gaining access. It was password-protected and all her files were encrypted, but she knew that wouldn't stop an expert. He was young and technologically savvy. Maybe they had even trained him in such techniques.

Angrily, she strode into his bedroom—laptop in hand. "You've been hacking into my computer."

He rolled over onto his back. "I try to find Ahmed."

"Who did you contact?" she shot back. Her voice rose to a shout. "Tell me, you bastard. Tell me who you contacted." Her face grew red with emotion. He had promised her that he wouldn't go online.

"Nobody," he replied. His voice was even and measured. "Your laptop is locked."

"That doesn't mean anything—not if you know how to bypass it," she said with derision. "Empty your pockets."

"What?" he asked.

"Do as I tell you. Empty your pockets."

"No."

"No?" She was livid.

"No," he repeated.

Daniela was stymied, and he knew it. She needed to know if he had anything in his pockets, perhaps a root kit—something that would confirm he had gained access to her stuff. She stormed out of his room, then turned back. "You have put us in danger, Yussef, letting our enemies know where we are. By your actions, you have placed our jihad at risk. Maybe you have put our whole mission in jeopardy.

"How can I trust you, after this?" she asked, slamming the door behind her.

Mossos Headquarters

"Where the hell did they get this stuff from?" demanded the new chief. He spread the pages of the newspaper across his desk: *"Huge Slush Fund Missing After Barcelona Terrorist Attack."*

"It's even more of a story on the radio and TV stations," said Antonio, as he speed-dialled a private number. "It has to be a leak from somewhere. Let's find out.

"Hola Roberto," said Antonio, as soon as his call was answered. He was anxious to get past the pleasantries.

"You want to know my source, is that it, Toni?" asked the newspaperman, also not wasting time. "Well, I'm sorry, compañero. Not this time."

"I don't want his or her name," Antonio shot back. "We're going to get it through the courts eventually anyway. What I need to know, Roberto, is if this story came from Madrid or from here—from my own backyard. Surely, you can answer that?"

"Hmm." There was a delay in the newspaperman's response. Then he spoke slowly. "We are a Catalan newspaper, that's true. We accepted the story from a reliable source. Impeccable source, in fact. That person does not speak Catalan, and that's all I'm going to tell you, Toni. By the way, I'm going to be calling you back shortly. Officially, that is. I will want you to confirm or deny that it's true."

"That's easy, Roberto. It's a complete fabrication. Don't worry about calling me back; I'll call you when I find out who is behind this rubbish and what they're trying to achieve. You can print that if you want—and quote me too."

He called off. "You heard, sir. Roberto is a friend. He was telling us that his information came from a source in Madrid."

The chief nodded. "Well, his newspaper certainly got some of its facts right; that's for certain. There's a lot of guesswork in the article too. The journalist rounded up the value of Aladdin's Cave to a billion euros. That's about right—from what the chauffeur revealed under pressure to our colleagues in Madrid. The problem is, Antonio, this story is going to bring us a lot of unwanted attention. Not just from the public and our bosses, but internationally too."

The chief's phone rang. "It's Madrid on the secure line," he mouthed to Antonio, who nodded and left the room. He was impressed that the chief was proving adept at dealing with the powder-keg politics currently running red hot between Barcelona and the federal capital. He respected his new boss and enjoyed working for him too. For Antonio, it was very different from the old days of reporting to his own father. He loved his dad but was happy he'd retired. It was better that way.

Pressing the elevator button, he headed down. Antonio had kept the same office. Despite his promotion to inspector and his new mandate, he wanted to keep things as close as he could to the way they had been before. Realistically, there wasn't much chance of that happening, he admitted.

Everyone on the force knew he was a changed man—angry and determined to put things right. No one said anything openly to him, but he was aware of the gossip behind his back. The golden boy of the Mossos Homicide Squad had come crashing down to earth, several detractors asserted—and it wasn't just said in whispers. All because of Daniela, they added caustically. She had beguiled him, fooling him into believing her story.

Now she was on the run—an international fugitive and the focus of a massive manhunt. Meanwhile, Antonio had been promoted. Ha! Isn't that always the way it works, the gossips said with exaggerated contempt. Family connections had got him to where he was. Now, his political connections ensured that he was untouchable, with an additional stripe on his uniform to bolster his self-esteem.

Physically, his appearance had changed too. Gone was the excessively long, floppy blonde hair. In its place, a utilitarian, quasi-military cut that looked harsh and unflattering. His hairdresser had been severe.

His behaviour had altered too. He no longer stopped by the desks of colleagues to chat casually, and he'd ceased his flirting with the gaggle of female admirers in the office—who now saw him as vulnerable and, therefore, somehow less desirable. Only a few hopefuls among the young women still coveted his attention.

Antonio knew all about the backchat. The things that people no longer said to him—the confidences they no longer entrusted to him. He took it all in his stride, telling himself not to take it personally. If anything, it motivated him. He became even more resolved to find Daniela and make sure she got a long prison sentence in a high-security facility.

Worst of all, it was whispered, he was no longer fun to be around. For the most part, his friends remained steadfastly loyal, but working with him these days was hard work. Not like the past, when he had been the natural and fun-loving leader of a cadre of officers who admired and respected his uncanny insights as a detective.

Xavi stuck his head around the door and raised his eyebrows in enquiry. "Amigo," said Antonio, using a nickname that he'd used for Xavi since their schooldays watching cowboy westerns. He indicated a chair.

"Sir," said Xavi, who liked to taunt his buddy about his recent promotion. He smiled widely, knowing the effect his sarcasm would have. Antonio mouthed a Catalan expletive and held up a middle finger. Xavi grinned as he slid into the faux leather chair. "Anything new?" he asked. It was a redundant question, voiced to create a feeling of ease. If anything of significance had developed in the hunt for Daniela, he would have heard about it already from Antonio.

He received a quick shake of the head. His long-time friend passed a file across the desk. "You saw the slush fund story? The information about Aladdin's Cave is now public."

"Hard to miss it," said Xavi quickly. "The newspaper must have an inside source. They're not just reporting a rumour. The part I don't like is the disclosure of information about the murdered freelance journalist from Madrid, Francisco Rioja. And the newspaper has dragged the condesa's name into it too. Until now, their involvement had been kept under wraps."

"Well, we can expect a lot more pressure from the top brass to track down Daniela, that's guaranteed." Antonio sighed. "She's going to make our lives hell. Yet again."

After Xavi had left his office, Antonio sat alone gazing out of the window.

He needed time to think. He couldn't rid himself of the feeling that he was screwing up the investigation. It mattered little that other people still had faith in him—in his ability to bring Daniela and her terrorist associates to justice. He wasn't nearly as confident in himself.

He couldn't put his finger on what was troubling him. It was disquieting; he had a feeling that he was missing something. Something really significant.

Separating his progress on the investigation from things happening in his personal life had become a challenge. Time was what he needed, to focus on the investigation without any distractions. His recent failures—and, he conceded, his really poor judgment—were eating away at his self-respect. It wasn't a nice feeling.

Normally, Antonio was low profile on social media—preferring the privacy and company of close friends. Now he became highly selective. He continued to play tennis regularly, but under his new daily regimen, he left the club premises immediately after his games. He was aware that, sensing his discomfort, his colleagues were giving him more space. In a way, he was grateful—but he resented that it was even necessary. There was an element of pity involved, which he hated. Dinner parties were few. Instead, he spent long hours at the office. It was an abrupt and stark transition from his natural disposition as a fun-loving, relaxed—and popular—local personality. Worse still, he knew that he looked unhappy. There was little that Maria or his friends could do; in truth, he stubbornly resisted their efforts to help.

He knew that he was punishing himself.

Until recently, his career as a detective had been stellar. He was accustomed to receiving accolades for his intuition and uncanny ability to resolve difficult homicide cases. Over the years, he'd ignored the honours thrown at him, knowing that he'd started several rungs up the career ladder—thanks to his dad. He admitted he'd enjoyed the trappings of success. He recognised that he was conceited enough to enjoy the praise and being the centre of attention.

He was a good policeman. Inwardly, he believed that he was a brilliant detective—at least when it came to homicide. Working on espionage, he was less sure. Months ago, he'd been thrown into the investigation involving al-Qaeda. It had happened by chance because his father wanted the Mossos to work with their long-time rivals, the federal police. Maybe working with the feds wasn't such a good idea, Antonio had said at the time to Xavi.

Dealing with espionage, maybe he was out of his depth. He didn't really believe that he was but conceded that his refusal to admit it was just his ego at work. It was possible that he was screwing up because he didn't have what it takes to be effective in espionage. Maybe he should leave spying and terrorism cases to the federal police—specialised units, such as GEO, and people like Diego. Yet, something told him he was being overly self-critical. He was getting things out of perspective. The fact was that he'd screwed up his judgment about Daniela because he'd allowed his personal life to interfere with his work. It wasn't a good mix. He knew his natural instincts were to focus dispassionately on the facts, and not be driven by emotions.

Not wanting to be disturbed, Antonio leaned across his desk and switched off his phone lines. He keyed his devices to silent and texted his new personal assistant to hold his calls. Disciplining his mind to a single focus, he reviewed the investigation from the beginning. As impartially as he could, he reassessed what was known about Daniela—and her role in the attempted bombing.

The bomb was more than two tonnes of high explosives. If it had detonated as the terrorists had planned, the force of the explosion would have ripped apart the building and the only thing left, apart from the rubble, would have been a deep crater at the centre of Barcelona. Many hundreds of people would have died, and countless injured. It was more than five times the explosive force used by al-Qaeda terrorists at Madrid's Atocha train station bombing in 2004, one report had noted. The report asked a blunt question: Why had such a large explosion been planned for the bombing attempt at Mossos Headquarters?

It was a question that had haunted Antonio since he and his fellow officers had thwarted the attempt. Why so much explosives? One conclusion that kept coming back to him was that the terrorists had intended massive destruction—but that they'd also wanted to send a stark message: We can hit you where you are most vulnerable. We can hit you when you are least expecting it.

We can hit you big.

Soon after the thwarted bombing attempt, Antonio had reviewed the documentation. He'd read the Mossos's internal reports, the federal police counterterrorism reports, and the crime scene investigation analyses. At the time, he was certain that the terrorists must have had local help. It had been corroborated by the evidence. The investigators were convinced that it was just too big an operation and too meticulously executed to be anything but a specifically targeted and well-planned attack.

Daniela had been linked definitively to Raphael Robles. There was no question that she must have been fully aware of the bombing attempt—and had motivation to make sure it succeeded. Reading again through the files on his screen, Antonio found it difficult to refute the evidence. Moreover, it came from multiple sources.

As routine procedure, the Mossos bomb squad had carried out forensic analyses. They knew that every explosive device has its own fingerprint. The source of explosive materials can be traced—often to its manufacturer, and sometimes to the perpetrators. After the bombing attempt, Antonio had been copied by the forensics people and had read their reports closely. Keying into his protected files, he reviewed them again.

On a hunch, he called the sergeant who'd headed-up the Mossos's bomb disposal squad on the day that Antonio and Xavi helped disarm the bomb.

"All the assessments are in," confirmed the sergeant. "All except one report. Within the Mossos, we don't have the laboratory capacity to analyse the detonators. They didn't fire, but I can't imagine they were duds. We sent them to Madrid where they have the proper facilities. Actually, it's been on my mind. I checked last week with the lab there. It's still in process, sir."

"Is it normal for the lab results to take such an extended time?" asked Antonio.

"Not really. It's taking longer than I thought. That happens sometimes when Madrid's workload gets backed up. I can follow up with a personal phone call if you like, sir?"

Antonio had a lot of respect for the Mossos bomb disposal squad—and for this officer in particular. The man had proven himself to be professional, not to mention selfless and brave. Maybe a call to Madrid from the sergeant would get the results quicker. Intuition stopped Antonio from asking him to proceed. For a few moments, Antonio mulled over an orphaned thought that had been bothering him.

"I tell you what, Ernesto," he said, choosing to address the man by his first name. "Leave it for the time being. I don't want to flag the laboratory analysis in Madrid as an urgent item. Keep an eye on it for me, though. I don't imagine they're dragging their feet deliberately, but I need the lab results as soon as I can get them. By the way, use the number I'm texting to you. I've changed over to a new high-encryption device. I want to keep our conversations completely private."

The Missing Billion

At his modest private mansion within the Royal Palace in Madrid, the grandee pushed his chair away from his ornate wood desk and walked to the window. In the square, three stories below, the ceremony of the changing of the guard would take place later. It was a spectacle of which he never grew weary, but it was rare for him these days to watch the full event.

Nowadays, the royal family resided outside Madrid at the Palace of Zarzuela. Many decades earlier, Franco had chosen to reside at El Pardo. In the absence of royalty, the Royal Palace lacked the stiff formality and reverence of its glorious past. Now in his eighties, the grandee had become a pragmatist. The world had changed: people of his breeding had been swept aside by the relentless march of democracy.

He'd been a courtier to the former king. During his many years of service, he'd made sure that the royal household had been enriched wherever possible. Returning from exile in Italy, the king had been penniless. The coffers today were much fuller than a generation earlier, and were increasingly filled from a broad base of sustainable sources. Reflecting on the responsibilities of his office, the grandee concluded that his task of enriching the Household had been abundantly accomplished.

The grandee was satisfied that he had been able to shield the family from some of the worst of their own stupidities. It was pitiful, really, he reminded himself. Numerous times, he had been forced to step in, often asking favours from loyalist members of the government, when the monarchy had to be protected from itself. Even today, he was still dealing with several of the older members' foolish endeavours.

He stepped back from the window and returned to his desk.

A newspaper had just been delivered. It was positioned next to his favourite hallmarked silver tray along with his regular morning carajillo, which had been fortified on this chilly day with a shot of Luis Felipe Gran Reserva brandy. He appreciated beautiful artefacts and, in a brief instant of sensual pleasure, ran the tips of his elegant slender fingers around the tray's intricate inlaid gold artwork created centuries earlier by a gifted craftsman.

His carajillo was perfect, as he was entitled to expect.

Moments later, his focus on it was lost as he read the tabloid's account of the public uproar over the theft of the riches of Aladdin's Cave. Reading the article for a second time, his carajillo went cold. It was soon matched by his mood. This very public attention to the fund amassed by the general and his entourage did not please him.

He had not been directly involved but had been given hints of its existence. Years earlier, his friend, the count, had intimated its purpose. The grandee had been sworn to secrecy; he'd said nothing to the royal family about the matter. It was better they didn't know. He preferred that they should observe the unfolding of events from a safe and protected distance. A few months earlier, news of an attempted coup had been suppressed by the government. He had heard that General Bastides had been arrested, along with many of his supporters. Tragically, the count had died.

Today's newspaper article, although speculative, was the first public confirmation that the fund was not in the hands of the government. It had been stolen. The grandee was already aware of that information. He'd received a briefing from an unimpeachable source here in Madrid. The name of the girl who had stolen it—an alleged jihadist, said the newspaper—was familiar to him.

Measures had been taken by loyal subjects to prevent the riches of Aladdin's Cave from leaving Spain. The girl had to be stopped, he'd been instructed. He'd personally issued the orders for her to be killed. Regrettably, the assassin's bullet had missed. The money hadn't been recovered. Now the media was running with the story.

The grandee considered it his sacred duty to get every peseta back where it belonged—but this time it would remain under his watchful eye. It did not belong to the government. It belonged in the hands of those who fought for a more enlightened country.

The Old Spain.

Langley, Virginia

Robert Errol Scott Jr. came from a long line of distinguished military officers. It was expected of him that he would continue the family tradition. At high school, he'd been a promising quarterback, with a strong arm that foreshadowed a promising career in college football. He'd dreamed of the NFL and spoke of nothing else.

Scouted by several Division 1 schools, he'd started his freshman year at Clemson. During a routine practice, a late tackle resulted in a serious knee injury. Physically, he recovered, but his confidence had been shattered; his game-sense deteriorated. He was relegated to backup. They encouraged him to stay on, but everywhere there were constant reminders of what he might have become.

West Point was delighted to accept the new recruit, and his parents were ecstatic. He excelled at foreign languages. Four years later, he graduated with distinction.

His army career, by comparison, was mediocre. Yet, he advanced quickly to the rank of major and, after Operation Desert Storm—in which he played a minor non-combat role—to lieutenant colonel. His early promotion to full colonel a decade later occurred without any of the exceptional active service or intelligence operations achievements that normally propel outstanding officers to the hallowed O-6 pay grade.

On the eve of his retirement after thirty-five years of service, Colonel Scott was recruited by the CIA. His resume was impeccable. Reinforced, some of his screeners noted enthusiastically, by his family's history of service to the nation. It helped that his great-grandfather, grandfather, two uncles, and a cousin were buried at Arlington. His years in administration had been unremarkable, which pleased the review board. He was a family man. On his record, they saw no combat censures or disciplinary reprimands.

Impeccable.

Still tall, a little more stooped, he had a wide Jack Kennedy smile, which gave reassurance and elicited a deep sense of bonhomie. Throughout his career, he had done nothing, said nothing, been nothing, and offended no one. He spoke five languages fluently, with perhaps a slight Virginian lilt. Prior to joining the CIA, he had only once visited Europe—in his later teens. Unsullied by years of pro-European biases typical of more seasoned competitors for the posting, the review board unanimously decided he was an ideal appointment.

He was given an office at Langley, then posted immediately to Europe as acting director of covert operations. That was a year ago. Despite his penchant for languages, and his all-American smile, Scott found it difficult adjusting to a much less friendly Europe than he'd toured as a teenager. It was not worth the effort, he confided several months later to his ill-at-ease wife. He told her he'd find a way to orchestrate their return to Washington—just as soon as this current posting was over.

This damned covert operation too. It had hounded him since his posting to Paris. Glancing at his watch, he saw that it was ten minutes past his appointment time with the deputy. He knew that the operation was a pet project of hers. In contrast to his own view, she supported the young Spanish female officer, codename Felix—their frontline operative on the case. He also knew that the deputy was an unabashed advocate of gender equality in the service. Her strong feelings on the topic presented him with a bit of a problem.

He had full confidence in the male CIA field officer with line responsibility for Project Catalyst. The man was a Navy lieutenant commander seconded to the CIA and a fearless operative. Scott had no confidence in Felix, for whom the lieutenant commander seemed to have an almost deferential respect. Scott knew it would be hazardous to criticise the young Spanish woman in front of the deputy.

The story about the money from Aladdin's Cave had broken wide open a day earlier in Spain. The risks of failure of the covert mission already seemed to him to be outrageously high. If by a fluke it succeeded, he was canny and nimble enough to take the credit. If it failed, the I-told-you-so conversation he was about to have would be on record.

He'd learned how to handle the deputy. Now it was time to win her over.

Calculating that the eight-mile distance between his office in Langley and the White House was equivalent to just over fourteen thousand passing yards, he was mindful that his Patriot's hero QB had thrown more yards than that in three seasons. Scott took it as an omen. Only sixteen thousand yards to make the distance as a congressman, and he would have an eventual shot at the presidency.

Scott had friends and, unusually for Washington, he had made no powerful enemies.

Touchdown!

Antonio

"Well," said the chief. "Here's the situation. I've agreed a new set of priorities with Madrid. Whatever else you're doing, Toni, I want you to focus instead on this slush fund fiasco. It's an embarrassment for Madrid—being completely in the dark while the general and his friends diverted all that corrupt money into funding a coup and a terrorist campaign.

"Then Madrid carelessly allowed it to be whisked away from under their noses—stolen by a former junior officer of the Civil Guard, who, it turns out, also is an al-Qaeda agent. And she was also one of our officers—thankfully, only for a short time," he added, frowning at Antonio.

"It's an embarrassment to us here at the Mossos," he continued. "We haven't been any more successful than the feds. We haven't been able to apprehend the suspect—or recover the money. Madrid says it's possible the stash is still here in Spain. Well, there's been a shift in policy. They aren't interested any longer seeing us waste our efforts chasing the girl; they want the money back. Not just that, but Madrid is getting a lot of pressure from our European Union partners—and the Americans—to seal the leaky borders being used by drug gangs, money launderers, and terrorists.

"Madrid is convinced there's massive money laundering continuing under our noses, despite our efforts to patrol the border between Catalunya and Andorra. We have a special Mossos anti-terrorism unit working on it, of course. And, yes, I know what you're going to tell me." He looked sternly at Antonio. "You're going to assure me that they're working closely with the police corps of Andorra and our colleagues in France—and with the international agencies, including FATF, the financial task force network.

"But it's not good enough, Toni. All this talk of slush funds finding their way into the hands of terrorists is freaking out our politicians. The public is in a foul mood, and national elections are likely again soon. Tempers are at breaking point." He stopped ranting and paused—looking out of the window to gather his thoughts.

"I know you're in Homicide, not the Terrorist Financing Prevention Unit, Toni. But you've had a lot of exposure to that side of things recently. Just as I've said, I want you to drop everything else you're doing. Hand those files over to someone else. See if you can nail some of the bastards involved. I need a photo op. I need photos of our boys hauling in criminals and seizing large stockpiles of laundered money. We must show the public that we're starting to win the war against the bad guys. That's the only thing that will get the Generalitat and

Madrid off our backs. We have to show that we're making progress," he added for good measure.

"Sir, it's going to ruffle a lot of feathers among the people at the TFPU. I mean, having someone from Homicide come in and look over their shoulders," said Antonio. His tone was polite but sceptical.

"It's not a turf war, Toni," interrupted the chief irritably. "I received my orders directly from the Minister of the Interior, and they're supported by our own government. I'll appoint you as head of a new task force, if necessary. We've made progress on the money-laundering problem over the past few years but not enough. It's got away from us, Toni. I want a new effort—and I want quick results." The chief left the room abruptly and slammed Antonio's office door on his way out.

"Yes, sir," said Antonio, speaking to an empty room. He speed-dialled Xavi.

"We need to talk, amigo. The gods are getting restless. Drop by my office when you can. Come to think of it, give me half an hour. I need to talk to our colleagues at the TFPU and make sure we don't piss them off. I need friends, not more enemies."

CHAPTER 6
A New Boss

Diego heard about the newspaper reports just as they were hitting the streets. At 0400 hours, he'd been awakened by a phone call from the duty officer at GEO Group 60. The cat was out of the bag: the theft of the stash of laundered money was a front-page item—sensational and syndicated.

It had taken him only a few minutes to relay the information to his new boss. She hadn't been pleased. It didn't impress her that the story had been scooped by a newspaper in Catalunya and was now making front page headlines—globally. She wasn't looking forward to addressing the Minister of the Interior—at whose office she would be arriving shortly.

Claudia Ramirez was a divorced mother of two children, now both in their late teens. A former army colonel and officer in the Civil Guard, she'd been recruited into GEO Group 60 to replace Raphael Robles. To her colleagues, it seemed that her career had been one success followed by another—an unsullied chronology of outstanding performances.

In itself, this might have been unremarkable. But none of her appointments had been easy, as the minister had learned when he'd first read her file. In fact, quite the opposite. Early in her career, Claudia had excelled at investigations in which men with twice her seniority and experience had admitted defeat. Her leadership qualities were legendary. She'd quickly become recognised as an outstanding administrator.

Stepping out of the chauffeured bulletproof sedan from the GEO carpool, Claudia glanced skywards. The gathering clouds looked menacing, and she was glad she'd chosen a sensible fleece-lined, ankle-length imitation fur coat. It was ideal to keep out the ice-chilled biting winds that had blasted Madrid for the past several weeks. It was supposed to be early springtime and warm, she reminded herself—hugging the coat closer to keep warm. She was grateful that the cold winds had at least kept away the rain. As much as she liked to take her children on skiing trips to the Alps, she hated the thought of more slushy snow here on the ground.

Climbing the steps of a side entrance to the executive building, a uniformed commissioner doffed his cap to her respectfully. She was a regular, but she made his job easier by flashing her security pass. "Señora." He smiled gratefully, holding the door open for her. She was glad to get inside the building and wipe her eyes—removing the creases of moisture from the bitter chill.

"He's waiting for you," intoned the minister's administrative assistant, indicating a large heavy wooden door. It seemed like the forbidding entrance to a fortress.

She knocked and entered. "Minister," she said pleasantly, as she approached his large heavy wood desk. It was a heritage piece, crafted from Honduran mahogany, beautifully inlaid with ebony—no doubt a trophy from Spain's imperialist history, she'd noted on a previous visit. The high-ceilinged room was large and cavernous. Along with its dark wood furnishings, it contributed to an imperious atmosphere of colonial power and historical exploitations.

She smelled the stench of a recently smoked cigar. It was an aroma she detested—part of Old Spain and the empire, she thought. Apart from the minister's regrettable habit, Claudia had always liked the room. This morning, however, she was not looking forward to their meeting.

"Espresso?" he enquired. "I would, if I were you. This new-fangled machine is remarkable; it comes out piping hot. You'll need it after being out there." He pointed to a large window, where the freezing wind was buffeting hard against the glass. "Keep your coat on if you wish. We both might need a little fortification." He added a good measure of Spanish brandy before handing the loaded beverage to her. "Although perhaps not for the reasons you may be anticipating, Chief Inspector."

He offered a bone china plate of imported Italian biscotti as a touch of luxury. Claudia declined politely; she was intrigued by his opening words and waited.

"The Brits," he said, taking a long sip, "called me this morning. I have something to tell you, Chief Inspector, which must be kept within a very tight need-to-know circle. Extremely tight," he added, looking over the heavy rim of his glasses. He held her in his gaze. "It's about the slush fund . . . the one which created headline news here and around the world this morning."

Next day, Claudia travelled to the nearby Torrejón Air Base, riding in the same limousine she'd used to visit the minister. The journey, using the M-30 and A2, was accomplished by the GEO driver in a crisp twenty-two minutes. He appeared unconcerned about attracting a speeding ticket.

"Faster than I can get out of the city at rush hour," remarked Diego, sitting comfortably across from her in the vehicle's plush leather seats.

Their journey was confined to small talk. It was department policy. Earlier, in her office within the GEO annex, she'd taken time to brief Diego. He had the feeling she hadn't told him the full story. That was fine with him: everything they were dealing with was classified, ultra-high security.

A short time later, they boarded a Spanish Air Force jet.

Diego was impressed. The hybrid Falcon 900B was emblazoned with the distinctive crest of the *Fuerza Aérea Espanola*. Its three powerful jet engines looked formidable, he thought, admiring the aircraft's clean lines. There were seats for about twenty, he guessed. But, today, they were the only passengers. The crew of two clearly were accomplished flyers—although Diego thought they both looked about nineteen years old. Age didn't seem to be an issue these days, he observed. Younger people seemed to take on jobs which in his generation would have required years of training—and seniority.

The younger, a second lieutenant, came to the back and saluted them. "Señora y señor," he began. "You are no doubt familiar with regular commercial aircraft. This one is high performance. Please, it is vital that you keep your seatbelt fastened until we inform you otherwise."

They both nodded, mentally conceding that he was in his operating environment and they were not.

"Any medical issues? Do either of you have a head cold? Excellent! Enjoy the flight and I'll be back soon with more information."

The aircraft speeded down the active runway and took off at a rate of incline that Diego had not experienced before. He felt his body slam back. His head was pinned to his headrest with such a strong G-force that he wondered if they were approaching the speed of sound. His ears popped several times. Soon, they levelled out and he was able to relax a little. Glancing over at his boss, he saw that Claudia was already at work on her tablet. She seemed perfectly at home with the subsonic flying experience.

Not to be outdone, Diego opened his laptop and tried to study some files. He felt like a young kid enjoying his first experience of flying. He felt . . . well, special. At that moment, he acknowledged that he had been very lucky. As an immigrant, he was grateful. Pride swelled his chest, and he could feel the exhilaration of blood rushing through his body. Yes, he admitted to himself, he felt excited and a little bit giddy. Under his breath, he vowed a renewed oath of loyalty to his adopted country—just as many people do when they experience at first hand the might of their nation's armed forces.

"We'll be landing in about fifteen minutes," said the second lieutenant. "Just a few statistics, if you are interested. Our top speed capacity is 510 knots—about 950 kilometres per hour. We are rated about two hundred and fifty below MACH 1. On our journey from Madrid, we've been cruising at around 480 knots at a ceiling of just over twelve thousand metres. That's comfortably above the civilian traffic lanes," he added. "It's a short journey."

"Where are we landing?" asked Diego, immediately regretting his question. The officer glanced at Claudia and received a nod.

"We will be arriving at Rota Air Force Base, sir," he replied, glancing at his watch, "in about eleven minutes. It should be a smooth, but steep, descent—perhaps with a little turbulence. Stay buckled up, please."

Well, thought Diego, it had taken them not much more than twenty minutes to get to Cadiz on the southern tip of Spain. Some years ago, he had driven to the area with his family. He recalled that their driving time had been over seven hours. His smile was a blend of pride, exhilaration, and awe. Once again, he felt privileged.

Fifteen minutes later, they disembarked and Diego beamed an involuntary rookie grin at the crew. A vehicle whisked them away to a waiting room adjacent to a hangar. He found it difficult to hide his excitement. They were ushered through the waiting room door—where a massive US Forces helicopter and its aircrew were standing by. Handing them ear protection, a crewman escorted them on board. Diego selected one of the many empty seats and strapped himself in.

"It's a Super Huey, in case you folks are wondering," said one of the Americans pilots as he checked their non-standard seat belt double-clasp buckles. He was black officer with a happy, broad smile and laughter creases around his eyes. "It's a combat aircraft. Don't worry, we're not armed. You're going to enjoy the travel experience," he predicted with a belly laugh. It relaxed them and they smiled in return. "Just a short journey. Real quick!" he added in his southern twang before returning to the flight deck.

The aircraft was towed from the hangar. Within a few minutes, its rotors started punching the air. Through his earphones, Diego could hear a muted conversation between the flight crew and the control tower. Minutes later, it lifted off the ground. It swayed, moved forwards, made a slight tilt sideways and finally climbed powerfully into the air.

Rota Air Force Base is also a naval base. The passengers were treated to a bird's-eye view of the naval dockyard with numerous Spanish vessels and several others belonging to allied nations. Huge cranes and containers lined the dockside. Diego could make out the shape of a powerful smaller ship, which he guessed was a destroyer. Several others, he thought, might be frigates or auxiliaries. The largest vessel was a camouflaged cruiser flying the ensign of the US Navy. Its bow lines were being cast off as the crew prepared to sail.

The helicopter swept forwards through the docklands and across the bay, making its approach towards what Diego saw was a giant of a ship. As the helicopter neared its landing spot on the wide deck, he was able to make out the name of the aircraft carrier—USS *Bataan*. Already impressed by the equipment he'd seen, Diego was in awe of the American vessel. It was massive.

More than that, it was formidable.

At the same time, he thought, it was reassuring. If you were on the right side, politically.

USS Bataan

Diego looked at his watch. It was amazing, he thought. So much had happened already that day, yet it was still only 0950 hours. Here they were, aboard one of the world's most modern and sophisticated aircraft carriers. Everything was unmistakably American. Both he and Claudia felt as though they'd flown directly to the United States.

A young deck officer with a Bronx accent escorted them from the flight deck to a mess room, where a good-looking man in his late thirties was sitting. He was in the process of texting and stood up as they came into the room.

"Ah, you must be Chief Inspector Ramirez and Deputy Inspector Abaya," he said in Castilian Spanish with an unmistakably cultured English accent. He extended his hand. "I'm James Garwood. We're waiting for our host. I understand he'll be here in a few minutes. Please help yourselves to refreshments." He waved in the direction of a coffee pot and an array of soft drinks. "How was your flight?"

Diego was still wondering what role the Englishman had on board ship when the door opened. A tall man ducked under the metal bulkhead frame as he stepped into the room.

He was no ordinary person, the visitors quickly noted. The man was a giant. Wearing the uniform whites of a navy lieutenant commander, his face was deeply tanned—confirming that he spent a great deal of time outdoors. Most likely in areas where the sun was harsh and relentless, thought Diego. He was young, possibly mid-thirties. His flawless, short-sleeved shirt was starched and crisp. In place of epaulets, he wore shoulder pads displaying his rank. A gold star above the stripes revealed that he was a line officer. Diego thought it would be hard to mistake him being anything but a man of action.

You couldn't miss the man's flaming Celtic-red hair and beard, and laughing aqua-blue eyes, thought Diego. Abundant strands of thick straight hair were swept back without a parting, pushed away from his broad, strong forehead. His flaming red tresses looked damp and freshly washed, as if he had just stepped out of the shower. He looked clean and handsome. Along the sides of his face, his hair blended neatly into a well-trimmed and unblemished flaming red beard.

Diego felt a strong pang of masculine envy and admiration. The man had a relaxed presence—the bearing of one who is confident in himself and at ease with his surroundings. He looked sophisticated, with a graceful elegance. A slight downturn of his mouth suggested that he was mildly amused by the formality of the gathering. Diego admitted to himself that he felt more than a little envious: his own stature, although muscular, being short and unremarkable.

The naval officer sat down and placed his cap on the table in front of him—gesturing for them to take a seat.

Glancing at the Englishman, he broke into a wide grin and his eyes lit up with pleasure. "Top of the morning to ye'all," he said, laughing. "Oi bet that scared the living bejabers out of yuh, myself comin' in like tat. Now admit it. Oi did, didn't Oi?" He searched each of their faces in turn for signs of response; he was like a schoolboy wanting his mates to enjoy his practical joke, thought Diego. "Now don't be judging me from this git-up, will you now?" He laughed with his shoulders until his whole body began to shake. He stopped abruptly and began speaking fluently in a dialect of Arabic, which Diego understood perfectly, conceding that the man sounded like a native speaker.

"Show off," the Englishman interrupted with just a hint of disapproval. "What Lieutenant Commander O'Flaherty is doing," he protested, "is demonstrating for us just two of his many disguises. I happen to know that he speaks the Queen's English better than I. He's Marlborough. Double-first at Oxford and an American citizen from Boston. I'll leave it to him to explain the purpose of this meeting."

The Englishman continued, "Among *my* other roles, I'm with a special ops counterterrorism unit at GCHQ in the United Kingdom. This is an American naval vessel. As we are in Spanish waters, it is appropriate to introduce—and thank—Chief Inspector Claudia Ramirez. She is, I understand, with GEO—the special operations arm of the Spanish National Police. So, too, I believe, is her colleague Deputy Inspector Diego Abaya. I'd also like to thank the US Navy for its hospitality. Very kind. Lieutenant Commander O'Flaherty is our host, so I'll turn the meeting over to him."

He turned his head towards the naval officer who had been deep in thought and was toying with his beard. It seemed to the visitors that their host was playing a role not unlike a Shakespearean actor—in the midst of changing costumes and characters between acts in a stage play, concentrating exclusively on his next lines.

"As you've heard, I'm Michael O'Flaherty," he began. His voice was cool and even. "I'm regular Navy, attached to the CIA at Langley." He paused. "As my good friend of many years, James, has explained, my work requires me to assume various disguises."

The Englishman passed around a single glossy photograph. It was a headshot of O'Flaherty. Taken against a desert background in a combat zone, it provided a very different view of him. He had the same flaming red hair and beard, but neither appeared to have been trimmed or combed for years. He looked unwashed; his face wore a scowl and displayed the countenance of a violent man with an irritable disposition.

Diego suddenly remembered. Of course! He had seen this man's photo before. It had been in Ceuta, when he and Antonio had met the colonel at National Police Headquarters. This was the same man—the CIA officer who had been caught in the sweep of a madrassa in Morocco, but then immediately released back into the field. As he gazed at the photograph, half-listening to the naval officer, Diego racked his brains trying to recall what else he knew about him.

"All of us around this table have been briefed by our own people on the confidentiality of this meeting," O'Flaherty was saying. His voice was soft and reassuring. As he spoke, he looked at each of them in turn. It was a collegial look—an invitation from the head boy to a few favoured juniors. His tone was collective: we are in this together.

"If you will permit me, I will start by making certain assumptions and open them for discussion. They're not cast in stone." He looked at Claudia. "We can make changes for the record, if that is the wish of your government. However, señora, if we can broadly agree on the assumptions, I'd suggest we move on to the real substance."

Claudia nodded.

"Assumption number one," O'Flaherty continued, "is that, as allies, we are united in our resolve to fight and thwart terrorism. I realise how sweeping that statement is—and I recognise that we, ourselves, are in the terrorism business. Our hands are not clean, not by any means. We'd be hypocritical to claim otherwise. On the other hand, we'd be naïve if we thought it wasn't necessary for us to be the adversary in certain circumstances. I'm referring to the particular brand of extreme terrorism which our respective countries, and the Global Coalition, identified some years ago. Over sixty countries, including ours, collaborated on a plan to defeat ISIS and deny them 'a safe haven,' to quote the agreed wording at the time.

"Assumption number two relates to the funding activities of ISIS—IS, ISIL, or Daesh, if you prefer their alternative names. To state the obvious, their activities require access to finance. In contrast to al-Qaeda, which has been starved of funding in recent years, ISIS has proven adept at creating its own sources of income. I'm referring to kidnappings and sales of Iraqi oil to the al-Daser regime and others. Among other nefarious deeds, ISIS has stripped priceless antiquities and works of art and sold them on the black market. In short, unlike al-Qaeda, ISIS—despite its recent defeats—knows how to run a profitable business enterprise. As we know, it also has become highly proficient at exploiting online communications through social media and the internet."

Diego studied O'Flaherty carefully as the naval officer looked at each of them. He didn't think that anything the American was saying would be regarded as controversial. They were close military allies, after all. He had no doubt that James Garwood and the British government would support the Americans. London was a long-term military partner. O'Flaherty would be less sure about the Spanish government. He guessed that the American had read the CIA files on Claudia. He would know she was a senior and experienced officer in Madrid with an enviable service record. O'Flaherty no doubt had also read his CIA file. He would have found out that Diego was considered a bit of an enigma. The record would show that he was a first-class officer, but he guessed there was a cautionary note in his file that he could be truculent.

He was aware that O'Flaherty was glancing at him cautiously. He would be looking for any changes in their body language . . . eyes narrowing, mouths hardening, fingers clenched tightly, or arms folded. Claudia and he were too well trained to reveal their thinking in such an obvious way.

"In addition, ISIS and its friends in al-Qaeda have exported their terrorist skills—selling them around the world," O'Flaherty was saying. "That includes the recent bombing plot in Barcelona—which, thank goodness, was foiled just in time. I'm speaking of the attempted bombing of the Catalan police headquarters. I expect you'll want to address that later," he said, anticipating that Claudia might want to comment on the incident.

"The validity of assumption number three depends to some extent on what happens in the immediate future," O'Flaherty continued. "The efforts of the Coalition—and, more particularly, the entry of the Russians on the side of President al-Daser—have greatly assisted the Syrian Army and regime to rout ISIS from the country. As an effective force, ISIS has been defeated—on the ground at least. Al-Qaeda, globally? Far from it!"

"Neither group has been defeated in the minds of millions of people who believe in their cause," said Diego, interrupting the American.

Claudia frowned a glance at him, but O'Flaherty was ahead of her. "No, you're absolutely right, Deputy Inspector. You've nailed one of the most important points that I want to reinforce at this meeting. ISIS may have been defeated on the ground, but it hasn't gone away in the Middle East or elsewhere—including large parts of Africa and Asia. Not just that but, as you infer, the causes and beliefs driving the two groups are still as strong, if not stronger, than they were before. In addition, in Afghanistan, we have to contend with the Taliban.

"What I was going to say," he continued, "is that when the Russians entered the two wars in Syria—I mean taking a back door role in the civil war, as well as the fight against ISIS—it was a decisive strategic move by the Coalition's traditional enemy. They have filled a political vacuum, just as ISIS had done.

"We created that vacuum. By *we*, I mean the Coalition—but a large part of that was a shift in US policy. For its own reasons, Washington decided to disengage actively from the Middle East and from Syria in particular. It was US policy, with the agreement and support of the Coalition, to defeat ISIS in the war against terrorism. As Americans, it was not our intention, in the process, to abandon support for our friends in the civil war fight within Syria, even though it might seem to some observers that we have.

"One of the realities we face is this: Russia is not constrained politically in the same way as we are in the Western democracies. They can do things we can't—particularly with money. It's the same for China. In the United States, we are required to go through the presidency, and usually Congress, to secure the funding we need for special operations. OCO, or *Overseas Contingency Operations,* funding is limited in scope and subject to congressional oversight. It's largely unhelpful for clandestine operations. The point I want to make is this: as Americans, we're working hard to overcome the vacuum we created in Syria when we withdrew military support for the northern paramilitary rebel groups we had been supporting. Several of those rebel groups, we believe, are vital to keep permanently in place. Why? Because the Coalition is determined to prevent Iran, and its ally Russia, from gaining a permanent foothold across Syria and Iraq—from the Persian Gulf to the Mediterranean."

"Are you saying that the allies, or at least those countries that will support it, should help create a Sunni Muslim buffer state in northern Syria and Iraq?" asked Diego. "A buffer state that would help counterbalance the creation of the so-called Shi'ite Crescent, that would geographically and politically unite the interests of Iran, Iraq, al-Daser's Syria, as well as Lebanon?"

This time, Claudia looked on approvingly at his interruption.

O'Flaherty sucked in his breath between his teeth. He seemed to realise that achieving his purpose here today would be no easy task, thought Diego.

"If only it were that straightforward, Deputy Inspector," he replied. "As far as I am aware, that is not *officially* an objective of the allies and the Coalition. The Turkish government clearly wants a buffer zone to protect its southern border. American policy has been unclear, but generally, we support Turkey as a NATO ally in that objective. Even though ISIS is weak, we have no desire to create a void that might help al-Qaeda achieve the same territorial result as ISIS by winning over people in the region who hate the West.

"We know that Iran, aided and abetted by Russia, has ambitions to control the region," he continued. "They are fiercely opposed by the Saudi Kingdom, which essentially fights for Sunni rights—not just in the Arabian Peninsula either. They are strong allies of the West. But I'm telling you things you already know. My point is that a territorial void has been created in the region, and that several interests are uniting together to fill, occupy, and control that void.

"The Turks have worked on improving their relations with the Iranians," O'Flaherty continued. "Neither of them wishes to see an independent Kurdish state on their doorstep. Yet, you are right. Turkey is also worried about Iran's expansionist ambitions and the explosive growth in Shi'ite power in the region.

"Unfortunately, the Coalition's efforts to destroy ISIS inadvertently have weakened our paramilitary allies. We have allowed the Russians to eliminate many of them. The Turks are doing the same. Worse still, under the pretext of fighting ISIS, Russian warplanes have pulverised the rebels. In effect, they are doing what al-Daser wants in the civil war—achieve a total victory. He is determined to regain full control over Syria.

"In considering our own interests, we'd be naïve to ignore the importance of Israel and the Saudis in the regional balance of power." O'Flaherty's face grew dark. "That's not where it ends. Longevity of our NATO bases in Turkey is not assured. We are being pushed out of the Middle East. It's a systematic—and, so far, successful—campaign by our adversaries. The Arab Spring failed. The trappings of the Western world no longer appeal to emerging nations. We are losing the culture wars as well."

Claudia spoke. "Allowing Russia, Iran—and perhaps China, eventually—to establish alternative gateways to Europe is not in our best interests. This was agreed within the Coalition some time ago, Lieutenant Commander. As a member of the Coalition, Spain has full membership in the executive councils. Also, as a member of the European Union, we are well aware of the dangers of not remaining united within Europe." She glanced critically at James Garwood.

Sitting back on her chair, she gestured at their surroundings. "We very much appreciate being hosted in such an impressive venue. Your aircraft carrier is magnificent—and intimidating. Our journey here, and the clandestine helicopter ride, added to our excitement and awe. Well done! Like the English, you Americans do intimidation very well. I say that with sincere admiration, Lieutenant Commander. We Spaniards have a long imperial history of intimidation. Longer than yours, in fact. So, when we are the target of that particular black art, we recognise and admire it. As Spaniards, we are your allies." Her face became serious. "Now, what exactly is it you want from us, Michael?"

"Olé!" exclaimed the delighted American. "Forgive me, señora, if I have appeared condescending."

His apologetic offering was accepted with a shrug from Claudia. He soon realised that her smile had disappeared and had been replaced by an ice-cold stare. "Before you answer, Michael, keep in mind that we do not like being manipulated. By you or anybody else." She included the Englishman in her glance. "There must be something else you are not telling us. So, what is it—what are you asking us to do?"

O'Flaherty rearranged his naval cap on the table in front of him. "Money," he said quietly, making eye contact with her. "It's about money. Let me explain. For some time, along with our counterparts in Britain, we have been carrying out a special operation in Syria and Iraq. We have been providing support for certain rebel groups—just a few of the many hundreds of Syrian paramilitaries that existed until recently. There are some we believe are likely to survive through the endgame of the two wars. They have the local support needed to consolidate the remaining rebel groups, including the Free Syrian Army, and win the support of the people. Together, they can form a post-war government of a new protectorate in northern Syria.

"You referred to it earlier as a buffer state," he said, speaking directly to Diego. "In effect, I suppose it would be—if it can be achieved. Our operation is code-named Project Catalyst."

"You mean that the US and the Coalition have been providing arms and money to the rebel groups? But a lot more money than we've been aware of?" asked Claudia. "And, I suspect, a lot more money than our governments have agreed to—at least as far as the public knows?"

O'Flaherty nodded in agreement. "The attitude among voters in Western countries has shifted negatively against intervention. There have been too many years of tough economic times—particularly in Europe, but also instability in the Americas. Massive numbers of refugees flooding into Europe have changed the demographic—and the politics. Voters are no longer willing to continue to support seemingly endless fighting in the Middle East. There are too many problems at home.

"The difference is that, with the tacit agreement of several governments, we have been diverting confiscated funds from global money-laundering operations," said O'Flaherty. "The money has gone towards helping fund Project Catalyst."

"You want us to redirect laundered money from Spain into covert US military operations?" interjected Claudia, her eyebrows raised.

"Coalition operations," corrected the Englishman.

"That involves at least two issues that I imagine might be of concern to my government," shot back Claudia. "Most importantly, the money—or at least part of it—belongs to sovereign governments, including ours."

"Some of it does," the Englishman intervened. "Part of the dirty money was obtained through corruption and bribery. Cash has been illegally diverted; taxes have been avoided. You're correct, señora. Properly speaking, that money belongs in the hands of governments. But, apart from dirty money, we are talking about the equivalent of over a trillion euros equivalent of other funds that are laundered every year. Large sums of money coming from the drugs trade. It's a moot point whose government that money belongs to."

"Secondly," Claudia continued to ignore him, "haven't we seen this movie before? I mean, covert financing of terrorists from slush funds has been done before—sometimes with unfortunate results." She looked at O'Flaherty. "I'm thinking of Oliver North and the Iran-Contra Affair."

O'Flaherty flinched but said nothing.

She continued speaking. "If this is an official request, I'll have to convey it to my superiors in Madrid." Her face indicated that she didn't think much of the idea and probably gave it little chance of success. She glanced at Diego, and both seemed ready to leave.

There was a pause, which seemed to last for a long time.

"I think it *is* important for you to discuss it with your people in Madrid," said O'Flaherty eventually. "They will inform you that we are talking about a *fait accompli*. We are already doing it: we are using the money. Our respective governments have been cooperating for some time on the clandestine use of some of the laundered funds flowing through and around Europe, and internationally.

"The precise sources of the funds have been kept secret. They've been contributed from various Coalition anti-money-laundering operations. Confiscated funds. Some from the UK," he continued, glancing at Garwood. "Some from the United States. A significant amount from our friends, the Canadians. France and Germany, too. Spain has made confiscated illegal funds available to us—intercepted transfers of laundered money controlled by drug cartels, formerly hidden in banks within Andorra. But let's set aside this direction of discussion. It's not my intention here today to discuss the sources of illegal funds, or to debate the rights and wrongs of using them for this purpose. Actually, we have some highly confidential information to reveal to you."

O'Flaherty's measured voice continued to provide a calm atmosphere of assurance and control. "For the last three years, I've been operating undercover, mostly in Syria and Iraq. At the CIA, with the help of James Garwood and his colleagues at GCHQ, we've been tracking a particularly powerful and dangerous set of jihadists terror cells. They are linked directly with al-Qaeda leadership, and particularly with the emerging leadership: the next generation. Those cells have roots in Spain," he said, directing his gaze at Claudia.

"You are referring to *Operation Ferrol*," she replied without hesitation. O'Flaherty nodded.

"My colleague Deputy Inspector Abaya was instrumental in bringing several aspects of that investigation to a timely conclusion—thankfully. Avoiding what could have been a major catastrophe at the Mossos Headquarters in Barcelona." She gestured towards Diego.

Diego considered that his boss was being far too generous in her praise of him. It had been the Mossos themselves who had foiled the attack. He lowered his eyes.

"You're correct," intoned the Englishman. "But it's much bigger than *Operation Ferrol*. It was, of course, a great relief to us all when the Barcelona terrorist bombing attempt failed. It was fortunate that the detonators used by the terrorists did not function as they were intended." He paused and glanced at O'Flaherty. "But we should not fool ourselves into thinking that al-Qaeda has been driven out of Spain—you know that better than we do." He looked at Claudia.

She shrugged her shoulders. "We are aware that several of the terrorists, at least members of jihadist extremist cells that we know about, still have not been apprehended. We have some knowledge of who they are. A manhunt is under way."

"The principal target of that, we understand, is a woman—a close collaborator of the former mastermind of *Operation Ferrol*," said the Englishman. "I'm referring to your former boss, Raphael Robles, aka Mustapha," he added, looking at Diego. "You've apprehended him and he's locked away securely, we understand. But his girlfriend accomplice remains at large."

"I met the former junior officer from the Civil Guard—Felix—in Iraq. I think you know that," said O'Flaherty. "There are certain things we have not told you," he continued, looking defensive. "One of the purposes of this meeting is to correct that unfortunate oversight.

As allies, we need to have a coordinated approach to defeating the extremists. Here is what's happening . . ."

Claudia

Claudia and Diego had spoken little to each other after leaving the aircraft carrier.

They'd waited briefly in the private airport lounge after the US helicopter crew had transported them the short distance back to Rota Air Force Base. The Falcon 900B and its boyish aircrew of the *Fuerza Aérea Espanola* had been on standby, waiting to take them back to Madrid. Within minutes, they were airborne.

O'Flaherty and the Englishman had trusted them with highly sensitive intelligence. They were still processing it—thinking through its implications and how they would have to change the focus of their investigation.

Diego had noticed the change in Claudia's mood. During parts of the meeting, she'd become very quiet. She seemed troubled, and he could only guess what she was thinking. On their inbound flight, Diego had felt like an excited schoolboy. Now, preoccupied with the new information, he was lost in thought. Puzzled by what he'd learned, he was revising his understanding of some important events of the past few months.

He thought back to the meeting on board the carrier. It was clear that the American and Englishman knew each other well. They had interacted with ease. He had the impression they didn't keep many secrets from each other. Another cosy-cousins relationship, he thought. The American's role was easy to understand. It was the Englishman's function he struggled to understand—he seemed to be old-school British, a throwback to the days of the Empire.

Claudia must have read his thoughts. Moments later, she passed her tablet to him. The page displayed a brief biography of both men—gathered by the Centro Nacional de Inteligencia and classified as highly restricted. He read that Garwood had a special role within British Intelligence, providing a link between the national security services and the British and American governments. It also turned out that he was a member of the British peerage—his title was Lord Garwood.

Well, that explained a few things, thought Diego, handing the device back to Claudia. As he gazed through the passenger windows of their jet, more questions nagged at Diego: How would he deal with his department's relationship with the Catalan police? What would he be able to tell Antonio? Based on the information he'd been entrusted with, he didn't see how he could say anything to his Mossos friend.

They had deplaned and were striding across the tarmac at Torrejón. Diego saw that their official car was waiting, engine running, to whisk them into the city.

"I phoned ahead," Claudia told him quietly. "You'd better come along to my meeting with the minister. I need to talk to him about what we heard this morning. Also, he wants to hear directly from you about your interrogation of Raphael Robles. He's got your report and has some questions. Let's hear our instructions from the horse's mouth," she added.

⁓⌒

They sat on the narrow, heavy wooden benches outside the minister's office. Dark panelling made the anteroom seem gloomy and austere, thought Claudia. Several heavily framed ancient oil paintings adorned the walls, adding to the sense of formality—imposing a deep sense of history and tradition.

In the background, through a door leading to the minister's secretariat, several members of staff were diligently at work. Muted phones rang occasionally, and they could hear the scraping noise of a metal filing cabinet being closed. Voices were kept low, as if in respect for the minister's high level standing within the government. The great man was an influential member of the prime minister's inner cabinet. Not much happened in Madrid that did not at some point find its way across his desk.

A late middle-aged assistant materialised and stood, feet astride, in front of her. Her faded brown hair, turning grey, was clipped tightly into a bun behind her head. She seemed like a severe old governess, thought Claudia. With her thumbs thrust under her leather belt and her exaggerated—almost comical—facial movements, the woman reminded her of a photo she'd once seen of a strutting Mussolini. A faint smell of mothballs lingered around the woman's dull clothing.

"The minister will see you now, Chief Inspector," she announced. Her colourless pinched nose upturned, she sniffed at the air. Glancing contemptuously at Diego, she made it clear that he was not the sort to be invited into the great man's inner sanctum.

Claudia stood up and turned to Diego. "You'd better wait here," she said to him, rolling her eyes at the assistant's rude and dismissive attitude. She took her time getting up, forcing the woman to wait. Dragging her feet, she slowly followed the condescending assistant through the heavy wood doors.

"Can we trust him?" the minister asked moments later.

"Sir?" asked Claudia, puzzled.

"I mean, he's not . . . not one of us," replied the minister irritably. "He's an immigrant and a Muslim. Can we trust him with such sensitive information?"

She had not been expecting the question, and it took her by surprise on several levels. "I have every confidence in Deputy Inspector Abaya," she heard herself say in a clear and confident voice. Her tone was matter-of-fact and measured—although, in truth, she felt annoyed with the minister. He had shown himself yet again to be entrenched in the Old Spain, unwilling to think outside traditional boundaries.

The thought flashed across her mind that she could understand his question from a security perspective. The classified information they'd received from O'Flaherty was highly sensitive. There was no room for error. It must be kept confidential; she understood that. In context, his question about Diego was not unreasonable. It was just the way the minister had framed it. His careless racial slur surprised and irritated her.

As far as she knew—and she had made it her business to be well-informed on the issue—Diego's loyalty and dedication to his job were beyond reproach. He had been given the highest possible security clearances evaluated by a group of hard-nosed, incorruptible service officers at the CNI. Before his appointment to GEO Group 60, Diego's security clearance status had been reviewed at the intelligence centre for counterterrorism and organised crime. His record and background checks were unimpeachable.

In what was uncharacteristic for her, Claudia threw caution to the wind. "I'd trust him with my life, sir," she said, looking directly at the minister.

"Well," he huffed, "I hope it doesn't come to that." It was his turn to be annoyed. He paddled his fingers dismissively in the air, indicating the door to his office. "You'd better bring him in. I want to hear more about what he got out of Robles.

"Before you do that, what's your reaction to what you heard this morning from our allies? Do you understand how this new information changes the nature of your investigation—how it might affect you personally, Chief Inspector?" He looked at her meaningfully, with just a slight hint of a threat.

"I understand, sir," said Claudia, her eyes dilating almost in fear.

"Good. I'm glad we are in agreement. Don't worry, I have no intention of saying anything. You did what you thought was right at the time."

"Thank you, sir," she replied in a defensive voice. His reference was to an operational decision she'd made before she was appointed as the new head of GEO Group 60. It had involved an assassination attempt by a trusted sniper—and it had ended badly.

"Before you bring in your Moroccan, there is something you can do for me." The minister reached for a cigar, then thought better of it. He walked back to his desk, gesturing Claudia towards a comfortable leather chair. He remained standing, pacing the room.

"The prime minister is worried about the latest developments in this Catalan separatist thing. It's gone on far too long. He has instructed me—as senior minister—to draw up a blueprint for a new national police force. We want to integrate these regional police contingents; they're far too independent." He huffed again. "They've started to follow the will of the people, of all things. You came to GEO from the Army and then the Civil Guard, Chief Inspector. You have an understanding of these regional police units. So, I'd like to send the blueprint over to you—for your comments, let's say? Our national security apparatus in Spain has far too many autonomous elements. Our policing has become an international joke. The PM intends to make changes, I can tell you. Not to be repeated, mind." He looked sternly at her.

"I'd be happy to look at it, sir," replied Claudia, aware of the minister's habit of delegating large parts of his workload. Leveraging his position, he was taking advantage of her. He was asking for much more than mere simple comments. There wouldn't be a draft to look at, as he'd intimated. Claudia would have to prepare it for him—a comprehensive report that he could then present to the PM. She knew she'd have to create a complete architecture of the new organisation without any help from the minister.

The minister sat down. "All right, you can bring him in."

"Deputy Inspector Abaya, sir," she introduced a few moments later, as Diego was ushered into the minister's office.

"Tell me about Robles," said the minister abruptly, ignoring Diego's salute. "Your report said he disclosed no new information of any use. What had you hoped to accomplish?"

"I worked closely with him for many years, sir," said Diego. "I thought that, by interviewing him, I might be able to detect inconsistencies. Perhaps even engage him in a line of discussion that might reveal information he had not provided to his interrogators. I was looking for small clues: little things that might reveal something more substantial."

"Did he?" demanded the minister. "Did Robles reveal anything new? Perhaps there was something you did not put in your report?" His eyes narrowed as he studied Diego's face for clues.

"No, sir."

The minister kept his gaze on Diego, allowing the silence to eat away at the policeman's resolve. Finally, he looked away and returned to the report on his desk. He stopped at a page flagged for attention. "You say here that he denies that anyone from the Government of Spain had any prior knowledge of the coup attempt?"

"I was following the list of questions I'd been cleared to ask, sir. Robles already had been asked most of them several times by his interrogators."

"You chose to ask that particular question, Deputy Inspector? What was the reason?"

"I was exploring for inconsistencies, sir."

"Did you find any?"

"No, sir. His reply to me was almost identical to the one he'd given previously to his interrogators. He claimed that no one within the Government of Spain had any prior knowledge of the coup attempt."

"His answer to his interrogators wasn't good enough for you, Deputy Inspector? Why was that?"

"It wasn't *what* he said, sir. It was the *way* he said it. He was daring me to offer names. It's one of his methods of extracting information, especially when he intends to give none in return. I've experienced it before."

"Did you suggest any names?"

"No, sir, I was under strict orders not to offer any information."

"Yet . . . ?"

Diego paused before answering. "I believe he is desperate to find out what we know, sir. He's frantic to glean that information in particular. He wants to know who in the government, if anyone, has been implicated in the coup attempt. I gave him nothing."

The minister seemed satisfied and once again consulted Diego's report.

Diego had noticed that Claudia was carefully observing their exchange. He got the impression that she approved of his handling of the question and was pleased he wasn't getting rattled. More revealing, she seemed particularly attentive to the minister's questions—noting his keen interest in knowing if Robles had talked.

To him, it appeared that the minister was trying to gauge if Robles was cracking. The minister appeared reassured by his answer. There could be several reasons for his question, thought Diego. He might simply be in damage-control mode, making sure that the PM was not blindsided by any new revelations—or it could be something else.

Claudia seemed to be thinking the same thing.

One thing was for sure, he thought. Despite the persuasive methods that Robles had been subjected to, he'd revealed very little—even when they'd resorted to the usual chemical methods of getting captives to break down. He'd talked, of course, but he was an anomaly in so many respects: a really tough nut to crack.

The minister looked up from reading Diego's report. "You asked him if he felt his life was in danger?"

"He'd been asked that question before, sir. I wanted to hear his answer. If he is protecting other people—powerful people, I mean—they might feel more secure if he was no longer alive to talk."

"What did he say?"

"He seemed indifferent, sir. I don't think he's worried about his personal safety."

"So, there's no evident threat?" supplied the minister. "If Robles doesn't feel threatened, it might indicate that he's not protecting anyone—at least no one who would rather see him dead than alive."

"Possibly, sir."

"Quite *probably*, Deputy Inspector!" shot back the minister. He sounded angry. "If some unidentified powerful people wanted to kill him, presumably they would have done so by now. They would have done so long before he was subjected to extraction methods that have yielded no useful information. So, your question to Robles was entirely speculative."

"Yes, sir."

Claudia watched the exchange without offering any comment. The minister's scowl left them both in no doubt about his views on the subject.

"You asked him about payments that were being made to al-Qaeda? Illegal transfers to a terrorist organisation made through the hawala system, you said?"

"Specifically, sir, I wanted to get him to talk about the sources of the money which became known as Aladdin's Cave," said Diego. "Almost a billion euros in total."

The minister flinched, and Claudia obviously did not miss the significance. Like Diego, she was well aware of the size and nature of the slush fund. It was yet another embarrassment for the government—especially because it hadn't yet been traced and recovered.

"We are still tracking the money, sir," continued Diego. "As you know, that's one of the things we have under way at GEO, and so do the Mossos. As soon as we learned about its existence, our investigators tried to find out where it came from. The person who could tell us, the conspirator Count Carlos, suffered a fatal heart attack before we had a chance to question him."

Diego saw the minister's eyes narrow at the mention of Count Carlos. He was aware that Claudia believed several senior and influential people in the federal government historically had connections to General Bastides and his gang. The full story had never come out. She must be wondering if the minister had known anything about the attempted plot, he thought. After all, he had listening posts everywhere.

"General Bastides and his banker friends seemed to know very little about the detailed sources of the money," Diego continued. "They left the accounting of that to the count. We interrogated all of them, and no one seemed to be holding back anything. They knew some of the money came from rigged construction contracts here in Spain, where cash was skimmed off in illicit fees. They admitted there had been illegal deals between land developers and local politicians. We know there were other large sums too. We weren't sure where they came from. So, when I interrogated Robles, I wanted to find out what the other sources were—and what underworld strings were attached. Who supplied the money, and why?"

Diego glanced at Claudia. With a quick movement of her head, she encouraged him to continue.

"Months ago, his interrogators had questioned Robles about General Bastides's connections to the royal family," continued Diego. "They had information linking several of his co-conspirators to the monarchy. If the coup had succeeded, the new government would have reinstalled the king as absolute monarch. That wouldn't have gone down well in separatist Catalunya or the Basque country. Maybe it would have been accepted—and likely might have been popular—in the rest of Spain. Had the vicious al-Qaeda bombings planned throughout the country been successful, the Spanish people would have been in no mood to argue. They would have supported the coup and the need for a strong and decisive government in Madrid," said Diego.

"This is preposterous," exclaimed the minister.

"I'm just repeating what General Bastides confessed after he was arrested, sir," said Diego. "It was one of the lines of questioning followed by Robles's interrogators. In my questions to him, I wasn't interested in the coup attempt. I wanted to find out where the money came from."

"Did Robles admit to any connection with the monarchy?" asked the minister stiffly. "Did he confirm any financial connection?"

"No, sir. Throughout my interview with him, Robles remained steadfast. He gave almost nothing away."

"He gave nothing away, or he gave *almost* nothing away?" demanded the minister. "Which is it?"

"It was just something he said to me, sir, when I had finished my interrogation. It's hard to explain. I made a brief reference to it in my report. During the several years that I worked for him, he always seemed respectful of the royal family. Yet, I had never thought he was much of a monarchist. It was nothing specific, sir—just his attitude. I always thought he was more of a—well, more of a globalist. I don't have the words to describe it," he said, looking at Claudia for help.

She said nothing and let him continue.

"He doesn't think in terms of individual countries," Diego ploughed on. "He loves Spain and sometimes he talked about its history, especially its early history. He asked my views. I told him that I wasn't much of a scholar. I said that I'm very grateful to Spain for allowing in my parents and our family as immigrants. We have been very loyal, sir," Diego added. He seemed anxious to reassure the minister, whose facial expression gave away nothing.

Diego continued his answer. "I had pressed the bell to summon the guard and was turning to leave. Two armed guards were stationed immediately outside the glass door to his cell. They were unlocking the door, and I suppose he thought the noise would drown out our voices. Robles came close to me and whispered in my ear. 'We'll win, Diego, you know that.' I said nothing and shook my head. His response was a sly smile. He said again, 'We *will* win, Diego.'

"It was almost as if he believed we were on the same side," Diego continued. "That we were fighting for the same cause—the jihad. We know that Chief Inspector Robles was a double agent, sir. We know now that he was also the head of al-Qaeda in Spain. At the jail, I thought he was playing me. I didn't get a chance to find out what he meant. We parted company, and the rest you know, sir. As soon as I could, I wrote up my report." He avoided looking at Claudia. "I included everything except for his last few words. I found it hard to explain them in writing, so I left out that part."

The minister stood up and walked across the room; he seemed deep in thought. "You know this is inconclusive, Deputy Inspector. He wasn't providing you with any new information. It doesn't tell us anything we didn't already know. He was playing ones of his games . . . playing you. I'm not prepared, on the basis of what I've heard here today, to place much credibility on what he said. I can't take this to the prime minister." He looked at Claudia. "You'll have to do better, Chief Inspector. Bring me something more substantive." He picked up a file and waved them away. "You and I will talk more about this," he said to Claudia. "That will be all . . . for now."

"That went well," said Claudia as they left the large, ornate government building. The note of sarcasm in her voice left Diego in no doubt about her real meaning. Even so, she didn't seem unhappy, he thought.

Their chauffeur was sitting inside their GEO pool car fifty metres away. The plaza seemed deserted. Claudia thrust her hands deeply into her warm coat and walked over to a large marble fountain where the cascading water would drown out their voices. Diego knew all about the listening capabilities of parabolic microphones. He hadn't seen one on the roof, but it was prudent to be cautious.

Standing shoulder-to-shoulder with him, facing away from the building, Claudia shared an interesting development: "The Robles interrogation tapes have been edited. Someone has been meddling with them. The royal family connection has been redacted from the official records. I want to know why. Nothing I heard from the minister today was reassuring."

"Do you think Robles's life is in danger?" asked Diego. "I mean, if he knows something, there are people who will want him out of the way."

Claudia said nothing. Her uncomfortable demeanour said everything that Diego needed to know. "The thing is, Diego, we are dealing with elected officials. They come and go; we don't. We are here for the long run. Our duty is to uphold the law even if it means embarrassing some important and powerful people. Even if, sometimes, it means sending them to jail. No one is above the law.

"We have the minister under surveillance," she said quietly. "I think he knows a lot more than he's telling us. That doesn't mean he's guilty of anything more than being strategically well connected. He's clever. However, I'd be surprised if he's mixed up directly in this situation. I could be wrong, but my instincts—and our investigations so far—don't point to his direct involvement. He's a survivor, politically. Politicians don't have clean hands, but who does?

"You spooked him, and we have ways to track what he does with the information you revealed," said Claudia. "It's not the last I'll hear about the meeting we just had. Maybe it's for the best. We need a break in this case—especially after what O'Flaherty told us earlier today. Anyway, this isn't the place to talk. We can continue to discuss it somewhere private—not my office. I'm never sure who has us bugged. For now, let's get back to work. We have a lot to do."

Claudia waved away the chauffeur who scurried to open the car door.

Diego hurried to the other side and scrambled in.

Neither spoke a word on the drive back to GEO Headquarters.

CHAPTER 7
An Education

The office directory on the wall of the lobby was momentarily confusing.

Antonio knew he had the correct address and he was aware that certain government departments preferred not to advertise their precise locations. He'd expected to encounter a creative euphemism for the Terrorist Financing Prevention Unit. Perhaps something like the classic "Import-Export S.A." Finally, he clued in. The directory displayed four floors, whereas the indicator lights above the old-fashioned cage elevator showed five.

He knew that visitors would be locked out of gaining access, so he phoned the receptionist. Moments later, he exited onto the private fifth floor.

Striding towards Antonio, a short, middle-aged bald man extended his hand and smiled. He had a boyish round face, pleasant and almost cherubic. His eyes danced with warmth. "It's a pleasure." He beamed. "I've heard all about you, Antonio." He reached up to place an arm around his visitor's shoulder guiding him into his office. "Coffee? Great work on preventing the bombing attempt—you saved a lot of lives that day," he added, fussing to ensure Antonio's comfort as they sat down.

Antonio flinched. He'd heard the same words from a lot of well-meaning people since the bombing incident and was embarrassed by them. Initially, he'd downplayed his role, denying that he'd done anything special. But people wanted to thank him. They needed a hero. He was swimming against a strong current of popular opinion, so eventually he'd decided just to go along with it.

"Thanks, Ramon. And thanks for seeing me at short notice," he replied, settling his tall lanky frame into a chair across the desk from his host. "I wanted to see you because my chief has given me a new assignment—and I think it crosses over into your jurisdiction."

The bald man held up a hand and waved away Antonio's attempt at conciliation. "There's no need to apologise, Toni. It's all been explained to me. We're here to cooperate, so don't worry about technicalities. Besides, adding another bright mind to the battle will help us all." His eyes sparkled. "Now, what can I do to help?"

Relieved, and nodding his thanks, Antonio launched straight into his topic. "I'm investigating the whereabouts of a large quantity of money. Its origin was a slush fund from the construction corruption scandal. It's linked to the jihadist terrorist bombing attempt on Mossos Headquarters—and a homicide case that's still ongoing. That's why I'm involved."

"You're speaking of Aladdin's Cave, a fortune worth a reported billion euros? Yes, I've read all about it in the papers. It's all over the media. Embarrassing for the government," said Ramon. "I was hoping while you're here that perhaps you could enlighten *us* about the money. What makes you believe it's being actively laundered? Have you been able to trace any of it?"

Shaking his head, Antonio replied that—as far as the Catalan police knew—there had been no sign that the money was back in circulation. "Actually, Ramon, I'm here to ask if you can suggest any useful leads for my investigation. We're working on the case with the National Police. But you know how difficult our relationship with Madrid is these days."

Ramon nodded his head in agreement. "It's incredible, isn't it. This whole separatist thing is pulling our country apart. Well, when I heard you were coming, I pulled some files of interest. Also, we have some sensitive stuff that isn't digitised." He patted several heavy paper files on his desk. "How much do you know about the money-laundering business?"

Antonio shrugged his shoulders. "I did some homework before I came here. Everyone knows about our money transfer authorisation procedures under *SEPBLAC*, of course. Otherwise, there's only general stuff on the internet. Some of our people at headquarters were helpful, but we are far from being experts. It's a hard subject to get a good handle on. I know the basics, I suppose. And, as a detective, I try to put myself in the place of the person who absconded with the funds."

Seeing a slight flicker of the money man's eyes, Antonio realised that he'd inadvertently supplied him with a piece of information he didn't have before. He decided to come clean. "It's classified, of course, Ramon. But we know who she is, and we are familiar with her modus operandi."

"Daniela Balmes?" asked Ramon. "I saw her name in the news. She hasn't been directly connected to the theft. Are you confirming that she is?"

"As I say, it's classified," said Antonio. "I can also confirm that the stash is a mix of gold and currencies—mostly euros. We don't know how many large denomination euro notes are included—such as the infamous five-hundreds." Antonio scowled. "Those aren't being minted any longer, of course. Everyone knows that the European Central Bank wants to keep them in circulation for now. They could be phased out anytime—and that's the risk that confronts Daniela Balmes."

Ramon nodded in agreement. "If I were holding aging paper money, I'd be worried about its obsolescence too. You're right. The central banks could render them worthless in the stroke of a pen. Personally, I'd put my highest priority on getting that kind of money into legal circulation damned quickly. Maybe we can help there. But I interrupted. Please continue."

Antonio handed him a memory stick. "Based on the dates during which the money was accumulated and some federal raids carried out, some of the banknotes are probably among this issue series. It's a wide range, of course. It probably took the launderers many years to pull together that kind of money, and it would have come from a number of different sources. From our interrogations of the people involved, we have good reason to believe that the billion-dollar stash comprises around three-hundred-and-fifty million in gold bullion, and the rest in cash.

"If we work together on this, Ramon, can I ask you to take the lead role in tracing the banknotes? We don't have the resources—or the expertise—to do it. You have the necessary global links, including the FATF network. We're not ignoring the cash, but there's a lot of gold too. Probably around eight hundred ingots, if it hasn't already been melted down and reshaped.

"It's a lot of weight—almost ten tonnes of the stuff. The perpetrators aren't going to move that around very easily. We think we may have better success using our Mossos security forces on the ground. I mean, if we focus on tracking the gold, it may help lead us to the banknotes as well," said Antonio. He looked enquiringly at Ramon. "What do you think?"

"I think that's a smart strategy. We *are* better equipped than any other department to trace the banknotes." He hesitated.

"But?" asked Antonio.

"I don't want to hold out any promises that we'll have success in tracing them," said Ramon. "Money laundering—just the cash part—is a global business worth over a trillion euros a year. Probably a lot more. That's larger than most countries are worth. It's bigger than the annual economic output of Mexico, for instance. In theory, every country in the world would like to eliminate paper money. Sweden has almost done it. In the future, centralised governments want everything in traceable and accountable digitised transactions. It's not just to prevent the tax dodging and laundering that's become an epidemic. Businesses prefer their employees not to handle cash. There's too much leakage.

"Then there are the vested interests. A lot of powerful people and institutions make fortunes from the money-laundering business. They deny it, of course, but it's a major and very lucrative source of income for nearly all banks. If they don't accept customers with dirty money, someone else will—with a nod and a wink.

"Speaking of which," he said, jumping to his feet. Going to a display cabinet, he took out a metal sieve and handed it to Antonio. "I use this to illustrate what we are up against in this department. The global monetary system at present is like a leaky sieve . . . a *tamiz con fugas*. Every time we manage to plug one of these holes, the money flows out somewhere else. It's almost impossible to seal up all the outflows.

"Not just that, new forms of money and creative ways to launder it are being developed all the time. Think of them as new holes in the sieve. Imagine the impacts of online gambling and shady real estate transactions. Then there are the cryptocurrencies—which we're only just starting to understand."

Ramon took his sieve and returned it to the display stand. "It's an almost thankless task. I'll be honest with you, Antonio. Unless we receive an inside tip, we won't have much to go on. We just don't have the investigative power, or the people to do the necessary systems programming to keep our tracking database up to date. I know that one billion euros from Aladdin's Cave sounds like a lot of money. But when we're dealing in trillions globally, it has to be placed in context. I don't want to sound unhelpful, Antonio, but that's the reality. We'll do what we can to trace the cash, I promise you. But don't hold your breath.

"Anyway, I think you're right to follow the gold, to misquote Deep Throat in the movie," he added with a grin. Pressing a button on his desk, he said, "Now, I want you to meet one of our brightest stars. She's our bullion expert. We might be able to assist with your case and help you trace the gold from Aladdin's Cave."

Minutes later, a vivacious young woman in her mid-twenties entered the room. She was well above medium height but wearing heels. It was hard for Antonio to tell if she was as tall as she was elegant. Her deportment was impressive—erect with perfect balance and poise. Weight slightly forward, she came towards them with almost no swing in her arms, her feet planted deliberately, left before right, one in front of the other. Her shoulders and long neckline suggested that she could, if she wished, have a promising career as a fashion model. In her case, however, the typically indifferent attitude and eyes-ahead haughtiness of supermodels were replaced by a vivacious engaging smile and direct eye contact. High cheek bones gave emphasis to her dark complexion, her generous lips forced outwards in a provocative pout.

He had no time to get prepared because she walked straight up to him. Her arm held in a V-shape, she offered her hand—almost at breast level—to shake his. Antonio was taken aback. He was so enchanted that he was late in his understanding and response. It was a failure that caused her amusement—her eyes twinkling as if she knew that she had immediately taken charge of their first encounter.

Her raised eyebrows asked many questions of him. She held his handshake longer than would have been necessary if she'd found him less attractive. Antonio didn't miss the significance. The lingering ghost of a smile on her now parted lips spoke silently of things that have been understood between a woman and a man since time began.

"Madame Périgueux," said Ramon by way of introduction, standing redundantly behind his desk.

Antonio took his cue and moved quickly to position a tall-backed chair so that she could sit comfortably and face them both. She gave his gesture no acknowledgement, intimating that it was the least a lady would expect from a gentleman.

Ramon seemed to be watching the ceremony with amused understanding, barely disguised. Without breaching any confidentialities, he explained to Madame Périgueux the essentials of Antonio's visit.

"The inspector would appreciate any help we can provide," he added unnecessarily.

It is said that the French invented flirting. It must be true, thought Antonio at that moment. The glance to which he was treated by Madame Périgueux elevated the ancient and skilled art of coquetry to a celestial level. To describe her flirtatious glance as evocative would be woefully inadequate. It had all the elements and implications of teasing, provocation—and an invitation. It inflamed Antonio's already aroused and fertile imagination.

Subliminally, it sent a message: You want me? . . . Come and get me. But bring your A-game.

Just as quickly, she switched to work mode. "We don't know how much gold there is in the world," she said, in a sultry French accent that would drive every hot-blooded male in the world insane with passion and desire. "But that is partly the secret of its value. What we do not know, intrigues us; what intrigues us, drives our desire. We want to possess that which we desire . . . a human characteristic already well established a millennia ago. We want gold for what it can bring us. It should not surprise you, monsieur, that the world's desire for it is insatiable. If you are fortunate enough to be involved in the complex and fascinating world of gold, you must accept one thing." She raised a seductive eyebrow. "Perhaps, monsieur, you know what that is?" she enquired of Antonio.

"Let me help you," she added, after just a momentary pause. "It is this. We are not in command of gold; it is gold that controls us. Throughout the history of so-called civilisation, man has been mesmerised by this yellow metal. *Aurum* in Latin. Just looking at gold does things to you." She sneaked a sidelong glance at him. "Women crave it. For that reason, and for other motives, men are willing to steal it. They love its feel. They use it for themselves—to prove their power and manhood. They dispense it generously to pay tributes and flatter those stronger than themselves. For thousands of years, it has been the hallmark of great rulers—a symbol of their greatness. Tutankhamun's tomb alone originally contained several hundred tonnes of gold. You knew that, didn't you?

"Why would that be?" she asked, not allowing him time to answer. "Doesn't it intrigue you?" she challenged, her dark eyes flashing. "In the entire world—in fact, in the entire *history* of the world—we do not know how much of this yellow metal has been produced." She paused and looked over to him. "In over seven thousand years of recorded human history, the so-called experts tell us that only two hundred thousand tonnes have been mined.

"How ridiculous! Circumstantial evidence alone contradicts the finger-counting of narrow-minded accountants and bean counters. As much as two million tonnes? Possibly. We don't know. That's one reason why this lustrous and lusted-after metal keeps its value: no one knows how much exists. In crass commercial terms, the open market supply is thin.

"I suggest to you, Inspector Valls, that the intrinsic value of gold and its ease-of-conversion are why the people with whom you are dealing most likely would choose to hide, rather than sell, it. Gold bullion is a safe store of wealth recognised—and revered—everywhere in the world." She smiled.

"Paper money is laundered. There is a myth that gold is not. Of course, it is! All tell-tale identifying marks on the ingots are easily erased; it liquifies without fuss. If you become its owner illegally, your first step in laundering gold is to remove any signs of where it was minted. With illegal gold, you erase all traces of identifying marks. Then, it becomes yours. If it is not already pure, you can further refine it; you can re-form it into pieces, larger or smaller. You can introduce impurities—adulterate it, so to speak." She smiled. "You can dissolve it in acids, hide it, and recover it again later."

"*Aqua regia*," added Ramon with wide eyes and an excited grin. He was as fascinated by her performance as was their visitor. "You must have heard some of the famous wartime stories?" he asked Antonio, not really expecting an answer.

She continued speaking. "I can tell you that most money launderers—the people who steal and cheat with paper money—long for the feel of gold. Once they have it, they hide it. They hoard the mesmerising noble metal. Rarely do they give it up willingly. To many of them, it is better than sex. It is more constant and reliable—more so than a close friend; sometimes, it is more important to them than food and water.

"Ramon has described me as an expert on gold." She smiled at her boss, clearly grateful that he had allowed her to speak so freely. "The truth is that I am only a student of the human mind—of the psychology of the metal. Gold, I concede, is the currency in which I deal. But the desire and the fever for gold is up here." She tapped the side of her forehead. "In the marketplace, it has a commercial price. Up here, it has inestimable value."

Antonio noticed that, as the Frenchwoman spoke, she played subconsciously with a leather cord and pendant, which hung low into her cleavage. Undoubtably, despite its dull lustre, it was high carat gold, he concluded. Yet, it was the shape of the pendant itself and the way she absentmindedly twisted and twirled it around her finger that fascinated him. He tried several times to get a closer glimpse of its shape, but the light in the room was subdued.

For a split second, he thought he recognised the shape of two numbers—a seven and a nine. Then he had to look away quickly. Since she had started speaking, her eyes had almost constantly held Antonio's. He was concerned that he did not want to be caught sneaking a voyeur's look at her delightful bosom.

Ramon spoke up. "What Aurelia is leading us to, Antonio, is this: In our department, we have spent years tracking gold and, in particular, illegal shipments of it. We search for its hiding places. We do not know, of course, where the gold stolen by your suspects is likely to be hidden. What we can tell you is that certain criminal elements operate gold laundering around the world. They make a nice profit as illicit bankers.

"For a fee, these criminals launder dirty paper money into untraceable laundered gold and other precious metals. They accept deposits and provide covert storage services—just like commercial banks do with safety deposit boxes. They are located worldwide. Occasionally, one of their operations is discovered and closed down. Their customers include regimes, warlords, drug dealers, mafia bosses, Russian and Chinese oligarchs, Swiss financiers, American bankers and industrialists, Israeli ministers, European nobles, and quite a few world leaders and presidents. Even several members of the Vatican," he added.

"In reality, there isn't much physical movement of illegally-sourced gold by its owners. Once they've banked it, they leave it there. They transact online, just like regular bank transfers. They like to keep a relatively small amount of physical gold close to them—for personal reasons. Its weight and lustre. Its touch. The feel of it. The power it gives them.

"Otherwise, they keep most of it in easy-to-access storage. We estimate that about half the world's supply of the metal is now held and stored by criminal operations—a lot of it on behalf of other criminals. Unlike Scrooge McDuck, they don't keep it under the mattress in their bedrooms," he added with a contagious laugh, clearly enjoying his own joke.

"What about the world's legitimate banks?" asked Antonio, already fascinated by the subject. "What about the big central banks?"

Ramon sneered with undisguised contempt. "Most countries sold their gold supplies many years ago. The reserve stockpiles they claim to be in their possession are largely a myth. How many people have actually seen—and counted—the fortune in gold supposedly stored by the American government at Fort Knox? The Bank of England stores gold for many countries, but even they have only five thousand tonnes of it. Frankly, as a basis for the world's modern monetary system, gold has long been irrelevant. There were times when gold was a vital currency of war," he continued. "The Republican Government of Spain, for example, shipped almost all of its gold reserves to Russia in 1936, ironically for safekeeping. That so-called "Moscow Gold" was traded into cash to finance the Spanish Civil War. Some of the gold also went to France—the "Paris Gold." Over seven hundred tonnes, they say. Most of it looted from Spanish colonies.

"Russia's royal gold disappeared many years ago. Most of it vanished around the time the czar and his family were killed. More recently, after the collapse of the Soviet apparatus, Russia's remaining gold has found its way into the hands of leaders and oligarchs. Nazi Germany accumulated huge resources of gold—much of which is still unlocated. Centuries ago, ancient civilisations lost untold shiploads of gold—still resting at the bottom of the sea.

"Countries and legitimate banks don't have much of the old gold," he continued. "As I've said, most of it is in the hands of criminal banks and their nefarious clients. President Putin is rumoured to have amassed a personal stash of gold worth many billions."

"You said that your department tries to track where all this illicit gold is hidden. Is there any concealed here in Catalunya?" asked Antonio.

Aurelia spoke up, her eyes bright with excitement. "Any?" She gasped. "Just on our doorstep, the Principality of Andorra has acted like the French–Spanish equivalent of Swiss banks for decades. It's been a money-laundering paradise. We know there were hundreds of tonnes of gold hidden up there. Some of it probably still is."

"You said 'were' stored up there?" queried Antonio. "Where has it gone?"

"Well," said Ramon, shrugging his shoulders. "You've asked us where the gold stolen by your suspects might be hidden. It depends. In the past, Andorra would be one of the first places we'd look. But don't spend too much time focused there, Antonio. The international community has forced the country to change its bank disclosure laws. They can't protect the identity of their criminal clients any longer. Gold has been secretly flowing out of Andorra to other safe places."

"The problem is," intervened Aurelia, "we don't know where it is."

Leaving the building, Antonio thought about Aurelia.

He made a call to Xavi.

"I'm heading back to the office, amigo. I need all you can find out about a young woman who works with Ramon at the TFPU. She's French, name of Aurelia Périgueux. Mid-twenties. I don't have photos, but she may be on file under another name. If you can put tracers on her, I'd be grateful. And, while we're at it, can you do an in-depth background check on Ramon as well? They may be good guys, I don't know. With what's at stake here, I want to know who we're dealing with. We're investigating a web of money laundering, and I don't want us to become the spider's victims."

Antonio called off and sat in his car thinking. He was aware that he was becoming a little paranoid. He was attracted to Aurelia, and he knew she was interested in him. If he was going to venture down that particular road, he needed to know that she wasn't anything remotely like Daniela.

If Aurelia had a dark side, he would find out.

Being blindsided by a beautiful alluring woman wasn't a mistake he intended to repeat.

Forensics

"Sir, I have some feedback on the results you were asking for," said the sergeant from the Mossos bomb squad. "I can come to your office if you'd like?"

"Let's meet outside the building in fifteen minutes," said Antonio.

"Yes, sir. I'll be there," came the brisk reply as they cut the connection.

Walking out onto the street, Antonio caught sight of the sergeant. They sauntered together towards an overpass where the traffic noise was heavy and sat down on a bench.

"The lab report on the detonators is now classified information, sir," said the sergeant, trying to make his voice heard over the traffic. "GEO is sitting on the information and won't release it. I talked to a colleague in Madrid, and he hinted that it might be better if I stopped my enquiries. I didn't push the issue, sir, worried that I might arouse his suspicions."

"Now that's interesting," said Antonio. "I would have liked to know why those detonators didn't work. Any guesses?"

The sergeant gave him a wry smile. "What's the saying, sir? There are many ways to skin a cat? I got lucky. Please don't ask me how, but if you knew that my sister-in-law works at GEO, you might be on the correct path." He winked. Taking out several printed pages from his jacket pocket, he passed them unseen to Antonio. "You didn't get these from me, sir."

"Hmm," exclaimed Antonio. "You've read them, obviously. Can you give me a summary?"

The sergeant nodded and waited until a large, noisy articulated truck had passed by. "Every one of those detonators had been rendered inert. The report says they had been injected with a chemical. Sorry, sir, I can't remember its name. The report says there was no way in the world those detonators were going to work. They were all duds."

"Meaning that someone knew about the attempted bombing of Mossos Headquarters and made sure the detonators would never work."

"That's my interpretation too, sir." The sergeant nodded.

"Of course, there was a minor explosion in the underground car park," said Antonio, now deep in thought. "But that came from the remote trigger that had been wrapped in TNT. We had already moved the amatol out of danger. None of the detonators worked, so none of it would have exploded anyway. The question is, who spiked the detonators—making certain they wouldn't work?"

"Maybe GEO has some ideas on that, sir," said the sergeant. 'I've been in the bomb squad for over twenty-five years and I've never seen or heard of anything like this."

Antonio looked at him for a moment. "So, you'd say that it was a fairly sophisticated level of sabotage? Not the kind of thing that your typical terrorist operative would be capable of doing?"

"I doubt it, sir. Whoever spiked those detonators had to have had access to the sophisticated chemical that was used and know how to inject it without causing them to deform or explode during the tampering process."

"Plus," said Antonio, "they would have had to have known well in advance about the planned bombing—and they would have needed the opportunity and sufficient time to spike the detonators. There was no room for error, and fortunately for all of us, the spiking worked perfectly. With those dud detonators, the amatol was never going to explode. The attempted bombing at Mossos Headquarters was never a danger. Leave this with me," he added. "You haven't discussed it with anyone?"

The sergeant shook his head. "No, sir, I came straight to you. The only other people who have this information would be GEO—and anyone they've told."

"Thanks, Ernesto!" He offered his hand to the sergeant, who shook it vigorously. "I won't let you down with this," said Antonio, patting the photocopied GEO document in his inside pocket. "You can trust me. If you hear of anything else that I should know about, please call. Anytime, day or night."

A Noble Relationship

The sudden death of her husband, Count Carlos, had been a profound shock for the condesa.

Just before his fatal heart attack, she had agreed to cooperate with the authorities and had helped them apprehend him—along with the general and his cohorts. She knew she was doing the correct thing, in the eyes of the law at least.

Fulfilling her duty to the state, however, did nothing to assuage her strong sense of guilt: the feeling that she had betrayed him. In the months following his death, she tried to come to terms with the shame of knowing she had forsaken their bonds as husband and wife. Remorse over her affair with the Russian, Pavel, made her misery even more wretched.

Carlos had been a man of great principle. In pursuing his love for his country, he had made serious and unforgiveable errors of judgment. Probably they had hastened his demise, the condesa reflected with culpable sadness. She knew now—too late—that her greatest betrayal of him had been her ambition. As a modern woman, she had no inhibitions about having a career. Besides, it was something that Carlos had encouraged and supported. Her regrets were that being away from home so much, she had not been there for him. Especially at those turning points along the way where perhaps she might have been able to guide him to the high road—away from his nefarious path to treason.

For a time, she stopped eating properly. It was a kind of penance. Malnourished, she lost weight and, at the worst times of her distress, looked almost skeletal. Her housekeeper, Hortensia, comforted and gently goaded her, forcing her to eat—a little at a time. The devoted woman had recipes for winter soups that were nourishing and restorative. Gradually, she convinced the condesa that no good would come to anyone if she sacrificed herself at the altar of abject contrition.

Hortensia's love and caregiving worked. Slowly, the condesa regained weight and came to terms with her self-imposed atonement. She worked in the garden that Carlos and she had loved so much, helping the gardener tend the springtime flowers now in their full glory. Eventually, she recovered and began to think about the future. Carlos had left her everything. She was a fabulously wealthy woman—far too young and vibrant not to be fully active.

She had received several visits from the police and security forces, especially in the days when the government was rounding up the general's gang. Perhaps it was her good standing within the government—and with the prime minister himself—that gave her a certain level of immunity; she wasn't sure. After she'd willingly handed over Carlos's private papers to the National Police, visits from the security forces had become fewer.

Her time of self-imposed atonement meant a withdrawal from public life. She gave up almost all her social commitments and spent most of her time secluded at their villa in La Moraleja. Hortensia was protective and defended the condesa's privacy. She fended off unwelcome and uninvited visitors, lunging into the fray with a snarling fury that would make a pit bull terrier seem mild-mannered.

One concession that the condesa made, even though she had declined other public appearances, was to accept an invitation to visit her former political constituency in Lleida. She did so even though she'd resigned her seat months earlier. She had always been popular with voters in the region, and well respected. It was not in her plans to revisit her former constituents—except that, one day, she received a call from the prime minister. Would it be possible, he asked, for her to support their replacement candidate for office in the local election made necessary by her resignation? Her response to him was immediate and positive. She agreed to throw her full support behind the new candidate . . . an aging former mayor of the city who had come out of retirement to run for the vacated office.

It was not all pure benevolence on her part. Despite her bereavement, the condesa was still a savvy politician. The election got her out of the house and, to some extent, out of the shadows and back into the national limelight. She was happy returning to the campaign trail, even though her role was merely to promote the new candidate. The media, aware of her unselfish championing of the less well-to-do throughout Spain and her reasoned approach to the Catalan independence issue, treated her like a hero.

The former mayor had personal credibility in the region—but, at his advanced age, lacked her energy and drive. The pair became known, affectionately by supporters—and disparagingly among the region's separatists—as "Granddad and his granddaughter." The condesa brushed it off with a broad smile and a laugh, turning the quip into a campaign slogan against Catalan separation from Spain: "*There's nothing that will separate us—we belong together.*" The prime minister was delighted and campaigned in the region. People were tiring of the ongoing protests and violence. He spoke of better times ahead for the working people. A more prosperous future—with Catalunya as a vital part of Spain.

During the campaign in Lleida, she had a surprise invitation from the bishop. They'd met on an earlier visit and he'd written a personal note consoling her on her bereavement. "*It is, of course, a late invitation,*" his note said. "*Are you able to join me for dinner tonight? There are some urgent matters upon which I would value your opinion and counsel.*"

His choice of dinner wine impressed the condesa.

Clearly, the bishop was a man of taste. His dining room was simple and located adjacent to the sacristy. With grace said and dinner eaten, he dismissed his kitchen staff for the evening. During their meal, he had regaled her with stories that had kept the condesa almost in tears with laughter. Now he seemed more circumspect—almost troubled.

"Forgive me," said the condesa. "I think I am keeping you from your devotions." She placed her starched white linen napkin on the table and got up to leave.

"No, please," said the bishop. "Stay, I beg you. I am simply struggling with how to introduce the subject that I very much want to speak to you about." For a few moments, he fingered his rosary beads—lost in thought.

The condesa sat back in her chair and waited.

"I would like to ask you about your view of the world today, dear lady," he began. "As a prelude, may I share some of my beliefs with you? I realise that the subjects I want to broach cannot be tackled easily—and are far less easily resolved. If you would permit me to talk, perhaps even sound off a little, maybe I can begin to approach the heart of the matter." He gave her a grateful smile as she lifted her glass and offered him the encouragement of a toast. He refilled both their glasses and began speaking.

"As a bishop of the Church, I think I can say—without fear of contradiction—that the world today is an ungodly place. In many peoples' lives, spirituality has taken a backseat to avarice and self-indulgence. In the process, many of the higher values we ascribe to civilised societies are being jettisoned. They are abandoned without thought, in favour of narrow-minded individual advancement. It is the age of entitlement.

"Of course, this is not the first time this phenomenon has occurred in the history of the world," he continued. "Records from ancient, as well as more recent, times tell us it happens rather too frequently. In the same way, the responses of various societies to excessive self-indulgence of its citizens are predictable. Forgive me, dear lady, for straying into your profession, but it seems to me that many of our Western governments are more than happy to fuel excessive levels of personal gratification among the voters."

"Without any concern for the consequences?" prompted the condesa.

"Yes. And, of course, as a priest, I am less concerned about the material consequences than about peoples' spiritual well-being." He stopped and looked boyishly contrite. "Am I boring you?"

The condesa shook her head. "Not in the least. Please continue."

"Speaking for my own ministry, the Catholic Church has become increasingly important to a large number of converts in what we used to refer to as foreign lands. Yet, we have become irrelevant to an even larger number of our traditional believers. We are not seen to be providing solutions. I'm not a graduate of Harvard, dear lady. But in business terms, compared with other providers of spiritual leadership, we are losing market share."

The condesa winced at his brusque businesslike characterisation but waited for him to continue.

"I am also aware that when a venerable ancient institution—such as the Catholic Church—has experienced such setbacks in the past, our response has been to engineer a raft of offshoot institutions with the purpose of refocusing on our fundamental beliefs. Our competitors—other faiths—have the same challenge," he added. "But *they* are finding ways to meet the spiritual needs of their followers. A few, of course, offer violent extremism."

"Such as the Salafists?" she enquired.

"Precisely. All mainstream religions ultimately are saying the same thing. We are preaching the need for humans to return to spiritual roots. We want people to refocus their lives. If not *abandon* their seemingly endless quest for material goods, then at least *moderate* it. Money for the sake of money. We are saying they need to recalibrate—retreat from the headlong pursuit of material wealth, and achieve a balance between it and spirituality.

"Our problem as clergy, however, is that we have blotted our copybook, so to speak. Our human frailties have let us down. Many times, in fact. Internal scandals are tearing apart the Church. As priests, we have betrayed the cause. Frankly, my dear condesa, we are lucky to have *any* credibility remaining."

"Is it that bad, Your Excellency?" she protested.

"It may be worse than you think," he replied, swallowing the last of his wine. "We need to turn the tide. The Church has survived for over two thousand years. If we make the right decisions now, we should be able to secure its future for the next two millennia."

"You think that I have a role in this? That I have a contribution to make?" she ventured.

"Think?" he exploded. "We know it, dear lady. Clearly, you are destined for high office."

"Just to be clear, Your Excellency. The conditions for your support—should I be foolish enough ever to run again for election and aspire to the office of prime minister—would be what exactly?"

The bishop looked startled. "There are no conditions. We have no right to demand any. It would be improper if we did. What I wanted to tell you is that there is a large group of us wishing to see significant reforms in the Church. We are gaining support in Rome. We believe we need to accelerate change and not revert to the status quo. We need to provide much better spiritual guidance—through example. We need to provide far better leadership than we have in past generations, especially in recent years."

"You need the financial support of our government in Madrid to achieve this goal—is that what you are saying?" she asked.

A look of horror crossed his face. "Good Lord, no! In fact, quite the opposite." He almost choked over his words in his haste to speak. "We fully support secularism—keeping religion out of government."

"Secularism is embedded into our political fabric—our Constitution," observed the condesa.

The bishop shook his head. "To an extent, dear lady, you are correct. But this is Spain, not France. Our constitutional court defines a positive secularism. It permits the national government to favour the Catholic Church—to protect its culture."

"Why is that a problem?" she asked. "Doesn't that benefit the Catholic Church? I mean, isn't that good for you?"

The bishop gaped at her with an unrestrained look of disappointment. "Throughout our history, the cosy relationship between the Church in Spain and the government has gone on far too long," he began. "It has alienated the ordinary people. Even today, the Church is allied with the monarchy and the powerful ruling classes. It is holding back the kinds of reforms that are essential. In the clergy, we need to find ways to become more relevant to the spiritual needs—of everyone. Our Heavenly Father knows that only too well. We are convinced that all government perks and favours that we in the Church receive should be cut off immediately. Totally eliminated! We've become too dependent on them. We've become soft in the process and have lost our way. The government is not helping reforms. It's hindering the process," he said, his voice high and excited.

The condesa began to chuckle. "You know, I'm constantly being petitioned for political favours. All kinds of people come to me and ask for something . . . money and interventions. It is part of the graft and corruption that plagues our country. Influence peddling is rife throughout our society. But you are not asking for that. You are making a plea for the opposite. For the Church's survival, you want complete separation of government from religion."

She continued, "It is startling to hear this, Your Excellency. Candidly, it's wonderful and I fully agree with it. Yet, it's such a surprise. Tell me, why are you so strongly in favour of secularism? Many of your less reform-minded colleagues are not."

"It is for our own protection, dear lady. As our society moves into the future and accommodates millions more immigrants and diverse religions, we don't want to see *any* religious group gain influence within the government. If the Catholic Church is permitted to gain favours from Madrid, inevitably there will be demands for the same privileges from other faiths and interest groups. The core of secularism is that it doesn't tolerate undue influence from *any* religious group—and particularly not the fanatics.

"There are far too many examples today of countries heading in the opposite direction," the bishop continued. "Turkey is an example. Our country, Spain, is a young democracy. The duty of the state is to look after the economic and social needs of its citizens. Thus, it should deal urgently with the epidemic of corruption in the country—which, to your credit, you have campaigned against vigorously.

"For its part, the Church needs to become much better at understanding and meeting the spiritual needs of the country and the people. If we don't, the attractions of radical extremists will continue to pull away our young people. Extremist elements will capture the hearts and minds, not just of this, but many future generations."

The condesa knew the young bishop's reputation for being a bold reformer within the Church. His rapidly growing influence in Rome and his popular frequent appearances in the media and evening talk shows were earning him the reputation of being an evangelist. Yet, she was surprised by the nature of his quest and his intensity. To her experienced politician's ear, he seemed brash. Yet, she acknowledged, reformers often are. And this young prince of the Church clearly was on a path to change things.

"Well, Your Excellency," said the condesa, "you can expect that any administration of which I'm a part will continue the path to a secular state within Spain, and Europe too. Any other path would be unacceptable. To my regret, my husband fell into that trap. I won't."

With a swirl of his cassock, the bishop strode forward and took her hands in his. "Then we believe in the same principles. Yet, let us not be naïve. There are many in our country, and elsewhere, who will continue to line their pockets at every opportunity. The road ahead of us will be difficult. Regrettably, that is the nature of reform.

"Now, to more immediate priorities. If I may be so bold, may we discuss the possibility of your return to politics—and a campaign, in the not-too-distant future, to re-elect you here in Lleida? I have a few ideas how it can be accomplished.

"Some more wine, dear lady?"

CHAPTER 8
Daniela

Online, Daniela was reading the newspaper's header a second time. She sighed. It was a deep exhale—almost a groan of anguish. "Damn!" she said eventually, followed by a colourful expletive.

Somehow, the journalist had unearthed even more facts on the Aladdin's Cave story. The new disclosures were full of errors, yet there were enough truths to create serious problems for her. Although the newspaper was now linking her directly to the heist, its main target was the government in Madrid. The article alleged that senior ministers were embroiled in the corruption scandals, reaching right up to the monarchy. Here was evidence of yet another egregious act of graft and malfeasance, the journalist asserted—adding fuel to an already blazing fire.

It wasn't the exposure of the slush fund scandal that really worried her; it was the way the authorities were likely to react to the bad publicity. The public would demand answers and swift action. There would be blame-seeking questions from publicity-seeking politicians. They would demand to know how the slush fund had been created and how it had been stolen from under the watchful eyes of the police.

The police themselves were an equal target for the newspaper. Next to unflattering photographs of federal police officials and the new Mossos chief, there were scathing comments about their incompetence. Why hadn't the terrorists responsible for the attempted bombing of the Catalan police headquarters been identified and arrested, the newspaper screamed.

The article provided details of the ongoing dragnet and speculated on Daniela's role in the bombing attempt on Mossos Headquarters. They speculated on her whereabouts. There was an old photograph of her, and one of her late aunt's house. Bring these criminals to justice, the editorial demanded.

"Well, this changes things," she said aloud, as Yussef was passing nearby. He stopped and looked at her. He was defensive. She still hadn't forgiven him for tampering with her laptop—and they hadn't spoken much since. "Come and see," she said, indicating the newspaper online. "They are talking about the money we took from Aladdin's Cave. It's fortunate that we moved it when we did."

"Is this bad for us?" he asked, struggling to understand many of the newspaper's words.

"Unfortunately, yes." Daniela's voice sounded choked.

"The hiding place for the money. It is safe?" asked Yussef.

"The money is safe; we are not," she replied. "Maybe we will have to leave this region. We should leave Spain and go somewhere safer. Someplace where the police aren't looking for us. Maybe it is time for us to go to Syria," she added, searching his face for a reaction. She would need his support.

At first, Yussef's face brightened: he seemed happy at the prospect. Then his features clouded over. "What about Ahmed? I cannot leave my brother. Maybe he is still here. We have to rescue him. You have money. We can buy help . . . perhaps some soldiers."

"Yussef, this is Spain—you cannot buy soldiers here. There are gangs; it is true. But few mercenaries. Besides, we do not know if he has been captured or if he was able to avoid the police."

"You have money." Yussef became aggressive. "With money, you can buy anything. It is the same everywhere. I will not leave until I can help Ahmed. I do not care for myself—just for him." His voice sounded shrill, but his tone was resolute. "I will do anything. We will pray. Allah will guide us. Please Daniela!"

She was surprised to hear him use her real name. She had become used to living under an alias. He didn't often call her Daniela. She was rather taken aback by the sound. Then she realised that no one had spoken to her using her real name . . . not, it seemed, for a long time. It sounded unfamiliar to her, but nice.

"Yussef, listen to me. I have promised that you will see Ahmed again. If he is alive, I swear on the blood of my family that we will find him. But the authorities are searching for us. The newspaper story is bad. It creates more problems. It is no longer safe for us to remain in this country. What good will it do if we are caught?"

"The police. They were watching the apartment. If they did not capture him, maybe he is free," said Yussef—his voice full of youthful hope. "If he is free . . . the apartment, he will go there to look for me. I will go and wait. Hide and wait for him."

"Yussef, use your brain!" she yelled at him. "You are not stupid, yet you are acting like a stupid person. Do you not think that the police will be waiting there too? Think of what he would tell you to do. Would he tell you to go running straight into their trap? That would not be using your mind. I will tell you what he would say. He would say, 'Yussef, be smart. Listen to the woman sent by Mustapha; she is our friend and ally. Has she not protected us many times? She is accepted by Jamal. He speaks well of her; he says that we can trust our lives to her.' You know what I say is true," she added.

Yussef said nothing in reply. He kept his eyes fixed on her, as the eyes of a trapped animal remains transfixed on its attacker. She could see his mind processing what she had told him. "You like this man—the one they call Jamal?" he asked suddenly, ignoring what she'd said.

Without being aware of it, Daniela had placed her hand protectively around the blue sapphire necklace that Jamal had given her.

"I have seen you do that before," said Yussef, pointing the necklace. "He gave this to you. I am sure of it."

Daniela was surprised by his remark and the intensity of his emotion. It was almost as if he was jealous of Jamal. She knew that Yussef had never met him, although his brother, Ahmed, had—several times. They were from the same neighbourhood in Homs. A thought flashed across her mind. It was the opportunity she had been waiting for—and now, inadvertently, Yussef had presented it to her.

"The gold and the paper money—they belong to the jihad," she said. "We must get them to Jamal. If something happens to me, promise me that you will find a way to give them to Jamal. He will know what to do with them."

Yussef's eyes narrowed, and he continued to look at her with suspicion. "How can we trust you?" he asked simply. "You are not one of us."

Daniela knew that he was challenging her; she knew that she must not flunk this vital test. Despite all they had been through together, after all she had done in support of the jihad, he still had doubts. Looking at him, she realised that there was something eating away at the boy's resolve. Perhaps it was nothing more than just a base instinct, yet it was deeply troubling to him. She knew that she must not allow it to fester. It was a cancer of doubt in the deep recesses of his mind. It would spread; ultimately, it could result in her downfall.

If Yussef had been older, full of the egotistical vanities that maturing men accumulate over their lifetimes, her response would have been predictable. No man among her many lovers had ever had a better fuck. Of that, she was supremely confident. It came naturally to her; she used her body as a finely crafted tool, to torment, withhold, punish, and finally release them—reducing even the strongest and most virile foes to a shuddering, ejaculative, and ultimately servile state of weakness and submission.

They adored her like a goddess. For her, it was easy. She enjoyed the pleasures of the flesh, but she didn't seek the physical satiation that is mere superficial lust. Daniela wanted to control their bodies, yes—but, much more, she wanted to command their minds. She was not interested in friendships; she demanded a cortege of adoring and willing foot soldiers. She required a retinue of lusty lovers: men . . . and women, if necessary. A congregation of worshippers, doing her bidding.

Except for one. There would be one special man in her life: her equal. She had chosen him from among all the others. Together, they would conquer the world. For Antonio, she would keep her best.

If Yussef had been an ordinary adult male, Daniela would not have been concerned about his doubts. She would take command of his body, as she had several times in the past, and win his mind. But he had known too few women. Sexually, he was inexperienced and had no basis for comparison. With Daniela, he had experienced the ultimate pleasures of the flesh—without knowing anything else.

She conceded, without any emotion, that the power over men that deft use of her body almost always guaranteed might, on occasion, have to be supplemented by less subtle weapons.

Leaving him standing there, she went to the kitchen and selected a sharp knife with a long blade. Returning, she stood in front of him and looked into his eyes. Raising a finger in front of his face, she drew the blade sharply across the tip of the finger—causing a fast gushing of warm blood. It ran down her finger and splattered onto the floor. Without flinching or taking her eyes from him, she swept her bloodied finger across her throat in a wide arc passing across her throat and windpipe.

With open palms, she offered the knife to him—holding it close to his face. Defiantly, she held his gaze. "If you do not trust me, our code says you must kill me," she said. "You will have possession of the gold; you know where it is located. So, just do it! Cut my throat. It is your duty. *Inshallah!*"

It seemed like minutes that they stood there, facing off against each other—eyes locked in combat. Daniela's gaze never wavered; Yussef did not blink. She had thrown his challenge back at him; now he must respond. Gradually, his pupils widened until his eyes turned jet black—deep with the atramentous hatred of a thousand generations. It was a wild look that cut into her soul and began to terrify her. Had she pushed his immature emotions too far? It was a moment of absolute terror. He seemed possessed by a primordial force, driven by some ancient tribal ritual.

She tried to stop herself shaking. Gritting her teeth hard, her lips parted. She breathed in deeply, preparing herself for slaughter. Her head trembled. Involuntarily, her teeth began to chatter. Her stomach ached from muscle cramps. She felt weak and powerless. From somewhere came the memory of a time, many years ago on a farm somewhere, when her uncle had sliced through the neck of a squawking chicken. She recalled how his eyes had blazed with excitement, as he held aloft the bird's severed head and neck in his bloodied hand. Even without its head, the chicken was not completely dead. Landing in the floor, the carcass had run about headless. For a few last dying moments, its short-circuited nerves had propelled its legs in a frenzied dance of death.

Slowly, Yussef reached towards her, took the handle, and lifted the knife into the air. Daniela saw the vicious, ominous, and uncompromising look that was now chiselled into his determined features. He leaned his face closer to hers, peering deeply into her eyes—as if making one last check of her soul. He curled his finger around the joint of hers, above where her blood still gushed. Moving the knife in a sharp cutting motion, he sliced open his own flesh. His blood spurted, running down her wrist and arm. He squeezed their fingers tightly together.

"Now," he said, his eyes blazing with primitive passion. "Now, Daniela, we are tied by our blood."

He turned and walked away, dropping the lethal blade with a loud clatter on the tiled floor.

~

Daniela knew that she often fed off her own adrenaline. Yet, the incident with Yussef in the kitchen had drained her. It made her realise how much danger she'd been in—only a half step away from being brutally decapitated. Her bluff had worked—just. There was a price to be paid: the dynamic between them had been altered, and not for the better.

Before the incident, Yussef had been predictable. Now she wasn't sure of him; he'd moved beyond her control in unforeseeable ways.

Until now, she'd been able to reason with him because of her connection to Mustapha and their mission. Respectful of the established lines of command, he'd calmed down after they'd argued outside the apartment in Barcelona. Reluctantly, he'd accepted her warning that a full-frontal attack on the police to search for his brother, Ahmed, would have been a suicide mission. Later, he'd been compliant in helping move the gold and banknotes. Now he was becoming withdrawn. Stubborn and obstinate. He was challenging her, and she needed to get ahead of him. Several steps, not just one. The dynamic had to be shifted yet again—this time, so that she would remain in control. But how?

They were mentally tired from an excess of each other's company, yet both knew they had no other choice. For the immediate future, they depended on each other. He was a bright kid, she conceded. What he lacked in experience, he seemed to make up for in street smarts. His intuition was sharp. Now she would have to be vigilant, watching for tell-tale signs that would forewarn her.

His agenda was fairly simple, she was convinced. Yussef desperately wanted to find his brother; he'd do almost anything to achieve it. His only other loyalty was the jihad. He would remain resolute in his pursuit of those two objectives. She had no inhibitions that, if the dynamic changed again in his favour, or if she stood in his way, he would have no compunction killing her.

He'd probably already concluded that she was manipulating him, she thought. That was tolerable. She could get away with it, so long as he believed she was helping the jihad. But that meant she would have to take decisive action very soon and advance their plans.

Yussef was important to her in ways he could not imagine; one thing was for certain—she couldn't afford to lose him. Not just yet.

The knife incident with Yussef was still bothering Daniela, and it made her think about the sniper who'd almost taken her life not many weeks earlier. That had been another close call with death. She'd covered her tracks well after that confrontation. It had been a relief to find that the sniper was not working for Antonio. In fact, at the time, she'd felt not just relief but elation at the revelation. Since the attack, she hadn't had much time to think about it. Who had the sniper been working for?

Going into the bathroom, she retrieved the gold pendant she'd snatched from the neck of her unsuccessful sniper. She kept it hidden at the base of her travel bag. With such distinct markings, it was an unusual piece. Tracing her finger over the shape of two numbers, a seven and a nine, she wondered about its origin. Its uniqueness probably increased her chances of being able to trace its owner, she hoped. As badly as Daniela wanted to know the identity of the assassin, she had no intention of trying to find him—not yet at least. Not until her circumstances were very different.

She returned the gold pendant to her travel bag.

Daniela decided to take a hot bath. In the middle of the afternoon, she was now luxuriating in the suds of the scented foam. It was an indulgent extravagance; she didn't care if Yussef disapproved.

The oils in the foam lubricated her naturally tanned body. She glanced at her now bandaged finger, keeping it out of the water. Her emotions had run high, and he had truly scared her. It had turned out all right in the end. Now, in the warm bathwater, her skin glistened and she found the combined effect quite arousing. She allowed her uninjured finger to explore lower until her body stiffened and her eyelids became heavy with the pleasured sensation.

Breathing deeply, she imagined herself with Antonio. She fantasised about his muscular body. Several times, months ago, when she had run her flattened hands over his chest and around his waist and his shoulders, she had become aware of how sensuous he was—especially when provoked and aroused.

She liked that.

Recently, she had not spent any time in the sun. She rarely sunbathed anyway and really there was no need for it. Her skin had a healthy natural hue. It was quite dark, in a way. Many times, as a young teenager, she had thought that genetically she might have Arab blood. In Spain, with nearly eight hundred years of Muslim dominance, Arab extraction among parts of the population was quite extensive. She knew all about al-Andalus.

Running a damp forefinger across her tight nubile breasts, she smeared the bath oils and foam into a shape. Then she modified the shape and washed it off, watching it drift like a slow-moving amoeba down the bath to the hair above her crotch. She could never understand how some women were eager to have such sensitive hairs ripped out so violently. Natural evolution, she thought, had provided women with alluring bodies for their own pleasure, not just to be slaves of men and the self-focused, hurried satisfaction of their superficial masculine carnal desires.

Her ears picked out a sound to her left, and she turned her head quickly. Yussef was standing there watching. Overcoming her initial surprise at being disturbed, she tried to interpret his expression. He was not looking at her face and seemed not to want to talk. She followed his gaze to where her fingers lay playfully against her clitoris.

"You should not do that," he said sternly. "That is for man." His voice was deep with disapproval.

Daniela remained motionless. At times, she knew, Yussef could become broody and almost threatening. Earlier that day, she had thought he was capable of the ultimate violence. Now he was being creepy. She wasn't sure what he'd do next. There was silence for a moment as he gazed at her. Then he left the room as quickly as he had entered.

Her mood ruined, Daniela reached for a long bath towel. She didn't like the changes she was seeing in Yussef. Not only was he becoming more assertive, more critical of her, he was far more possessive too. He was reverting to the attitudes typical of many men from his culture. He expected Daniela to be passive and obedient. More orthodox Islamic.

She wondered if she'd been wise to enlist his help in moving the treasures of Aladdin's Cave. There was no other way, she told herself—if she were to prove her loyalty to Jamal and the jihad. Living much longer with Yussef, however, would be fraught with dangers.

She had to make a strategic move—and quickly.

Mediterranean Cruise

Yussef had accepted her insistence that Spain was no longer a safe place for them. The longer they stayed, the greater the chance they'd be caught, she'd told him. She needed to make plans for their escape.

Daniela faced a dilemma. If they travelled overland from Spain to Syria, a road distance of four thousand kilometres, the risks of being caught by security forces or border patrols were high. Even if she used some of the euros still in her possession to secure the services of a reliable smuggler, she knew there would still be hazards at the major borders.

Flying and passing through airports, even with well-forged documents, involved an even greater set of risks. The global database of persons registered as flight risks was just too comprehensive. Almost certainly, she would be on the international no-fly list. She researched private planes and the possibility of leasing a corporate jet travelling between remote airports. Even those options left her unconvinced. What she needed was a means of transportation where she and Yussef could combine the advantages of a quick journey with reduced risks of being detected by police and border guards.

Eventually, she figured out a daring but promising solution.

Picking up her phone, she keyed in the numbers displayed on her laptop screen. Yes, the agent answered with pleasure, the ambassador's suite was still available. And, yes, they had several cabins adjacent to the suite. The agent positively gushed with pleasure. It would be wonderful to welcome such a well-known celebrity aboard their cruise line.

Daniela, now quite at ease with her new persona as Susan Garcia, cautioned the enthusiastic agent. "He will not be travelling under his celebrity name. This is a sensitive situation. Unless you are able to handle this booking with complete anonymity, he will not proceed with it."

The enthusiastic agent, fearful of losing such a prestigious booking, was clearly concerned. "Could you hold for a moment, please, madam," she requested. "I am going to put you through to our vice-president of passenger services. Rest assured, Señora Garcia," said the woman, "we will handle everything with the utmost discretion."

After a fifteen-minute conversation with the senior person, Daniela was satisfied. "His stage name J2 Browne will never appear on our records," the woman promised. "We will use the passport name that you have given us: Mr. Pedro Martinez. He and your party will receive our very highest level of service," she gushed. "We are used to protecting the privacy of such guests. The premium fee you are offering on top of the standard tariff, for additional services, is more than generous—thank you!"

"So, there will be no problem if J2... excuse me... if Mr. Martinez wishes to bring his own chef on board?" asked Daniela. She sounded as though she was working her way through a list of his requirements. "He will not want to eat with the... eat in public," she added. "In addition, he has certain hygiene requirements. He will use his personal laundry on the beds. His valet will take charge of sanitising the bathrooms. We will bring the necessary supplies and equipment on board with us," she added. "Is that acceptable?"

"Good! I will give you a credit card number," she said, after hearing the senior supervisor's approval of the arrangements. "Would a Diamond Elite card be okay?" Daniela asked, aware that its exclusivity would impress the woman. "I'll give you a hundred thousand Euro deposit. We can fix up the details and adjust the balance later." Daniela read off the numbers from one of the two private client cards she'd received from Nicolas at the Banco de Familia Tarragona. Thanks to her, his bank was still operational. Thanks to him, and limitless bank credit, she was now part of that distinguished global group of people who have access to privileged and incognito ultra-prestige travel.

"It is the least I can do," the smiling Nicolas had assured her when he, and the armoured car driver from his bank, collected the wooden boxes of euros from the farm. The overnight transfer of nearly six hundred and fifty million euros had worked like a charm. It had boosted the cash reserves held at his bank past the minimum levels required by the central bank authorities. Daniela had put most of the vast fortune from Aladdin's Cave to strategic use.

She was content.
Nicolas was ecstatic.

Days later, at the Port of Barcelona, a dark limousine pulled up alongside an exclusive gangway leading to a private embarkation deck of the luxury cruise liner. Two people—one wearing sunglasses and an oversized hoodie—were quickly ushered on board. They were escorted to an elevator that had exclusive access to the ambassador's suite. Thirty minutes later, a stream of commercial vehicles arrived at the secluded gangway. It would be several hours before regular boarding would commence.

Deck officers supervised the loading of pallets of bottled drinking water by Lanjarón from Granada, organic foodstuffs by Holland & Barrett from Marbella, and a variety of personalised items required by the celebrity. They included a water filtration machine, sanitised deck chairs that Daniela had ordered for him, personal soap, towels, and bedsheets. J2 Browne was a global celebrity—and was well known for his germophobic revulsion of touching anyone or anything that might expose him to infection.

Embarking the vessel several hours later, the ship's other passengers were completely unaware of his presence on board. The ship was scheduled to sail for the Greek Islands, with a final stop eastbound at Limassol, Cyprus. From there, it would return westward towards Venice, visiting Malta en route home.

Daniela knew that, at its farthest point eastwards, Cyprus is no more than two hundred kilometres from Syria and only a little further to the coast of Lebanon. That knowledge had inspired her plan to reach their destination. There was traffic in illegal migrants between Syria and Cyprus—but it was a one-way flow of political and economic refugees from Syria to the safety of the European Union. She and Yussef would be travelling in the opposite direction, and with the money at their disposal, they would not be travelling migrant class.

When the cruise ship finally cast its lines and departed Barcelona, Yussef quickly shed his designer clothes. He had the assurance of complete security of their locked suite but wore sunglasses and a hoodie—as Daniela had instructed. He was uncomfortable in the make-believe role and the need for such fake play-acting. For several days afterwards, as the vessel made its way east, he remained secluded in his cabin, avoiding contact with anyone. Daniela let him stew for a time. She knew that without her, he wouldn't have a chance.

A week into their cruise, she called him to her stateroom. Taking out a map, she reminded him of their plan to get to Syria. When she'd first proposed it, not long after the kitchen knife incident, he'd seemed unimpressed. His response was flippant and critical. Now that they were well into their journey, and with time in his cabin alone, he seemed more cooperative.

She traced for him the magnitude of the journey they were undertaking and took the time to impress upon him the message that if she failed, he too would fail. It seemed to have an impact. "You have an important part to play," she told him. "Here is a camera. On the next stage of our journey, you will act the part of a photographer. Practise with it. Get to know the controls. I haven't asked much of you. Recently, you've been liability and an asshole. Now I need you to help me—and do your part."

She was pleased to see that he responded positively. He quickly mastered the camera. His artistic talents were broad-based, she noted. She'd witnessed his impressive skills as a painter; now, it seemed, he had a natural flair as a photographer. It was a skill she knew would be important on their clandestine journey from Cyprus to Lebanon.

Prior to boarding, Daniela had carried out hours of research. To make their cover story convincing, she had hired and prepaid for an entourage, comprising the celebrity's chef and valet. The arrangement enabled Daniela and Yussef to eat in private. The hired hands had no inkling of Daniela's scheme and rarely saw the celebrity up close. They had no way of knowing that Daniela planned to announce, after the cruise ship reached Limassol, that he had contracted a virus and would be travelling immediately by private plane to a clinic in Rome for treatment.

Daniela planned to advise the cruise line concierge that they would require the return of their passports. She knew they would protest and tell her it was against regulations and would mean there could be no refund. That was not a problem, she planned to say. A generous additional tip left for the cruise line staff would make sure they were well compensated for the inconvenience. After all, Daniela would remind them, the celebrity's health and well-being was at stake—they would not want the bad publicity if he became seriously ill on board.

The journey was not without incident. A senior officer, a stubborn Dutchman, hearing the rumour that J2 was on board, became quite insistent. He wanted to be able to tell his children that he had met the celebrity. He wanted a selfie. Things became tense. Eventually, Daniela fobbed him off with a photograph of the real J2. She'd had the foresight to bring along several copies. Her rendition of his autograph *"To Niels, from your buddy J2"* would have passed even the closest scrutiny.

Several days later, she told Yussef that Limassol in Cyprus would be their next port of call and, for them, their last day aboard the ship. She instructed him on what to bring ashore, leaving behind the clothes and belongings that she knew he detested anyway. He seemed to have reverted to his resentful ways. Their relationship had been strained since the last days in the cottage. Now he only went along with things for the sake of the jihad.

Just prior to disembarking, he seemed particularly irritated. He stood glaring at her. Glancing at her watch, she understood the meaning. It was close to the time for *Dhuhr*—the midday prayer. As was required of her, she withdrew to a separate room while Yussef prepared himself.

Mindful of her role, Daniela followed his lead in similar fashion. She guessed that, in addition to his normal devotions, Yussef would be offering special thanks for this chance to return home and, *inshallah*, meet again with his brother. She imagined that he would ask forgiveness for the charade that Daniela had created. It was obvious that he considered it a waste of precious money. Perhaps he would acknowledge that it was necessary to ensure his safe passage home, yet it would make him feel ashamed. Daniela knew that Yussef considered such frivolous extravagances as typical of life in the debauched and unspiritual West.

She knew that Yussef tolerated her. Maybe, to some extent, he respected her. Even so, he would find it difficult to forgive this excessive indulgence on his behalf—while millions of his people starved and were being persecuted. After his *salat*, no doubt he would pray again for atonement. Respectful of his time at prayer, Daniela worked out their next steps in intricate detail.

So far, it had been comparatively easy.

Now, the really tough time was starting.

Turkish Republic of Northern Cyprus

Departing from the cruise ship—with a minimum of administrative obstacles—had not been as difficult as Daniela had feared. Money spoke, and it spoke loudly.

At the dockside, their Greek limousine driver had been instructed by the cruise line steward to take the guests directly to the airport, where the celebrity and his assistant would catch a private jet to Rome. The celebrity's entourage would remain on board and return with the bulk of his luggage to Barcelona.

With the generous advance tip he received from Daniela as they pulled away from the dock, the limousine driver decided that he could take the rest of the day off work—and the following week, for that matter.

Daniela had plans, and they didn't involve the airport. She spoke to the driver. He smiled broadly. The change of destination was not a problem, he assured his young passengers. He was quite happy to go along with the new instructions that Daniela had just announced. Yes, of course, he would be delighted to take them to the border point with the Turkish Republic of Northern Cyprus, at Nicosia. His company was authorised to cross the border to the vacation resort in the TRNC at which Daniela and the gentleman had confirmed reservations.

If they wanted, he could drive them directly to their hotel. It was frequently done. On the island, we depend on tourists—and so do the Turks, he told them. Maybe the offshore oil and gas discoveries would bring them new wealth, he said. There were almost no controls now at the border, he revealed. It was quite open. There might be a slight delay if their papers were checked by the Turkish authorities. But so long as they had European passports and proof of a return date and travel documents back home from the Greek side, everything would be fine.

"I need to buy some personal items," Daniela said to Yussef as they parked in the centre of Nicosia. "I'll be back soon." She saw no reason to share the true reason for asking their taxi driver to stop in the city. There was always the danger that the boy would get into some kind of trouble while she was gone. Telling the driver to wait, she said quietly to Yussef, "Remember our deal. Don't go on the internet and stay away from the cyber cafés. We're fugitives. They are still looking for us."

Taking her backpack, she walked along Ledra Street, mingling with the tourists until she found what she wanted. She recognised the name of the bank and asked to see a manager. Minutes later, she was seated inside his office. "Certainly, Señora Garcia, we will be happy to open an account for you—and later, we can help with the purchase of the property your parents wish to buy. We will need a passport, of course, and you do realise this has to be a non-resident account? It's government policy here in Cyprus. But we like new investors," he added with a charming Greek smile. He took the five thousand euros in cash. "I'll deposit this for you."

Girl On The Run

"There is one other thing I'd like," said Daniela. Opening her backpack, she took out a small framed picture she'd purchased minutes earlier on the street and displayed it for him. I purchased this for my parents as a gift for their new property when they arrive. "Do you have a safety deposit box?"

"Well, you'll need a premium account to fit that one." A forced frown momentarily clouded his handsome and tanned young face.

"No problem," said Daniela, thinking that in other circumstances she might like to get to know him better. "I'd be happy to pay the fees for a larger safety deposit box. My dad will probably need it anyway."

The young manager smiled at his success in upselling the young American. It had been a long, slow recovery at the bank since the financial crisis. The prospect of acquiring this new investor, and her family's account, would help his promotion prospects. "We do have a special safety deposit facility—a sealed room, out of the public eye. It's a little more expensive . . ." he said.

Ten minutes later, in possession of the digital code to a high-security safety deposit box at the bank, Daniela left the building with an empty backpack. Inside the deposit box, she had placed the twenty-euro painting—and six hundred and fifty million euros in untraceable and negotiable bearer bonds she'd received from Nicolas. The money was safer in Europe than where they would be going, she reflected. She liked Cyprus and knew it would be easy to return there.

Now, there were just one or two details she needed to complete on her way back to the taxi. She was aware that Yussef would be suspicious about her unexpected shopping expedition. Stopping at a pharmacy, she picked up some deodorant, make-up, condoms, and a pack of sanitary pads. She guessed that, sometime during their journey, Yussef would find an opportunity to search her travel bag. Attention to detail is vital, she reflected as she climbed back into the waiting taxi. She smiled at Yussef.

Men are so predictable.

Three hours later, they were welcomed to their hotel in the Turkish Republic of Northern Cyprus. Executive class rooms had been set aside, the elderly male receptionist told them. He was charmed by Daniela's ability to speak several phrases in Turkish. Yes, of course, he smiled, they could be assured of complete privacy during their stay. A private printer sent up to their room? It would be there within thirty minutes. Yes, the Wi-Fi connection to the suite was secured. He handed a business card to her. If there was anything they needed, here was his personal phone number.

It seemed to Daniela that now they were no longer on the cruise ship, Yussef had become increasingly happy at the prospect of returning home to Syria. She had cautioned him about what to say while they were staying at the hotel, warning him not to call attention to himself or arouse suspicions. There will be spies, she warned. "We are nearly there, Yussef," she told him. "We will find Ahmed." She knew it was a bold promise but not rash. In any case, she observed, Yussef seemed reassured by her words. Maybe it was just that he needed encouragement; she wasn't sure.

In any event, she needn't have worried about his behaviour at the hotel. Her concerns were replaced—within a few hours—by other developments that worried her even more. Yussef's mood seemed to be continually shifting. He was distant and prayed more. It seemed to her that he had been rejecting the ways of the West—systematically, day by day. Consciously or not, he was reverting to the patterns of behaviour that he knew would be required in his own country.

Long ago, under the uncompromising tutelage of Raphael Robles, Daniela's young teenage mind had been influenced in favour of cosmopolitan ideologies. She rarely thought about them now, but they remained entrenched in her psyche. One manifestation was that she had rejected the Middle Eastern stereotypes popular in the West; she had the ability to transition quickly and convincingly to the ways of an educated Arab woman.

It was easy for her to understand Yussef's strong feelings. He wanted to fit back in quickly with his own people. She knew that once they reached Syria, she too would have to act differently. His role as a male would become dominant: he would become her chaperone. Adapting was not difficult for her; she had spent extensive time there undercover. In the Arab world, she knew her role as a woman and how to act properly—how *not* to attract attention.

But she worried about Yussef. He was inexperienced in moving about his country in the company of a Western woman. Several times, she had suggested they talk about the transition—and perhaps rehearse some situations in which, almost certainly, they soon would find themselves. He resisted her suggestions, dismissing them as unnecessary. Aware that the shores of Syria were only two hundred kilometres from their hotel in Cyprus, he seemed oblivious to the fact that the most perilous step of their journey was yet ahead of them.

"Is it your plan to denounce me to the authorities when we arrive?" she finally asked him, speaking brusquely. She had to get his attention. "Surely, you know that ISIS has been routed from your country. While you have been away, Yussef, there have been many changes." She strode over to the large TV in their suite and keyed the remote. "Watch this; you will see of what I speak.

"If we are to reach safety, we must work as a team—not in conflict with each other. There will be eyes everywhere, and many spies working for the regime. If we do the wrong thing or say the wrong things, they will know very quickly. In the hands of the regime, you will be tortured and most likely killed for your association with the caliphate. I will too—for the same reasons. Even though I am Spanish, that will not help me; it offers no protection.

"Do you understand, Yussef?" She shook his shoulders. "This journey is not about you, and it is not only about finding your brother, Ahmed. It is about our jihad. You must behave like an actor. You must think like a Syrian who supports the al-Daser regime. I know you have seen much pain and violence in your country. But do not look at al-Daser's people and supporters with hatred in your eyes—for they will see it. Come, please, let us talk about this. It will be the most important thing you will be doing to help our cause."

They spent several days at the hotel, always ordering only room service. Daniela did the talking, not allowing Yussef to speak to the room service attendants. She told him to wait in the bathroom until it was safe to emerge. They watched television news channels as much as possible, and it was soon evident that her concern had been well placed. While living in Spain, she knew that Ahmed had shielded Yussef from the worst of the news about the decline of ISIS. Their mission was to remain in Spain and work with al-Qaeda agents, he had instructed Yussef. Ahmed had not wanted his younger brother to become depressed by the unfolding events at home.

Here in Cyprus, TV channels were available. Some broadcast programs from Syrian, Lebanese, and Israeli networks. Yussef seemed shocked at how quickly things had changed, realising that Daniela was right. They would have a difficult time when they got to Syria. Crestfallen, he agreed to be schooled by her. He would practise how to conduct himself and what to say.

Yussef was not the only challenge facing Daniela. She had a plan to get from Cyprus to Syria, but it would need of lot of careful execution to be effective. Dropping into a travel agency, she booked a day tour for them to Beirut, leaving the following week. She had no intention of joining the tour; it was a back door way of getting their passports stamped with a visitor's visa to enter Lebanon.

She used the printer a lot and spent several hours a day in a local Turkish-Cypriot town. As a tourist from Spain, and without Yussef accompanying her, she achieved most of what she needed to do within a few days of their arrival. She explained her plan to him, and they rehearsed his part in it.

Early the next morning, they left their hotel—leaving behind the remainder of their luggage. Wearing warm clothing and waterproof jackets, they took a local taxi down to the harbour. In their inside pockets, they carried identification papers—and the premium credit cards supplied to Daniela by Nicolas.

"Good morning," said a cheery English voice as they approached the locked slipway leading down to where a large, powerful boat was about to cast off. "You must be Susan Garcia? I'm Tom Savage."

They shook hands, and Daniela introduced Yussef. "My assistant," she explained. "He speaks Syrian, so he will be useful when we get to that side. He gets a bit seasick. He'll be okay if he can find somewhere quiet. By the way, thank you for allowing us to come out to the rig with you," she added.

"Well, the emails from head office told us to give you the red-carpet treatment. You're a writer for Bloomberg's investment newsletter, so you have our full attention, Susan. By the way, what you'll be seeing today isn't a rig. It's a drillship. If we strike fields of oil or gas that show commercial promise, we use heavier and more permanent equipment. Have you been on a rig or a drillship before?" he asked with a smile.

"This will be the first time," said Daniela with an equally nice response. "I don't usually cover the commercial desk—so I don't know much about the oil and gas business. It's really a human-interest story that I'm writing. We may syndicate it. You know . . . *Life Aboard the Big Rigs*. It all depends on my editor."

"Well, let's get moving," he said. "We'll be casting off in a few minutes. We're a supply boat, so there's no one else on board. It's a fast ride to *Discovery 8*—that's our most successful drillship to date. It's relatively calm today, so about an hour and a half's journey. I'll brief you on the way. But first, I have to ask you to go through our security procedures. We don't allow alcohol, drugs, or any ignition materials on board or on the rig. Company rules. Visitors have to go through a physical screening. Smoking is allowed, but only in designated secure areas.

"I see you've both brought cameras along. That's fine on this journey. There's nothing on the drillship that's secret or proprietary. Take as many photos as you want." He pointed to a woman approaching them from the cockpit. "If you can go with Carol, she'll do your security screening. I'll look after your colleague," he said, inviting Yussef to stand up. Daniela glared at Yussef, her blazing eyes warning him to cooperate with the oil company man.

Their journey to the drillship was uneventful. Yussef appeared to sleep most of the way, as Daniela had instructed. At times, the ride encountered rough water, forcing the boat to reduce speed. They saw a few other vessels and a large LNG tanker to the west. "That's heading down to its base off the Israeli coast," explained the oil man, handing binoculars to Daniela. "The Israelis are already self-sufficient, and they are a big exporter of natural gas. You should see the Tamar field and their big rigs. That's where all the excitement is in this region.

"I hear that you'll be taking our sister boat on your other journey," added the oil man. "It will take you to Beirut. There's not much exploration activity happening off Lebanon just yet, so I don't know how much of interest you'll find over there," he observed.

"Just doing what Bloomberg tells me to do." Daniela smiled in response. "We really appreciate your cooperation. If you give me your email, I'll make sure you get an advance copy of the article."

They spent several hours aboard the drillship, after which Daniela thanked the captain and crew. She was popular on board, and there was a lot of laughter and good-natured backchat. Several of the men shouted out proposals of marriage, all of which she accepted in fun. Yussef proved to be useful—saying little but taking what turned out to be professional class photographs. Some of them were amazing, thought Daniela.

Later, they boarded the sister supply boat that would take them to Lebanon.

The oil company's sister supply ship approached the port of Beirut and was met at sea by an armed patrol boat. The water was choppy and both boats rolled in the afternoon swell. Overhead, the sun was hidden by rain clouds coming from the northeast. The patrol boat travelled alongside them for a time. Daniela, on the bridge, wore a baseball cap and was obscured by the skipper as she eyed the hostile-looking soldiers scrutinising their boat. The skipper was busy on the radio, talking to an officer on the patrol vessel.

"Sometimes they come aboard," he said to her. "We're coming in from the rigs for supplies, so they don't usually bother us. Doesn't look like they will today either. So, I'm afraid you will have to miss out on that bit of excitement."

Daniela looked back at him with an appropriate level of disappointment. For her, it was a complete stroke of luck. She had a good cover story explaining why she wanted to enter the country, but she was not sure that Yussef's forged Spanish passport would have been enough if the soldiers had boarded and started to question him. She didn't have much confidence that he would hold up under pressure.

Minutes later, there was a bark of strong engines, as the Lebanese patrol boat accelerated back towards the coast. It produced powerful bow waves, which rocked their boat. The skipper turned to Daniela and grimaced. "They're not bad to deal with most times. Mostly young guys on those patrol boats. They can be a bit trigger-happy. Anyway, we've been cleared to enter the harbour. We should be there within fifteen minutes. Excuse me, I have to radio my controller."

When the deckhands started to moor the boat, he turned to them again and asked, "You've got a hotel fixed up here?" It was obvious to Daniela that he was concerned he'd be dropping them off in a conflict area.

"Yes, it's all arranged by Bloomberg. There's a meeting point near the customs building at the harbour. They're sending a car to get us. We'll be fine." She smiled, pointing at Yussef, who appeared to be waking from the fitful sleep he'd been in since they'd left the drillship. "But, thank you."

She was grateful to the skipper. Like everyone else they'd met from the oil company, he'd been genuinely helpful. Mind you, she had made sure of a successful outcome through the forged emails of instructions she'd sent from their London headquarters. She figured that, by the time the oil company people found out they'd been duped, she and Yussef would be far away. She felt a pang of guilt. The skipper was a nice man and showed real concern for her welfare—almost as if she'd been his daughter.

"We're going to be picking up supplies of fresh food and vegetables, then heading back out," he told her. He looked concerned. "I'll be here for a few hours. Here's my cell phone number. It works well near the harbour. If you need any help, Susan, just call me. I can always take you back out to the drillship, and they can get you back to Cyprus.

"Just watch where you go here," he advised. "Generally, it's safe for Westerners . . . people on business, like you, and tourists during vacation season. The hotel people are very friendly. But it's best to stay away from the city outskirts. Your company will advise you better.

"Good luck," he called, as she and Yussef disembarked.

It was the first time Daniela had visited Beirut. She knew it to be a beautiful capital where the women seemed to dress even more fashionably than in Rome or Paris. Recently, it had seen hard times. Under any other circumstances, she admitted, she would have stayed and enjoyed the city—taking in its historic buildings, legendary Arabian jasmine scents, and deeply rooted culture. And its amazing food.

Today, she and Yussef wouldn't be spending much time there, so they decided to remain casually dressed as they were—to avoid attracting attention. Later, as they journeyed northwards to Syria, they could decide if they need to change into more conservative apparel.

Leaving the port area, they walked to the nearby Charles Helou Bus Station. At an enquiry desk, Daniela asked about buses going to Latakia that evening. Two express coaches had departed earlier, said the booking clerk, but there would be another express going in about five hours. As tourists, he suggested they look outside for a shared taxi. Daniela considered the situation and went outside to check out their options. There were risks either way, she figured.

An older man and his wife wearing backpacks with a maple leaf flag were standing next to a five-seater cab, negotiating with the driver. It was obvious they were out of their depth. "Are you Canadians?" asked Daniela.

The man and woman glanced guiltily at each other. "Sort of," said the woman. "We like to wear the Canadian flag when we travel. It's safer over here than our American flag. I'm Chuck, and this is Martha," said the man, sticking out his hand. "Where are you guys from? We're trying to get to a beach resort in Syria. We'd fly, but Martha has developed an ear problem. Don't want to risk a burst eardrum. Lord only knows what the hospitals are like over here." He laughed.

"Latakia?" asked Daniela, introducing herself. "We're going there too. He knows the area," she said, pointing to Yussef. "We can share the ride, if you'd like?"

"We have a bit of luggage," said Martha. "But it would be good to travel with you two young people."

"We don't have much baggage—just backpacks," said Daniela. "Why don't you use the washrooms while you can. It's about a four-hour journey, plus the stop at the Tartus-Arida border. Go while you have a chance." She laughed. "We'll negotiate a rate with the driver. Take your luggage—you never know who you can trust."

"Oh, we'd trust you any day, honey," said Martha, leaving their bags and hurrying off. "Come on, Chuck."

"Sixty euros each," said Daniela to the American couple when they returned about five minutes later. It included the tip that Yussef had negotiated with the driver, she told them. "If you don't mind, we'd both like to sleep. It's been a tiring day."

It was close to midnight when they arrived at the border town of Arida, where the crossing straddles a river. There wasn't much traffic on the road, mostly a few trucks. Looking at their passports, the Syrian border guard seemed to take a particular interest in Yussef—and ordered all four passengers to get out of the taxi. A second guard examined their luggage.

Minutes before they'd stopped, Daniela had noticed that Yussef had taken off and retied his shoe. When he got out of the vehicle, he was hobbling badly. The border guard was yelling at him.

Chuck intervened. "Hey," he shouted. "We are travelling together. I'm an American, and if you want to get nasty, you'd better do it with me. We are going to our hotel in Latakia." He held out their travel confirmation documents. "If you continue to harass us, I'll call the American consulate; they won't like it."

His aggressive outburst seemed to help quieten the hostile guard.

"Can't you see that the boy has a leg injury?" Chuck demanded, breathing in deeply so that he now towered over the guard. "We are tired, and we want to get to our hotel. Here," he added, handing him a large denomination Syrian banknote. "This is payment for our entry visas. Give your boss a call and see if he thinks you should prevent legitimate tourists from travelling into your country."

The guard gave him a resentful look and glanced viciously at Yussef. Then he waved them back to their taxi and through the barrier.

Latakia, Syria

"Well, that was the best ten bucks I ever spent." Chuck laughed several minutes later. "It was a great deception of yours, young fella," he said to Yussef. "I used the same trick myself back in my army days." Yussef was laughing, but the two women seemed puzzled.

"My guess is that our young fella here would be a perfect recruit for the Syrian Army—if he hadn't got such a bad leg injury. Smart kid. But don't leave that stone in your shoe too long," advised Chuck. "You'll get a blister." He and Yussef continued laughing for several minutes.

The Americans' good spirits and generosity continued when they arrived almost two hours later in Latakia. "Unless you two kids have better plans, I can book you a room at our resort. It's late, and we all have to get some sleep. It's our treat, so don't say no." Chuck smiled. "Then you can go to wherever it is you're heading in the morning, after a good breakfast. What do you say?"

The hotel receptionist was only too happy to expand the reservation for Mr. Conner. Yes, all on the same bill, the receptionist confirmed, handing over their room keys.

Daniela and Yussef did not stay for breakfast. They knew they were taking a risk being there. Leaving the hotel early, they made their way back into the city centre. She left a thank-you note for the American couple, adding lots of kisses. They were lovely people, she admitted to herself.

Yussef knew the address of a cousin, and they made their way to his apartment. Visiting his relative unannounced involved taking some chances, Daniela was aware. But she didn't have a better idea. Here at least, she acknowledged, Yussef spoke the local dialect.

Knowing that Latakia is a well-known stronghold of defenders of the al-Daser government, particularly within the inner city, she hoped that Yussef's cousin was not a supporter of the regime. So far, they'd been fortunate. If they were going to be successful finding Yussef's brother and Jamal, they needed good fortune on their side.

They needed to stay lucky.

⁓◎

Yussef's cousin didn't seem overjoyed to see them, thought Daniela.

It wasn't a good omen.

He wasn't hostile, yet he made it clear that Yussef had arrived unannounced and his visit clearly was unexpected. Daniela had a bad feeling.

When she emerged from the washroom to see that Yussef's cousin's wife and children were no longer in the room, she quickly grabbed her things and shouted to Yussef that they should leave immediately.

They were met on the staircase by a squad of heavily armed police.

CHAPTER 9
Khmeimim Air Base
Latakia, Syria

Daniela slept sporadically in her jail cell. She alternated between sleep, brought about by complete physical exhaustion, and semi-consciousness, caused by the alarm signals sounding in her brain. Several times, she forced herself awake, knowing that soon they would interrogate her. In one of her twilight moments of consciousness, she figured they must have drugged her—depriving her of the opportunity to prepare herself mentally.

A heavy pulse from her carotid artery beat a rhythmic throb in her right temple; it contributed to her disorientation, not allowing her to gather her thoughts. She fought against the desire to relax by squeezing her muscles and gulping deep breaths of air to increase the oxygen to her brain. In spite of her attempts to achieve a strict mental discipline, her thoughts remained confused and disorganised.

"Your name?" the man sitting across the interrogation table demanded.

She rolled her eyes, as if in a dreamy state. She needed to play for time to determine where she was and who was questioning her. Bright lights glaring into her eyes made it an almost impossible task. A disjointed recollection crept into her awareness. At the apartment of Yussef's cousin, she had stuffed the passport identifying her as Susan Garcia deep down the side of the sofa. The American woman's ID had served its purpose. It would be dangerous to be caught on the streets of Latakia with two passports.

"Your name?" the man repeated. He sounded Russian, she thought, knowing that she could not stall much longer.

"Daniela Balmes," she answered, knowing that no good could come from trying to prove either identity. She had a vague grasp of a single detail—that being a citizen of the European Union might place her in a slightly better position than the alternative.

"Not Susan Garcia?" The man almost smiled.

"No."

"Tell me, Daniela, what is it in Syria you are doing?"

She was aware that her mental faculties were becoming slightly less unfocused under his questioning. Her headache was dreadful, and her head throbbed. If anything, she thought, the pain could work in her favour. For now, she could concentrate only on a single thought at a time. It was like waking with a heavy hangover; her body needed time to recover. Looking across the table at her interrogator, she could discover nothing from his appearance. He was tall and thin, wearing a plain blue dress shirt with a button-down collar. No epaulets that might have indicated military. He wore his watch hidden under his right wrist, so she could not identify its make or origin—or the time. His hair was short but styled. A senior officer, she thought.

"Daniela?" he repeated. His tone was brusque, but she had a feeling that he was not being combative.

Her instinct was to tell him the truth, despite voices of caution at the back of her mind. Or at least tell him a version of the truth that might be plausible. They had captured Yussef too, she recalled. How much of the real truth would *he* have told them, she wondered, knowing that their captors would compare their explanations very closely. She was aware that she needed to make credible statements and gain her interrogator's trust. Just stay away from confessing your real purpose in Syria, she cautioned herself.

How long had she been in a drugged state? she wondered. Had they carried out background checks on her? What did they know about her?

"No, not Susan Garcia," she repeated, playing for time.

"I will ask you just one more time," said the thin man, now raising his voice. "What you are doing in Syria?"

"I am helping my friend find his family," she answered. It was partially true, and she hoped that Yussef would tell them the same thing. It was the cover story they'd agreed in Cyprus. "We were able to locate his cousin. We had just arrived at his apartment when you . . . when you arrested us."

"Why do you help this friend?" the man persevered.

"I wanted to help him—now that the war in Syria is coming to an end. He wants to be reunited with his family, if they are still alive," said Daniela.

"How you know this friend?"

"I worked for the police in Spain. He needed help," said Daniela, knowing that her answer would invite more questions. She had no idea what they already knew about her, but she had a feeling that mentioning her background in the Mossos and Civil Guard might help. It gave her status and possibly leverage. Hopefully, she thought, it might divert her interrogator's attention.

"You here are on official business?" the man asked, his eyebrows arched. "You here in Syria working for Spanish police. You are spy?"

"No," she answered emphatically.

"No?" he shot back quickly. "No? You say you not working for Spanish police. So, you must be spy."

"I am here as a private citizen," said Daniela just as quickly. "I am not a spy."

"Then why you not apply for entrance visa and enter Syria legally?" he questioned. "Why you enter from the Lebanese border, bribing the guard? What you doing on board those oil drilling ships? What you doing in Cyprus?"

"My friend no longer had his Syrian passport, just his Spanish one. We had to get back here so he could find his family."

"This you have told me already," said the man. "All Spanish police, they personally escort Syrian refugees back to homeland? That very generous. Surely you not expect me believe such a story? You are Spanish citizen, you say. Maybe best action for us is hand you over to Spanish authorities. They arrange you taken back to Spain. What you think, Daniela? That be good for you, yes? Back to Spain with armed guard? Or, you tell me truth?" He looked hard at her. The raised eyebrows on his chiselled but handsome face were mocking and challenging. "Before you answer, think this. We have much time to interrogate your friend, Yussef; he told us many things. Now your chance it is to tell us the truth."

She knew better than to believe on face value everything he told her. It was possible that Yussef might have said nothing. Yet, this was wartime Syria; coercion and oppression were the norm. Daniela guessed that the boy would have talked. Talked, yes, but not blabbed. He would not have told them everything; his brother and the jihad were too important to him.

They would have questioned his cousin and each family member. Had someone in the cousin's family betrayed them to the authorities? The Syrian Army troops must have been given information by someone. Was it the border guard? The family knew they were looking for Ahmed and for Jamal—both known members of enemy forces. Daniela knew that her response to the interrogator's question would have to be convincing.

She knew also that anything she revealed might be used in their questioning of Yussef. It was vital that the boy must not stray from the purpose of their journey; it was equally important that Yussef must be confident she would not betray their cause.

Another thought gnawed away at her: Why was she being interrogated by a man who sounded Russian? There were no Syrians in the room, and she had not seen any since the army troops had arrived at the cousins' apartment. The thought emboldened her, and she decided to take a risk. "Why are you questioning me?" she demanded of the man. "You're Russian; you don't have any authority here." The man's face remained impassive, but Daniela thought she saw a flicker of his eyes.

"What interest do you have in us?" she continued with gathering confidence. "What interest do you have in a Spanish policeman and a teenage boy—one who was forced under gunpoint at a young age into combat. But he escaped. He is a legitimate refugee in Spain. All he is trying to do now is to find his family, to see if they are safe . . . to be reunited. If we have committed a crime, it is a minor offense at a time of war. We are not spies. We mean you no harm."

The man sat back on his chair and started to applaud. "Very good, Daniela. That was good acting performance. But you see, we know much more about you than you think." He turned his wrist and glanced at his watch, again preventing her from seeing it. "You have two high value credit cards. Very unusual, except maybe for very important people—and drug dealers." He held up the cards for her to see. "Question it is this: maybe I give another chance you tell me truth, or maybe I give you to Syrians—let them extract information. Their methods, I know them. They are not subtle. It is bad for men; for women, is agony. What my decision should be, do you think, Daniela?"

"You seem like a reasonable man, sir," she replied. "Perhaps even a kind man. You may have children, I don't know. But I doubt you are in such a senior position merely because you may appear to be reasonable and kind. You are interrogating me, and I think that you are weighing in your mind the probabilities of success of your future interrogations. Some of those options may not be pleasant for me. Well, that is your decision. Yet, I suspect that you have a special interest in me, and my friend. That is the only explanation why we are in your custody—not in the hands of the Syrian secret service."

"Tell me Daniela," he said, leaning forward across the table—until his face was close to hers. "Tell me, what is special interest you speak about? What is meaning of it?"

She shrugged her shoulders. "I only suspect it, sir. You know it. Why don't you tell me? I will cooperate. I am willing to help—to tell you everything I know." They were brave words, she knew. Sometimes, being bold was the best way. Unsettle the interrogator, force him to depart from his script. It had served her well in the past. But if her hunch about him was wrong, it would not be long before they would use more forceful methods of extraction. Ones against which she would have little or no defence.

The man opened a thin paperboard folder that so far had remained closed in front of him. He took out an enlarged photograph and slid it to her across the desk. Even before he had opened the folder, Daniela had a strong feeling that she knew who it would be. In spite of the split-second forewarning, she gasped as she saw it. He had been badly injured and his face was in pain. He looked emaciated and old.

"Jamal," she uttered. "Is he still alive?"

The man said nothing but took out his smart phone. He scrolled through a photo gallery, allowing her to see photographs he'd taken of the badly injured Jamal trapped in the heavily shelled building in Taybat al Imam. She could not believe that his condition had deteriorated so much since she had last seen him. He withdrew his phone and asked, "You ask me he is still alive? What interest you have in him, Daniela?"

"I knew him, some time ago," she replied. "Did he survive . . . that?"

"You were courier from Spain to the rebels, we know that is true. You worked with Jamal as jihadist. It is true, yes? You can deny if you wish. It is no use; we know it." The man scrolled again through the gallery on his device. He showed a series of more recent photos of Jamal to her, moving through them slowly. "You see, Daniela, Russian medical treatment best in the world. He is not fully recovered, but great progress he has made."

Seeing the photos of Jamal, Daniela's mood changed instantly. She smiled with relief. Her excited laughter was like that of a young girl. Her eyes were bright and joyous, even though she was almost in tears. Her body seemed to fill with renewed energy. "Is he here? Where is he—may I see him, please?"

The Russian closed his phone and took back the photograph. "You have received news that makes you very happy. That is good. Now perhaps we talk. You will answer my questions—truthfully, please."

On the Beach

The Russian officer drove Daniela to a quiet part of a long sandy beach near the town. He stopped at the end of a sand-blown concrete promenade where there were few other vehicles. Peering through the windshield, Daniela saw a lone figure standing a long way down the beach, close to the sea. Her heart rate increased as she recognised him. The Russian officer opened the passenger door for her.

"You worried, I think, we listen to your conversation with him?" He smiled. "You think we have no feelings." He offered a helping hand as she climbed out. "That not our intention. You can walk together anywhere on beach. If you wish, you can swim too—but the water, still it is not yet warm enough. We offer you full privacy," he added. "Believe me, or do not believe me. It is your choice, Daniela."

She ran as fast as she could down to the water's edge.

Jamal extended an arm to embrace her, but she stopped a step or two away—her heels digging deeply into the soft sand. With his other hand, he was leaning heavily on a metal cane to support the left side of his body. The happiness and relief on their faces at seeing each other was something hard to describe, she thought. He looked so much older and battle-scarred . . . but it was her Jamal. Carefully, not wanting to injure him even further, she reached up and put her arms around his head. Gently, she kissed his mouth.

It was a long kiss; it was a kiss of passion, yet cautious and caring—knowing that not long ago, he had been close to death. He responded eagerly but flinched several times from the pain of his wounds. She could feel his abdomen throbbing uncontrollably with emotion. Seconds later, around their entwined mouths, she could taste the salt from his warm tears.

She pulled her head back and giggled with intense delight—looking at his war-beaten face. She wiped away his tears and laughed again. "I did not know if you were still alive." She hugged him again until he breathed in sharply and winced with pain. "Oh, Jamal! I'm sorry," she cried. "I did not mean to hurt you. I'm so happy to see you."

With difficulty, he adjusted his metal cane on the sand and, wincing again from the sharp pain, shook his head. "Daniela, you could never hurt me." His mouth was turned down, and his lower lip quivered as it jutted out; he breathed deeply, trying to stop his blubbering. "You are here," he said through misted eyes. "It is hard to believe." He shook his head in disbelief. "Just like before, you have come back to me. It is wonderful. A gift from Allah."

"Have I changed?" She was anxious to know. "I must look awful." She brushed back her hair and laughed nervously. Then she ran her fingers gently through his thinning hair. Towards the back of his head was a deep scar. "What happened?" she demanded, tracing the wound with her fingertip.

"I am alive," he said simply. "There are many who are not."

"But we are," she replied quickly.

With his good arm, Jamal reached over towards Daniela and took her face in his hand. He said nothing, yet the tenderness in his eyes told her everything she wanted to know.

"We are still alive, Jamal," she blurted out. "We can go on together."

He nodded, but his tears again clouded his face. "Al-Daser has won," he said without emotion. "With the help of the Russians," he added. His voice had lost all its energy.

Daniela knew it was true.

"What of Mustapha? What of my friend?" Jamal asked eventually. He dragged his leg awkwardly, as he struggled to walk on the soft sand.

"Mustapha was captured, so was the general. Almost everyone, except for the boy, Yussef, and me," answered Daniela. "Maybe Ahmed escaped, I do not know. Our bomb—Ahmed's bomb. You heard that it did not work? I was working for the police at that time. I was not there, but I heard that the police cameras observed Ahmed entering the Mossos Headquarters car park.

"Ahmed armed the bomb and escaped. I don't know why, but he decided not to remain in the building and detonate it immediately. He tried to detonate it outside where he would be safe. In the delay, the Mossos were able to defuse the bomb. There was a small explosion. It was not enough to detonate it all. Why did Ahmed delay the explosion, Jamal?" she demanded angrily. "He should have remained with the explosives. Our lives are not important; his mission and the jihad . . . they were more important than his life."

Jamal looked at Daniela. "He could have remained there. He could have died, or perhaps he might have been captured. I know nothing of it. Our agreement with Mustapha was to carry out six bombings in your country on different dates. We would be paid for six attacks. Thanks to you, Daniela, we were paid for the first one—even though it was not successful. We received that money. Yet, our bombing effort, it was a failure, yes?"

"Not a failure, Jamal. The general talked with Mustapha," said Daniela. "Mustapha insisted that our partnership must continue—despite that one setback. We planned five other targets . . . five other opportunities."

Jamal interrupted her. "Our first attempt failed. Now the general and Mustapha, they have been captured. What is the future for our partnership, Daniela?"

"Mustapha was not pleased. It is true. He was angry that the Barcelona bombing attempt had not succeeded as planned," said Daniela. "Maybe the Spanish security forces knew something. Maybe we were betrayed. I don't know. I was employed by the police, so I was protected for a short time. Then they discovered that I, too, was part of the bombing attempt. They tried to kill me. The bullet was this far from my head." She opened two fingers to show the distance of a centimetre and held it against her forehead. "The assassin's bullet missed me. If it had not, I would not be here today."

"*Alhamdulillah*," said Jamal. "It is His will that you are alive and now returned to me."

"*Alhamdulillah*," she repeated.

Both were silent for a moment, reflecting on their thoughts—aware that life is transitory. Daniela waited, sensing that Jamal had many things to say. Also, in deference to him, she was aware that he should speak first.

"I must hear the full account from you, Daniela," he said at last. "I have many questions about what happened in Spain; perhaps they can come later. For now, we are here together. We are here because the Russians are allowing it. Do you know why, Daniela?" he asked, searching her eyes.

"I can tell you what I know, Jamal. But it is not much. I came back here to Syria to find you—to bring news of the money. Yussef, the younger brother of Ahmed, I brought him with me. I needed his help to find you. It is too difficult in this country for a woman alone. Are there other reasons? Yes, I will describe them to you. Most importantly, after Mustapha was arrested, Yussef and I stole the money belonging to the general.

"I did not know then that I was under suspicion too. I knew only that Ahmed and Yussef were in danger. I gave them money to escape from Spain. We do not know where Ahmed is, but Yussef has been with me every day. Now, the Russians have captured him too. I have not seen him since they raided his cousin's apartment here in Latakia, where we were hiding. I am convinced that we were betrayed—maybe by his cousin, I do not know. I was drugged and remember nothing more.

"When I awoke, I was interrogated by the tall, thin Russian—the Spetsgruppa officer. I tried to pretend at first that I was just a Spanish policeman helping a young Syrian boy to find his parents. The officer was amused. He knew all about me. He knew that we had travelled to Cyprus and he knew how we journeyed through Lebanon to Syria. He knew so much about me that I am convinced now that I must have been under surveillance for some time."

"What did he tell you, Daniela?" asked Jamal. "Why has he allowed you to meet me? After all, it is the Russians who are helping our enemy—the al-Daser regime."

"Jamal, I do not know what game he is playing. Why did al-Daser's soldiers hand me over to the Russians? Maybe he wants me to admit I am a spy—so they can justify killing me. That does not make much sense. I am in this country illegally. No one in Spain knows I am here. I am just another jihadi: an idealistic Western woman volunteer who wants the world to be a better place. Why not just kill me now?"

They had reached a flat area of rough concrete at the top of the beach. Jamal's breathing was laboured, and Daniela could see that he was sweating. The hand in which he held his metal cane was unsteady, and she feared he might fall. She took his other arm and guided him to a bench. The wind had picked up and blew small gusts of sand at them. The beach area was still deserted, but she did not trust the Russians. It was likely they were under close surveillance, despite the Russian officer's assurances.

Jamal slumped onto the bench; he leaned forwards struggling for breath. She made a motion to warn him about listening devices, but Jamal shook his head and managed a weak smile. He took her hand in his. She ran her hands over Jamal's chest and arms. "You feel so thin," she told him. There was no sign that he was wired. She doubted he would try to trick her voluntarily, but Jamal might be under duress, she thought.

"You are safe." He smiled knowingly at her. "They are not listening; there are no microphones on me."

"The Russians want me to become a traitor," he said eventually. "They have offered me an opportunity to help my people—in the peace process. The civil war, it is almost over, Daniela. Al-Daser has been allowed to win." As he said these words, Jamal had been holding her hand—almost pumping it with his strong grip. She could see that he was visibly distressed; pained emotions scoured his battle-scarred face.

"There is a plan for peace, the Russians tell me." Jamal laughed. "They are lying. There will be no peace, just a stalemate. Maybe that is what they intend. My days as a fighting soldier are finished." He looked at his leg and grimaced. "But the Russians think I have other uses. They tell me to become a statesman. *You* know what I am, Daniela; I am a surgeon. The war forced me to become a fighter. There was no other choice. But I am not a politician."

It was Daniela's turn to squeeze his hand. She did so gently, with tenderness.

Breathing with difficulty, Jamal continued to speak. "Al-Daser knows no compromise. He will not surrender any Syrian land. The Turks will not tolerate Kurdish and other peoples who shelter the YPG. It has been a threat to them for generations. I do not believe that any country fighting in this conflict will permit a new state to emerge.

The people of northern Syria, they want peace. But it is only the resistance fighters in the northeast who have the capability to govern themselves. ISIS is almost gone; it is hated. But the people—they will support al-Qaeda. It is a passion for us. To expel the foreign infidels. "For myself, I have doubts. Yet, I think anything is better than this constant fighting—the atrocities, the genocide. We must begin to rebuild this country." Jamal's cheeks were covered with streaming tears. "There have been too many deaths, too much violence. So much pain. Such a waste." His voice choked as he sobbed.

"There is support for this peace plan?" asked Daniela, her voice betraying surprise. "I understood that the negotiations at Astana and Geneva had achieved no results—nothing of substance."

He shrugged. "In Yemen, there is mass starvation—a famine, caused by the conflicts there. The Red Crescent no longer is effective. No humanitarian agencies can help. When those things happen, the world takes notice. The Western powers use it to justify invasions and take control. It is not just supplying aid; they want military control too, Daniela. Here in Syria, conditions already are very bad. Unless the famine which threatens us in the north is averted, al-Daser will realise his own greatest fear—increased military intervention by the West . . . or the East. He does not want that. Our people have suffered enough," he said flatly. "We do not want Western Crusaders to return. We do not need new masters from the east."

"You are a great man, Jamal. You are an inspired leader among your people. You will do the right thing . . ." Her voice trailed off. "Yet, there will be a price to pay. I know it."

Jamal looked at her sharply and gave her a half-smile. "Daniela, you are a clever politician. Always it is this way. You see things more clearly than other people. Yes, there will be a cost for this support from the Russians. They, too, want political and military control. I have a chance to bring short-lived peace for my people. The price is heavy. I will have to sell my soul to the devil."

"How could you become a traitor, Jamal? It is not in your nature. It goes against everything you believe, everything you have fought for. Whatever it is they are asking, you must not betray yourself. Do not do that, I beg you."

"The Russians say that they will allow us time together," said Jamal. "I would like that, please. They tell me that they will not confine you. You may return to Spain, if you wish. But they think you can help me. I, too, believe it. Stay with me. I must recover my health."

He smiled at Daniela. The merriment in his dark eyes reminded her of how she had fallen in love with him—the first day they'd met. He gazed at the blue sapphire necklace she was wearing and seemed pleased. "I gave you that. You have kept it all this time? Perhaps you will help me, please, to get better—just as you did in so many ways before. Do not think I did not know what you were doing for me. I will always be grateful to you. Now, again, I ask for your help. Please, Daniela, think about it."

Jamal struggled to his feet. With difficulty, he balanced himself upright. Raising his walking stick in the air, he signalled a car waiting for them several hundreds of metres along the road. She held onto him tightly, fearing he might topple over. As the vehicle's driver started his engine, moving slowly towards them, Daniela stood in front of Jamal—her face stiff and determined.

"Jamal, I will stay here and help you recover. I love you, and I will make sure you become well again. But I will never allow you to sell your soul. I cannot. It will kill you. It will kill you faster than any of al-Daser's bullets. I will not allow you to do it."

"He spoke many times of you when he was delirious and near death," said the Russian officer. "I myself was there when we found him trapped in ruins of the building. He is strong man. In this country, only strong and the paranoid can survive. You very important to him, Daniela."

"Is that how you knew who I was—why you arrested me?" she asked.

"Many things are known; even more things are not." He shrugged. "We are in the same profession. You understand."

"You are his handler," she stated, not seeking confirmation of her guess.

"We not have such expression in Russian." He laughed. "Not for people, only for trained dogs. Yes, you are correct—he is my assignment. But yours also, I think, Daniela. He is your assignment. He does not know these things, of course. But I know. Your secret with me, it is safe. For both of us, it is necessary for him to be alive. Even though we are different sides, they have a plan . . . our handlers." He smiled. "We cooperate and work together. For him, there will be no torture. Just good Russian medical treatment. Bring him back to life—and return to work."

"Because his people trust him, because they love him?" asked Daniela. "Because they will do what he says, is that it?"

"That is it," he confirmed. "That *is* it, very precisely, Daniela." He paused. "Will you help us?"

"Sir, I have a question. What plan do the powerful people have?"

"We can only guess, Daniela. Even then, most likely, both of us will be wrong. Over time, maybe we understand. It is not important. For now, we have our orders. They are simple to understand."

"Yet, such orders may be difficult to carry out," she said.

"He trusts you," the Russian repeated.

"May I see him again?"

"Of course, anytime you wish."

Daniela thought that the Russian was right: don't overthink the situation. Maybe it was just that simple. Jamal needed her help—not only for the jihad but to restore his confidence in himself. Help nurse him back to health—mentally and physically. Jamal needed someone who loved him. Someone who would care for him. She was aware that the Russian was watching her attentively, patiently awaiting her answer.

"I will provide you with a list of things I will need," she said eventually. "If you will permit it, I will walk with him each day—it will assist his rehabilitation. Good nutrition too. And a first-class physiotherapist. Those things are for his body. For his mind, you and I must decide what is best, sir. Our goal is clear. Mentally, he must return to the man he was. If it takes months, so be it. At one time, he had a vision of his destiny. We must restore his faith and confidence in that vision. What do you think?" she added.

"Our file it describes you as remarkable woman, Daniela." The Russian smiled. "Complex and remarkable. I must seek authorisation from my superiors. You understand? For myself, I consider your proposal good. It is the only possible plan. For Jamal to return and lead his people, it is the only way. Thank you," he said, starting to get up to leave the room.

"One other thing, sir, please," she called out. "The boy, Yussef. What have you told Jamal?"

"Jamal knows only that both of you were apprehended. Soon after you entered Syria illegally—not more. To meet, we have not allowed them—or talk together in any way. It is best, no?"

"I think you should allow them to meet; it will help his convalescence," she said.

"And you, Daniela, do you wish to see Yussef?"

She shook her head. "It is not important that I do. The boy has served my purpose; I no longer require him. But I think he can be a good foot soldier for Jamal in the future."

The Russian officer looked at her with interest and nodded; he continued towards the door.

"Your mission may be even more successful, sir, if you can reunite him with his brother, Ahmed."

The Russian's eyebrows arched skywards. "That is more, how you say, problematic," said the Russian. "We could not intercept him. Ahmed has returned to the fighting, we think. Maybe he is dead, maybe not. I enquire, Daniela. Now, please, restore the sick man. Medicine, it can help a lot." He tapped his head. "The real recovery, it begins up here."

Not long afterwards, the Russian officer reported the conversation to his superior.

"Will it work?" the senior officer asked. With his index finger, he pointed to his ear and then to the walls and the lamp on his desk—indicating the room was bugged.

"They are Moscow's orders, sir," answered the tall thin officer who had interrogated Daniela. "She is clever, but also she loves him. Whatever else her purpose here in Syria, she will stay to help him recover. Our instructions are to not detain her. We need not worry. She will remain with him until he is able to do what we ask of him. Maybe four months; maybe six. Only time will tell. Then he will be fit again."

"Keep me informed," he ordered. "Prepare your report and send it to Moscow.

"Be careful, Alexei. This is a dangerous game."

CHAPTER 10
Diego's Brother-in-Law
Barga, Galicia

Diego was disturbed by the phone call he'd just received. He was in his office, finishing work for the day, when his wife called. Zineb sounded upset; she asked him to come home as quickly as possible. He asked what was wrong, but she wasn't willing to talk over the phone. So, he had no inkling of what it was about.

"Are you all right?" he asked, his voice rising with concern. "Are the children safe?"

"Yes, we're fine," she whispered. "It's something else. Come home soon . . . please!"

To get there, he exceeded the speed limit in their modest sedan. It was already exhausting thick blue smoke: the engine was burning too much oil. They would have to buy a newer model soon. Pushing the speed of the vehicle to its limits was not helping. Swearing, he exited the autovia. Now he was only five minutes from their apartment complex west of Madrid.

He didn't waste time parking in their underground parking slot. Leaving it on the street, he rushed upstairs—getting his front door key ready as he leapt up the steps. He headed to the kitchen. Zineb came to meet him, her face looking strained. As he kissed her briefly on the forehead, she twisted around and pointed to a middle-aged man sitting at their kitchen table. "Lucas is here," she said, confirming what was already evident to Diego. He had recognised his brother-in-law immediately.

"What's up?" he demanded, hearing the brusque tone of his own voice.

His wife ushered Diego towards a chair. "He wants to explain it. I'll make sure the children are okay. I'll be back in a few minutes."

"You've got a problem, Lucas?" Diego demanded. Then he softened his tone. "Is it something we can help you with?" His eyes had already taken in some important information. A large and ancient cheap suitcase was standing upright by the far wall. It didn't have airline tags, so Diego guessed his brother-in-law had arrived by rail or bus—and, most likely, intended to stay. A heavy overcoat lay over the back of a chair, along with a scarf, suggesting that Lucas had travelled from his home on the Galician coast of northwest Spain, where the weather recently had been quite harsh.

On the table was an open bottle of a strong liqueur, alongside a single glass. Neither Diego nor his wife drank alcohol, but it was clear that Lucas had been in need of something fortifying. They kept the bottle at the back of a cupboard, just for visitors.

"Has something gone wrong with your job over there in Barga?" Diego asked, and watched as the man's eyes widened in surprise. He knew that his wife's brother was not the sharpest of people, but at least the man was good at his job. For more than twenty years, he'd held the post of harbour master at the small port town. It was a sleepy place, which normally woke up only for the tourist season—a favourite destination for the few brave travellers willing to traverse the tough mountain roads into that desolate part of Galicia.

"My job? How do you know that?" asked Lucas, almost in alarm. "Has something been said?"

"Look, Lucas, why don't we just top up your drink. I'll sit and listen, and you can start from the beginning." Diego tried to sound reassuring. Placing his hand on his brother-in-law's shoulder, he gave a friendly squeeze and poured a generous portion of the thick and sticky amber liquid into the glass. "I suppose you've already told Zineb about it," said Diego. "She's looking after the children while we talk. You and I, we'll talk man-to-man. How's that?" He forced a brief smile. "Start at the beginning," he repeated.

Lucas nodded gratefully and swallowed almost half the drink. "A few years ago, I got to know some men. They're good people, and we became friends. They're from Madrid. They rent a cottage just outside the village, west of the harbour. On that hill, we've climbed a few times together . . . you know the one.

"They told me that one of them had won a small amount of lottery money. He had a ticket on El Gordo. Not the winning number, a much smaller prize. Enough to retire, anyway. We had a few meals together and some drinks," he added, glancing at his glass, grinning with a slight look of embarrassment.

"As harbour master, I was able to do them a few favours. Nothing big. They needed an extra permit for one of their boats . . . that kind of thing. Then, one day, I was telling them about my son, Hugo, and the university place he'd won in Madrid. I guess I'd been complaining about the tuition and living costs because they offered me a loan. No interest payable, just between friends. I said no, of course. I didn't want to be obligated to them in any way. But when it came time for Hugo to go to Madrid, I said yes. I didn't tell anyone about the loan—and they never mentioned it again."

"Until?" prompted Diego.

"Well, a friend of theirs had a boat coming into a harbour up the coast. The berth up north was too small; they needed something larger. It was a large fast motor launch. We had just the right place for it. I'm supposed to report all new boats coming in from offshore to the regional customs office. My friends had a problem with that. They told me they weren't insured to moor the boat at my harbour and they'd get into trouble with the owners if they were found out."

"So, you agreed to say nothing?" prompted Diego.

Lucas nodded and took another gulp of the liqueur. "Everything was fine. The boat stayed for a day or two, then departed. That was the last we spoke of it. Then, a few weeks ago, they had another friend with another boat. It was coming from Venezuela, they said. They wanted another favour. Nothing much, but I started to wonder.

"Their friend's boat arrived in the middle of the night. A gang of motorcyclists arrived in town at the same time to unload it. The operation was carried out very efficiently. By then, I had started to get worried. For my friends, I don't mind turning a blind eye to waiving permits and making the docking regulations a bit easier for them. Up there in Galicia, everyone survives by doing a little business on the side. The fishermen, they used to dive for razor clams. Scallops and crabs too—until the seafood mafia took over." Lucas frowned. "It used to be just a local thing until the gangs took control. The restaurants are in on it too. So, we turned to other things to make a living."

Seeing Diego's eyes harden, Lucas quickly returned to his story. "It was starting to worry me that these friends might be running drugs—big shipments, not the small stuff that everyone does. Everyone knows that cocaine comes from South America into Europe through the Spanish coast. It's part of the local economy. Smuggling helps us all, just a little bit of it."

"Did you think of reporting this to the Civil Guard?" interrupted Diego, with an impending feeling of dread at what Lucas's answer would be.

"Of course. Well, I did think about it. But then one of the men suddenly asked for full repayment of the loan. He wanted it right away, and I didn't have the money. He brought someone else along with him: a big, muscular guy—a biker. He asked how Hugo was doing in his studies at the university in Madrid. He said they had a friend there, and the friend might drop by to say hello to Hugo.

"I'm not dumb, Diego. I knew he was threatening me. Then he became very friendly and said not to worry; he'd find the money he needed somewhere else. The biker was terrifying. He said there was another boat arriving soon. He said not to be concerned about Hugo's studies. Everything would be all right.

"A few days later, it was late at night and I couldn't sleep. I'd gone down to my office at the harbour. I needed to have a smoke and a drink or two; you know that Salma doesn't like me to do that at home. I sat in my office in the dark—thinking. My friend's boat had arrived, and I knew I had to find a way out of the mess I'd got our family into. I had to stop it somehow.

"Then I heard some voices. Two men unloading my friends' boat were sitting on the dock next to their motorcycles. Looking through the window, I saw that they had a number of packages with them. Bundles of something; I guessed it might be cocaine. I knew the men hadn't seen me because I'd kept my office lights turned off. Then I had a stroke of luck. Both of the men went back to the boat. I walked over to the bundles and quickly took two of them. They didn't see me."

"That was stupid," scolded Diego, becoming alarmed. "Those hombres are bad dudes. What did you do with their cocaine?"

"I thought you could sell it for me," said Lucas. He looked earnestly at Diego—seeing his shocked face. "I couldn't sell it locally. Anyway, I don't know who to sell it to. You're a cop. You bust up drug dealings all the time. I thought that you'd be able to sell it for me—here in Madrid. Then I can pay the money back. They are going to want a hefty interest payment as well, I know that. But then I'll be free of them. We can stop worrying."

Diego rubbed his forehead vigorously with both hands. It was a violent frustrated motion, as if he was trying to figure out how to explain the facts of life to his brother-in-law. The man was living in a fantasy world. Then Diego looked up, his eyes blazing. "Quite apart from being the most stupid thing you have ever done, apart from the fact you've pissed off a bunch of bikers by stealing their merchandise, doesn't it seem obvious to you that when you give the men back their money, and with interest, they'll wonder where you got it?"

"I can say it came from one of our relatives," replied Lucas hopefully.

"Then you will involve them," said Diego. "Don't you think the bikers will check? These guys are in the business; they are professionals, Lucas! I hope you found a safe place to hide that stuff. You didn't keep it at home with Salma. You didn't, did you?" Diego glared at his brother-in-law.

"No, of course not," said Lucas. "I brought it with me."

The blood drained from Diego's face; he felt nauseous. "Not here? You didn't bring it here, did you? Into my house?" He stood up in recoil and backed away from Lucas. "You can't be that fucked up."

Lucas eyes strayed towards his heavy suitcase. The giveaway look was so obvious that no one in the room could have missed it.

"Caramba! You bloody stupid idiot, Lucas."

Diego's shout was so loud that Zineb came running back into the room. She said nothing but looked at the two men. Her emotions were in a turmoil. She understood the situation. Now she was torn between loyalty to her husband and her need to protect her brother. "What's wrong?"

"What isn't wrong?" said Diego. His voice sounded desperate. Turning, he pointed to Lucas's suitcase. "*That* is stuffed with cocaine. Your dumb brother stole it from a mafia gang and brought it into our house. He wants me to sell it for him. How selfish and stupid can you get?" It was not a question.

Diego reached for his phone.

His wife stifled a scream. "Diego, no! Please don't turn him in to the police. It will ruin everything for him." She rushed over and tried to grab it, but he held it away from her grasp.

"If I don't report him, it will ruin everything for us," Diego shouted at her. "Right now, he's in deep trouble. But if we don't report him, all of us will be in even deeper shit."

"They'll kill him," yelled Zineb. "You can't let them, Diego. He isn't a bad man; he just made a mistake, that's all."

"Some mistake," said Diego, trying to think.

"You're not staying here, Lucas," said Diego after a few moments. "And neither is that." Diego pointed at the suitcase. He opened his wallet and took out several large bills. "Take this. Get yourself a hotel. Take a taxi. I'm not going to contaminate my car with that stuff."

Going through Diego's mind were the implications of what Lucas had told him. It would be in character for his brother-in-law to embellish some aspects of his story and leave out other parts—avoiding things he felt might get him into trouble. He wondered what other skulduggery Lucas might have been up to. If Lucas had not been his wife's brother, Diego would have taken him to a deserted place somewhere and thrashed the full truth out of the man. As it was, now he was being forced to take a series of unsavoury risks. He didn't like it, and he didn't trust Lucas. His instincts told him he was wise to get the man out of the house while he figured out his next steps.

He looked hard at his brother-in-law. "I'm going to need some time to think about what you have to do. Now listen to me. Book into a hotel under a false name and stay in your room. I'll find you. Room service only. Don't contact anyone. Is that clear, Lucas?"

Lucas nodded. It was obvious that he was completely terrified of his brother-in-law but relieved and grateful for not being reported to the police. He nodded his head vigorously and took the money. "Thanks, Diego. You're being really decent about this. I'm sorry; really, I am." He turned to his sister, kissed both cheeks, and hugged her. She looked scared and close to tears.

"Do what Diego tells you, Lucas," she implored him. "He is a smart man; he's family. Listen to him."

Diego was moved by the obvious love she had for her brother. He placed his arm gently around her shoulder and detached her. "Zineb is right, Lucas. Now remember what I said. Don't contact anyone. Don't phone home, not even to talk to Salma." He saw a guilty shadow pass over the man's eyes and guessed that phoning his wife was exactly what Lucas had planned to do.

It was exasperating, thought Diego. Mentally, his brother-in-law was like a child: always thinking that he could sneak something by you. "Don't do it, Lucas," he repeated. "Drug dealers kill people. If anyone has a phone tap on your house and office, you'll be in even greater danger. Your family is already in danger. Don't make it worse."

A Dilemma

All evening, Zineb had pleaded with Diego.

"Please do not tell on him," she begged. "They'll put him in jail. He made a mistake, that's all," she repeated. "He will not do such thing again; I promise it."

Diego's instincts were to report his brother-in-law; let him live with the consequences. He might not have to go to jail for long if he gave evidence against the drug smugglers. Such an outcome, he knew, was wishful thinking. If life were only that simple. They'd find a way to get their revenge against Lucas. For sure.

His brother-in-law had been crazy; naïve to have done such a thing. Absolutely stupid.

For hours, Diego tried to figure a way out. He'd thought of the witness protection program. If Lucas could help the police break up the smuggling gang, maybe Diego could help negotiate a relocation for Lucas's family. Somewhere safe—a long way from Galicia. Problem was, thought Diego, he didn't think that Lucas was smart enough. He couldn't pull it off. He talked too much.

Maybe the narcotics squad wouldn't be interested in offering Lucas a deal? They might already have the gang under surveillance, biding their time to capture the whole network. Lucas would be implicated—collateral damage. No matter which way he tussled with the lawful options, Diego couldn't come up with a solution.

His thoughts went to the dark side.

Despite the shady environment that Diego invariably worked in, stooping to do anything seriously illegal was alien to him. Since his family had emigrated to Spain, when Diego was thirteen, he'd proudly regarded himself as being Spanish. He had many memories of Morocco: some good, some not quite as nice. To him, the laws of his new country were to be respected above all else. He'd thought several times over the years that it was why he'd become a policeman and worked so hard to rise through the ranks at GEO.

In the poor area of Madrid where his parents settled, he had excelled at school. In his neighbourhood, there was never any prejudice against immigrants—because all the kids were from immigrant families. Gang fights made up for it. Whenever he didn't earn respect and was pushed to the point of retaliating against the bullies, Diego took physical action. His adversaries nursed their wounds for weeks. After that, they steered clear and left him alone.

It helped that he worked out—following a regimen that athletes would find punishing. At nights, as a kid, he would climb over the wall into a builder's yard and lift concrete blocks—hour after hour. He was not a tall youth, but his barrel chest, well-muscled arms, and closely cropped hair projected an appearance that was physically intimidating. Maybe that would come in useful again, he thought, as he tried to figure out how to deal with Lucas's predicament.

Diego loved his wife. He knew he'd lose Zineb's respect if her brother went to prison, or worse. She, too, was from a Moroccan immigrant family. Their cultural code dictated that family must look after family. There was no other way. For Diego, it was a test of his manhood and family standing.

There was always a solution on the dark side.

Just this once, Diego told himself.

―∽―

Many kilometres away, in the Galician harbour town where Lucas lived, two irate bikers were struggling to figure out how someone had stolen the cocaine. The wild unkempt men, roughly dressed and sporting untrimmed beards, had quickly discovered their loss—on the night that Lucas had seized his opportunity and disappeared with two of their high-value bundles.

It had been dark at the time. Looking at each other accusingly, the angry bikers soon realised that someone else had made off with their coco. They'd searched the area for anyone walking on the streets. There was no one. Soon, they turned their attention to the small boats moored against the jetty that jutted out into the harbour. One boat was showing a cabin light. They boarded it and kicked in the door of the hatch leading to the living quarters.

A young man was doing his best to service a well-endowed young woman. The youngsters were startled . . . embarrassed to be caught *in flagrante delicto*. It was obvious they had been nowhere near the bikers' stash.

The hapless youth, less well-endowed than his girlfriend would have liked, quickly grabbed a cushion and covered his modest manhood. The girl seemed unconcerned, impressed instead by the fearlessness and muscularity of the intruders. She sat shamelessly nude on the edge of the messroom table, her shapely legs dangling to the floor, as the bikers pushed aside her boyfriend and searched the boat.

As they left, the taller of the two bikers moved towards her and traced his finger in a circle around her breasts—giving one of her nipples a quick squeeze. With more time, he reflected, he would have treated the girl to an unforgettable shag. She would beg for more. But right now, there was other business to take care of.

They wanted vengeance against the bastards who had stolen their merchandise, and they wanted their goods back. The tall biker made a mental note of the name of the lusty boat. Giving the girl a lecherous leer, he recognised from experience the meaning of her raised eyebrow and the briefest of smiles on her face. She would be an easy *comer*. He would come back later, he'd decided.

That was several days ago, and they were still no closer to finding the stolen cocaine. They had a few suspects, including the harbour master. His wife told them he'd gone on a few days holiday. They had threatened several other suspects, but none seemed the likely thief.

The two bikers were on their way to revisit her. The noise of their bikes carried inside the house as they revved their engines outside. They knew that noisy intimidation scares people. This time, they were determined to make her talk.

Lucas the harbour master was their man; they were convinced.

But where was the bastard?

⸺

"Curse Lucas!"

Diego had become so frustrated with his brother-in-law's antics that he was almost willing to let him suffer the full consequences. But he knew he couldn't.

There was only one thing he could do.

He knocked on his boss's office door.

Claudia listened and shook her head. She walked to the window, deeply in thought.

"No, I'm not going to let you resign over this, Diego. It's a noble thing to suggest, but you're being foolish. Your brother-in-law did something stupid. He has to take responsibility. I'm not going to let misguided family loyalties ruin the career of one of my best officers. You're going to take time off—and I'm instructing you not to contact him, or his wife."

"But, ma'am, I can't just let him take his chances. We both know the consequences," Diego protested.

"Well, the only thing I can do is talk to my opposite number in Narcotics," said Claudia. "If they can't do anything—or aren't willing to—there's not much we can do. It's the best chance we have. You've done the right thing, reporting it to me. If we're lucky, they might be willing to charge him with a misdemeanour. At minimum, they are under an obligation to protect him and his family. That's the most important thing—make sure that innocent people are not the target of gang retribution.

"We have to act quickly," she added. "In the meantime, I have to remove you from the situation. I'll need your badge and gun, Deputy Inspector. Sorry, but we have to do this by the book. Go home, Diego. Look after your family first."

Two days later, he received a brief text from Claudia and immediately reported back to work. Without a word, she handed over his badge and gun. He knew then that Lucas and his family were safe and nothing would appear on his own service record.

Already determined, he resolved to work twice as hard to justify her trust in him.

Fixing the Irredeemable

The grandee had returned moments earlier from an audience with the king.

A crisis meeting. The scandal involving his majesty's father had covered the front pages of the tabloids all week. It was well beyond an embarrassment. Police investigations had been announced; fraud and corruption had been alleged; even worse—tax evasion.

The king had been angry. Furious. In recent months, he had been reassured that his father's indiscretions were a thing of the past. Hardly youthful indiscretions at his advanced age—but perhaps understandable, possibly even partially forgivable, now that the former king had been forced to step aside. News of illegal payments to the old man—millions of euros from foreign powers—had now thrown fuel onto the fires already consuming the family's collapsing credibility.

Going to his liquor cabinet, the grandee poured himself a single malt Scotch. There was nothing single about the amount. He ignored the distilled water kept in special bottles stored at room temperature.

Once again, the royal family had to be saved from itself—and he knew precisely how to do so. "Thank goodness for the new generation," he said aloud to the empty room as he swallowed the remaining contents of the elegant cut glass. He loved the weight of its base—pure lead crystal, from a set that was a gift from the king of Sweden. The girls were being brought up properly, he thought thankfully. Modern thinking, from an intelligent mother. Not his first choice, he'd admit. Not at first. But, in the short time since their marriage, the queen had proven herself many times over. There was hope yet for the monarchy.

Pouring himself another generous portion, the grandee considered how he could implement his plan. It had to be disconnected completely from the family. Of that, there was no doubt. They'd be the ultimate beneficiaries, of course. But they had to be able to deny any knowledge of what he was scheming. The fact was that the condesa had inherited a substantial fortune; all of it was Carlos's money. Every single peseta. She had been an opportunist; she'd diverted funds from Spain's aristocracy. By birth, she had no right to do so.

The family needed money.

Desperately.

The grandee was determined that repossession of the condesa's inheritance—following the tragic death that he planned for her—must be handled appropriately. Preparing himself for an early night, the grandee resolved to wake at dawn and review his plans for a final time. He would tell no one. Not even the grand master.

It was time for the condesa to be eliminated.

Isabel

Breakfast time. Isabel was sipping a hot espresso, staring out the window at nothing in particular.

She had been thinking about men. In her view, to say that she had reservations about the men in her life was an understatement. Her brother was an exception: Toni was special. The rest, including her father, were a disappointment. She preferred the company of women, in bed as well as out.

Julia, cup in hand, shuffled past in her dressing gown, hair untidily arranged above her neck. "Good coffee," she observed.

"Men can be so . . . frustrating," said Isabel.

"Tell me about it," replied her partner. "It's that missing chromosome." She picked up a day-old copy of *El País* from a side table and sat down to read.

"The worst thing is they don't even think like women. They go off on tangents that have no logic," continued Isabel.

"Any man in particular?" asked Julia. "Or are you just doing your usual stereotyping?"

"They're such hard work," Isabel pursued her crusade. "Most of them are like little boys—they need a mother, not a female partner. As a species, they just haven't matured biologically or mentally. I don't know why I bother with them."

"Go into politics. You'd be good at it," said Julia. "You did a great job fighting our bloody landlord. If it hadn't been for you, he would have evicted us and everyone else in this building. He thinks only about the higher rents he can extract from the short-term tourist trade. Bloody offshore developers are pushing out families who have lived in this area for generations. Greedy pigs," she added, throwing down the newspaper to clear away the breakfast dishes. "I'd like to see you in politics. You'd sort the bastards out."

Isabel knew what she was getting at. Anything would be better than what she was doing. Julia didn't like her chosen profession as a courtesan. Isabel's parents were the same, and so was Antonio.

When their landlord had hiked their rents, Isabel had spoken up. Determined to pursue the issue, she had spent time researching in libraries and government offices. It had reaped a big reward. With the help of an aging Catalan professor from the university, she had unearthed an old municipal statute. The residents of their building had tenure and were protected. With the help of a lawyer friend, she had won the court battle. Now, her friends were pleading with her to run for the upcoming neighbourhood elections. Julia, in particular, was begging her to put her name on the ballot. For weeks, her partner had been saying she was a natural spokesperson for the community—and incredibly popular. She could look after the neighbourhood far better than the loud and outspoken but ineffective people who dominated the council at present.

"What's stopping you?" Julia asked.

"Money," Isabel replied. "I have to earn a living."

"The existing lot of politicians don't seem to do too badly," said Julia, removing their empty cups.

Girl On The Run

"Ha!" Isabel protested. "They're just as bad as the rest. Most of them have got some kind of scam going. Some of them are in bed with the property owners. Literally, in some cases."

"Well, do something about it," said Julia. "I've got a steady job; it's enough to support us both." She glanced at her watch and winced. "I'm late. I've got to get going."

"Do you think they're going to want a former prostitute in their midst?" scoffed Isabel. "That would be a laugh."

"Courtesan," corrected Julia. "You're selective. You're a courtesan, darling. And yes, you're just the person to shake them into action. Stir things up a bit. Stop all this talking, get things done."

"I might give it a shot," said Isabel, kissing Julia. She looked at her watch. "You're right. We'd both better get going. I have one of my regulars this morning. That young guy from Madrid is in town again."

"I know he's hot and virile, but I can't imagine why he wants to fuck this early in the day."

CHAPTER 11
Maria

His booming voice almost made her cell phone shake.

"Hola Maria, my love. How's everything in Barcelona?"

Sergio always had an agenda, and invariably she felt terrible after his phone calls. Feeling her body stiffen, she dreaded what might come next.

"It's your birthday next week," he continued. "I have a nice surprise for you. You remember Enrique Mendez? He's having his thirtieth birthday party, three days before yours. He's in Barcelona performing, and he's invited us to meet him after his concert, to go for dinner. I said I didn't know if you'd be busy, but I promised to call and find out. You recall the fun time we had together a few years ago? You and I went backstage after one of his concerts. His recent album just hit number one in the charts. He wants to celebrate with us."

Of course, Maria remembered Enrique! He had a soft and sultry voice, which she often listened to when relaxing at home. He was a charming and modest person—unlike Sergio. She couldn't understand how the two men had remained such close friends for so long.

"I'd love to," she replied happily and thanked Sergio. She felt elated. After the call, she opened a new bottle of wine . . . a really good one. Sometimes drinking alone isn't so bad, she told herself. Now her life had just turned a new and exciting corner. "Yes!" she shouted out loudly to the empty room. "Yes!"

Who knew what the evening could bring?

Girl On The Run

The day arrived.

Maria could hardly disguise her excitement. It felt like a first date.

Sergio acted like a gentleman, and Maria almost forgot how much of an asshole he could be. He collected her from the narrow lobby of her apartment building and complimented her numerous times. It was obvious he was quite taken by her new hairstyle. Minutes later, he held open the passenger door for her and drove at about half his usual breakneck speed to the concert hall. He over-tipped the concierge parking attendant, securing an overnight space for his vehicle. Within minutes, they were milling in the crowded theatre lobby with a long stem of cava in hand.

Enrique's concert tour had been reviewed as "brilliant" by the critics—adding extra spice to the buzz around the building. Last-minute fans were desperate to buy tickets; none were available.

"Where are we sitting?" asked Maria, sipping her wine, her bright eyes sparkling with excitement. Behind them, an open door allowed the haunting chords of the guitar accompaniment to escape—elevating the thrill of anticipation from the ecstatic audience to an even higher pitch.

Maria squeezed Sergio's arm. "Oh, this is so exciting! Thank you for inviting me." She held onto his muscular arm and surprised herself how comfortable she felt with him.

"I didn't really," said Sergio. His smile was kind. "Enrique insisted." He took out their tickets to show her. "Third row, in the centre . . . the best seats in the house." He laughed. "We should have an excellent view of the maestro. I'm sure he knew that when he sent the tickets over to my office."

Their seats were fabulous. The concert was magnificent; almost every number sung by Enrique received a standing ovation. His voice was modulated to perfection. His lyrics captured their souls. The deliriously happy and adoring audience was drawn in even closer by the maestro's conspiratorial flirting with the ladies—and many of the men—who gladly would have given themselves to him in those moments. Several times, he waved directly at Maria and blew her a kiss. His power over his audience was palpable; his godlike status, unmistakable. As they rose as one to their feet in the dying stanzas of his finale, their capitulation was complete.

What a night! Oh, what a performance! Bouquets flew through the air, and female personal items too. He laughed with joy, applauding his adoring audience in return. No recreational drug could have achieved such bubbling euphoria and happiness. The accolades later awarded to Enrique by the critics spoke of the performance of the century. It was a sublime experience that no one who saw it would forget. The consummation of his creativity; his was a voice that would live on forever.

They stayed in the theatre long after the fifth brilliant but exhausting encore—refusing to go home, milling with the other worshippers, laughing, intoxicated by their shared camaraderie. All of them pregnant with pleasure. What a climax!

Propelled forwards on a hoverboard of gravity-defying joy, Sergio and Maria found the nearby restaurant where Enrique had promised to join them later. They could hardly stop talking, each good-naturedly interrupting the other, reinforcing and elaborating their praises. Over more wine, they sang refrains from their favourite pieces, repeating memorable phrases from Enrique's lyrics.

Holding off ordering food until their illustrious guest arrived, they drank more and more wine. As the evening grew long, their elation over Enrique's performance quite naturally began to flag—gradually nudged aside by the euphoria of the grape. As it often does, the wine made them reflective and perhaps even a little bit maudlin. They talked about the old days when they had been together—content as man and wife and optimistic, so long ago, about their future together.

Enrique called Sergio, apologising profusely. He simply could not get away from the theatre. Would they like to . . . sorry about the background noise . . . would they like to come and join the party? "Not to worry," Sergio reassured him. "You were amazing, awesome, brilliant, and incredible. We loved every moment." And, yes, they would try to make it back to the theatre to join the celebration. They were a little drunk, Sergio told the superstar. So perhaps they would eat something first. Not to worry if they didn't make it tonight. Everyone wanted to be close to the maestro. They could catch up again soon. "Love from Maria, by the way. She, too, thought you were magnificent. Fantastic! Well done!"

Deflated but resilient, they finally ordered food—and more wine. Slurring their words, they took extraordinarily polarised viewpoints on topics of no consequence, alternatively laughing out of control, then arguing unreasonably with inebriation-assisted passion. The rest of the night was a blur.

Next morning, Maria could not believe that she had slept in Sergio's bed at his hotel. Gallantly, he had slept on the narrow couch. Her wristwatch did not lie: she was late for work. Horrors! She couldn't arrive there in the stunning red evening gown she'd worn the previous evening. At the office, her gold sequin purse alone would have given the game away. There was nothing else for it: she would have to go home, shower, and change.

The elevator down to the lobby was crowded with hotel guests checking out. Try as she might, Maria could not avoid their knowing glances. Normally stunning, her mascara had smudged, and her dress was creased. She looked like a tired lady-of-the-night. Worse still, the last available taxi pulled away from the forecourt just as the doorman pushed the revolving doors open for her. One of her high heels caught in a crack in the pavement and she lurched forwards—just managing to recover her balance on time.

Oh no! She looked up to see a familiar figure walking towards her.

"Maria," said Antonio in surprise. "Are you all right?"

He didn't say it, but his shocked look told Maria what he was thinking—that she looked terrible. His first concern had been for her safety; he had seen her catch her high heel and trip over. Now, he was staring at her evening clothes and tell-tale purse. Mouth open, no words would form.

Then a catastrophe.

Sergio came rushing out of the hotel's swing doors. He was calling to her, saying that he would give her a ride to her apartment. He stopped suddenly when he saw Antonio. Sergio's creased shirt and dishevelled appearance confirmed the worst in Antonio's mind. He looked at them both for a moment, then shook his head and strode up the street.

"Toni," called Maria, running after him. She grabbed him by his arm. "Toni, it's not what it looks like . . . honestly . . . is there somewhere we can talk? I can explain."

"You need a ride home," said Antonio in a curt, formal tone. He pointed at Sergio frozen motionless in the hotel forecourt. "He's the ride you want." Antonio continued striding up the street, leaving Maria standing, close to tears.

"See you," he called over his shoulder. "Have a good day."

Borbón Connection

"You were right, Toni," announced Xavi, as they met on the second floor of the Mossos Headquarters building. "It's not her original name.

"Her mother died when she was seven. Soon after that, her father officially changed the family's name to Périgueux. According to her employment records, Aurelia didn't make any secret of her name change. Her human resources file at the TFPU contains a copy of the official document."

Antonio nodded. "Let me guess: her father didn't want to continue with their real family name. Obviously, neither does she. So, now you're going to tell me who she really is—and from the excitement in your voice, amigo, it's going to impress me."

"Well, hold on a minute; it's more complicated than that," cautioned Xavi. "Her father's name was Marchand. It's commonplace, really; not much reason to change it to something more distinctive like Périgueux."

"Without a reason," added Antonio.

"I traced her father's background," said Xavi. "After his wife died, he went downhill rapidly. He used drugs heavily. He gave up Aurelia's younger brother for adoption. Aurelia looked after her father—remarkable really, for someone so young. The social welfare people normally don't allow that, but someone pulled influential strings. A powerful person with friends in high places, I'd guess. Someone was paying for a full-time housekeeper and the kids' education."

"So, the family secret is something to do with their mother's side of the family. Something they wanted to conceal, perhaps?" asked Antonio. "Making it hard to trace."

Xavi laughed. "A lot of families would like to do that if they could. Here's the exciting bit. What makes Aurelia's family secret different is this: In the official records, except for her mother's death certificate, there is no trace of her background. Absolutely nothing. It's as if she didn't exist. No names of parents, no grandparents. Nothing.

"I thought it might be a case of someone being sheltered within a witness protection program. It isn't," Xavi added. "William came up with the answer. I don't know how he does it. He hacked into a high-security database somewhere."

"And?" asked Antonio.

"Does the French family name *Dampierre* mean anything to you?"

"Wasn't she a relative of Louis-Alfonse, the Duke of Anjou—who today would be the rightful king of France, if France hadn't become a republic? He's a cousin of our king here in Spain, Felipe VI."

"You've got it," Xavi sounded impressed. "But Aurelia's mother is only distantly related through the same family. It still makes her part of the House of Borbón—even though she's far removed from the throne."

"Well, it's fascinating in a way," replied Antonio. "If you're connected to any famous family, you probably wouldn't want to draw attention to it—not constantly. But it's interesting that someone powerful stepped in and took a personal interest when the kids were growing up. I guess those Borbóns look after their own."

"William figures that Aurelia is well down the pecking order in the line of succession," added Xavi. "That's a good enough reason to stay out of the limelight."

"I'd be interested in knowing how Aurelia got into the gold-laundering investigation business," said Antonio. "I guess I could ask her myself," he added, mindful of the French girl's flirtatious enticements. "Did you have time to find anything about her boss—Ramon?"

Xavi shook his head. "William is still working on it. I reminded him not to leave behind any traces when he's doing his snooping. Same for Aurelia. The feds might be screening us. It's best they don't know we are looking."

He received an appreciative nod from Antonio.

The Condesa

He decided he could wait no longer.

The condesa's accident had been carefully planned. Now was the time to act.

It was really quite simple, thought the grandee. Travelling home to La Moraleja from the city each Wednesday, she always took the same route, he'd been reliably informed. It was a forty-minute journey using the M30 and M40—both busy motorways at rush hour.

The truck driver from Romania had readily accepted the offer of money that would be deposited into his bank account when the job was done. He needed it badly. His cover story was solid. His log book would show that he'd driven only an hour more that he was permitted—a minor infraction carrying a small fine. He'd be tired but still capable of controlling his big rig of steel bars. Importantly, he knew the route well.

To cover his tracks, the grandee had a follow-up plan. Soon after the motorway accident that would demolish the condesa's car, the truck driver would be released from police custody. It was standard procedure, even with traffic fatalities. The guilt-ridden truck driver would be found dead at his motel the next morning—in a distraught state having succumbed to an excess of alcohol and drugs. The police investigation would confirm that drugs had been found in his cab.

No criminal blame would be attributed. It would be a cover-up that had been perpetrated many times before.

The grandee made a note in his diary—to send a fittingly thoughtful wreath to the condesa's funeral.

―⊙―

Months earlier, the condesa had spoken to several friends at her country club in La Moraleja.

"I'm setting up a trust fund and foundation—in Carlos's name," she told them. "As you know, he loved music. Spanish classical, to be precise. With the wealth of resources already available to that field of art, I'd like to focus on a neglected but deserving group and a different genre—young immigrant children and the indigenous music they bring into Spain. It enriches us all, I think."

She had received overwhelming support from the group—and later, from a variety of generous sponsors. Since then, a board had been elected, staff had been hired, and a series of scholarships and bursaries had been disbursed. The centrepiece was the trust's acquisition of a former industrial building in a working-class area of Madrid, where extensive renovations were now taking place. A music school for immigrant children would be opened within a year. Her board of advisors and fundraisers met regularly at an office adjacent to the site.

Today, she had completed her meeting and was approaching her reliable but aging Fiat—parked on a side street. It was more appropriate to the neighbourhood than the opulent Mercedes she'd inherited from Carlos. Her board members had followed her example and also drove modest vehicles to the meetings, or shared rides.

The condesa had been outspoken about their need to fit into the district. "It's hypocritical, in a sense," she'd declared candidly. "But this is one case where the end justifies the means. We each contribute substantially to the foundation. We're not seeking to gentrify the neighbourhood—rather the opposite. There's no need to undermine our purpose by inviting ridicule. There are enough detractors out there already."

Opening the Fiat's door, she glanced around. There was no doubt it was a rough area. Several older buildings were derelict; graffiti covered many others offered for lease. Among the remaining premises—a mix of immigrant-run shops and residences—garbage was piled outside, spilling onto the street. She wondered, not for the first time, if her choice of location was the wisest.

Further up the street, a shiny recent model dark blue luxury sedan was parked—engine running. It had dark-tinted windows. It stood out and caught her attention. Her first thought was one of annoyance: someone within their group wasn't sticking to their informally agreed arrangement. She made a mental note to mention it discreetly at their next meeting.

The condesa drove towards the approach road for the motorway. Traffic flowing north was light; she could be back in La Moraleja within the hour. Behind her, unnoticed by the condesa, the dark blue sedan followed at a distance. Clearing the outskirts of the downtown area, the condesa's thoughts were preoccupied with details of the construction schedule for the school. Speeding up, she was careful to move to a centre lane, allowing a convoy of new traffic to merge.

Glancing in the rear-view mirror, her instincts told her that something in the traffic pattern looked awkward. Ahead of her, a long flatbed truck occupied the slow lane. Behind her, a sleek dark blue sedan was almost tailgating her. She'd seen it before—outside the school. A blue flashing police light on the dashboard of the sedan and a siren signalled her to pull over. It was an unmarked police vehicle. She knew she'd been speeding a little, but only for traffic safety reasons.

Accelerating past the heavily-laden flat-bed truck, she was surprised when the truck driver looked directly at her. It was a strange look, not a glance but a calculated assessment. It was a look that stayed with her—and alerted her senses.

Immediately in front, the condesa's access to the hard shoulder was blocked. Accelerating past the traffic travelling in the slow lane, she was forced to travel over a kilometre in the process. The blue flashing light in the dark blue sedan had been switched off, but the vehicle still tailgated her and its siren still sounded. She wanted to throw up her hands in protest—it was almost impossible to do what the police vehicle was instructing her to do. Eventually, at a faster speed than she would have liked, she steered over onto the hard shoulder and began to slow down. The dark blue sedan moved ahead of her, blocking her way. It was an unusual procedure she thought. Then, behind her, she caught sight of the flatbed truck—barrelling at speed towards her in the slow lane. Suddenly, it veered onto the hard shoulder.

She added up the tell-tale signs: it was a set-up.

The road ahead was blocked by the dark blue sedan. Behind her, the closing distance of the flat bed was now dangerously short—and the truck driver was not slowing down. There was a screech of tyres as the dark blue sedan shot forwards, accelerated to safety—leaving her vehicle directly in the path of the heavily laden truck—its horn blaring a deafening blast.

Knowing that her life was in her own hands, the condesa gunned the Fiat's engine. The underpowered engine screeched and lurched forwards, fishtailing as she tried to keep control. She tried not to look in her mirrors but could sense the collision about to happen. With its heavy load, the truck would demolish the Fiat—and her.

The blast of the truck's horn was now continuous. The flatbed was only metres from the back of her vehicle and showing no signs of attempting to slow down. Her foot was hard down on her accelerator. Desperately, she shifted down a gear to gain more speed. She could see the image of the truck driver in her rear-view mirror. It was not a kind face.

Perhaps it was divine intervention. Possibly, the bishop had prayed very earnestly for the results that he and the condesa had discussed over dinner. Whatever the cause, divine or simply good fortune, she was able to keep the Fiat just ahead of the truck. She heard a bang as the truck demolished an exit sign—but it kept after her relentlessly, like a wayward Exocet missile.

Metres ahead, she saw the off-ramp. Gritting her teeth so hard that she later developed a toothache, the condesa managed to shake off the flatbed and accelerate onto a side road. The whole incident had taken less than a minute, although it seemed like hours.

Parked, keeping her engine running, the condesa breathed in deeply and exhaled several times. She was unable to control her shaking. That had been no ordinary road emergency.

It had been an elaborate set-up. She knew for certain now that she had been the target.

Someone was trying to kill her.

A Puzzle

Normally, he wouldn't receive traffic reports.

They rarely crossed Diego's desk. This one was different. It was sent by a female civilian working in transportation services—the staff specialist who months earlier, at his request, had tracked the condesa's Fiat after she'd visited the lodge. Her covering note was brief. She'd kept the Fiat's licence plate number on active file. Yesterday, the vehicle had been involved in an incident on the motorway near La Moraleja. It had been caught on CCTV and reported to her.

She'd pulled the footage. The deputy inspector might want to know about it. The truck driver had reported to police that his brakes had failed. Unfortunately, she had been unable to lift a licence plate number from the dark blue sedan involved.

Looking through the footage, Diego came to the same conclusions as the staff specialist. The condesa had been set up. Fortunately, her presence of mind had probably saved her life. Yet, he wondered why she hadn't reported the incident and filed a complaint.

Diego decided to copy Antonio on the report. They'd been out of contact since he'd visited the USS *Bataan* months earlier.

He felt he owed the Mossos detective a favour or two.

Lab Results

Sitting alone in his office at Mossos Headquarters, Antonio thought about the National Police and wondered about Diego's GEO Group 60. Were they behind the withholding of lab results? If so, why? It was obvious that someone in Madrid was making sure the Mossos wouldn't find out about the spiked detonators. He had the feeling that someone there knew a lot more than they were saying. Without their cooperation, it was going to be difficult for the Mossos to determine who had spiked them.

Robles was on his list, but Antonio crossed out his name. The man was an unrepentant jihadist, and anyway, thought Antonio, he would have needed an accomplice. Daniela? Well, she was a candidate. She would have known about the plan and the timing of the bombing attempt. She'd turned out to be a double agent, and the evidence was that she was closely tied to Robles.

In Syria, she'd helped Jamal. But why would she sabotage the detonators? She had worked at Mossos Headquarters and had friends there. Was that enough motive? Maybe she had been thinking of him ... knowing he'd have been caught in the explosion if the bombing attempt had been successful. He dismissed the thought; it was too absurd—even for Daniela's twisted mind. Besides, she didn't seem likely to have the expertise or the opportunity.

The sabotage meant, of course, that everyone's efforts—his, Xavi's, the bomb squad members'—had been in vain. They were not to know that, and Antonio decided he would sit on the information. Until he had more answers, there was no point in fuelling speculation. Meanwhile, there was other urgent work to do—other leads to follow.

There were more ways than one to skin a cat, as the sergeant had said.

Even if it was an evil, fiendish wildcat named Daniela.

William

"Toni, how's the hunt going?" barked the chief. He wasn't asking a question, thought Antonio. He was demanding positive news.

"We're hopeful of making a breakthrough soon, sir," Antonio replied, invoking the department's standard defensive response.

The chief wasn't having it. "You know that we need results, Toni. I'm getting it in the neck from both governments. They want action. Call me tomorrow—with some real news." He severed the connection.

Antonio called William at home. "Walk me through what you've uncovered on the Andorra connection," he instructed the talented nerd. "Do you have any ideas about where the Andorran outflows of laundered money are going?"

"Funny you should ask, boss. I was working on the transportation angle this afternoon. We have six months of back data. Some traffic patterns are beginning to emerge. The bad guys love their routines, don't they?"

"Tell me about it," said Antonio disdainfully.

"Think of the geography of Andorra; it's fascinating," William continued. "If you were going to move a heavy load of laundered money by road, there are only two main routes out—unless you want to hike over the Pyrénées or take a very minor road, and that would be unsafe. The CG-2 connects with the N-22 into France through El Pas de la Casa. Then there's the N-152, which is a merging of two routes into Spain. Between the French police and ourselves, we mapped all the possibilities. Also, we figured that . . ."

"Give me the goodies, please," Antonio interrupted.

"Facts first or my interpretation, boss?" asked William.

"Go ahead. Give me your theory first," said Antonio. He tried to sound exasperated but smiled as he listened to his young protégé. William worked hard and put in incredibly long hours. Not much in the cyberworld escaped his notice. He was dedicated to Antonio and kept him informed. The geek had a manageable recreational drug habit. In a party place like Barcelona, that was all right.

"I've eliminated the legitimate truck traffic from suspicion," said William. "I'm left with a single conclusion. There's one trucking company that ticks all the boxes. It made numerous visits to our list of suspect banks. It's the most obvious candidate for smuggling money out of Andorra. Also, I've detected spikes in traffic shipments using twin axles and bigger trucks coming out of Andorra. They correlate closely with the announcement of new sanctions on non-compliant banks . . . you know, the new rules about disclosures."

"You mean, you have evidence that when they get spooked—by the fear of discovery—the banks and their questionable customers promptly move their money elsewhere?" asked Antonio.

"Yes, and the trucking company I'm talking about is on that list," said William.

"If you're right, where's it going?"

"Can't be certain, boss. But, if my guess and the CCTV tapes are right, some of it goes initially to a processing plant in a place called La Garriga. That's a famous civil war town; it's full of separatists."

"Whoa, just give me the facts," Antonio cut him off. "Your theory sounds like a bedtime story. I know about La Garriga's history. You've put together a shortlist of trucking firms—possibly crooked firms who have the physical capability to move the gold out of Andorra. Based on that, you're telling me that you've shortlisted a *single* company? That sounds kind of lucky."

"Well, I did some lightweight hacking, just to shorten our longlist. Guesswork really. But some of the French technology guys . . ." William stopped to laugh. "Some of those French guys are cool. They're geniuses. I've been learning a lot from them. We even hacked into Airbus in Toulouse together."

"William!" shouted Antonio. "I'm not interested in your social life or what you do in your spare time. Just reduce it down to something I can understand."

"Boss, I'll make it simple. If you and Xavi set up surveillance on the two addresses that I've just texted you, you'll find out who we think is involved in smuggling gold out of banks in Andorra. And that second ding you just heard on your cell phone? That was from me too. It's a photo of the guy who I think is masterminding the transfers. I got lucky on one of my visits to the darknet. He's also on record as being part of a mafia gang. His younger brother works at a green energy generating facility next door to some kind of monastery at a place called Montserrat.

"You don't have to increase my pay check, boss. Just say thanks when you arrest those guys.

"Call me if there's anything else you need."

CHAPTER 12
Going for Gold

Xavi was impressed.

If William's information gathering techniques could be described as creative, his sleuthing would qualify as inspired. Despite the solar panel factory's innocent-looking façade, William had identified it as a likely centre of money laundering. Xavi soon found that William's hunch was right. For several days, his team of Mossos plainclothes had been tracking every vehicle and person who entered and exited the site at La Garriga.

The factory was located on several hectares, separated from the surrounding farmland by a high security concrete-rendered brick wall and razor wire. Clusters of low-rise buildings could be seen inside the compound. The stake-out team had carried out around-the-clock surveillance. Xavi and a colleague were now sitting inside an innocuous-looking commercial services van, examining photographs and videos from a series of drone flights over the area.

In front of him, a photograph indicated that a large solar panel farm had been constructed on waste ground inside the compound. "They're using the cover of a legitimate business manufacturing solar panels and storage batteries," said a young officer. He indicated an area on the photograph coloured off earlier by a colleague. "These look like storage tanks. That building is for warehousing materials. That's my guess, sir. These ones are shipping facilities for panels and solar batteries being sent to customers. That part of the operation is legitimate."

"What about these buildings?" asked Xavi, pointing to an isolated cluster. "What's that?" he asked, looking closely at a brick chimney.

The young officer peered at the photos. "It's a reduction furnace left over from when this area was manufacturing metal goods a hundred years ago. Back then, they made boilers for the shipping industry and railroads. From the steam being emitted, it looks as though it's been brought back into use. They won't be using fossil fuels." He laughed. "It might be powered by an ecologically efficient steam turbine. Smelting of metals is expensive; it uses a lot of electricity, but they're generating lots of that.

"See this heavy barrier?" he added. "That's an internal security fence. Obviously, they don't want people snooping around there. This is a loading bay for deliveries and shipments." He pointed to a building. "We have photos of everything that goes in and out. We're tracking each vehicle to see what they're carrying. We think there may be a secondary site, not far away."

"Any idea where?" asked Xavi, his voice betraying his eagerness.

Finding a sheet of paper, the officer began to draw a sketch. "Here's a flowchart of what we think is happening, sir. It looks to us as though the solar panel and solar battery business is mostly legitimate, but it's also a front for some illegal operations.

"The gold comes down from Andorra and, we suspect, arrives from other areas of Europe as well. We can't tell, really, because some of it is probably shipped in along with legitimate materials needed to manufacture solar panels and solar batteries. They buy a lot of silicon panels, glass, base metals, plastics, and lithium cobalt oxide. Plus, a lot of electrical cables. Heavy traffic. All legitimate.

"It's perfect for a clandestine operation melting and recasting gold ingots. Lots of trucks, forklifts, and people coming and going. Several containers always on site. It's an important employer of local people, and the local officials really like the solar aspect—it's a green industry, very environmentally friendly.

"What we've discovered is that they ship some items from here to a car battery recycling operation near the airport at El Prat. It doesn't make solar products but seems to be a lead battery repairer and distributor. Nothing wrong with that, of course. They sell their legitimate products everywhere. We've set up a surveillance team to start tracking traffic in and out of those premises.

"That's about all we've got so far, sir. We're working on it 24/7, as you ordered."

"Do we have enough to make arrests?" asked the chief, the anticipation of success spreading across his face.

Antonio and Xavi shook their heads. They were aware of the pressure he was under to get results. "If we can hold on a little longer, sir, our team thinks we have a shot at identifying and bringing in the whole network," said Xavi.

"We have someone on the inside?" questioned the chief.

"No, sir."

"So, we don't really know what their thinking is, what their plans are?" queried the chief, with a heavy frown. "Aren't we taking a bit of a chance? I mean, they could close down the whole operation, and the bad guys would disappear into the sunset. Then we'd have nothing. Don't you have a Plan B? In fact, the more I think about it, I can tell you that I'm not happy. If anything goes wrong, I can't go back to the Generalitat and Madrid, and tell them that we had it within our grasp, only to lose it—again. What else do you have, Toni?"

Antonio knew that the chief was right. If the decision was left to him and Xavi, they would prefer to hold out and try to capture the whole network. The solar panel factory at La Garriga was only part of the operation. If laundered gold was being melted down there, the Mossos needed to know where it was being shipped afterwards. Surveillance of the battery plant near El Prat might answer that question, but Xavi's unit had only just been set up. It might be a day or two before they got any results. Maybe not even then.

At the back of Antonio's mind were two thoughts. He didn't think that anything they'd find by raiding the La Garriga factory would reveal anything about Daniela and the gold she'd stolen. She was far too smart to entrust her gold to a mafia operation. But he knew that the chief needed results—and quickly. He badly needed a photo opportunity—showing that the police were taking action and making progress.

Antonio was aware that he hadn't discussed their options with Xavi. He didn't want to undermine his squad partner's investigation. On this occasion, however, he'd have to do what the chief wanted.

"I think we should organise a raid for tomorrow, sir," Antonio heard himself say. He caught the sharp look that Xavi shot in his direction. "We will need to plan the raid carefully so that nothing goes wrong. That means tomorrow midday at the earliest. In the meantime, sir, Xavi and I are going to take part tonight in the surveillance of the secondary site near El Prat," he improvised. "With luck, we might be able to figure out where the gold is going. We are going to need some warrants, sir," he added. "Even under the terrorism legislation, we have to cover ourselves legally. With your permission, I'll ask Jose Miguel to arrange them."

"Good! Decisive action—that's what I like." The chief beamed.

"Well, I'd better not keep you two if you're going to work the night shift. Just one thing. This raid on the factory at La Garriga—I want the Mossos to handle it. I don't want anyone leaking information to the federal police. This is our turf. By law, because it's the proceeds of a crime, we should be able keep most of what we obtain from the seizures. Got it?" He glared at his two officers. "Keep me informed about tomorrow—and I mean regularly, Toni. I want to be there for the kill. Good evening, gentlemen," he added as he left Antonio's office, clearly now in a buoyant mood.

"What the heck was that about?" asked Xavi when the chief had left. He looked annoyed.

"Sorry, amigo. I should have consulted you before making a decision, but the chief's right. If we allow these guys to slip through the net, there'll be hell to pay. A raid tomorrow at La Garriga is not ideal, but somehow I don't think it's the wrong decision."

"He doesn't want us to bring in the feds," said Xavi. "Not that I care."

"We don't need to. If the feds get involved," said Antonio, "they'll be able to claim ownership of any laundered gold we find. The chief wants to be in control of that."

"And what's all this stuff about us participating in tonight's surveillance of the secondary site near El Prat?" asked Xavi, clearly still unhappy.

"You'll be off duty by then, so I'll do it," said Antonio with a shrug. "Don't worry about it, amigo. The chief is on the warpath; I thought it might buy us some time."

"I won't be off duty. The raid at La Garriga will take time to orchestrate," snapped Xavi with an undisguised glare. "This is unlike you, Toni. What's going on?"

Antonio shrugged his shoulders again and put his hands in the air. "Amigo, if it hasn't escaped your notice, I haven't been very successful recently. I dropped the ball on Daniela. I don't know where the hell she is. None of my other investigations have produced anything. I'm screwing up and I'm due for a bit of luck. Maybe tonight, things will change; I don't know. I just can't keep going like this—it's not fun."

Xavi wasn't about to tell Antonio to suck it up and persevere, but that was how he felt.

Girl On The Run

His buddy was becoming maudlin, and he wondered if he might be suffering from mild depression. He hadn't seen any signs of it before, he reflected. Never in the time they'd grown up together. It could develop later in life. He and Pilar had been talking about Antonio the previous evening. Pilar had met Maria for a coffee, and they'd talked several times by phone.

Maria was still really upset about her night out with Sergio, and the unfortunate incident outside the hotel—bumping into Antonio while still dressed in her clothes from the evening before. She'd told Pilar that she'd called Antonio, texted, and even written a letter to explain. He hadn't replied. Antonio was ghosting her.

It was a tough time, too, for Antonio. Xavi was willing to cut his friend some slack. "All right," he said after a pause. "Here is what I have in mind for tomorrow's raid at La Garriga." He outlined his plans and his partner seemed genuinely impressed.

"Sounds really good, amigo. You head up the raid. I'll just tag along," said Antonio. "Same for tonight at the stake-out. You're the field officer-in-command after all. It's your show."

Taking a back seat was not normally in Antonio's character. This time, he seemed anxious to follow, not to lead, thought Xavi. Maybe some success at tonight's stake-out at El Prat might help break him out of his despondent mood. If not, the raid on the solar panel factory at La Garriga tomorrow would be sure to produce some fireworks.

Hopefully, it wouldn't all blow up in their faces.

Stake-Out at El Prat

Xavi had decided on a small surveillance team to keep the battery-recycling operation near El Prat under observation. The two squaddies on the night shift were surprised when they got the call from their captain warning them that an inspector and his deputy from Homicide were about to turn up.

The four men settled down inside the unmarked van, which looked like it had seen better days. "Don't be fooled by this old wreck, sir," said the younger officer with a toothy grin. "It's fitted with a V-6 and fuel injectors. It can stay ahead of most things on the road."

"Let's hope we don't need that tonight," said Xavi. "What have you guys picked up so far?"

"Seems like a legitimate operation, sir. Just a few trucks going in and out. Mostly old car batteries for recycling and refurbishing. They deal in solar storage batteries too. They recycle the lead plates and battery acid as well. The acid is corrosive and a hazardous cargo. What exactly is it we are looking for here?" he asked.

"Not sure," Xavi lied. "We want to maintain surveillance on where they ship things to from here. Then we'll find out what they're smuggling." He glanced at the squaddie, who seemed unconvinced. There was no need to tell them everything, Xavi had decided. He looked like an honest lad. But Xavi knew that word soon gets around on the street.

"We have two officers around the back, sir," said the senior squaddie, "just in case our suspects spot us and try to flee. We can call for backup. They'll arrive here within a few minutes if we need them."

"Who's been tailing the trucks that leave here?" asked Antonio. "Where do they go?"

"To get out of here, sir, they have to join the autovia—even if they're going to local destinations. We have unmarked cars waiting for them—two parked at a service station for trucks travelling east. Two others are parked ready to pick up westbound vehicles. If it appears that the bad guys are travelling long distance, we hand over to our highway patrols, sir. It's a slick operation. We've done it before." He glared at Antonio, no doubt wondering why the senior detective officer was really there, thought Xavi.

Xavi witnessed the unspoken exchange and thought it was a pity. In the old days, Antonio had been one of the most popular officers on the force—always joking around with his colleagues. Silently, he cursed Daniela.

Glancing at the building, he wanted to take a walk and look around. Better not, he decided. It was an industrial area, and no one except for an occasional moto rider passed through. A lone pedestrian might draw attention and spook the suspects.

Just then, they saw the headlights of a slow-moving truck heading towards the entrance gate. As it passed by, they could see it was laden with a heavy cargo. The truck driver was being cautious as he neared his destination. On his approach, he must have made a phone call, thought Xavi, because the factory's heavy metal gates swung open immediately to allow the truck inside. Just as quickly, they closed and the street fell back into darkness.

"Well, that delivery is well outside normal hours," said the senior squaddie. "That doesn't make it illegal—just suspicious. I mean, it's not as though it's a high-value cargo they've hauled halfway across Europe. It's just a local delivery. Why would they be working overtime hours on a low-value product like lead batteries?"

Antonio voiced his agreement. He was starting to feel better, being back out on the street with the surveillance boys. It was exciting. "You got the licence plate . . .?" he started to ask Xavi, but his friend was ahead of him. The ownership check of the truck was already being run through their database.

"Nothing irregular," he said to Antonio moments later, sharing the ownership details shown on his device. "Everything seems above board. This could be a long boring night," he added. "Unless we catch a break."

They didn't have long to wait. Soon, the gates opened again and a different truck—much newer and electrically powered—pulled silently onto the road. It looked sturdy, and it, too, was heavily laden.

"I think we'll get back to our own vehicle and follow this one," Antonio said to the senior squaddie. "I've got a hunch it may be interesting. Tell your colleagues we are assuming pursuit. Here's my mobile number, if anything happens back here." Seconds later, he and Xavi climbed out of the darkened surveillance vehicle and ran up the road—following the truck's quickly disappearing tail lights. Their car managed to catch up with the truck as it approached the autovia travelling east.

"He's taking the B23 northwards towards Montserrat," said Xavi, a few minutes later. "Holy Saints! Those electric vehicles certainly can accelerate smoothly." For the next half hour, he and Antonio followed the truck—dropping back from time to time when there were no exits to avoid being detected. Antonio closed back up on the truck when they approached turnoffs. He'd recalled William's mention of Montserrat.

Eventually, the truck signalled and pulled into a service area. "It can't be to recharge that thing, can it?" asked Xavi with a laugh. It appeared that the driver was buying a soft drink and a sandwich. He came back out, then seemed to change his mind and headed for the washroom.

"Give me a minute," said Xavi, jumping out of Antonio's vehicle. Soon he was back in their car, sporting a big grin.

"What was that about?" asked Antonio.

"Tracking devices." Xavi smiled, opening his palm to show one to his partner. "Just in case we lose him."

"You had the foresight to bring those along, amigo? I'm impressed."

"It's not as good as the onboard diagnostic models, but it will do tonight if we need it," said Xavi, placing the tracking display screen on Antonio's dashboard.

Fifteen minutes later, the slow-moving truck, struggling under the weight of its cargo, switched to gasoline and powered at an improved speed up the mountain switchbacks leading to the monastery at Montserrat.

"The monks and businesses up here are very ecologically conscious," said Antonio. "That's probably why the trucking firm is using an EV. What I'm really interested in is what kind of cargo that guy is carrying. It could be legitimate, but the heavy load might indicate they are hauling gold. I guess it could be solar panel batteries too. They use a lot of them up here, I read somewhere. You think we may be in luck tonight, amigo?"

As they approached the monastery, Antonio parked his car in a deserted coach stop. "Let's continue on foot, Xavi," he said, starting to sprint. "That truck can't go any further. The road ends here."

Above them, to their right, the magnificent Benedictine Abbey of Santa Maria de Montserrat loomed heavily out of the darkness—lit by landscaping floodlights, giving it even more mystical permanence. It was late. The tourists were gone, or asleep, and the small community seemed deserted. The abbot and monks, their devotions completed, had retired for the night. The monastery and dorms watched silently over the steep sides of the mountain, guarding the valley below.

Running, they were just in time to see the truck reverse silently into a narrow space. Drawing his handgun, Antonio dodged inside just as the automated garage doors were about to close. Xavi, gun in hand, followed closely behind. The bright lights of the truck and banks of fluorescents stretching across the high-ceilinged room almost blinded them.

"Get the driver," instructed Antonio. "Don't let him use his phone to raise the alarm."

Antonio dodged around the vehicle and headed in the direction of a fat, ugly man with large muscles who was starting up a forklift truck and heading to the truck's tailgate doors. The man hadn't seen him. Antonio pulled him to the ground, yanking his arms behind his back. Keeping the big man's face down on the floor with his knee in his back, Antonio strapped his hands with zip tie handcuffs and stuffed a rag hard into his mouth. Using another zip tie, he bound the man's ankles tightly and looped the cord through the first. It was a standard police technique, guaranteed to keep the man immobile. He searched the man's pockets and confiscated his phone.

Spinning around, Antonio searched for movement—confirming that no one else was in the room. From the corner of his eye, he noted that Xavi had strapped the driver to the steering wheel of the truck and placed a piece of tape over his mouth. Antonio gestured towards a large closed door, and Xavi nodded.

They moved quickly towards it, observing that it was marked with several warning signs: *"Peligro Electricidad"* and *"Corrosive."* Handgun off safety, Antonio nodded to Xavi and threw open the door. It opened into a cavernous room without windows. It was an amazing sight. Several hundred industrial-size batteries were stored neatly in numbered lines across the concrete floor. Most were connected by wiring to what the officers figured must be transformers, inverters, and other control equipment.

There was a heavy electrical buzz in the room. By the far wall, a man in a white laboratory coat was sitting on a stool studying some papers. He had his back to them. Within a minute, he too was wrestled to the ground and handcuffed. He yelled loudly until Xavi hit him hard across the mouth.

"Let's take a look," said Antonio, examining the area. In a separate windowless room, which seemed to be carved into the solid rock of the mountain, they found vertical stacks of batteries. Evidently, it was a storage area and, with the constantly cool temperature of the rock face, probably ideal for the purpose.

"What the hell are you doing, *chingados?*" yelled the man they'd trussed up. "It's a generating room supplying current to the buildings. This is police brutality. You're going to regret it when my boss finds out." They ignored him and continued to search the area.

"It looks legitimate," said Xavi. He was beginning to doubt his partner's swift and aggressive action. But Antonio was walking through the nests of batteries, sidestepping the complex wiring which seemed to be everywhere. "Why aren't these connected?" he asked the man who'd yelled at them.

"Fuck off," came a swift reply.

Xavi, standing close to the man, took out his gun and thrust the end of the barrel into the man's mouth. "Answer him," he barked at the now terrified man.

"They're stand-by batteries," he spluttered. "We connect them up when the electrical charge from the others drops—they're called rotators. Just watch out for those connecting wires. We can't allow a sudden drop in the current." He nodded his head to where a series of dials indicated the amperage being generated and the drawdown demand from the circuits to the buildings.

"Can you untie me now?" he asked. "Please."

They ignored him.

"Xavi," said Antonio a few minutes later, "give me a hand over here. Lift up this battery. Then lift up this one. What do you think, amigo?" he asked, with a triumphant twinkle in his eye.

"Hell, they're both heavy—but this one is much heavier than the other," said his partner, gently placing the batteries back onto the floor.

"Try these," said Antonio, indicating a set of batteries not far away.

"Same thing," said Xavi. "Why the difference in weight?"

Antonio didn't reply but picked up one of the unwired batteries. With effort, he carried it to the side of the room.

"Hey, you can't do that," yelled the man on the floor. "You'll screw up our generation cycle."

Glancing around, Antonio saw what he was looking for. He grabbed a fire axe from its holder and stood legs spread apart over the battery. "Stand back," he said to Xavi, as he swung the axe high into the air.

"Hey, don't!" protested the man. "Those things are bloody expensive."

It took Antonio several swings before he had cracked open the thick plastic case of the battery. The man lying trussed up on the ground looked scared, and the reason why was soon evident. The outer coating had split open revealing its contents . . . pure yellow gold, gleaming where the axe head had sliced across the metal.

"Holy shit," exclaimed Xavi. "How did you know?" he asked.

"Remember our science classes at school, amigo? We learned that gold weighs more than lead." He gestured around the room. I think we'll find that the batteries painted with a blue dot like this are just cuckoos in the nest—*los cucos estanen el nido*, as we say. This place is a legitimate storage station for solar power generation. But it also stores laundered gold. It's ingenious, really. Who would have guessed?"

"Holy shit," said Xavi again, counting up the batteries with blue dots. "There must be over fifty of them here."

"Take a closer look inside the storage room we just went in," said Antonio. "I'm guessing there are hundreds altogether." Picking up the plastic cover he'd broken open, he pointed to a small metal label attached to the outside. "See this, amigo?" he asked. "That's a code number. It's just like a bank account number. Each one of these belongs to someone. This place is a deposit bank. I'll wager they charge the owners a significant fee for storage. It's a private and illegal bank—for laundered gold. Its operations are very cleverly masked by a legitimate and eco-friendly solar electricity facility." He laughed. "They probably make money on that too. You'd better check on our friends out there," added Antonio, pulling out his phone.

"Calling it in to the chief?" asked Xavi, who was surprised to see his partner shake his head.

"No, I'm calling Diego," said Antonio in a matter-of-fact tone.

"What?" questioned Xavi, looking stunned.

"I'm making an executive decision," replied Antonio, as his call got through. He spoke for a few minutes and rang off.

Xavi still looked stunned. "Hell, Toni. There's a fortune in laundered gold up here. Why bring in the feds?"

"Politics and prudence, amigo," said Antonio. "I've just agreed by phone with Diego that his people can take the credit for this raid. In turn, he's agreed to let the Mossos have an exclusive on the La Garriga site. By the way, we had better reschedule the raid for tonight. I'll have to let the chief know. He will want to get our people to arrange some media conferences for early tomorrow. Of course, he will deliver the good news to the president tonight.

"Now before Diego's people get here, we need to pump these goons for information. We want to know what they can tell us about the La Garriga factory. Don't be soft on them, amigo. We need all the intelligence we can force out of them. We can't afford to screw up our opportunity. After all, we have to outdo the feds." He smiled.

"Let's see now. There's two million euros worth of gold in each of the phony solar batteries—about four ingots. Each ingot being about half a million euros," said Antonio, doing a quick mental calculation. "We counted fifty of them on the floor, and maybe two hundred in that storage room. It's like a bank vault in there. Diego's National Police unit is going to be delighted. We've just handed those boys a haul of over half a billion euros in laundered drug cartel and terrorist gold. That should make Madrid feel good. They will arrest the criminals and recover the loot. This part of it anyway. We get the other part—and hopefully we'll get to keep it in Catalunya. *Esta bien, si?*" he asked, high-fiving Xavi.

Striding over to the trussed-up man on the floor, Antonio dragged him to his feet. He was still protesting his innocence. "I didn't have anything to do with it," he howled.

Antonio kneed the man hard in the testicles. "If you don't want to spend a lot of time in jail, you'd better talk—and fast, *caballero*.

"See what you can get out of the others," he said to Xavi. "Diego's local people will be here within an hour. We have to pump these goons dry. Then we have to drive like hell before those other birds fly the nest. "Good work, amigo," he added.

Xavi grinned happily.

This was much more like the old Antonio.

News Conference

The media was invited, and they came out in large numbers.

The chief tried to look serious. After all, he reflected, busting a major money-laundering operation involved handing out some harsh federal indictments and the prospect of criminal trials. But if you ignored the deliberate downturn of his mouth and serious face, you could tell from the twinkle in his eye that he was having a wonderful day. Standing alongside his Mossos colleagues and several federal police chiefs, he beamed. Leaning towards Claudia, he shook her hand with vigour—to the delight of the excited scrum of reporters and cameramen.

"Feds and Catalan Police Work Together: Millions in Illegal Gold Seized," said one newspaper's headline later that day, while another showed a photograph of the battery that Antonio had smashed—revealing the gleaming gold. *"Montserrat Strikes Gold,"* said another, with an editorial lauding the new era of collaboration between the two governments. A Madrid newspaper declaring *"Hope Yet for Catalunya to Remain in Spain"* was the chief's favourite.

"Where's all that money going? Are you guys in Madrid going to pocket all of it? Can we have some?" shouted one comedian, to cynical laughter from the media scrum.

Hovering at the back of the media room, Antonio, Xavi, and several of the other arresting officers raised their eyebrows as the chief, in his speech, upgraded the role he'd played. Somehow, his heavy dinner at a restaurant the previous evening had been forgotten. The chief revised his absentee role to an active one. Yes, he had been part of the raiding party, he informed the media. It was evident that he'd pulled off achievements that would have taxed the endurance of even the fittest of young squaddies.

As they left the building, Antonio said to Xavi. "The chief's happy, Barcelona is delighted, and Madrid is gloating. Now perhaps we can get on with the real work.

"Let's find that bitch Daniela."

Banco de Familia Tarragona

Antonio had a feeling that his luck was changing, for the better.

He'd received a call from Ramon at the Terrorist Financing Prevention Unit. Hearing Ramon's voice, he'd immediately thought of Aurelia. He had to force himself to concentrate on what the government's money-laundering man had to say.

"Nothing definitive, Toni," said Ramon. "I just thought I'd tell you. It's more of a progress report than anything else, but it might turn into a helpful lead. As you know, our unit screens all Spanish banks as a matter of routine—regularly these days. We're constantly on the lookout for unusual activity. Well, there's one bank in particular, a family bank, that I want to talk to you about. You should be careful. It's well connected and quite prestigious—so tread lightly would be my advice.

"Have you heard of the Banco de Familia Tarragona? It's owned by Nicolas Julio de Granada, the Marquis of Tarragona. Like a lot of the smaller banks, his business was scorched during the financial crisis. It recovered after the government bailout of the banking sector—lucky for them. But it seems that the marquis made some unwise investments soon afterwards. The scuttlebutt was that he was trying to make a killing financing a large number of construction projects. Most of them turned out to be scams.

"Anyway, about a year ago, we had signals that Banco de Familia Tarragona was running into cash flow problems. A month ago, it seemed like it might go under. A complete bankruptcy, wiping out his family's personal wealth too. He'd been careless, mortgaging his personal assets, and those of his wife, to renew some interbank loans and extend credit to some dubious borrowers.

"Then, a big surprise. He received new financing—a large amount of new funds. The official account is that his friends gathered around and clubbed in to help him out. They are in the form of repayable loans, so he doesn't lose control and ownership. We think the official account is bogus. Anyway, he met all the covenants. The bank's balance sheet improved significantly overnight and the marquis has been able to meet the bank's liquidity requirements—just in time."

"So, overnight, his problems went away?" said Antonio. "What makes you suspect it wasn't legitimate?"

"We can't prove otherwise, Toni, at this point. It may be completely legitimate. However, we have flagged it for greater scrutiny. It seemed to have happened very quickly."

"And you think it might involve money laundering?"

"I don't know that, Toni. We haven't dived in deeply enough yet. The old saying, you know . . . where there's smoke, there's fire. My call is just to keep you informed."

"Thanks, Ramon. I appreciate the heads-up. Let me know if anything else develops. By the way, what was the amount of money involved? How much did it take to bail out the Banco de Familia Tarragona on this occasion?"

"It's hard to be precise unless we get a closer look at his books," said Ramon. "We estimate that around six hundred and fifty million in fresh funding was injected overnight into his bank. He was easily able to meet his cash call requirements."

"Six hundred and fifty million?" asked Antonio.

"Yes. It could be a chance event—just a normal commercial transaction."

"Thanks, Ramon." Antonio called off and sat thinking about what he'd just learned. It didn't take a rocket scientist to figure out the math. Six hundred and fifty million was the amount of cash they'd estimated Daniela had stolen from Aladdin's Cave.

It seemed like a rather fortuitous coincidence.

After he rang off, Ramon made another call. It never harmed to cover one's tracks, he thought. Besides, his contact in the government was a senior person—well connected, and that was always useful. He told him about his suspicions about Nicolas, providing much the same information as he'd just provided to Antonio.

"Thank you," said the government person. "I won't forget this."

Ramon put down the handset of his secure landline and smiled with satisfaction. He considered it a good day's work. He liked to be helpful, and it was always good to have a few credits among the rich and powerful.

William

He had been trolling the web.

Bored with its mundaneness, William's intuition led him to a deep crevice inside the darknet. His thinking at that moment was driven by something Xavi had said to him weeks earlier about Daniela. Xavi's off-the-cuff remark had led William to a so-far-unanswered question: "If Daniela wanted to escape from Spain, where would she go?"

Figuring that Syria was a strong possibility, he recalled that was where she'd met Jamal. So, William set some electronic trap lines for her, and a few chatter snags, in case she tried to use any of the communication conduits she'd favoured in the past. His efforts had yielded nothing so far.

The high from his most recent dose had passed, but he was still on a plateau of creative exploration. Russian intervention in Syria was foremost in his mind. It led him to check the communications traffic in and out of their air force base near Latakia. Even when he had worked in China, Russian language skills had eluded William. But a darknet acquaintance in Kazakhstan was a genius—and had offered help. Her handle was deceptive, and William guessed from her several exploratory transmissions that she was trans. Silently, he'd wished her well—and good luck. Her location was not the most tolerant in the world for them.

He glanced again at her most recently encrypted message sent to him in a trusted-host modified dialect. It was clumsy but workable, William reflected. What he saw caused him to download the text and go offline—immediately. He'd instantly recognised the importance of the intercept he'd just made. It was a Russian military transmission from its Khmeimim Air Base in Latakia to Moscow Control.

Roughly translated by his friend, it revealed that permission was being sought to assist Daniela Balmes's return to Spain.

In a separate portal, using a sanitized laptop, he asked his contact to continue her surveillance. He was out of luck. Her terse reply said, *"Fancy Bear on my trail."* It was a reference to the infamous GRU cyber espionage group APT28—and indicated that her activity had been detected. The channel had been shut down. Not wanting to risk using his phone, William took the elevator to Antonio's office.

"The Russians are helping Daniela get back to Spain," said William. "That's all I know. I wasn't able to get any intel on how, or when, she will arrive. Sorry, boss!"

"We can't monitor every flight that lands in Spain," said the chief. "Madrid would never agree to it. Besides, if it is Daniela, she may fly to somewhere else in Europe and then sneak over the Spanish border. Now, if we knew how and when she's getting back—and who is helping her . . ." His voice trailed off, and he looked disappointed.

Antonio wasn't prepared to give up. "I doubt that anyone connected to the Syrian regime is helping her. So, who the hell is? Maybe the Russians are creating a smokescreen. There may be another agenda at work here. We are still working in the dark, sir."

"Look, Toni. There isn't a lot of political pressure on us any more—to find her, I mean," said the chief. "Both governments are happy now that we've shut down the mafia's money-laundering operations. Let me be clear, I don't want you spending your time investigating Daniela Balmes."

"Sir," Antonio began to protest, "we still haven't recovered the huge stash of gold and currency she stole from Aladdin's Cave. This information from the Russian intercept is the best chance yet we've had to get a fix on her location and potentially the money."

"I don't know, Toni." The chief shook his head. "It's been going on for a long time. Madrid has lost its enthusiasm for chasing her and recovering the gold and money from Aladdin's Cave. In fact, we've been ordered to withdraw from the case. Besides, we just don't have the resources to keep this investigation going—not on a full-time active basis anyway. Look, I'll give you until next week. After that, you have to get back to your duties running Homicide. Understood?"

Antonio was tempted to tell the chief he'd be willing to take a leave of absence and pursue the case in his own time. But he said nothing. It would only confirm to everyone what he himself knew—that he was on a personal vendetta.

Cast your nets sparingly, his instincts told him. Daniela had numerous routes to get into Spain undetected. What he needed to figure out was why she was coming back, and where she was heading. It must have something to do with the gold.

If he knew where the gold was, he could set up a trap.

He had no inkling that he was about to get one—from an unexpected source.

Suspicions

Antonio's grandfather had been thinking about Susan Garcia. She was a lovely girl, he admitted, and very thoughtful. Yet, he had a nagging feeling that something didn't quite add up.

There were a few things that bothered him about her. Several times, he'd thought that her Spanish language skills were better than she'd made out. A few phrases that only native speakers would use. By itself, that meant nothing—after all, her parents in New Mexico were Hispanic, she'd told him.

She was articulate and confident for her young age, and quite worldly. There were a lot of other small things, too, that he'd wondered about. Little things, not significant on their own. Still . . .

He had a lot of time on his hands. A lot of time to think. Too much, perhaps.

The old man thought he might check out some of his suspicions. From his army days, he still had a few useful contacts. He'd been an officer in the Mossos too, and there were a few old hands who would still know him. But he didn't want to bother any of Antonio's friends.

That morning, he'd received an email reply to one of his enquiries. Yes, his contact said, Susan Garcia was from New Mexico. She had a younger brother who was handicapped and the details about her parents were true. His source had been able to find out that Susan Garcia had been in Spain some months ago, on a cycling tour. She'd returned home early.

Antonio's grandfather had thought about the reply from his contact. It wasn't perfectly accurate, but most of it fitted the story that Susan had told him. Prior to leaving, she'd ridden her bike over to his house to tell him that her dad was ill and that she and her brother would have to return to New Mexico. Susan had told him that she'd keep the rental house going—planning to return as soon as she could to continue with her painting and art studies.

His contact said that he hoped the information would help. He offered to keep checking.

Before Susan had left the cottage, Antonio's grandfather had offered to drop by and make sure the property remained secure. She'd said there was no need. The place was safely locked up and it would be fine until she got back. "But thank you," she'd said. "You're very sweet."

"Walk?" he asked Trieste, and the dog leapt into action. "No, not that way," he shouted, as the dog started down the path. "We're not going on our usual route today."

Daniela's cottage was locked up and everything seemed fine, thought the old man as he approached the building. He felt guilty prowling around her place. After all, he was just an old man with a suspicious mind. He was about to turn back, but thought he might circle around the back to make sure. All the windows were shuttered and secure—the actions of a responsible tenant, he observed.

Peering through the shuttered blinds of the main room, he was able to make out the shapes of several paintings. Two were on easels, and obviously a work in progress. Paint brushes were still on a palette and tubes of paint lay to one side. With the sudden news of her dad's illness, it was understandable. Mostly likely, she and her brother would have been in a hurry to get home.

He checked the driveway to the garage. There were faint tread marks—evidently, the tyre marks of a large vehicle. It was strange, he felt. Susan had not owned a vehicle, and the property owner had not been there for a long time.

He scolded himself for his suspicions. Once a policeman, always a policeman, he said to his dog as they made their way back home.

"I'm too old for this," he muttered.

Two days later, he received another reply from his contact. Not much fresh information, his contact apologised. But he was attaching a copy of a photograph of Susan Garcia that had appeared in her town's local paper in New Mexico. She'd won a cycling trophy, the man added.

Downloading the paper clipping, Antonio's grandfather reached for his reading glasses and peered again at the photograph. Susan Garcia was smiling, holding a trophy high over her head. She appeared fit and happy. But one thing for sure: it certainly was not the young woman who had been masquerading as Susan Garcia here in Catalunya.

The Susan Garcia he knew was an impostor. A total fraud.

He found his cell phone and called his grandson.

Crime Scene

Not far from the cottage belonging to Antonio's grandfather, blue lights were flashing.

White-and-blue squad cars were moving at fast speed in his direction. There was no indication of the vehicles, not at first. The sound of their oscillating sirens was drowned out by a strong summer breeze blowing away from him down the valley. Trieste, slumbering on the cool of the tiled floor, heard them first. Her ears perked. Getting to her feet, she barked. Once, then several more times.

The old man heard them too and got up from his kitchen table. Glancing at his watch, he noted that it had taken the Mossos less than five minutes to get units on site after he'd made his call to Antonio. Soon after, a text message arrived from his grandson saying he'd be flying in by helicopter. He'd be there soon. "Stay safe," Antonio had instructed his grandfather. "She's dangerous."

Mossos officers from the local garrison arrived first. Their first action was to surround and seal off Daniela's rented cottage. They took down the door. Satisfied that the place was unoccupied, the police sealed off a wider area and began a systematic search. Within a few minutes, the forensics team arrived in a series of specialised vans. In combination, the vehicles formed a travelling laboratory. Plastic covers for shoes, gloves, overalls, and honeycomb hairnets made them look like surgeons busy at work in an operating room.

Xavi and Antonio's helicopter arrived thirty minutes later, landing on a nearby flat strip of farmland. Met by a local Mossos squad car, they were driven down a fork in the dirt road leading to the old man's house. Antonio's grandfather was waiting outside with Trieste. "Yes, that's Susan," he said when Antonio showed him a photo of Daniela—but his grandson already knew it. Satisfied that his grandfather wasn't in danger, he posted two armed squaddies outside and drove the remaining short distance to Daniela's cottage.

"Next door to your granddad," said Xavi, as their vehicle bumped and lurched over the unpaved dirt track. "What the hell is she up to?"

Antonio wasn't going to voice what had been on his mind since he'd received the call from his grandfather. He knew that Daniela was doing it to get to him. She had been living right under his nose all this time, the bitch. His stomach churned as he thought of what she might have done. At least his grandfather was safe now. The thought of the alternatives made his blood boil. She was calculating and intrusive. How dare she involve his family!

As a hideout, he had to concede that the cottage was ideally located. From its vantage point on a slight rise, all roads leading to the place could be easily observed and monitored by the occupants. Yet, it was hidden from observation by a grove of widely spaced trees. Strategically, she was very smart, he admitted.

He and Xavi walked the immediate area. They were met by the senior forensics officer as they approached the cottage. "Sir, they certainly weren't trying to hide anything, that's for sure. There are prints and DNA everywhere inside. Hair in the showers too. Their clothes are here, and some oil paintings. Even some video games—which tells us something about who was here. There's non-perishable food in the cupboards. They intend to come back, I think.

"A couple items of interest, sir," he continued. "We've found bloodstains on the tiled floor near the kitchen. Two sets. We'll test them in the lab in a few minutes."

"We want to look around inside," Xavi told the officer. "And we need you to leave the crime scene exactly as it was when you found it. You know the procedure. If she comes back, we'll have a stake-out ready for her."

Antonio and Xavi put on shoe covers, separately walking the place—stepping around the army of forensic specialists, floor markers, and police photographers. They met again outside with the forensics officer. "We found these in the garage, sir," he told them. "There are minute traces of gold on these work gloves. If I had to guess, I'd say they've been used to lift gold ingots. Oh, we've found two recent sets of fingerprints," he added. "A woman's and a man's. There are some older prints, too, but they've been there for a long time. I've eliminated them from any connection to the recent occupants.

"You might want to hold onto this, sir." He held out several enlarged photos of the tyre marks of a vehicle. "By the width and tread, I'd say it was a pretty heavy-duty vehicle. I'll try to get a better description for you when my people are finished with their other work." He held up two sample bags containing a woman's shoes and another pair. "I'd say the occupants were a young woman in her twenties, and a boy in his late teens."

"You can tell all of that just from two pairs of shoes?" asked Xavi.

"Not really, sir. There are personal items in the bedrooms and the bathrooms. They help us construct and fill in a complete picture. They were sleeping together too," he added, failing to notice the stiffening of Antonio's body. "I'm still puzzled by the blood stains we found on the kitchen floor. Some of hers and some of his. We see some strange things at crime scenes, as you gentlemen know. I'm stretching the known facts here, but it almost seems like they were carrying out some kind of ritual."

The two officers nodded their thanks and left instructions with the CSO to advise them when the scene could be vacated. "From the outside, I want it to look like no one's been here," Xavi told him. "That only matters from the outside. Forensics can leave the dusted prints and things inside. They're a giveaway that we've been here. It doesn't matter. If those two come back, we won't be giving them time to go back inside.

"What do you think, Toni?" Xavi asked. "We can stake out the property from those trees over there and from across the fields. It would help if we knew when exactly she was arriving, but we don't have that information."

273

"I've been thinking about it, Xavi. My bet is that she's going to be back in Catalunya for the anniversary of the referendum," said Antonio. "Not because she's nostalgic—she's not a separatist—but because the streets will be crowded with people. She will use the demonstrations as cover for whatever she's trying to do."

"There'll be lots of police and security forces as well," added Xavi. "We'll be busy and preoccupied in the city."

"It plays into Daniela's hands," agreed Antonio. "She's already proven she can elude even the most elaborate and widespread of police dragnets. The referendum anniversary is in two days. Obviously, she hasn't been here yet. It could mean she's still on her way. I've got an address for the agent who leased this place to her. Let's give him a visit. See if he knows anything."

"We should organise a few female officers and plainclothes to circulate locally—see if any of the other neighbours know anything," he added. "Try the village too. Oh, I don't want any news leaking out about this raid. I want it to look like it never happened. Close down any media enquiries. Make up a plausible story and shut down any local gossip as much as you can. I'm going to take a closer look around my grandfather's place. I've got a suspicion that Daniela had other reasons for locating herself and the boy here."

Apart from harassing me, he thought but didn't voice it.

It took Antonio only a few minutes to figure it out.

The tyre marks found by the forensics people at Daniela's cottage were a dead giveaway, he thought. They indicated that a powerful vehicle had been used to haul a heavy load. After a quick inspection, he found traces of an identical tread alongside his grandfather's empty garage.

Pulling up the oil-stained old wooden boards from the inspection pit, he found the gold.

"Aladdin's Cave," he said to himself and called Xavi.

"We're in business, amigo," he told him. "Let's get a photographer down here—someone who can keep his mouth shut. I don't want news of this discovery to get out. I'm certain now. She's on her way here."

He allowed himself a rare smile.

"It's taken a year—but now we'll catch the bitch."

CHAPTER 13
Khmeimim Air Base
Latakia, Syria

Jamal had grown a beard.

His peppered grey facial hair made him look elegant, Daniela thought with pride. With her help, he had achieved impressive physical changes over the past months. Several times a day, they had worked out in a private gym at the Russian air base. With exercise, and first-rate nutrition, he'd put on weight and muscle.

His emaciated frame from months earlier had given way to the muscular physique that Daniela recalled from their first meeting. He was a very good-looking man: memorable and attractive. Anywhere else in the world, he would project the physical appeal of a celebrity. Except for his leg, he showed few visible signs of his injuries.

Every day, they spent time together walking and talking. For security, they were restricted to their private exercise area. "You look like a young man again, Jamal," she said, kissing him. "Maybe I should be jealous that other women will throw themselves at you. You look so handsome."

Jamal liked her praise. With fewer stresses in his life, his personality regained its charm. He had regained his sense of humour. Over the months during his recovery, they had talked secretly about Aladdin's Cave. He'd been impressed by her resourcefulness and the size of the stolen fortune. "One billion euros, Daniela," he had whispered in astonishment. "I am sad that Mustapha was not able to achieve his vision. He is a true believer and a friend. For the jihad, it is indeed a world of riches sent to us by Allah. I must think of how we can use this unexpected gift."

Daniela had respected that Jamal had not pressed her for details of where the money was hidden. She knew that Yussef would have confirmed to Jamal all the details of how they'd stolen and secured it. Of course, Yussef didn't know what had happened to the euros taken by the banker, Nicolas. She needed to keep that ace card up her sleeve. As for the gold, the young Arab boy knew exactly where it was hidden.

She fully expected that Yussef would denounce her to Jamal as a spy. It was regrettable, but in the scheme of things, it didn't concern her excessively. Jamal would be aware that the boy distrusted all infidels. He would know that the boy had a strong distaste for self-determined women. He was a youth, rabidly focused on a violent jihad—and finding his brother.

Jamal could make up his own mind. He would regard Yussef as useful to his plans, she hoped, but would disregard the boy's extreme views about her. Jamal knew better and would discount Yussef's denunciations and criticisms. The boy's account of what had occurred in Spain and on their journey would give Daniela more credibility with Jamal than she herself could achieve. This outcome was what she'd planned; it was what she needed, she reminded herself. It was a question of playing the probabilities—balancing what people wanted to believe, and their suspicions of her, against what she actually did to support the jihad.

Daniela had adopted the role of nurse and caregiver, never once probing for information about Jamal's plans. She reflected that he was a survivor in a land where ordinary citizens, the majority of whom were decent and law-abiding people, were secondary to the politics of power. Political intrigues were woven every day into a fabric of lies, deceit, and duplicity. It was the same everywhere.

Despite his protests that he was just a simple surgeon, and a reluctant soldier, she knew that he was also a shrewd politician. He was perfectly capable of turning the cards he'd been dealt to the benefit of his beliefs and the jihad. Now, assured of the immense riches of Aladdin's Cave and the Russians' protection, his hand of influence had become unexpectedly strong.

She had no doubt that if it became necessary, Jamal could be as duplicitous as the most conniving and cunning of his people. He was an old and experienced fox with the ability to sniff the winds of change and an instinct for how the game would play out.

After all, she thought, for millennia, this land had given root to myriads of intermingled tribal and family loyalties, jealousies, and almost constant violent conflicts. It had survived the horrors of countless infidel invaders and despotic rulers. Yet, it retained and cultivated a deep and unwavering spirituality. Robles believed in its power. He had told her many times when she was growing up that with enlightened leadership, Islamic spirituality would help unite its peoples.

Daniela felt reassured knowing that Jamal's actions would remain true to the values she knew he held close to his heart and soul. She was aware too that at any time, he was equally capable of redefining who were his friends. And his enemies.

She didn't want to be on his wrong side.

Someone at the Russian air base must have succeeded in smuggling a message to Jamal, Daniela suspected. Almost overnight, his demeanour had changed. There was a new sense of urgency in his voice. He questioned her several times about the money. "Tell me again, Daniela, what must we do to transfer the funds so that the jihad can control them?"

She guessed that most likely he'd received instructions from al-Qaeda high command. She'd had suspicions that over the past several months Jamal had been smuggling out messages—telling the high command what she had told him about the bearer bonds and the stash of gold. Now he was being told to seize the prize.

"The bearer bonds are in the safety deposit at the bank in Cyprus," she answered—providing the same information and advice that she'd done several times before. "They are the easiest. They can be transferred quickly and without fuss. Think of them as liquid funds, Jamal. They're almost like cash but much safer. Banknotes can be withdrawn from circulation; bearer bonds cannot—provided that they are issued by a bank that is solvent and able to pay. Believe me, they will be honoured by the Bank of Tarragona. I promise you."

Jamal seemed satisfied and asked about the gold.

"That is more difficult to transfer to the jihad," said Daniela. "To retrieve the gold, we will need to work much harder. It, too, is worth a fortune."

"It is a tempting opportunity," Jamal agreed. "But we need to know that it still exists—that it is still hidden where you and Yussef concealed it. Are you confident we can secure it for the cause?"

"Jamal, it's so well hidden, I'm confident it's still there. But you are correct—we must confirm it. Over the past months while the Russians have allowed us to be together, I have thought of how we can move it from under the noses of the infidels." She looked around to check again for indications they were being watched or bugged. "It's heavy and dense. We should not transport it very far," she whispered, with a hand cupped over her mouth. "We have many friends and soldiers of the jihad in Morocco. There are ways we can transport it there without detection. We will need their help, of course—and that must be organized."

Jamal said nothing, but his preoccupied mood confirmed to Daniela that he was giving it a lot of thought. A week later, he quietly made his announcement. "We have an agent in Barcelona. He is a sleeper, as they say. A decision has been made that you should return to Spain. You must meet with him—and show him where the gold is hidden."

The two of you—you must think of a plan, a way to retrieve the gold and deliver it into our hands."

It seemed like such an obvious and over-simplified request that Daniela had to stop herself from crying in dismay. "You know that I would give my life to serve our cause, Jamal. I respect your instructions. Yet, I can do nothing—we are both prisoners of the Russian military."

Covert Collaboration

Within hours, several encrypted messages were exchanged between the tall thin Russian officer in Latakia and his Spetsnaz headquarters in Moscow. They were followed by several exchanges between the Kremlin and Washington. The Russian officer was authorised to arrange Daniela's release—at a time and in a manner that would reinforce her cover story.

The Russian officer was creative; he told Jamal a variation of the truth.

"No longer I can detain her here, commander of al-Nusra," he announced. "You are important Syrian people hero. You are hated by Syrian government, but Moscow says you are vital diplomatic asset in peace negotiations. Needed to help rebuild your country. Maybe long time you have to wait. We Russians patient. You remain our guest for many years, I think.

"Daniela Balmes is not important. Now you are nearly recovered. No more need help from her, says my commanding officer. The Spanish authorities, they are shouting loudly. They demand her extradition to Spain. They insist her release. We have no reason to take orders from Madrid. My orders are free her—but not to Spanish authorities. We will arrange escape route for her. She will be safe.

"Two days more you have together. She good-looking woman. Very sexy." He clenched his fist and bent his arm in a crude male gesture. "Enjoy your time with her, Syrian hero."

Daniela

The Mercedes with Syrian diplomatic plates, flying the Syrian national pennant, slowed to a stop where a sign indicated the border was two kilometres ahead. Another road sign indicated, in Syrian and Turkish, that travellers crossing the border would soon enter the town of Yayladagi.

"You are ready?" the tall thin Russian GRU officer asked, looking kindly at Daniela. "No need we stop at Syrian side. I take you Turkish border, then return to Latakia," he said. "You get out. You walk to Turkish guard station. Show your papers. When they give permission, you will proceed through barriers. Is clear? Your contact, he is waiting for you other side. That is all I am knowing. Good luck, Daniela." He smiled. "I think you have been places before where things not look good. This place not dangerous for you. They know you are coming. You will be treated well, I think."

Stretched across the road, a blue sign—correct in Arabic but misspelled in English—carried the message *"Good By Thank You for Your Visit."* It was an old sign . . . from a past era when travel was normal. Despite her concerns, Daniela could not help being amused by the English language spelling error—grateful for the spirit of goodwill that was intended. The Russian officer's driver continued to edge their vehicle forwards. The road was narrow, jammed between two rocky hills covered with pines. Glancing through the heavily-tinted side windows of the Mercedes, Daniela saw stern-faced heavily armed Syrian soldiers in lookout towers—examining the vehicle with binoculars.

Moments later, the pine trees gave way to a barren strip of land marking the border. They drove slowly, without stopping, past the Syrian side of the crossing. It was empty, except for two young guards who saluted as the diplomatic vehicle passed.

In the distance, beyond the thirty-metre stretch of no man's land, a much larger contingent of Turkish uniformed border guards and heavily armed troops watched as the vehicle approached and stopped short of the barrier.

There were no other vehicles or travellers on foot. They would be kept away until she had passed through the checkpoint, thought Daniela. She knew she was the focus of attention. Getting out, she turned to the GRU officer. "Thank you, Alexei," she said in passable Russian. "Please look after Jamal for me. I have promised to return." With her free hand, she gathered the folds of her dark-coloured robe and pulled her headscarf across her face.

Staring intently at the ground in front of her, Daniela walked along the rough concrete road leading to the Turkish side. Behind her, she was aware of two huge red, white, and black tricolours of the Syrian Arab Republic. Ahead of her, she saw the bold red Turkish flag, with its white crescent and star. Again, not one flag but two. Large and intimidating. In the near silence of her footsteps crunching against broken gravel, the flags flapped noisily. It was as if they were defending their ground, declaring their separate and inviolate sovereignties. The flapping was an eerie sound, she thought—one she would remember for the rest of her life.

The entry papers she held tightly in her hand rustled slightly in the cool breeze of the early morning. Keeping her forehead low, she permitted herself a quick glance. It was clear that the Turks controlled the crossing. Alexei had told her that since the massacre of innocent Turkish locals by terrorists some years earlier, the border crossing had been heavily fortified. Today, he'd said, was one of the few days this month when it would be open.

Shivering, she continued forwards. Her headscarf caught a gust of wind. Catching it quickly, she held it close to her head with her free hand. "*Merhaba,*" she said to the Turkish guard. Seeing her passport and the entry papers, he took them from her grasp.

"Wait," he ordered in English. Turning, he went inside the security booth. Two armed guards, their feet spaced wide apart, stood with determination in front of her, staring with emotionless neutral eyes. Daniela yearned to look past their shoulders, to see who was there to meet her. It was not wise to provoke them, she reminded herself. As a woman, she must keep her eyes low. The golden rules were submissiveness—and silence until spoken to. A cool blast of air again caught her headscarf and she pulled it tighter.

Eventually, a senior guard emerged. His brown uniform was heavily decorated. He looked at her indifferently. "Luggage?" he asked.

"Just this." She held up the well-used leather satchel she'd been carrying. "My laptop and a few personal things."

He opened the bag, searched it, and handed it back. She waited as he conferred with a colleague inside the booth. The second man was speaking on the phone. The door of the guardroom slammed in the cool breeze, and the senior guard again stood in front of her. He returned her passport but said nothing.

"*Teşekkür ederim*," she mouthed, giving him a slight bow.

Thirty metres away, she could see a parked vehicle that stood out from the rest. Its engine was running, and as she approached, a passenger rear door swung open. The black Lincoln Navigator was huge, she thought, almost like a fortress. She hesitated. No one got out to meet her. Was this vehicle here to pick her up? Cautiously, she peered inside the opened door. There was a single occupant, whom she recognised immediately. "Get in, Daniela," he invited.

The vehicle drove away smoothly from the checkpoint. As her body sank into the thick leather cushioned upholstery, she felt she'd never experienced such wonderful comfort. It was luxurious. In the background, soft classical music oozed from the loudspeakers. A large TV screen and game console were set elegantly into a sealed bulkhead behind the driver. Next to her armrest, chilled bottles of water and cans of soft drinks were available.

"I don't think you'll be needing that any longer," said Michael O'Flaherty, leaning forward and taking her passport. "We have a new identity for you. It will be better—much safer—for you to use when you fly back into Spain." He handed her a well-used Spanish passport. "There's plenty of time on the journey to become familiar with your new ID." He gave her a big smile. "I'm glad you're safe."

"Help yourself to refreshments, and bring me up to date. There are fresh sandwiches and fruit in the cooler by the way. Oh, and some Western clothes. We are heading straight to Incirlik. Two guys with the 39th Air Base Wing will accompany you to your destination. Sorry, that part of your journey won't be as luxurious as this. In fact, you might find it a bit rough.

"How the hell are you, Daniela? It's a long time since we talked. Bring me up to date on Latakia," he invited. When she glanced with concern at the glass window separating them from the driver, he smiled. "He hears only what I want him to hear. He may be dressed as a driver, but that is one heavily armed, mean hombre. He's West Point. You needn't worry, Daniela. He's secure."

"How did you get me out?" she asked. It was a question that had been burning away at her since the Russian officer had told her several days ago.

"Sometimes, we and the Russians have aligned interests." O'Flaherty smiled. "I'll tell you the details later. For now, I need to get some information from you—and advise my boss."

He listened carefully as she detailed the events of the past several months, interrupting her only for a few items of clarification. He seemed particularly interested in Jamal's recovery, his mental health, and physical condition. He showed little obvious interest in the Russians or the GRU officer. Daniela wondered what he already knew about Alexei and if O'Flaherty had been directly involved in arranging her release from Russian custody. He grilled her closely on what Jamal had said to her.

"What about the money?" he asked. "What instructions did Jamal give you?"

Satisfied, he asked several other questions. "I'm sorry. You must be exhausted. Take a break," he invited. She shook her head.

"I'm still puzzled about the Russians," she began, but her voice trailed off as she lost concentration.

Feeling sleepy, she gazed out the side window. Their vehicle was entering the outskirts of Antakya. The sprawling city trapped in the valley shadows of the Nur Mountains to the north had long outgrown its ancient boundaries. They were forced to reduce speed as the streets narrowed, passing through an area of ugly concrete apartment blocks, straggling farms, and plastic-tarped greenhouses. They slowed again as they approached the outskirts of the congested old city.

A buzz in the control console cautioned them that the intercom was being activated. Their driver, speaking in a twangy southern US accent, told them the city bypass was just ahead.

"Antioch," said Daniela, giving the Christian name for the ancient city.

O'Flaherty looked at her with interest.

"The Cypriot, Saint Barnabas. They told us about him at school," she continued dreamily. "The defender of the Gentiles. Quite a city." There was something she wanted to ask O'Flaherty, but she couldn't focus her mind. Now that they were out of the cold mountains, the temperature was higher. The soft leather car seat and the rising heat of the day invited relaxation.

By the time she awoke, several hours later, they were approaching Adana and had turned south towards the Incirlik air force base. Armed US guards allowed them through.

O'Flaherty returned the salute of two airborne officers who joined them in the flight's assembly area. "Your escorts," he said. "They'll make

285

sure you arrive safely." He turned and gave Daniela a hug. "You ready for this?" he asked, at which she nodded and smiled.

He returned to his car without a wave. She felt strangely alone.

"Have you flown in a C-5 Galaxy, ma'am?" asked one of the aircraft's flight engineers as he nodded to her two escorts. "You're going to need these." He handed Daniela a pair of noise-cancelling heavy earphones. "We're light on cargo today, but we have a full payload of personnel. I'll have to stow you in the rear compartment. We call it the Cave. Nice and cosy in there." He smiled.

Daniela heard hardly a word he said. She could not believe the size of the aircraft. It was more like a multi-storied building than a plane. Through a forward hatch, a large contingent of fully equipped ground forces was lining up to board.

"Can't tell you much about them, ma'am. Tight security," he said. "But they're happy 'cause they're on their way home."

Daniela felt like a complete outsider. Even though she was not unfamiliar with the military environment, she was unused to this magnitude of scale. Everything was huge. She was in awe of her surroundings, the military personnel, and the journey she was about to undertake. Her escorts obviously regarded it as routine.

Her time with O'Flaherty had been brief, and she wished, in retrospect, she'd had more time with him. Dozing off on the journey from Antakya had been unintended. He'd been kind. He'd allowed her to sleep for too long. She'd been a lot more run-down than she'd admitted to herself. A lot had happened in a short time. She wasn't burned out, she told herself. Just chronically tired. She was grateful to the American; he always looked after her. He did so in the protective way she sometimes imagined her father might have done, had he still been alive.

Forcing away the memory it evoked, Daniela settled into her seat for take-off, her escorts strapped in either side. The flight engineer was right; they did need ear protection. As the pilots revved the engines, reaching take-off speed, she could feel the powerful aircraft fight against its brakes—the huge superstructure was trying to lurch forwards. The noise was overpowering; the four powerful engines screeched and whined. Then, suddenly, as the pilots began their journey down the active runway, a fear came over Daniela: How could something this big even fly? It wasn't possible. She gritted her teeth and counted the seconds as the aircraft gained speed, faster and faster. Then the noise changed. They had lifted off—almost vertically, she thought. It was amazing. It had been just nine seconds from a standing start to being airborne.

After they had levelled off, she dozed again . . . exhausted. Transitioning to her dreams, she wondered what would happen when they arrived. She was going home, but she wasn't going be welcomed by everyone.

To hell with that, she thought. The only person who counted in her life now was Antonio. It had been a long time since she'd seen him.

She wondered what he was doing at that moment.

"Ma'am, this is as far as we are authorised to take you. Our orders are to get you here safely, then return to base on the rotation."

Daniela could see that the senior escorting officer was struggling. He wasn't sure if they should be saluting her or not. Her escorts were in uniform; she wasn't. She guessed they had talked together, wondering if she was military or not. They must have known that she had some kind of special status—she'd arrived at Incirlik with a senior officer in a chauffeur-driven vehicle with diplomatic plates. Was she an officer out of uniform? Hesitating, then making up their minds, the escorts gave her a smart regulation salute.

She glanced at the mob of soldiers—ranks and officers—disgorging loudly from several doors of the huge Galaxy. They were in a light-hearted mood and enjoying the fresher Spanish weather. It felt good.

"There are plenty of military buses taking personnel to various places. You're authorised to hop on. It will take you to where you are going, or close enough. Just look out for the right one; some are express." One of her escorts grinned. "Don't get aboard one of those station hoppers. You'll burn up your leave just getting home."

She thanked them and joined the throngs of uniformed forces heading towards the fleet of buses. She found one—an express to Barcelona.

"Where are you heading, honey?" Daniela turned to see a stocky woman in her early thirties. The woman's USAF uniform bore some markings that Daniela tried to look at quickly.

"Second Airborne," supplied the woman. "Curtis, Leonora. Lieutenant, Supplies."

"You?" she enquired.

"Can't say, Lieutenant," replied Daniela, the words spilling easily from her mouth.

The woman's pencilled eyebrows rose, and she smiled. "Oh, Special Ops, eh? Got it. I was wondering why you aren't in uniform. Saw you climb on board that baby," she added, gesturing at the Galaxy. "Got it: no questions. Just thought you might like a bit of company on the journey up to Barcelona."

"I'm going to sleep, thanks," said Daniela, hoping that the limpet mine would detach itself from her.

"Okay," said the woman and went to the side of the bus to stow her gear.

Minutes later, Daniela had secured a window seat and stowed her leather satchel under her legs. The bus was crowded.

"Me again," said the woman. "No more seats left. If you want to sleep, just rest your head on my shoulder," she padded her beefy frame. "I know this place, so stick with me, honey. I'll take care of you. Water?" she offered. "I have a hotel booked in Barcelona, if you need a place to kip."

"No thanks," replied Daniela. "I don't want to be unsocial, but I *am* a bit tired. Thanks."

She rode all the way to Barcelona with the lieutenant's body closely pressing against hers. After an unpleasant five-hour trip, the woman got off—handing her a scrap of paper. "My number and address in case you change your mind. This is a fun town, honey. It helps to know a few people." She squeezed Daniela's upper arm, winked meaningfully, and got off the bus.

Ten minutes later, Daniela grabbed her leather satchel and got off with several others. She wouldn't be noticed among the group, she figured. And the place was close enough to where she wanted to go.

A disembarking platoon of junior ranks noisily took out their stowed gear from the luggage area under the bus. As they pulled out their heavy travel bags, Daniela leaned inside and retrieved a kitbag that looked like it might belong to a female. Exiting behind the bus with her trophy, she hoped the luggage she'd just borrowed might contain a servicewoman's uniform. She might need a disguise, she figured. After all, the police would be unlikely to stop or question an active-duty servicewoman wearing the uniform of the US Air Force.

Not just that. In her pocket, she had the military papers and ID of the amorous lieutenant who'd glued herself to Daniela's body for the past five hours. They'd been easy to slip out of the woman's bulging breast pocket while she'd napped.

Thanks, honey, thought Daniela. I guess that makes us even.

Stake-Out

He had done everything right.

If Daniela came within ten kilometres of the cottage, Xavi figured, she'd be scooped up in the elaborate security net he had placed around the area.

Under his orders, the Mossos vehicles were unmarked. He didn't want to spook her before she arrived at the cottage. Squaddies were disguised as civilians; a sniper was concealed up in the bell tower of the village church, while plainclothes female officers mingled with the summer tourists.

"I can give you forty-eight hours," the chief had told him. "After that, I won't be able to justify it to the president. It's an expensive operation—I need results."

They waited.

They were ready for her.

Daniela thought that someone in heaven must be looking after her. When she opened the military kitbag she'd stolen from the bus, she couldn't believe her luck. It contained the complete uniform of a second lieutenant in the US Air Force—the airborne division.

Looking at it carefully, she saw it was larger than her size. No matter, she thought, the military never tries to make fashion statements out of the uniforms it designs. It would do her nicely, she decided. Dumping the rest of the contents of the kitbag, except for a tactical uniform hat embroidered with the words US Forces, she stuffed what she needed into her leather satchel and hurried out of the area. She needed to put some distance between herself and it.

Daniela knew exactly where she was heading.

The Humvee that she and Yussef had used to drive to Barcelona was stored in a rental car park near the waterfront. She had left a deposit for long-term parking, but there would be a stiff additional charge for the extended length of time it had been left there. Hopefully, it hadn't been towed.

Her luck held.

The vehicle was filthy with dust but otherwise fine. She was glad now about the new industrial-sized battery the young salesman had fitted into the vehicle. Before their cruise, she'd decided that carrying the keys with her would be a liability. Scrambling underneath the vehicle, her fingers grasped the plastic shopping bag that she'd jammed tightly into a space above the vehicle's rear axle. The keys were intact. She was thankful once again for her attention to detail.

The tank was full. Just the way she'd left it.

The Humvee was an attention-getter, for sure, she thought. And a gas guzzler too. But she figured that when you're trying hard to avoid attracting attention, sometimes the best defensive strategy is to be blatantly obvious. Security forces wouldn't be expecting it. Soon, she would be wearing the stolen uniform.

Using a washroom, she morphed into her new role. She had the amorous lieutenant's ID and papers. Memorising the details, she started the drive out of Barcelona.

The city looked different—almost like it was under military occupation. There were political posters and referendum anniversary signs everywhere. The separatists obviously were confident of a good turnout. Any worries she'd had about the Humvee and its military connotations were soon dispelled. The federal government had been flooding the area with its security forces ahead of the Catalans' anniversary march in a few days. There were military vehicles everywhere; no one seemed to give her a second glance.

Stopping briefly, she picked up some equipment at a store. GI Joe's sold military surplus. It was easy for her to walk in off the street and buy the items she wanted. They might not be necessary, she conceded, but they might help her cover story if she was stopped.

Her natural caution told Daniela to approach the cottage with care. She had been out of touch. She didn't think it likely, but it was possible the Mossos and the feds had been successful in tracking her down. It was just a precaution she told herself: never underestimate your enemy.

She was pulled over in a surprise roadblock about ten kilometres from the cottage, but seeing her vehicle and uniform, the Mossos squaddie waved her through. Forewarned about what might be ahead, Daniela drove off-road. The Humvee took easily to the rough terrain. Parking the vehicle in a sheltered area alongside some trees above the village, she trained the high-grade military binoculars she'd just purchased onto the community below.

A sniper was lying flat on his stomach in the bell tower, fully clad in fatigues despite the warm sun—probably looking forward to the end of his shift, she thought. As she micro-focused the glasses, she saw that he was talking on his radio. A quick scan of the buildings around the village confirmed that he was the only one in his profession on duty. She swung the glasses to examine the remaining landscape. Even in her limited reconnaissance, she identified three unmarked Mossos vans. No doubt they're filled with heavily armed squaddies waiting for her to make an appearance, she thought. "No such luck guys," she muttered under her breath.

Swinging the binoculars, Daniela saw that the cottage was deserted. The blinds were drawn, and the place seemed no different from when she had left it. But, of course, they would want her to think that, wouldn't they? Shifting her focus, she saw several Mossos assault troops—convincingly disguised and well-armed—entrenched in the copse of trees near the cottage. She would have been walking into a trap.

Curious about the old man, Daniela turned her binoculars in the direction of his cottage. For a brief moment, she felt badly about having deceived him. Her regrets didn't last long. Antonio had discovered her secret, and there was no doubt he had laid this trap for her. She had to adjust the binoculars' focus to be sure of what she saw. The garage doors at the old man's cottage were wide open. It was what she had always worried about—that they would discover the hiding place of the stolen gold.

Yet, her attention soon was not on the contents of the garage. It was unbelievable, she thought. Antonio was standing next to his grandfather, talking. Next to them was a young woman holding a gold ingot in her hand. She was using a magnifying glass to examine the object.

All of Daniela and Yussef's hard work had been for nothing: the gold had been discovered.

A few minutes later, something shocked her even more. The girl replaced the gold bar inside the garage, and Antonio closed the garage doors behind them. The old man had walked back to his house while Antonio escorted the girl to a waiting squad car. As he opened the passenger door for her to get in, the girl leaned over and kissed him. It was a lingering kiss. He did not resist. Daniela couldn't believe it. He'd wasted no time in finding himself a new girlfriend. Worse still, she was beautiful and alluring.

To Daniela, the kiss seemed to last for hours. Her blood pressure soared. As the girl climbed inside the squad car, she turned to wave to Antonio. Daniela's binoculars caught the unmistakable flash of a gold pendant. She gasped. Adjusting the lens for a close-up look, she saw that it was identical to the one she'd snatched from the sniper's neck. It had the same leather thong.

Daniela had examined the sniper's pendant numerous times. It was a skilfully crafted and beautiful piece of jewellery. The artist had intertwined the numbers seven and nine into a single elegant piece. Seventy-nine. Daniela knew it was the atomic number for gold.

Her interest lay less in the beauty of the piece than in finding the sniper—and determining who he worked for. It was unusual and valuable—far from being costume jewellery. Now, quite by accident, she had found its twin. She'd also established that there was some kind of connection between the sniper and Antonio's new girlfriend.

Had it been Antonio, after all, who had ordered her assassination? She couldn't believe it. But the evidence suggested some connection to the sniper. She would have to rethink that later, she told herself. For now, she had to get away from the area. The gold had been found, and she could no longer use the cottage. She had come very close to being captured. It was time to move again—to reassess her plan of action.

Time for another change.

Several hours later, a Mossos patrol car cruising forty kilometres away—within Barcelona's city limits—found an abandoned Humvee parked on a side street. Inside the vehicle, the patrolling officers found various pieces of military equipment and the discarded uniform of a US Air Force female officer.

An hour later, a report showed up on Xavi's phone. A Mossos squaddie had reported that he'd stopped the vehicle earlier—driving away from the location of the stake-out. The squaddie had demanded to see the woman's identification. She was a US Air Force officer, he reported. Very good-looking. He hadn't paid much attention to her vehicle. He remembered it was dust-caked from being driven off-road.

The squaddie had reported to his captain that the female American officer claimed she was stationed at the Santa Eulalia barracks not far away—part of a small US presence related to NATO exercises. He admitted that he'd been quite impressed. His brother was in a Civil Guard battalion stationed at the barracks. "Did she know him?" the squaddie had asked. She'd shaken her head. "Sorry," she'd said in almost perfect Spanish, "the barracks are big. But, if he's as cool as you are, maybe I should get to know him."

Her papers were perfectly in order, said the apologetic squaddie. Naturally, he'd let her drive on.

"Oh, one other thing, sir," the squaddie had told his captain. "She said that she knows a senior officer in the Mossos. They're good friends, apparently. She wrote down his name and asked me to make sure her message gets to him—Inspector Antonio Valls."

"Oh God," said Xavi aloud, as he keyed in the captain's phone number. "Don't tell me," he mouthed as the call was being connected, wondering how he was going to tell Antonio.

"The name she wrote down for Inspector Valls," he asked the captain. "It's Daniela, isn't it?"

"Well, it's hard to read, but, yes, that looks like the name she wrote down," agreed the captain. "How did you know?"

"That wasn't an American Forces officer your squaddie allowed to get away," said Xavi, gritting his teeth.

"That was the Devil."

CHAPTER 14
Checking In

Daniela sat at the back of a dimly-lit café on the outskirts of Barcelona and considered her next move. She told herself that the Mossos's discovery of the gold shouldn't be a complete surprise. Hiding it near the cottage had always involved risks. It had been safe there for a long time, until now.

She wasn't even surprised about the Mossos's stake-out. In a way, it didn't really worry her—it just wasn't what she'd planned. Now she would have to think of a convincing explanation for the al-Qaeda operative whose name she'd been given by Jamal. The network in the Maghreb would be expecting the shipment. It was vital that the gold remained in play and accessible. It was one of her ace cards with Jamal.

Racking her brains, she tried to think of an external event that would explain the need for a delay. Even her fertile mind couldn't create any plausible ideas. She needed to talk to Michael O'Flaherty.

Taking out the secure phone he'd given her, she dialled a number. Moments later, she had a callback. A recorded voice informed her that enquiries for lost passports should be directed to the American consulate at the following number: 93 280 2227. Listening carefully several times to the intonation of the recorded voice, Daniela confirmed the information she needed. Eight was code. It gave her the location of a meeting point where a contact would be waiting for her. Calling back twice and keying in some numbers, she messaged a time. She'd used the system before. Years earlier, she'd memorised the coded locations.

The numbering series was rotated regularly, on a basis known to field agents and their handlers.

The disorientated young woman who approached her in the park an hour later seemed stoned out of her mind, Daniela observed. Murmuring words of disapproval, several people steered clear of the young addict. She collapsed as Daniela was walking past. Moving quickly, Daniela helped her sit down on a park bench. Several other people gathered around to lend a hand. None of them saw the message the young woman slipped to Daniela.

Armed with fresh instructions for her meeting place, Daniela walked away from the park and continued on her way.

"The Mossos have found the gold," she told the duty station officer thirty minutes later. He was a man she knew from previous meetings. Bill Yates was a balding, long-time fixture at the Barcelona CIA station. A quiet, unassuming man, solid and reliable.

"We saw that. In fact, we had immediate intel about the fleet of vehicles they sent to the cottage," he replied. "Fortunately, you weren't there when they arrived." He smiled kindly at Daniela. "Do you want to tell me what you've been up to, Felix? You've been gone for a long time. Good thing we knew where you were."

She liked him. He was old school—doing a difficult job. "Can you put me up for a few days?" she asked. "The Mossos and the feds have me on their public-enemy-number-one list. We need to talk to Michael. I'm overdue on my call to the al-Qaeda contact that Jamal gave me. I need a believable story for not organising transfer of the gold.

"In the meantime, Bill, you should copy down this number. It's the access code for the safety deposit box in Cyprus for the bearer bonds I received from Nicolas. I don't want you to think that I've absconded with the loot. Six hundred and fifty million is a big temptation. Especially for a poor Catalan girl." She grinned.

"Oh, and I'm going to need some new clothes and a few other items. Switch on that recorder and I'll tell you exactly what I've been up to," she added. "Is there anyone around here who can make a good carajillo?"

Catalunya's 1-O Anniversary

The first of October, 2018—a special day in Catalunya.

The dawn heralded the first anniversary of the historic day in 2017, when the separatist Catalan regional government had defied federalist Madrid. The regional government had organised a popular, but constitutionally illegal, independence referendum. Millions of impassioned Catalans had taken to the streets to express their aspirations—voting to become the Republic of Catalunya. To protect Catalan culture; to protect the Catalan nation.

It was the day on which millions of other Catalans who supported Spain mostly stayed at home. They were far from indifferent. For weeks, they had felt intimidated by the more vocal and assertive separatists. They had stayed away, trusting that the rule of Madrid's constitutional law would prevail.

Everyone had known there would be violence. Few had expected the brutality and bloodshed that had caused the outside world to gasp in horror. Hundreds of voters, mostly demonstrators, and some police had been injured. When the history books are written, said many, it will be remembered as a dark and shameful day for democracy in Spain. Heavy black shadows of Old Spain once again had been cast across the region.

Separatists held Madrid's rule in disdain. They claimed that the history of a thousand years was on their side. Autonomy survived and thrived in the hearts and minds of many whose ancient families had fought for this land long before Spain existed. The legitimacy of Madrid's claims to other parts of the country also were debatable, they said.

In the weeks leading up to the illegal vote, the scene had been set. Madrid was clear in its message: voting must not take place. Catalan separatists were equally clear: Madrid's legalistic amendments forced through several years earlier were unconstitutional. They'd been drafted and enacted by a powerful self-interested elite. An elite determined not to permit the separatists' creation of a regional republic. The separatist minority seemed determined to dictate the future of the many. Or was it in fact only a minority? Perhaps it was the many who would lead the few. Put it to a vote. "*Referendum es Democracia,*" said their signs and banners. We have a democratic right.

Madrid thought very differently and was determined to undermine the insurrection—to stop it completely. In the event, a vote of sorts had been taken. It heartened the separatist government which, almost immediately and unilaterally, had declared its independence. Under recent amendments to the Spanish Constitution, legally it counted for nothing. It was an outlawed and illegitimate vote.

Afterwards, the Catalan government was given a chance to comply with the law. Instead, Catalunya's separatist government had decided to defy the strong arm of Madrid. Soon after, direct rule had been imposed. Catalan government leaders—cited for insurrection, sedition, and treason—were arrested and detained.

Their leader, the president of the autonomous region of Catalunya, had fled in the middle of the night to seek sanctuary in other parts of the European Union. Madrid had prevailed, but the Catalan rebellion was far from over.

Some declared that it would never be over.

Today's anniversary of 1-O would test the strength of the separatists' resolve.

Josefina was a little bit slow for her age.

Hers had been a difficult birth, and the old village doctor attending her mother had been late in realising that it was not going well. An ambulance rushed them to the local hospital. Josefina was delivered without further problems. It was several months before her mother heard the whispered words . . . developmental disabilities.

Her parents' love and devotion, and wider family support, made up for any other disadvantages the young child might otherwise have experienced. They moved from their village to Barcelona where the health care system is regarded as one of the best in Europe.

"We should take her today," said the father that morning. "She's Catalan, and she needs to see what it means. It's a historic day for us."

"We should go. But I'm not sure about Josefina," reasoned her mother, smoothing her child's hair with a soft brush. The child was now six years old, and the neighbours agreed that she was one of the happiest young creatures that God had created. Her energy for life was contagious; her laughter was so rich and deep, it was heart-wrenching. She ran everywhere. Be careful of the roads, her parents would shout—running after her to keep the child out of harm's way. She would suddenly stop, turn, and screech with joyous laughter. Keep tight hold of her, he implored his wife; she's oblivious to danger. Today, he prevailed in his wish to take Josefina with them. They took her to witness the referendum anniversary march.

Unfazed by the throngs of well-behaved citizens crowding the streets, and the phalanxes of heavily armed police, Josefina smiled at everyone. Overhead, helicopters flew low over the rooftops. They moved back and forth, their threatening noise adding to the tension. It felt like a coup was under way—and, in many ways, it was. But who were the aggressors and who were rightful defenders of liberty? the people asked. They were determined to continue the struggle. Only one outcome existed in their minds: independence from Spain.

"Do you think they will allow us on the streets?" Josefina's mother asked her husband in a hushed voice.

"Let them try to stop us," he cried out, his proud eyes wide and defiant. He laughed and several others in the crowd joined him, echoing the same thoughts—yet with a wary eye on the grim-faced Mossos and defiant federal troops.

"It is our day!"

―○―

Across the region, in cities, towns, and small villages, like-minded Catalans gathered to celebrate the big day. Some came straight from home. Others had been to church: to pray for supplication, light an extra candle, and offer a pious penance. Men and women of all ages, alongside their children and grandchildren, walked the streets good-naturedly but with determination—waving flags and banners, chanting their slogans for independence.

There were several other groups alongside them: the Catalan police—historically, friends of the people; more threatening, there were two tough and uncompromising federal police forces—the Civil Guard and the National Police. In total, tens of thousands of strong, armed, and determined law enforcement officers ordered into the area by Madrid. They were primed for action, resentful of the daily taunts in the streets from vocal and implacable separatists.

"Madrid will not be able to silence us this time," said the people.

"Be careful," cautioned the Catalan police. "Stay calm. We are your compatriots, but we must uphold the law. We cannot be seen to be taking sides, as we did at 1-O."

As the early October morning temperature rose, so did the fever of the crowd. Extremists became bolder, even while the multitude preached caution. A global news team arrived at the Rambla del Raval—just as the beginnings of an open conflict were under way. Three vehicles supporting a platoon of about twenty civil guardsmen in full riot gear were being swarmed by an angry crowd. Minutes earlier, the guardsmen—wearing helmets and plastic visors, holding riot shields, and wielding batons—had advanced towards them, forcing the leaders back.

Amid deafening sounds of sirens and approaching reinforcements of police vehicles, a smaller group of Mossos squaddies was struggling to prevent a separate clash—with little success. The thickly knotted crowd of men and women jostled forwards, trapping several of them against their vehicles. As a news crew started filming, a cameraman leaped into the middle of the fray. His colleague was only a few steps behind him. Camera rolling, they pushed their way through the yelling crowd—managing to position themselves near the police vehicles and close to the squaddies now pinned with their backs against the wall.

There was a loud bang as a jagged concrete brick hit the side of a police van. Demonstrators ducked and pushed back. Fearing a clash, they tried to retreat to safety, but the size of the crowd prevented movement. Guardsmen held their riot shields high to protect themselves. Several wielded night sticks, hitting out at demonstrators, while others brandished semi-automatic weapons. In retaliation, they yelled at the now terrified and retreating crowd.

Within minutes, several additional missiles hit the police vehicles. A female guardsman, furious with the separatists, advanced alone towards the demonstrators and fired several warning shots of rubber bullets into the air. The sound of the gunshots deafened even the bystanders, loud discharges only metres away. Videotaping the clashes, the cameraman recorded the muzzle flashes. A tall Texan newsman made his live commentary for NBC News into a handheld microphone. An interviewer behind him was on her phone, yelling at someone for backup coverage. The conflict—they knew for sure—was going to make big international news.

Moments later, the guardsmen were ordered by their commander to retreat in close formation and consolidate their ranks. Heartened by the switch of police tactics, the crowd incorrectly sensed a weakness—a turning point. If the guardsmen were firing in the air and retreating, the crowd reasoned, it was an opportunity to press their advantage. Moving again towards their enemy, shouting insults, coaxing, and goading, extremist demonstrators tried to push the troops aside to reach the police vehicles. They were intent on destruction. Anarchy.

A smaller squad of Catalan police positioned themselves between the federal forces and the people. They yelled loudly, warning the crowd to avoid a direct conflict. Several demonstrators angrily turned on the Mossos—moving threateningly towards them. Scared and intimidated, facing taunts from both sides, and ducking stones thrown directly at him, a young officer fired several shots in the air as he retreated. The cameraman caught the moment on his videocam and captured the terrified face of the young officer in his moment of near panic. It was a video that went viral that day and would for many more years to come, as the world reviewed the tragic events of the day.

More violence was just seconds away.

Additional shots were fired as the federal guardsmen began discharging rubber bullets closer to the crowd. And then, when they were threatened by a few advancing demonstrators wielding makeshift weapons, the police fired several shots directly at them—only metres away. A demonstrator was hit in the forehead.

A close-combat confrontation was developing between a rabid demonstrator—thrusting a birdie finger centimetres from the grim face of a defiant but well-disciplined guardsman. Then a gunshot. Seconds later, an aging demonstrator—blood pouring from his face from a ricocheted rubber bullet—was hustled by friends away from the scene. The ferocious anger in the faces of the crowd confirmed the worst.

This was not just a battle. From now on, it was outright war.

The images were captured by the cameras of the global news teams.

"It's getting out of hand," shouted the chief. "It's as bad as last year."

He was standing in the control room at Mossos Headquarters, watching a bank of video monitors, looking on with horror as the morning's events unfolded. Large-screen network TVs were showing real-time reports of clashes in several parts of the city. Rural stations were broadcasting similar ugly scenes.

Antonio was standing next to Xavi in a portable command post close to Plaça de Gràcia. Xavi had been feeling despondent all morning. He knew that his team had blown its opportunity to apprehend Daniela at the cottage stake-out. Unlike Antonio, he wasn't convinced she would attend the demonstrations and continue to risk her neck. There were thousands of Mossos and federal security officers looking for her. If she risked going out on the street, she'd have to be incredibly fortunate to avoid being caught.

Over the previous several days, every on-duty Mossos officer had been briefed to watch for her. A wanted photograph and her description had been circulated to all detachments. Xavi's team had made personal calls to the border patrols and field commanders. Plainclothes officers were out in force on the streets. Their mission: find and arrest Daniela Balmes. Throughout Catalunya, she was their primary target.

If she was out there, they reasoned, they'd find her.

She couldn't continue to have such an unbelievable run of luck.

Daniela, at that moment, was not far away from Antonio and Xavi.

She was mingling with the crowd, following events on the streets. Her minimal disguise seemed to be working. Wearing a blonde wig, she passed easily for a tourist—one of many tens of thousands venturing onto the streets that day, taking photographs and witnessing the events first-hand. There was a great deal of empathy among tourists for an independent Catalunya. Why, they weren't sure; they just loved the Catalans. They loved the appeal of revolution, the narcotic attraction of anarchy. Despite her devotion to Catalunya, separatism was not a sentiment that Daniela shared. She had seen its dark side.

Ahead of her, an area had been road-blocked. She saw that the barriers were preventing a large angry knot of demonstrators from spilling onto a road being kept free for traffic. An isolated contingent of Mossos squaddies was being forced back against the barricades. It seemed like another violent conflict was in the making. In the background, she could hear police reinforcements arriving. The crowd jeered. Sirens blaring, the cavalry were arriving—led by an escort of several police motorcyclists.

As they approached the barricades, the noise of their sirens and horns—and loud powerful engines—scared the demonstrators, forcing them to scatter. Citizens scrambled to both sides of the road as the heavily armed contingent hurtled towards them. In near panic, families pushed against each other to get out of harm's way. Mothers and fathers scooped up children, scrambling to safety.

One of the belligerents threw a plastic chair in front of the police motorcyclists. Trying to avoid the object, the leading officer swerved awkwardly and fell. Rolling helplessly forwards on the road, his motorbike slid out of control towards the retreating crowd. A newsman filmed the incident.

A gasp of horror came from the bystanders. The still spinning motorbike bore down on a young child who had been separated from her parents. It only took a few seconds, but the incident seemed to be taking place at painfully slow speed . . . frame by frame. The child seemed unaware of the danger and the need to get out of its path. Above all the other noises, an anguished scream came from the helpless mother. "Josefina!"

From the crowd, a young woman was sprinting—trying to reach the child. The motorbike—its engine running, wheels spinning, and its bent metal frame emitting a shower of sparks—was just metres away. It seemed, for sure, that it would scythe down the poor child.

Everyone's eyes were upon them. Collectively, they gasped—their words unspoken, like a silent prayer—watching in agony, the nanoseconds ticking away.

At the last moment, when an awful tragedy seemed about to unfold, the young woman leapt into the air with amazing agility, leapfrogging over the still-spinning juggernaut. With no time left, she lifted up the young child and performed an acrobatic somersault, rescuing them both from the path of danger.

There was a stunned silence.

Then the crowd broke into a spontaneous eruption of relief and appreciation. Running forwards, the child's mother took her from the arms of the young woman. "Josefina, Josefina," she cried. Her tears flowed without restraint as she hugged the child—almost squeezing the breath from her. Reaching out for the rescuer, grabbing her arm—her face, distraught but ecstatic, conveyed a silent message of intense gratitude that mere words could never articulate.

The cameraman was just feet away and yet another near-tragic incident from that day became recorded history. This time, it had a fortunate and happy ending. The crowd spontaneously applauded the bravery of the young woman, who had lost her blonde wig in the process.

"It's her," yelled Antonio, watching the real-time feed on the monitor. "It's Daniela," he repeated. "*Vamos*, Xavi, I know where that is." They ran out of the command post and jumped onto Xavi's moto, accelerating rapidly down a nearby street.

The tall Texan newsman, wanting to scoop the story, reached Daniela. She was pushing through the grateful crowds, trying to get away, but they wouldn't allow it. "You're a hero," he yelled to her. "That was incredibly brave. What made you do it?" He thrust the microphone at her and glanced sideways to confirm that his cameraman was still rolling.

Daniela pushed him away and tried to muscle her way through the crowd. She had injured her leg. Her progress was impeded at every step as women leaned forwards to kiss her and men reached out with hugs. The applause for her was loud, long, and sustained. Her unselfish bravery had transcended the day.

Giving up his pursuit of Daniela, the big Texan returned to interview the still-sobbing mother. He was just in time to see the Mossos officer who had been thrown from his motorbike reach the woman and embrace her. The officer took hold of the child and held her aloft for all to see. Thanks to God, she was safe, he seemed to say. Thunderous applause from the jubilant crowd confirmed their unanimous emotion. "The Mossos—our home town boys, our heroes," they chanted happily.

Metres away, it took only seconds for Antonio to jump off the back of Xavi's moto and catch up with Daniela. She was limping from the scene. It took him even less time to apprehend her—throwing her to the ground, yanking her arms behind her back. In seconds, he had locked his handcuffs around her slender wrists—hauling her roughly to her feet.

He was confronted by the furious crowd. "You fucking bastard," yelled a man in his mid-twenties as he took a swing at Antonio—catching him a solid blow below his left eye.

"Stop," shouted several others, pushing at Antonio, who was struggling to find his police badge. "She rescued a child. Leave her alone—she was incredibly brave."

"Typical bloody cops," yelled a middle-aged woman, stabbing at Antonio's neck with the metal spike of her folded umbrella.

"Mossos," yelled Xavi, as he arrived to help his partner. "Get back!" Holding his badge high above his head, he pushed several aggressive male combatants away—facilitating their reluctant retreat with several choice words in Catalan.

Ten minutes later, hands still shackled behind her back, Daniela sat on a chair in an interrogation room at Mossos Headquarters. A female doctor was examining her swollen lower calf muscles. "It's a muscle tear. She'll need hospital treatment," the doctor said to Antonio. "She should have an X-ray too."

Antonio's grim face revealed his feelings. As far as he was concerned, Daniela could damn well suffer. "She's not leaving this room, so they'd better come here," he said gruffly.

As she left the interrogation room, the doctor scowled at Antonio with undisguised contempt. She wanted to remind the bully that prisoners had rights and that injured suspects with obvious physical injuries needed proper medical treatment. Rarely had she encountered such an uncompromising arresting officer. On many occasions later, she would repeat her feelings to anyone who would listen: Inspector Antonio Valls was a hardnosed, intractable son-of-a-bitch.

On a TV monitor, the doctor had seen a rerun of the remarkable street-scene video. The prisoner had rescued the child from almost certain serious injury. She'd been incredibly brave, risking her own safety.

The doctor was unaware that the prisoner also had sacrificed her personal liberty; she'd risked almost certain arrest in order to save the child. The doctor wondered what the prisoner could have done that was so bad. She hoped that the prosecuting authorities would be more understanding of the circumstances than Inspector Valls.

Some policemen are just monsters, she concluded as she left the Mossos Headquarters building. Bastards!

CHAPTER 15
An Inquisition

Daniela's right leg had been put in a temporary brace. She looked up when Antonio entered the interrogation room. "Hi," she said hopefully, as he sat down across the table from her and switched on the interview videotape.

Glancing at her, Antonio thought she looked tired despite the tan, which suggested she'd been somewhere in the sun recently. "How's the leg?" he asked in a matter-of-fact tone.

She shrugged.

"Let's talk about the money you stole, shall we?"

"What money?" she replied just as quickly.

"The billion euros in gold and cash you stole from under the chauffeur's nose at the farm at El Canós. We found your fingerprints all over the place—you didn't try to hide them. Why was that, Daniela? We also found them on the stolen stonemason's truck you parked at the house you inherited from your aunt. It was the vehicle you used to transport the gold to your new hiding place. We found that too."

Antonio's tone was cold and uncompromising. "It was clever of you to think of disabling the odometer on the truck. I guess you thought that if we didn't know how many kilometres you'd driven, we wouldn't be able to trace the money to your new hiding place. But we did," said Antonio.

She shrugged again.

"We found fingerprints belonging to your young friend, Yussef." Antonio paused, allowing her time to process the information.

Even though she didn't respond, it was clear she was following every word. He was careful not to risk losing the initiative by making claims he couldn't substantiate. For now, he stuck close to the facts—knowing he'd have to take some risks in his questioning later.

"We've found the gold. Why don't you tell me what you've done with the paper money?" he asked again.

Daniela said nothing.

"It doesn't matter," said Antonio. "I was just testing your cooperation. We know that you did a deal with the banker, Nicolas Julio de Granada, to recycle the cash. What did you do with the bearer bonds?" he pursued. "Robles can't help you any longer. Anyway, I doubt you'd be seeking his help. You two fell out some time ago, didn't you?" He searched her face and eyes for a flicker of recognition, but there was none.

"You used the bonds to advance the jihad?" he ventured.

Again, nothing from her.

An hour later, Antonio still had not managed to break her resolve. He had attempted several different approaches, but she remained resolute—and had said almost nothing since the beginning. She didn't appear remorseful and seemed indifferent to having been captured. The prospect of spending most of the rest of her life in jail didn't seem to alarm her. She had remarkable self-control, which he'd expected. She didn't appear scared or even subdued by the prospect. If anything, he thought she seemed a bit bored.

He'd expected the interrogation to be tough. Now he was being reminded how difficult it really was. Counselling himself that he'd have to be patient if he was going to break her down, he consoled himself that this was the easy first stage of her interrogation. Later stages would be less easy on her. "You haven't asked for a lawyer," he said eventually.

"I don't need one, Toni," she shot back.

"You're a non-cooperative suspect, Daniela. We have more than enough evidence to bring several heavyweight indictments against you—including domestic terrorism. The charges against you have been sealed by a judge; we don't have to make them public. We can hold you for as long as we want. The justice system will put you away for a long time. Why don't you consider cutting a deal?"

She shook her head.

"I'll give you time to think about it," he said, standing to leave. Terminating the taped interview, he nodded at her two female guards and left the room.

Daniela was escorted back to the holding cell. Three hours later, after she had dozed off to sleep, she was awakened and hauled back into the interrogation room. Antonio was not there. His place had been taken by an older officer who reminded her of the caretaker at her convent school. Two hours passed, and she still declined to talk.

The routine was repeated later—but, this time, Antonio was there. He'd changed into evening clothes. Daniela looked at him with barely disguised appreciative eyes.

"Sorry about this. Maria and I had a dinner date with friends," he lied. This time, he caught not just a shadow of recognition—but a spark of jealousy and resentment. Well, thought Antonio in surprise, she hadn't tried to hide those emotions. "Maria's doing well," he continued, keen to exploit Daniela's weakness. "I'd like to say she says hello—but, quite honestly, that wouldn't be true. Still, she'll be pleased to hear that you're on your way to prison. I guess there are a lot of people who feel that way. Do you have *any* friends left, Daniela?"

Over the next several hours, no matter how much he tried to goad her, her self-discipline remained. It was now after midnight, and she

311

seemed to be getting tired, thought Antonio. "Do you want to talk about the money?" he asked.

She seemed indifferent to his line of questioning. Perhaps a little frustrated and impatient, he thought—as if she was losing patience. Antonio was encouraged and decided to take some risks in his questioning. "We know about the money, Daniela," he began. "That was a smart hiding place you created—at my grandfather's. That was a lot of gold to move." He laughed. "Anyway, we have it back now. And we have your friend Nicolas, the banker, in custody. He's talking."

"So, why pretend to offer me a deal—if you know all this, Toni?" she asked.

It was Antonio's turn to shrug. "Old times, I suppose. If you had cooperated with us, maybe I could have helped get your sentence reduced. Well, I guess that's gone. So, it's time for me to say goodbye, Daniela. I'll hand you over to the professionals. I don't think you'll like them very much. Anyway, I gave you a chance." He waited, taking one last shot at testing her reaction. She remained impassive. Damn, he thought. She's a strong woman. Despite his anger, he felt some of the old physical attractions.

"I have a question for you," said Daniela, calling after him.

Antonio turned and shrugged.

"On the day we were travelling together to the academy—the day I forced you out of the car on the autovia—did you try to have me assassinated?"

Antonio was a professional. He was practised at not giving away information, especially not during an interrogation. Even so, her question clearly had taken him by surprise. He thought about it, but only for a split second before replying. "No. Why the hell would I want to do that?"

She looked at him closely. "I didn't think it would be you. Someone tried to kill me that evening. A professional sniper. I saw him, but

I don't know who he is. If you want to help me, you can track him down. I can tell you for certain: someone wanted me dead.

"There's a gold pendant among the possessions your people took from me when I was arrested. It belongs to the sniper. I've tried to trace it, but I can't. It's quite old and looks like pure gold. Quite valuable, I'd think. Maybe you can find out where it's from and who the sniper works for? Maybe ask your new girlfriend. She wears one that's identical—she might know." Daniela dug the knife in deep.

Antonio's face flushed. He said nothing, but his mind was working overtime.

"There was a government serial number on the sniper's headphone set. It was on the battery pack." From memory, she recited the serial number. "That and the pendant might be your best clues."

"Where did this attempt take place?" he asked, not sure whether to take her seriously.

At that moment, the door of the interrogation room swung open noisily. The chief walked in. He was followed by Diego and a man whom Antonio didn't recognise.

"You can release her, Inspector Valls," said the chief. He placed his hand on Antonio's arm. "Sorry, Toni," he added. "It's out of my hands. She's free to go." The chief turned and nodded to the female guards. "Okay, you're dismissed—thank you." They saluted and left the room.

Antonio was blindsided. "What the hell is going on?" he demanded. He glared at Diego and the other visitor. "What the hell are they doing? We can't just release her. You know how long it's taken to apprehend her, sir!" he appealed to the chief.

Diego spoke up. "Antonio, I'm sorry, but you have to let her go. Neither of us has jurisdiction." He turned to the stranger. "This is Colonel Scott. We are under his orders now."

"What the hell?" asked Antonio, glaring in turn at each of them.

313

"Toni, she's CIA," said Diego quietly. "She has been since the beginning. We couldn't tell you." He glanced at the colonel before continuing. "I only found out about it myself recently. With all the Madrid versus Barcelona political conflicts, I was under strict orders. I couldn't say anything. I wanted to, but I was forbidden to tell you."

Antonio slumped back into his chair. His legs felt weak, and his head was spinning trying to absorb the information. He looked at Daniela. "Is it true?" he asked. "Has this just been a charade since the beginning?"

Her face was crimped with pained apology. Her look said, *"I tried to tell you, Toni, that we are on the same side."*

"I really don't understand," said Antonio, now completely deflated. "Will someone explain this, please?" he appealed to his chief.

It was the colonel who spoke. "Inspector Valls, there are things happening that I'm not at liberty to divulge. I can imagine your surprise at tonight's developments and—quite frankly—I find it reassuring. Your ignorance of our agent's mission is gratifying. However, her cover may have been blown by her hasty action this afternoon." He stared hard at Daniela, who lowered her eyes and looked at the table. "It was a commendable action for anyone, except a deep undercover agent.

"I've spoken to your chief, and we agree that Deputy Inspector Abaya can brief you on the bare essentials." He nodded towards Diego. "I don't need to remind you that you are still operating under the Official Secrets Act. Do not, I repeat, do not talk about this to anyone. Am I clear, Inspector?"

Antonio's answer took several seconds to articulate. "Yes, sir," he said eventually, his voice flat and unemotional. His world had been turned on its head. He was struggling to adjust to the new reality, knowing that his personal feelings had to be set aside. This was heavy and serious stuff.

"If you'll hand me those tapes, please," said the colonel. "We can't afford to be careless. There are spies everywhere. We have to protect our asset." He nodded towards Daniela. She stood up and collected the interview tapes.

As they left the room, Diego paused at the door and came back to the table. "Sorry, Toni. I can't explain it right now."

Antonio looked forlorn. He threw up his hands to stop Diego from speaking. "Holy shit," he said to no one in particular, as the group exited the room. "I can't believe it. Holy shit!"

⌒

A pained look from Diego alerted Daniela.

Colonel Scott was in a foul mood. His displeasure with her recent actions had been obvious in the interrogation room at Mossos Headquarters.

Sitting in the front passenger seat of their unmarked military SUV, the colonel hadn't said anything to either of them. Instead, he stared out of the heavily shaded windows. His mouth had hardened. In the back of the vehicle, Daniela could tell from the movement of the American's jaws that he was grinding his teeth. Whatever he intended to say, he was going to hold back—until he could unleash it upon her with maximum impact. It wasn't going to be pleasant.

"What the hell were you trying to do, Felix?" he yelled at her, moments after they'd entered the high-security bunker at the American Consul General's residence in the Sarrià district of Barcelona. "You realise what you've done? You're a compromised asset. Our entire project is now at risk!

"It was a stupid thing to do. I can't even imagine what was in your head. That little girl—there was no need for you to expose our whole set-up just to become the hero. Somebody else would have rescued her if you hadn't. It wasn't necessary for you to get involved. Besides, what were you doing there anyway? Why would you attend something so public as a street protest? There were cameras everywhere. Everyone could see that. Why?"

Scott paced backwards and forwards across the floor. Daniela and Diego were seated at a long narrow wooden table. At the other end was Bill Yates. All three listened silently as the colonel continued his rant.

In the SUV, Daniela had anticipated an unpleasant encounter. She hadn't met Colonel Scott before, but she knew he was acting director of covert operations in Europe. He had the power to abort her mission. She also knew that he wasn't enthusiastic about Project Catalyst. Michael O'Flaherty had told her that Scott was strongly opposed to their clandestine operation. She knew she'd have to be careful not to antagonise him further. Let the colonel vent his pent-up anger without arguing back, she decided. Being contrite was just the first step; she'd also have to win his support.

"Well?" he demanded at last.

"I'm truly sorry, sir. It was an impulsive reaction," she heard herself say. "I was wearing a blonde wig and heavy make-up. They were an effective disguise. The little girl? Well, for an instant, she reminded me of myself at the same age . . . separated from her parents. I didn't think about the cameras; it was just a gut response."

"Which may well have cost us the project," seethed Scott. He looked around the room as though he'd rather be somewhere else, and then breathed out heavily. "Now that you're here, you may as well brief me on what you've been doing since you talked to Fidelity in Turkey."

She gave him a detailed chronology of her activities over the past several weeks.

He listened but said nothing.

Diego had not spoken during this time. Now he took the opportunity. "We, and the Mossos, received your request not to remove the gold hidden at the cottage outside Barcelona. Can you tell us what your plan for it is?"

"Yes," said the colonel. "But this is not the right time."

"With respect, sir, I need to have some instructions from you," Diego responded quickly. "I'm under instructions from my commanding officer to obtain your orders. How do you want to handle the laundered funds? At present, the gold is being held in its original location. It's under heavily armed guard—which is wise, considering its value. Eventually, police activity at the cottage will become known, even if only locally. Already, I understand, questions are being asked.

"There's another problem," he continued. "Our officer needs to have a convincing story for why she isn't arranging the transfer of the gold to al-Qaeda in the Maghreb. Unless she contacts them soon, they'll be asking questions. That won't go well.

"Then there are the bearer bonds that she has deposited into a bank in Cyprus," said Diego. "Along with the gold, that's about a billion euros in laundered funds. A billion euros that, by mutual agreement between our respective countries, have been earmarked for the CIA's Project Catalyst covert operation against al-Qaeda."

Scott looked uncomfortable. Daniela was aware that Diego had been appointed by the Spanish authorities as their acting representative on the case. Inter-agency protocols were involved. Scott would have to tread warily.

He paced the room several more times before replying. "I don't like these types of clandestine operations," he announced eventually. "But this one is supported strongly by Langley. Also, by your own government," he added, looking deliberately at Diego. "It's complex. You know that."

Daniela glanced at the two men, with growing anticipation of a showdown.

She knew that Diego wasn't a fan of hers, so it was a surprise that he seemed to be standing up for her. Michael O'Flaherty had informed Diego that she was an undercover officer—playing the role of an al-Qaeda sympathizer and covert jihadist volunteer. Before that, Diego had set in motion a series of events that had placed her life in danger. Now—in a complete reversal—he was glaring at Scott; his mouth twisted into a shape that made no pretence about his feelings. He did not seem impressed by the colonel's dressing down of a valuable and valiant field employee.

"Our officer may be unconventional sometimes, sir," said Diego. "I'll concede that. With respect, I have to remind you that she's also a highly respected officer here in Spain. Moreover, she has expertise and experience in the field to which few others can lay claim—with the full trust and support of our government.

"She has spent the past year deep undercover in a violent war zone," continued Diego. "That's a lot longer than most people could endure. Her life has been threatened—several times to my knowledge. If you believe her cover has been blown, then I believe my commanding officer will request that her secondment to the Agency and this project be terminated immediately. We do not wish to place her life in any more danger. Equally, we do not wish to prejudice the safety of any other officers in the field working on the mission."

"Is that an official point of view, Deputy Inspector?" asked Scott, glaring back at Diego.

"Yes, sir, I believe it will be."

Scott seemed surprised by Diego's pushback. Daniela was astonished. It was clear that she hadn't anticipated the depth of passion behind Diego's intervention on her behalf.

When she thought about it later, she would realise that Diego's unequivocal endorsement was the first official acknowledgment and praise she'd ever had of the work she was doing. She'd received a few accolades when she'd returned from Turkey, after her posting as a jihadist in Syria and Iraq. But, in her mind, that had not been real; it had been a necessary ploy. She'd had no choice but to continue the charade in order to protect her cover.

Daniela had been a lone wolf for so long, operating solely on her wits, that she'd almost forgotten what it was like to receive any recognition for what she was trying to do. Now, coming from someone like Diego, who knew the true nature of her mission, she was grateful. Here was a senior officer from the National Police, an immigrant from Morocco, praising her conduct and providing his unequivocal support. He was no pushover, and she could see that Diego's words were having an impact on the colonel.

At the beginning of the meeting with Scott, Daniela had prepared herself to do battle—to fight for continuation of the mission. Now she could step back. Unexpectedly, Diego was doing it for her. By nature, she rarely allowed herself any emotions. If she had, she might have described her frame of mind at that moment as a euphoric feeling of belonging. She felt incredibly proud of being Spanish—of being part of a nation that, despite its many faults, could promote a Muslim immigrant to such a senior position of trust and influence.

"It's not my decision, Deputy Inspector," she heard Scott reply to Diego. "It's above my pay grade. I'll present the facts to Langley, and we'll go from there. Would *that* be acceptable to your commanding officer?"

Daniela thought she detected a sly, contemptuous half-smile on the colonel's face.

"In the meantime," he continued, "I think we can conclude this meeting. For her own safety, she will remain here until the matter is decided. I'll let you know the outcome, Deputy Inspector."

Diego stood up. Physically, he was many centimetres shorter in height than the American. But, as he moved towards him, Diego's barrel-chested muscular physique seemed to overcome the difference. Diego said nothing but continued to stare down the colonel.

Turning, he looked at Daniela. "You will come with *me*, please," he announced. To the American, he said, "Our officer has an appointment tomorrow morning to report to her commanding officer. In addition, as a result of her act of bravery, she has sustained injuries to her leg and foot. They need immediate medical treatment. Thank you for your hospitality, sir. Please convey Washington's decision to us through official channels. Oh, and don't worry about giving us a ride. I texted earlier for a secure vehicle to wait outside," he added.

"Good day, sir," he said curtly—as he and Daniela left the room.

Bill Yates followed them out to the main entrance.

He could see that Diego was fuming with rage. The Madrid policeman was speaking on the phone, giving instructions to his driver to pick them up. Bill glanced at Daniela. In contrast to Diego, she didn't seem upset by the encounter with the colonel. She shrugged her shoulders and gave him a pained look. It worried him that she was being caught in the middle of the ugly spat. He was aware that she'd just been doing her job—and a very tough one at that.

"Don't worry, Bill," she said quietly while Diego's back was turned. "I'll talk to Michael. He'll know what to do."

Bill winced. It was not in his place to interfere. Yet, he felt protective of the young girl—as tough as she was. "Daniela, be a bit careful about Michael," he said. Seeing her raised eyebrows, he added, "Michael operates in a different space than the rest of us.

"Just be alert, that's all I ask."

Sitting at the end of the long wooden table, Bill Yates kept his eyes fixed downwards.

"I'll let her stew for a while," Scott said eventually, using his hand to brush away imaginary dust from the end of the table. "That's the problem with these joint operations. The United States doesn't have full control. Let's keep her in the dark for a while. If we nix this operation, it might reflect directly back on us. I'm going to boot it upstairs and let them decide. Be smart and follow my lead, Bill. Don't stick your neck out on her behalf.

"I think she's blown," he added. "She's been stupid and, in the process, she's burned herself. Send a message to Fidelity. Tell him to await my instructions. Amateurs like Felix work outside the system. They're nothing but a bunch of cowboys. Let Langley decide," he said, as he headed for the door.

"You and I, Bill . . . we are just paid hands.

"The idea of delivering a billion euros into the hands of al-Qaeda—it's just madness.

"Dumb madness."

EPILOGUE
Diego

When I helped Daniela deal with the bullying Colonel Scott, I was trying to make it up to her.

She'd stolen the billion euros in the line of duty. Soon afterwards, she had nearly been killed by an assassin's bullet. Indirectly, I was partially responsible for that—I had alerted Antonio to her connection with al-Qaeda. I wasn't told the full facts about her mission until later. So, I wanted to put things right. Not many people knew how she'd ended up working for the CIA. Like most aspects of her life, she'd kept that a well-guarded secret too. For her, it had started soon after the March 2004 Atocha train station bombing in Madrid—when she was orphaned. She was eight.

Soon after the attack, CIA intel had identified Rashid al-Muhasib as the mastermind behind the attacks. They'd found out his name—but that was all they knew.

His vicious actions bumped him up several notches on their global most-wanted list. Within al-Qaeda, he kept a low profile, and so the Agency's file on him remained thin. Despite the CIA's best efforts, only trickles of new information were gleaned. Building a profile was frustrated by the violent deaths of his field operatives. Systematically, or maybe by chance, almost everyone closely involved in the bombing at Atocha train station was lost in action or eliminated.

Rashid al-Muhasib was adept at covering his trail. Whereas his mentor, Osama bin Laden, embraced publicity, he shunned it.

Around the time that Rashid first came up on the CIA's radar scope, Michael O'Flaherty was a junior staff officer at Langley, seconded from the US Navy. He was on the Agency's profiling desk—a reward for his exceptional field service during the 2003 invasion of Iraq. Speaking fluent Arabic, he was already an accomplished undercover officer.

With Iraq occupied by coalition forces, the Agency ordered a new approach to supporting the administration's strategy for the region. Al-Qaeda was no longer just a hit-and-run global terror group. In the eyes of many suppressed people living in the region, it was becoming a legitimate statement of the region's aspirations. Atocha in 2004 reminded the world of its global reach. O'Flaherty was one of several bright new minds recruited to track al-Qaeda and provide the intelligence needed to prevent future disasters. Rashid al-Muhasib's file was among those for which the young O'Flaherty became senior investigator.

It took years for the rookie CIA staff officer and his team to discover al-Muhasib's alias—*al-Amin*, the trusted one. It was the name by which he'd become known within a very tight circle in the Islamic world. In the Western counterterrorism world, he was dubbed "the Accountant." The CIA's codename for him was Alpha. They knew he was powerful and influential, but they had no idea what he looked like or where he was hiding.

The Arab Spring uprisings in 2010–11 presented new opportunities for Western-style democratic reforms. They also provided an excuse for violence and brutal repressions. Regionally, the status quo was vigorously defended—the uprisings were a direct assault on established Islam.

Subsequent withdrawal of US troops from Iraq changed the dynamic—and created the widely reported vacuum that encouraged al-Qaeda to implement its plans for Mesopotamia and the fertile crescent. Al-Qaeda in Iraq became ISIS, which subsequently broke from its parent and pursued the goal of establishing a caliphate. In the process, it perpetrated a level of violence that shocked the region—and the world.

Now there were two wars. Alongside the civil war in Syria, a coalition of Western nations launched a counterterrorism war against ISIS, as did Russia and Iran. It took years—and many lives—to subdue the emerging caliphate. They say ISIS has been routed. Personally, I doubt it.

Michael O'Flaherty had been promoted to lieutenant commander. While working in Langley, he'd authored a daring plan to capture Ayman al-Zawahiri—Osama bin Laden's successor as supreme leader of al-Qaeda. Other events made his plan obsolete. The rapid rise of ISIS and its ascendancy had eclipsed the influence and, temporarily at least, the importance of al-Qaeda in the Levant.

But CIA senior command had liked O'Flaherty's idea. So, when the power of ISIS waned, O'Flaherty was told to dust off his plan. This time with a new target—the man who seemed likely to succeed al-Zawahiri . . . al-Amin.

A man of action, O'Flaherty ignored the dangers. He volunteered to place himself in the position of greatest danger—to go undercover and track him down. For the next several years, in Iraq and Syria, the Western jihadi with flaming red hair and a terrifying presence became legendary within ISIS and al-Qaeda. Yet, he could never get close enough to al-Amin. He was unable to confirm his target's identity and complete his mission.

O'Flaherty rethought his plan—and, this time, he included Daniela.

She had appeared in several classified reports issued by the Agency's office in Madrid. Her links to Raphael Robles were already known. The CIA was actively monitoring his activities. By then, she was seventeen and attending university. O'Flaherty befriended her. He began to groom her as a recruit—only to be presented one day with a dossier she had prepared. Inside were several names and photos.

He asked where she had obtained them. Her answer wasn't a surprise, yet it impressed him. She'd hacked into Robles's laptop and obtained the names and locations of members of an active al-Qaeda terror cell operating in Madrid. Her intel proved accurate. O'Flaherty put her through a series of screening tests and concluded she was legitimate.

He couldn't figure her motivation until she told him about her discovery—that Raphael Robles had been lying about the death of her parents and brother. She wanted to avenge them. Retaliation.

Recognising that even at her young age she was ideal for undercover work, O'Flaherty asked if Robles had mentioned the names Rashid al-Muhasib or al-Amin. He hadn't, she said. Eventually the CIA revealed the facts to her: Daniela's uncle, Raphael Robles, was a traitor who would soon be apprehended. Through Jamal, he was directly connected with al-Qaeda—and al-Muhasib.

Daniela was given an offer. Did she want to work with O'Flaherty and capture the mastermind behind the Atocha bombing? She was warned that it would be a deep undercover, long, and dangerous assignment. She had accepted in an instant.

I'd learned all this aboard the USS *Bataan*. Sworn to secrecy, I couldn't breathe a word.

Antonio had spent a year chasing down Daniela. Through determination and smart detective work, he'd succeeded. But he'd never suspected her real agenda.

To convince al-Qaeda, Daniela knew that her cover had to be perfect.

Neither Daniela nor I were aware that another agenda was being advanced. It was one in which she and Michael O'Flaherty would play major roles—and which would shift the balance of power in the Middle East.

325

Read on for a sneak peek at

GIRL WITH A VENGEANCE

BOOK THREE OF DANIELA'S STORY

BY PETER WOODBRIDGE

CHAPTER 1
Recalibration

He sat at the bar for his first three drinks, then moved to the seclusion of a booth at the back.

As long as he was able to pay his bill, thought his waitress, he could sit there all afternoon if he wanted. And all night, too, for that matter. It was a pity, she thought. He was cool but in some kind of a dark mood. Too morose and locked away in his own personal world of hurts.

She flirted a little with him at first. He was a lot older than she was. Not harmful, she decided. Just another ordinary guy hitting a few speed bumps along the road.

If he gave her any encouragement, she'd be tempted to go home with him, she admitted to the bartender—half in jest. Her colleague was surprised; she wasn't the type to sleep around. But he knew she'd been through her own wars recently. Some really tough breaks.

He switched to hard liquor and was gripping his hands tightly around his glass. He studied the ice cubes, using them as the focal point for his thoughts. From time to time, he would grit his teeth, grinding them in an act of frustration. His eyes never once looked up to scan the room. Romantic opportunities seemed the furthest thing from his mind. She wasn't even sure he was aware she existed. A man consumed by his own thoughts. But an interesting man—intriguing.

"Another round?" she asked. Was that a "yes?" She placed it on his table anyway.

Her maternal instinct kicked in; she wanted to help him. She was familiar with the signs. Women, if they can't be lovers, revert to being mothers. He hadn't ordered food, so she put a plate of appetizers on his table. He nodded politely. Brief eye contact but no recognition—even less commitment. Whatever magic it was that he held for her, she wasn't able to keep her eyes off him.

He went to the washroom. By the time he returned, she'd placed several fresh tapas on his table. He ate them, oblivious to her thoughtful gesture.

The evening crowd was drifting in. Other customers needed to be served. From time to time, she found herself glancing over at him—sitting alone at his table. Keeping an eye on him, she needed to make sure he was all right. She had no way to know what he was thinking, his problem. He was so deep.

Unreachable.

Hours later, he was still binge-drinking but seemed in control. The bar had rules. "Are you driving?" she asked.

He looked up at her. "I know what you're asking. No car keys; I left them at the office. I'm all right. Honestly, I am. If I'm in the way, if I'm disturbing anyone, I'll leave."

She shook her head.

An hour later, she ignored his request for another drink, concerned that he was spiralling downwards so fast in freefall that he had to be rescued from himself. "I'm off duty soon. No conditions. You want to come to my place? . . ."

From the cloud of his intoxicated state, he managed a weak smile. He said nothing; his thoughts weren't connecting any longer. He was too far gone.

"You're coming with me," she told him when she checked out from her shift fifteen minutes later. "I'm Caterina."

"Antonio," he announced, as if he were seeing her for the first time.

"What do you do?" she asked.

"Me?" He laughed. "I screw up peoples' lives. Don't mean to," his words were slurred, "just happens."

Half an hour later, they were in her apartment. "Just sleep if you want to," she said.

"Do you have any wine?" he asked.

She shrugged her shoulders. "Do you want some?"

"Not really," he conceded, managing a smile. "Sorry. Not much use to you. Very sorry, really. You're nice."

She undressed him and helped him into her bed. He lay face down on the pillows, breathing heavily with the saturated stench of alcohol on his breath. Worried that he might throw up and choke, she rolled him onto his side.

"Night," she said to his prostrate snoring form. Taking a pillow, she headed for the couch. Whatever burdens he was carrying, she thought, he seemed like a decent guy.

Heaven knows, there are few enough of them around.

Antonio woke up naked in her bed. She was sitting on the edge, offering him an espresso.

"Morning," she said simply.

No fuss. No loaded glances. He felt relieved. "Sorry about last night. Thanks. You rescued me."

"Seemed like it was something you had to get through. Apart from the hangover, are you feeling any better?"

"Give me a few days, and I'll be able to tell you." He grimaced as he leaned forwards, then managed an embarrassed smile. "I wasn't very good company, was I?"

Her eyes flashed a look of disappointment and resignation. "When I served you in the bar, I thought you were nice. You drank a lot. I don't know why; it's none of my business. But I was intrigued. You were really intense. But I knew you just needed to sleep." She took his empty cup from him. Moments later, she was back and stood at his bedside.

She caught his glance at her thin nightdress. It was temptingly short, ending just below the top of her shapely tanned legs. "You're probably wondering. No, we didn't. You were so far gone, you were useless to anyone." He tried to take hold of her hand, but she pulled away from him. "By the way, you snore. I slept on the couch." Making a grimace, she rubbed the back of her shapely neck. Then another smile . . . and a catchy laugh.

Antonio had woken up in these situations before. Usually, he couldn't wait to get out of the door and away from the scene of the crime. This was different. He felt relaxed and unhurried, strangely free in a way—without any responsibilities. Maybe it was the events of the past few days; maybe it was . . . he couldn't recall her name.

He'd resigned from his job, although he knew this was only in his imagination. It *had* crossed his mind last night that he would resign. He'd been crapped on from a great height. Important people had let him down. They'd deceived him—kept him in the dark. They'd allowed him to pursue a complex investigation that turned out to be completely unnecessary. He'd put his heart and soul into it.

He'd tracked down and arrested Daniela. In the midst of her interrogation, the chief, Diego, and Colonel Scott had entered the room. "She's a CIA officer," they'd told him. "She has been since the beginning." He'd had no idea; they hadn't trusted him enough to share the truth. "Let her go," he'd been ordered.

He'd been made to feel like a fool; that was the worst part.

Fuck them.

"Another coffee?" she called from the kitchen. Her voice was young and clear.

He looked at his watch and saw that it was past eight. Picking up his trousers, he retrieved his phone—still on mute. Lots of unread texts and messages. He slipped it back into the pocket and decided to ignore the world. His resentment was still raw.

She returned with a glass of water. "Rehydrate," she instructed. Her voice was kind.

"Thanks," he said, taking it. He felt embarrassed.

"Caterina," she supplied, sensing his discomfort. "You're Antonio."

He nodded.

"You don't look like a breakfast guy," she continued. "In case you're hungry, I have some things on the table. Help yourself. You didn't eat much last night. I have to get dressed; I have classes," she announced.

"You're a student?"

"Sure." She laughed. "Working in a bar isn't how I see my life unfolding."

Her tone was light hearted, he thought. She wasn't being intrusive, not asking for any explanations. Most of all, she wasn't trying to lay claim. She'd looked after him last night—at a time when he was not very safe with himself. He'd been lucky. She was probably the least complicated and most undemanding female encounter he could have made.

Reaching out to her with his arm, he pulled her towards him.

She came easily and sat on top of him, pushing his strong shoulders back into the pillows. Leaning over him, her long auburn hair covered his face and head. Then she leaned back and pulled off her top—arching her shoulders, baring her firm breasts. She invited his hands to sweep upwards over them, squeezing them together.

"Last night in the bar . . ." he began to say.

"Yes," she replied with a laugh. "They look different, don't they?" She jumped off the bed and returned carrying her push-up bra. "If I hadn't worn this to work, I wouldn't have got the job. But they're mine, and they're both real."

Her words were smothered as he pulled her down on top of him, his mouth swallowing each of her breasts in turn, moving his tongue in circular motions around her nipples. She gasped, and he felt her buttocks draw closely together. Seconds later, she split her legs apart and began to grind her clitoris into his lower abdomen, forcing his shoulders back onto the bed. He watched, fascinated, as she closed her eyes and threw back her head and her long mane of hair. It fell back in a cascade between her narrow shoulders. The pulsating motion of her body as she thrust herself into him kept him spellbound.

Her lids opened, and he saw her eyes lift upwards, almost disappearing, in a state of absolute ecstasy.

Antonio watched in fascination. He wondered, had he not been there, if she would have derived the same pleasure from another man's body. Evidently, it was not him that she wanted; it was the opportunity for arousal. It was the stimulation of her fevered imagination and her lust . . . the sensations that her uninhibited exploitation of his undeniably muscular and masculine frame could deliver. Her fantasy.

Again, she was working herself up into a fever pitch. Thrusting . . . it was a grinding rhythmic vibration. Antonio had never experienced a woman who was so self-centred, so intent on her own sensual pleasure. She became wild, groaning ecstatically. Her nails dug into his shoulders—so deeply that they cut into him. Still, she continued . . . on and on and on. He heard a scream as her rapture reached and then surpassed its peak, her body pulsating with uninhibited female pleasure. The overwhelming ecstasy of her release. The pure, joyful gasp of happiness that escaped from her mouth was almost inhuman.

Her climax seemed to liberate a beast trapped within her.

She pushed away from his body and rolled across the bed—her body continuing to shudder as she twisted and groaned. Wrapping her arms around her knees, she drew into a foetal position. Moments passed. Slowly, she rose to her knees and crawled back on top of him. Thrusting her mouth over his, she forced his lips apart, stretching him, searching every crevice with her stiffened tongue. Digging deeper.

Until now, Antonio had been involved merely as a fascinated bystander. No woman he had ever known had performed such gymnastics using his body—treating him solely as a secondary object of her desires. Released temporarily from the sexual incarceration that had trapped her passions, she proceeded to repeat her slow movements, rubbing her limbs against his muscles. This time, however, it was obvious to Antonio she was intent solely on his pleasure.

He was ready.

Slipping his hand between her knees, he forced her legs apart, delighted to feel her moisture—the lust, the wanting, the wetness that enticed him upwards to invade her. To possess her, just as she had taken command of his body and dominated him moments earlier.

Her body gave a cartilaginous click as the sacral column of her lower spine thrust upwards to meet him. Hardwired to satiate her demanding hormones and yield to his male desires, she arched her backbone towards him to facilitate his entry inside her. As they met in a unison of pure passion, her legs wrapped around his back controlling his body so that he had no power to move, or do anything that was not a part of their shared craving to consummate an act of procreation. It was mutual lust, an animalistic determination. A concentration of pent-up energy passionately liberated in pursuit of a single purpose.

He was spent.

Suddenly, her eyes widened. Grasping his hands, she squeezed them tightly in hers—not letting go. It was a gesture of possession. Instinctively, she wanted to keep him close to her—to prolong the moment. But she knew it was much more than that; despite the disregard for commitment that she had claimed, something within her had evolved.

They lay alongside each other, heads on pillows—staring without focus at the ceiling. Still breathless, but content. Set free.

Relaxed and happy.

Antonio woke up in work mode. He examined his watch.

Scrolling through his messages, he breathed out heavily in exasperation. A meeting was scheduled with the chief for early afternoon, and Xavi had called him numerous times. There were about a dozen more texts that could be answered later; the chief couldn't be kept waiting.

He uttered a Catalan expletive.

"You have to go," said Caterina.

He nodded. "I'm sorry."

"Don't be. I feel wonderful."

"So do I." He grinned and meant it.

Getting dressed, he heard the sound of her shower. The heavy splashes of water and soap on the tiles as she washed away their lovemaking. Wrapped in a towel, she looked young and fresh.

"No recriminations," she said, handing him a slip of paper. "My address . . . if you want to call a taxi. Around here, it's easier than trying to flag one on the street. We don't owe each other anything, you know," she added, sensing his discomfort.

"It's complicated," Antonio said.

Don't miss Book Three, the final volume of Daniela's Story, *Girl With A Vengeance*!

For more information, visit peterwoodbridge.com

BEARWOOD
PUBLISHING

CPSIA information can be obtained
at www.ICGtesting.com
Printed in the USA
LVHW101455230822
726674LV00005B/53